Lash is a former federal prosecutor, environmental litigator, and college president. *Rolling Stone* magazine profiled him as one of 25 ‘Warriors and Heroes fighting to stave off planet-wide climate catastrophe’. His book, *A Season of Spoils*, told the story of the Reagan Administration’s assault on the environment.

This book is dedicated to my beloved wife and partner. Her patient support, thoughtful reading, and wise advice have inspired and sustained me throughout.

Jonathan Lash

What Death Revealed

A Story of Virtue, Vice and Violence

Austin Macauley Publishers™
London * Cambridge * New York * Sharjah

Ordering Information
Quantity sales: Special discounts are available on quantity purchases by corporations, associations, and others. For details, contact the publisher at the address below.

Publisher's Cataloging-in-Publication data
Lash, Jonathan
What Death Revealed

ISBN 9798889107033 (Paperback)
ISBN 9798889107040 (Hardback)
ISBN 9798889107064 (ePub e-book)
ISBN 9798889107057 (Audiobook)

Library of Congress Control Number: 2024904233

www.austinmacauley.com/us

First Published 2024
Austin Macauley Publishers LLC
40 Wall Street, 33rd Floor, Suite 3302
New York, NY 10005
USA

mail-usa@austinmacauley.com
+1 (646) 5125767

Acknowledgements And Permission

Fun, Fun, Fun

Words and Music by Brian Wilson and Mike Love
Copyright © 1964 IRVING MUSIC, INC.
Copyright Renewed
All Rights Reserved.
Used by Permission
Reprinted by Permission of Hal Leonard LLC

The Tracks of My Tears

Words and Music by Smokey Robinson, Warren Moore and Marvin Tarplin

Copyright © 1965 Jobete Music Co., Inc.
Copyright Renewed
All Rights Administered by Sony Music Publishing (US) LLC, 424 Church Street, Suite 1200, Nashville, TN 37219
International Copyright Secured
All Rights Reserved
Reprinted by Permission of Hal Leonard LLC

I am grateful to wonderful friends, family, former colleagues, and mentors who read and commented on the book, including: Robin Barber, Ide Carroll, Dayna Cunningham, Ellie Donkin, George Hamilton, Emily Lash, Gary Milhollin, Florence Roisman, Annie Rogers, Cody Tannen-Barrup, and Will White. They made it better. The failings are mine.

Table of Contents

Prologue

November 1976: It is a few years since the fall of Saigon and the impeachment and resignation of President Richard Nixon; eight years since the assassination of the Reverend Martin Luther King set off riots that destroyed much of the center of Washington, D.C. and brought tanks rumbling into the city's streets. Now, the country has elected a gentle peanut farmer president. Congress has passed the Home Rule Act permitting the mostly Black citizens of Washington to elect a mayor and a city council. The advent of home rule is fraught with racial tension in the city's government, its police department, and on its streets. Below those streets, Washington's multi-billion-dollar, two-decade effort to build a subway system has been plagued by delays but is nearing completion and will ultimately help bring the city together.

WAMATA Lawyer, 28, Slain in Home

December 9, 1976. A 28-year-old lawyer for the Washington Metropolitan Area Transit Authority was gunned down in his home on Varney Street Thursday night. According to a Metropolitan Police report, Ernest Hills admitted two well-dressed men with scarves hiding their faces. One of the men tied up Hills' wife and son in their kitchen. The two men spoke briefly with the victim, pistol-whipped, and then shot him.

Detective Pete Phillips of the Homicide Squad said, "Unfortunately, there are a lot of killings in this city, but an execution-style killing like this isn't something we'd ever expect to see in a quiet Gold Coast neighborhood."

Washington Star, Section D, p. 3.

Chapter 1
Tourist in a War Zone

Early morning. Gray November light seeped in through the grimy basement window, mixing with the harsh glare of humming fluorescent tubes overhead. The office, used by whatever DA was assigned to 'paper' cases, was barren of decoration. There was nothing on the drab yellow walls or the dirty gray metal desk. A dark bearded man sat scowling on a metal chair that was dwarfed by his bulk. Sargent Larry Williams. Facing him from the other side of the desk seated on a creaking desk chair with cracked plastic padding sat a slight, young white man in a blue suit, white shirt, and red power tie. Assistant U.S. Attorney Jimmy McFarland. Behind Williams a pale shambolic white man leaned wearily against the door. Lieutenant Allen Dixon. In the corner, a very pretty, light-skinned black man watched intently with a half-smile. Detective Smallwood. The three cops wore stained pants and shabby sweatshirts, the 3rd District Vice Squad's uniform for 'old clothes detail'. They'd been up all night and showed little interest in getting to know a rookie prosecutor. Like storm-weary fishermen, they just wanted to process their catch.

McFarland was trying to figure out what to make of the trio in front of him. Williams appeared threatening and angry, but then he pointed to a small metal pot perched on the corner of the windowsill by a pitcher of water, a canister of coffee, and a jar of sugar.

"You the coffee nut?"

"Mmmhm. One cup espresso machine. I don't like the stuff down the hall."

"You carry that around with you?"

"When I have to come down here at seven in the morning, I do."

"Funky."

"It makes good coffee. Want some?"

"Uh-uh. We've been sucking down coffee all night."

"Lieutenant? Detective? Would you like a cup?"

Williams held up his big hands and the other two kept quiet.

"Let's get this shit papered so we can go home to bed."

"I gotta go to court," Dixon said, shaking his head, "Judge Gilman."

Smallwood groaned. "Oh, Christ, what a waste of time." Judge Gilman was blind, colorful of expression, and very liberal of politics. He was a hero for the public defenders. Not so much for the cops and prosecutors. He'd dismiss a case, especially a drug case, on any technicality.

Dixon laughed and said, "Hey man, he just can't see to send anyone to jail."

"Oh," said Smallwood, "he lock your sorry ass up if he could see you drinking outta that bag you take to court."

"Yeah, Ms. Burke said she'd tell him, but maybe I'd be a sweetheart and not show up for her client's case."

Smallwood smirked and responded, "Well, sure, for her you do whatever. That babe got it goin' on. You run into her yet, counselor?"

McFarland, listening to the exchange, grinned and said, "Mm-hm, tall, blond and ruthless. What do you have for me, gentlemen?"

Williams nodded to Smallwood who placed four case files marked 'District of Columbia Metropolitan Police Department' on the desk. The cover of each bore a defendant's name; an MPD case number; the date, November 15, 1976; the criminal code provision that applied—possession of a controlled substance with intent to distribute in each case; and the arresting officer's name, Detective Amel Smallwood. Williams and Dixon didn't want to go to court if they could avoid it and did their best to keep their names off minor drug arrest cases.

McFarland opened the top file and read the typed arrest form. It was the fourth carbon: the original went to the Third District Vice Squad, a copy to HQ, and another copy to the arresting officer.

The defendant was observed on the corner of 14th and U streets Northwest at approximately 2:40 am passing a glassine packet—a condom—to the driver of a late model blue Mercury Montego with Maryland plates. Having probable cause to believe a crime was being committed the detective, backed up by Sergeant Williams and Lieutenant Dixon, approached, displaying his badge. The car sped off. The defendant was searched and found to have five more *glassine packets containing white powder and a large sandwich bag full of a grassy substance believed to be marijuana hidden in the lining of his jacket. He had $1,256 in cash in his pockets.*

McFarland nodded and opened the second file. It described the same basic facts, with a different car and a different defendant. So did the third and the fourth. Smallwood saw McFarland wondering how to react.

"Busy night?" he asked Smallwood.

"The usual. We do our best to keep the nation's capital free of this shit and get the scum off the streets."

"How come these guys all pull the same dumb stunt when they've already seen you making arrests?"

"They ain't too bright to start with, Counselor, and mostly they're using."

"No offense, but could you tell me what actually went down?"

Williams leaned forward reaching for the files.

"Fuck that shit. We're going down the hall to someone who'll get this done."

McFarland pulled the files back. "I'll paper the cases, but I'd like to understand what's actually going on."

Williams rolled his eyes, "Hey man, we're cops, not teachers."

"I have to take these to the grand jury. They're going to ask."

"No, man, they ain't. These pieces of crap will plead out, and you'll never have to see 'em no more."

"Sergeant, my name is going on these papers. I need to understand what's going on."

"You don't want to know."

"Yeah, I do. I'm not jerking your chain; I just think it's my job."

Smallwood saw McFarland looking at Sarge, not angry but thoughtful. He coughed and said with a wan smile, "Dude wants to see, Sarge. Let's take him out so he sees what a night on 14th Street looks like. We've got a job too."

Williams examined McFarland intently. Sizing him up? Laughing inwardly? Calculating? Smallwood thought it was like watching a crocodile floating motionless by a riverbank deciding whether to make a lunge at a gazelle. Williams turned to Smallwood and gave a small nod.

Dixon roused himself from near comatose indifference and growled, "You ride with us, Counselor, you do the whole night, you keep your head down, you do what we tell you, and you keep your mouth shut."

"That seems pretty clear, Lieutenant. Tomorrow night?"

"No, we're off tomorrow. Thursday night. Eleven pm in front of Third District Headquarters. Wear old clothes."

*****

Two nights later McFarland stood outside Third District Headquarters dressed in jeans, layers of sweatshirts, and an old wind breaker. The night was dank and cold. He was wishing he'd chosen warmth over appearance. The leather jacket had seemed too posh, but it would have been warm, and he wasn't going to look as if he belonged here no matter what he wore. Smallwood drove up in a dirty unmarked Ford cruiser. No sign of Williams or Dixon.

McFarland gave a half salute and said, "Evening, Detective."

"It's Amel."

"Evening, Amel, I'm Jimmy. Where are the Sergeant and the Lieutenant?"

"They're already out there, Jimmy, *patrolling.*" The last word sounded euphemistic. "The lieutenant asked me to tell you, again, you gotta do what we tell you. That mostly means stay in the car. You start messing around playing lawman, you are gonna get yourself or one of us hurt. These streets are nasty and covered in shit. You don't need to step in it. The Court House is your turf, this is our turf."

"Got it."

They drove off slowly. The car smelled of cigarette smoke and greasy food, and groaned whenever they turned sharply to the right.

"What is this, Amel, a retired DC cab? It's a hunk of crap."

"Old clothes, old car. Anyway, you wouldn't want the MPD wasting taxpayer money on new cars for cops. Congressman Natcher makes sure that don't happen down on *his* plantation."

McFarland was surprised at the focus of Smallwood's disdain. He agreed but would have expected him to blame the department or the city. Congress's treatment of the Nation's Capital was appalling. More colony than beacon of freedom. Even as Congress enacted home rule legislation ceding D.C.

residents the right to elect a mayor and city council, Representative Natcher's Appropriations subcommittee held onto control of the city's budget.

They drove past shabby houses with small porches and tiny front yards, mostly vacant, some boarded up, front fences falling over. Some blocks were partially burned out. McFarland shook his head, "This…," he gestured toward the windshield, "this destruction is all the effects of the riots after Dr. King was murdered?"

"Uh huh."

"It's been eight years."

"Yeah, it has."

McFarland saw no sign of rebuilding. The wide, numbered streets that ran north and south were lit, but the east-to-west lettered streets were mostly dark, a few cars parked or abandoned, one on its side in a front yard. "How far does this wasteland reach?"

"You'll see a lot of it tonight."

McFarland wound down the window, letting the chill air splash on his face, looking at the shabby facades of the town houses. He turned to Smallwood and said, "I live a few miles west of here. I travel across the city to Judiciary Square every day. I suppose I knew Washington was still scarred, but I had no idea it was still in ruins."

"Why would you? That's our job—keep it contained." Smallwood pulled over somewhere on T street. "I gotta take a leak. You can get out if you want." He went into a nearby yard and urinated, then stood quietly and lit a cigarette. McFarland wandered over to the young detective trying to imagine this neighborhood a decade earlier filled with Black working-class families. Where had those people gone? Smallwood held out a pack of cigarettes: "Smoke?"

"No. Never have."

"Not even weed?"

"Man, I'm a prosecutor…"

"Lot of 'em do weed."

"Yeah, well, like the sergeant said, I don't want to know."

Smallwood chuckled. Back in the car, they drove slowly, windows down. The cold air smelled slightly rancid. Rotting buildings? Burning garbage? It was a grindingly bleak landscape twenty blocks from the Capitol, and even nearer to the White House.

"It looks," McFarland said, "like a damn war zone."

"It *is* a war zone. Most of us were in 'Nam and didn't count on coming home to this shit."

"Who's winning?"

"What's it look like? The dealers. The politicians. Seems like white folks do ok."

"Mayor Washington is black."

"Mayor Washington, the brand-new Mayor of Washington? Old Walter don't run the city. I told you, a bunch of Southern sonofabitch Congressmen control everything and let my man Walter Washington hang out and play mayor."

"Who do you work for, then?"

"Sergeant Larry Williams. He's in charge on these streets."

"Who's the enemy?"

Smallwood started to say something, stopped, smirked, and said, "We're cops. We don't have enemies. We enforce the law on an equal opportunity basis."

"Right. Sure. But you said it's a war."

"Well, you better see what you see, Counselor."

Back in the car the radio squawked, and Williams's deep voice drawled, "Smallwood, you active?"

"Twelfth and T, Sarge."

"Come on across T. Watch for your man Gatorade. Didn't want to say 'hello' to his old friend Sergeant Williams. He's dirty. I want to know where he's been."

"OK, on my way with my guest."

"Yeah. Keep it cool."

They drove slowly west, Smallwood peering into the dark, holding the radio mike in one hand while he drove. McFarland saw a movement in front of a house about a hundred feet down the block. Smallwood spoke quietly into the mic, "Sarge?"

"You see him?"

"Yeah. He went into the old shooting gallery at 1347."

"Good. Hang there. We'll come up the alley."

They waited in silence, Smallwood alert, engine running, lights off. McFarland was startled when Williams's low voice came from the radio. "The back door's open. Seems quiet. We're going on in. Don't bother with any motha coming out unless it's Gatorade. If there's no action in about three minutes, you come on in. You can bring your tourist."

Tourist? McFarland had a sudden vision of the MPD setting up a tourist division to generate cash. See the *real* Washington. Watch junkies shooting up. Drink disgusting coffee.

"Counselor?"

"Huh?"

"I am gonna be out here in case the vermin come out from their hole. You stay in the car 'til I tell you."

"Is this a raid?"

Smallwood grinned and shook his head. "Uh-uh. More of a business meeting."

He leaned casually against a car, but McFarland saw he had his gun in his hand in a jacket pocket. Sirens wailed in the distance, and the radio crackled with an exchange about a fire up North Capitol Street. T Street was quiet. Smallwood gestured for McFarland to come. They went up the front stoop. The door was off its hinges, and the narrow front hallway was dark. Smallwood had holstered his gun and gotten out a flashlight. Someone had been using the hall as a latrine.

They heard voices from the second floor and climbed the creaking stairs. In a front bedroom lit by a couple of votive candles, they found Williams and Dixon. Three figures were sprawled on the floor amid a litter of bottles, MacDonald's boxes, and what would be described in the next day's reports as 'drug paraphernalia'. Dixon was holding a man by the arms from behind, though it wasn't clear whether it was to keep him still or to hold him upright. Williams, almost featureless in the dark, stood in front of the sagging figure, emanating menace. McFarland thought that Williams was going to hit the guy. He imagined ribs breaking. But Williams didn't actually move, the violence just hung in the air.

"You *know* me, Sarge—just a broken-down junkie. Why you messin' wi' me?"

"You're dealing," Williams growled.

"No, no, Sergeant, usin'."

"Dixon, what did you find in the man's pocket?"

Dixon reached into the pocket of his old coat and pulled out a paper bag full of smaller plastic bags of white stuff.

"Merchandise, Sarge."

"Gatorade, we gonna take you to the station an' lock you up for dealin' coke…"

"Noooo!" he wailed, "That ain't mine, Sarge, you know it ain't mine. Why you settin' me up?"

"Takin' you to a nice clean cell. No dope there. Looks like you'll get clean."

McFarland watched wondering, 'Are they staging this for me?'

Abruptly Williams asked, "Counselor? What's the sentence for possession with intent?" McFarland was surprised he had a role in this little farce. He was sure Williams knew the answer to his own question. Apparently, he needed a straight man.

"First offense?"

"Oh, I don't think so," Williams rumbled peering at Gatorade. "I reckon it's a second offense—or maybe a third."

"That would be mandatory life."

"Ooooh, extended stay. See, man," he looked closely at the cringing figure in front of him, "The Congress want this city cleaned up, and they declared war on drugs. They want you in a cage."

"What you want from me, Sarge?"

"Like I said, I want to know what happened last week."

"Whaddya mean?"

Dixon rolled his eyes, but Williams didn't make a sound, he just stood and stared.

Gatorade lowered his head and put his hand on his crotch, saying, "I gotta go."

"Huh?"

"Hall, piss."

Williams nodded wearily. "I got him." The two men disappeared into the dark.

Dixon and Smallwood were joking about two female rookie cops. Dixon, suddenly animated, said, "They come to the Third District Headquarters their first night, all in clean blue, shiny badges, polished leather, and the captain calls them in and says, 'You ladies need to put on these clothes. You are going undercover. The Johns don't know you yet.' Undercover my ass! He gets them dressed up as street meat and says, 'Well ladies, it's undercover, but there's not that much of you that is under cover. You have to show the product to make the sale, and you gotta make the sale to make the arrest.'"

Smallwood laughed. Dixon rubbed his hands and was about to go on, but Smallwood coughed, looking at McFarland, and he never heard what had happened next in the hazing of the two new women cops.

Williams reappeared, alone. McFarland looked at him, perplexed. Williams said, "Let's go" and when they were in the hall turned to McFarland and said, "The man didn't want to be seen talking to me. He gave me what I needed."

"What was that?"

"Just some intelligence about who's trying to move into the turf."

"Worth cutting him loose for?"

"Like he said, Gatorade ain't nothing but a two-bit junkie."

"You believe what he tells you?"

"Some. He's got family in the business."

"Why's he hanging out in—places like this?"

"It's a business and they don't coddle junkies."

"Even family?"

"You are all full of——questions, Counselor. Drop it."

McFarland shut up. He wondered what would have happened if Gatorade had kept his mouth shut. All Williams had to do was bust him for dealing and list McFarland as a witness in an arrest report, as he should do, and McFarland would get sucked into testifying, caught between cops he relied on and defense counsel trying to find a hook to undercut their credibility. And how would he explain why he was out there? Would a jury believe he just wanted to see what was going on? He thought about how he would handle it as defense counsel: "You spent the entire night cruising around unofficially because you were *interested*?" He could imagine the scorn in counsel's voice. He could imagine his colleagues shaking their heads. He could imagine any of these guys spreading stories about him. And what would he have said about that bag of dope?

Smallwood coughed and said, "Maybe it's time for some dinner. You hungry?"

"Sure. What is there around here at 1:00 in the morning?"

"Popeye's by the bus station, or Big Mama's. We eat in the car either way."

"How come?"

"You kinda stick out."

"Big Momma's. My treat."

Smallwood laughed, "Forget it. She never lets cops pay." McFarland looked over at the young detective. Smallwood smiled knowingly, "You ask her about it, Jimmy. As long as I been here, Momma has served cops, and you know what? She ain't been robbed once."

Half an hour later they were parked on U Street, a hundred yards from the 14th Street intersection, lit by harsh streetlights and full of activity. The seat between them was littered with cardboard containers of fried chicken, pulled pork, pickles, biscuits, and fried onions. Smallwood was laughing so hard he couldn't speak or eat.

"What's the big deal? I don't see it. I was being polite…"

"Oh, man, they are gonna be telling that story to their grandchildren."

"What? What?"

"The brothers an' sisters hanging out at Big Momma's, the home of deep fat and cracklins, hungering for some late-night soul food. A very straight white dude comes in with a cop, introduces himself to Big Momma, shakes her hand for Chrissake, and asks what he oughta eat. She says, 'Honey, you need some feedin'. I'm gonna get you pulled pork an' biscuits', and he asks 'Does that come with a salad?' That ain't funny? You are even whiter than I thought."

"Yeah, that's probably right."

"Uh huh."

"Amel, did you grow up in DC?"

"Nope. Pittsburgh. I came here for Howard University. I was gonna be a lawyer."

"And…?"

"And? And I didn't get there. I quit because I was pissed off that the world's unfair and the system is rigged for rich white people."

"True enough."

"And for that I got to be a soldier in a fuckin' war that made no sense."

"Yeah."

"One thing, though…"

"What?"

"White boys and Black boys both got shot. How'd you stay out? Bad knees?"

"Nope. Educational deferment then a good lottery number."

Smallwood wiped his hands on a sheaf of napkins Momma had shoved in the box with their food, rinsed his mouth with soda, and lit a cigarette. He checked his watch and drove closer to the intersection. McFarland asked, "Amel, were you in DC when LBJ called out tanks to take control of the streets?"

"Naw, I was in Southeast Asia fighting LBJ's other war."

"The tanks must have come right through here eight and a half years ago. Now you watch young white professionals in late model cars with suburban license plates cruising through looking to score."

He could see half a dozen women in short skirts and tight tops looking cold on the east side of the street. On the opposite side, a couple of shabby figures lurked in the doorway of a boarded-up storefront. Most of the storefronts were boarded up. Amel said, "The east side's the meat market. The two girls in the boots are young cops. The one in the fake fur is actually a guy."

"Very convivial. The prostitutes don't know?"

"Oh they knew as soon as they saw them. Our girls are going for the Johns tonight and leavin' the hookers be."

"Do they make arrests out here? Wouldn't that scare off the clientele?"

"Mm, and the John's would say it was all a misunderstanding. The girls get in the guy's car and ride up to one of those motels on New York Avenue and bust them there."

A car stopped on the west side and a figure in sweats and a dirty gray overcoat scurried forward, speaking for a moment with the driver, then gesturing to another figure in the doorway. McFarland asked quietly, "You going to make an arrest?"

"Nah. That looked like a nickel bag of weed. Let's see what else goes down."

An hour later Smallwood had busted up several sales and made one arrest. He had him cuffed in the back of the car, whining and sniveling, forcing them to open the windows to let the smell out. He only moaned when McFarland asked why the hell he stayed there when he knew there were cops around.

Smallwood said, "Jimmy, you ever watch those nature shows. You see a big mother fuckin' lion stalking a bunch of antelope? They know the lion's there and they're jumpy as hell, but they don't bolt till the lion actually makes a move. They just keep grazin' and twitchin' their tails. That's what you got here. These people are desperate to make a few sales. Twitchy, but this is their place of business."

A couple of the women disappeared into cars with clients, one was back in minutes.

"Bad date?" McFarland asked.

"Probably a fast blow job."

Williams's voice broke in over the radio. "Smallwood, time to go. Get the women and get outta there. Make noise, run your lights, see if you can break up the party."

"Something goin' down?"

"We'll talk later. Get on it."

"Backup, Sarge?"

"Get your ass moving, Smallwood."

Smallwood picked a blue light up off the floor, plugged it into the lighter, and put it on top of the dash. He careened noisily into the intersection. Now the sedans scattered like frightened prey. The women on the east side of the street shifted uneasily as Smallwood pulled up. "Creighton…Abrams. You're done. Get in the car." They looked startled and hesitated while the other women laughed. "Goddammit, get your asses in here! We need to move."

The young officers finally grasped that this was their colleague, and he was dead serious. The other women looked uneasy. One shouted, "Amel, what's up?" He yelled for them to get the hell outta there, and from a block away they heard the sharp pop of a pistol. Smallwood pulled out turning onto U Street.

"What the fuck was that?" McFarland asked.

"Pistol, a twenty-two probably. Not MPD."

"Yeah, but what's going on?"

One of the women groaned, "Aww, Detective, this guy stinks like a shit house." Smallwood stared straight ahead and said, "Let's see what the sergeant wants to tell us."

The man who was the last of the night's catch asked, "One of you nice ladies got a cigarette?"

Yellow light flooded from squat brick district headquarters building as they pulled through the alley into a parking lot surrounded by a ten-foot chain link fence. The two women cops got out laughing. Relief? Smallwood led his arrest in through the heavy metal door and down the hall to be booked, though he seemed to know the way. Smallwood told McFarland, "That's it. You might as well get home and get some sleep."

"Are you shitting me? I want to hear what the sergeant has to say."

"Up to you. I guess it'll be a while. You know he's over your way all the time."

"He isn't going to tell me shit, is he?"

"Dunno, probably not."

"Will you?"

"We'll see."

"I appreciate you taking a tourist out with you. We'll have to do it again soon."

"Not too soon, Jimmy, everyone'll wonder what the fuck's going on."

"I'll take the risk."

Smallwood looked at him with the half smile McFarland had noticed two mornings ago. "Yeah, well I'm glad you want to see for yourself."

Chapter 2
Football Sunday

On a bright Sunday afternoon in November, Sergeant Larry Williams pulled up in front of his friend Ernie Hill's modest brick house on Varney Street, a quiet, tree-lined street in an upper middle-class black neighborhood in Washington, D.C. Varney Street was just to the east of Rock Creek Park, which divided the city. Black neighborhoods lay to the east. Williams gathered the six pack, bouquet of flowers, and carefully wrapped box sitting beside him on the front seat, paused for a moment, took a deep breath, opened the car door, and started up the path.

The door of the house flew open, and an eight-year-old boy dressed in perfectly pressed khakis, white shirt, tie, and checked sport coat leaped down the front steps.

"Uncle Sarge! Uncle Sarge! They're about to kick off. C'mon!" Eager as he was, the boy made coming on impossible by throwing his arms around his godfather's legs. Williams gathered the boy up along with his other parcels and shook his head.

"You are getting too big for me, kiddo."

"Noooo!" the boy laughed. "You're the biggest man we know. Daddy says you could be on the Redskins."

"Your daddy makes stuff up. Always has."

A smiling figure appeared on the stoop. "Ernie, let Uncle Sarge get in the door. How ya doin' man? You been keeping the great capital city safe?"

They crowded into the foyer. Williams crouched by his godson and held out the wrapped package. "I got you something, Little E."

"What? What is it?"

"Well open it."

The boy ripped the paper off the box and pulled it open like a tornado in a trailer park, shrieking with delight when he saw it was a kid-size football. Holding it tightly, he tore around the living room while delivering simultaneous commentary on his actions: "He hits the line, cuts left, sheds a tackler and heads for daylight!"

A sober figure in an apron appeared from the kitchen. "What's going on out here?"

Little Ernie stopped short looking at his mother with concern.

Williams grinned sheepishly. "Hello Claire. I brought him a football."

"Well, I can see that," she said sternly, "but he can't play in the house."

"I brought you these, too." Williams held out a bouquet wrapped in green tissue paper, and she smiled.

"You are too much, Larry. Thank you."

Williams turned to the little boy. "You know, that football is signed, Little E."

Ernie looked at the ball in his hands, turning it over, and his eyes widened. "Riggo?"

"And who is that?" his mother asked.

The boy rolled his eyes. "John Riggens, the Diesel. The *Diesel!* Whooo-whooo!"

He was off again around the room, ball tucked under his left arm, right arm straight out in front. Claire looked at her husband and Williams and shook her head. "You all go down and watch. Watching is fine, but that boy is not *playing* football."

"He's fast. He's coordinated. He's got good hands…"

"He's a good student, and he's a little Black boy, and I don't want him put in a box marked 'athlete'. I worked hard to get him into that school. He's there to be a student." She turned and stalked back into the kitchen.

Williams, Ernie, and Little Ernie descended the basement stairs to the den and began the happy ritual of watching the game, yelling at the refs, deriding opponents, and groaning about Billy Kilmer's wounded duck passes.

"Oh man, that's lame. Coach Allen," Ernie yelled at the screen, "you have *got* to put Theismann in."

Williams scoffed, and said, "Shut up, Ernie, they're moving the ball. The Eagles can't stop that boy running. Don't matter that he's white, he can run."

Kilmer handed off to Riggins who rumbled for twenty-two yards. Amid the crowd's roar they could hear the air horns fans had brought to salute their man, the Diesel. Little Ernie, seated between the two men clutching his football, put his head back and joined the crowd in the stadium. "Whoooo! Diesel! Diesel!" His father and godfather smiled.

Ernie asked, "Yeah, come to that, Sarge, how did you get that ball autographed?"

"Oh, I jes' helped keep a fella outta trouble. He was grateful."

"No lie? What'd he do?"

Williams looked at Little Ernie, smiled, and said, "Nothing really," and was rescued when a Kilmer pass fluttered into the hands of a big tight end who stormed into the end zone giving Washington the lead.

*****

Larry Williams would always be 'Sarge' to Ernie Hills, not Sergeant Williams of the Metropolitan Police assigned to the Third District Vice Squad, but Sergeant Williams of Charley Company, the man who swore he'd get Ernie home alive when, in 1967 near the end of their tour, Claire wrote that she was pregnant.

Williams had been drafted when he lost his football scholarship because of a knee injury. It was bad enough to keep him off the team, but not bad enough to keep him out of the army: "You're a big strong boy," the doctor for his draft board in Wilmington had told him, "You'll be fine." Williams had met Ernie, who'd been drafted the week after he graduated from Howard Law School, at Fort Bragg.

Williams was an incredible soldier. Cagey, calm, charismatic, and physically powerful. Ernie was a smart guy who courted trouble. They became friends. After Tet, they were blood brothers, along with their white stoner lieutenant, Al Dixon. All three survived, arriving back in the States in 1968, after a year and a half of brutal terror, to a country fractured by a controversial war and, for Williams and Hills, to their own communities convulsed by rage after the assassination of Dr. King.

Dixon, a Washington native, was from a Metropolitan Police family. His uncle, Deputy Chief Herman Dixon, got his nephew a place as a police cadet, and then an open road to promotions. Dixon persuaded Williams to join the force, too, telling him, "It's a decent living, the benefits are ok, and it's worth doing. You'd be a helluva cop, Sarge." Once he was Officer Williams, everyone knew he was going to be a sergeant soon, and he was.

Hills had a wife and child to support. Claire had had a very difficult pregnancy and there was not going to be another child. They doted on their son, and Hills wanted doors to open for him as he grew up. After he passed the bar exam, he found a job with the newly created Washington Metropolitan Area Transit Authority (WMATA, or 'WahMahTah'). As the region geared up to build a subway system and gradually overcame the pitched resistance of the highway lobby and the intransigence of members of Congress, who never intended to ride public transit preferring more highways, WMATA became a major player, a source of lucrative contracts, and an exciting place to work.

Once Little Ernie was in school, his mother got a job teaching fourth grade. She and Ernie managed to scrape together the money to buy a house on Washington's Gold Coast, though only after Dixon called on another uncle, a banker, to approve a pricey mortgage. Williams had told them they were crazy. Why go into debt, he had asked, when they could get twice the house for half the money further east. Claire and Ernie had been adamant. Their boy was going to grow up playing with the children of Washington's Black elite.

When Claire met Patricia Barnes at church, the woman who had created a fund to help talented Black children into Washington's elite private schools, she volunteered at the fund, helped with the flowers at church, and oohed and aahed over Patricia's hats until Patricia at last asked about Little Ernie. After meeting with their family, she connected them with the elite Beauvoir school, the elementary branch of the St Albans and National Cathedral Schools.

St. Albans was seeking to overcome an all-white history in a majority Black city. When the Hills went to visit the school, located among the trees and gardens that surrounded the National Cathedral in the heart of white northwest Washington, Ernie had deep misgivings. It was beautifully green, very rich, and still completely white. Although he and Claire wanted Little Ernie to get a fabulous education and go to a top college, he wasn't sure he wanted his son to be a pioneer. Little Ernie had no such qualms. His seven-year-old eyes saw a happy place, an amazing playground, and classrooms full of interesting stuff. He was not at all abashed by all the white faces.

Mrs. Crowley, the Director of Admissions was friendly and reassuring. St. Albans had decided to seek out and admit more African Americans, she said, and they would support the families they admitted. "We are a Washington school, and we need to reflect the whole community." *Or maybe a few blocks to the east of the park, anyway,* Big Ernie thought to himself while nodding agreeably. Little Ernie was polite and talkative. If he hadn't been just seven years old, his mother would have sworn he was turning on the charm.

"Ernie, did you have a good time visiting the classroom?" Mrs. Crowley asked.

"Oh yes, ma'am, it was fun."

"What did you do?"

"I played a game with two other boys, and the teacher read a story."

"Oh, that sounds lovely! What story did she read?"

"It was about a little donkey that makes a mistake and gets turned into a stone."

"Oh, was it about Sylvester the donkey?"

"Yes ma'am. He was really sad. He missed his parents."

"What happened?"

"His mom saves him. Her an' his dad have a picnic by the stone. She sees a pebble an' picks it up. She doesn't know it's the Magic Pebble. He wishes and wishes and then she drops it right on top of him."

"The pebble?"

"The Magic Pebble. That's how he got made into a rock. An' he wishes he was a donkey again, an' then he is. His parents were really happy about that."

Mrs. Crowley had met a lot of little boys whose parents wanted them to go to St. Albans, but she had not met many, Black or white, who were as bright or engaging as this child. She heard the same from the teacher who'd conducted the classroom interview of Ernie and five other children and said Ernie connected with everybody and was the instigator of their games. He was alert and he listened. Ernie was a keeper. The school offered him a full scholarship a few weeks later.

At the half, the Skins lead the Eagles 17-0. Williams followed his friend and godson up the basement stairs to a table laden with food. His flowers stood in a vase amid the bowls and platters, and he breathed in the rich smell of baked ham, which said, "Sunday" to him. Football talk was forbidden at the table, so he turned to Little Ernie to ask about school. It was obvious that he loved going. "What's your favorite class?" he asked.

“Science! We have snakes, and gerbils, and all kind of animals. And we do experiments and build stuff. Mr. Brown, the teacher, he’s really funny.”

Trying not to look like they were rushing, they emptied their plates and returned to the TV. Claire brought down pie and ice cream. The Skins were killing the Eagles and Riggo was running up and down the field. Pie and ice cream and football. Little Ernie was in heaven, sitting like a puppy on the sofa between his father and his godfather, his tie and jacket hung carefully over the back of a chair. Claire sighed happily and went to clean up.

It was dark by the time Williams made his way to the door. Little Ernie, finishing his homework at the kitchen table under his mother’s watchful eye, shouted his thanks for the football. Claire went to the door to give Williams a kiss. “Thank you for the beautiful flowers, and for being so good to Little Ernie.”

“Yeah, well he’s my favorite little boy. He’s gonna be something. You know I’d do pretty much anything for him—or for you.”

Big Ernie coughed and yelled, “You stop flirting with my wife!”

“I don’t know if you deserve her.”

“So says the bachelor. What’d you save my life for, Sarge? You could have left me.”

“We all saved each other. See you all soon.”

Chapter 3
Execution

Just past eight o'clock on the evening of Thursday, December 9, 1976, Professor Albert Tyrell walked into his study carrying a briefcase full of bluebooks. As he reached across his desk to turn on the tall goose neck lamp, he glanced out the window and saw his neighbor's wife, Claire Hills, in her kitchen washing dishes. He watched for a moment, turned back to his desk, switched on the light, sat down with a sigh, and lifted a stack of bluebooks from his briefcase onto the desk.

He was fond of the young couple next door. The husband, Ernie, was a bit brash, but Claire was utterly charming, and their son, Little Ernie, was a delight. The Tyrell's were childless, and Albert thought of himself as a grandfather to Little Ernie.

About 8:30 p.m., Tyrell was startled by two sharp bangs. He called out to his wife Evie, who was watching TV in the living room. "Did you hear that?"

She appeared at the study door her face creased into a mask of fear. "What was it? It sounded like…"

"Gun shots, that's what it sounded like. From next door."

"Oh God, Albert I hope they're alright. I hope that little boy is safe."

He told her to call the police and grabbed his coat.

"Shouldn't we wait for the police?"

He grunted and went out, around the little dogwood tree between the two houses and up the steps to the Hills' front door. He listened, heard nothing, rang the bell, and then knocked, shouting, "Ernie! Claire! It's Albert. Are you alright?"

Up and down Varney Street, neighbors pulled curtains aside or opened doors to look out. Several called 911. This was a neighborhood where people knew and looked out for one another.

Tyrell heard the siren of an approaching police car and remained at the door, knocking and calling. The car's flashing lights exposed the dark trees and cast momentary shadows across the scene. The driver directed his searchlight at the stoop, and Albert turned toward the vehicle, shielding his eyes. The driver rolled down his window.

"We got a call about gun shots?"

"Yes. I think from this house. It's the Hills'. I know they're home, but no one is answering."

The officer on the passenger side got out and walked slowly up the path. "Step back from the door."

"I'm Dr. Albert Tyrell. I live right next door, Officer. I just saw Claire through the window cleaning up the dinner dishes maybe half an hour ago."

The officer took in Tyrell's gray hair, tweed coat, and argyle sweater and relaxed.

"You sure it was gunshots"?

"Pretty sure. We need to get in there, officer. Now!"

They could hear a second patrol car approaching. The first officer's partner joined them on the stoop, rang again, then looked around and found a key under a large planter. He opened the door. There was a faint acrid smell. The first officer shouted, "Police!" and they heard what sounded like a moan from the kitchen. The officers stiffened and drew their weapons.

"You stay here," said the first officer, as the two men started toward the kitchen.

Ignoring him, Tyrell entered and turned to his left toward the living room. He gasped and shouted, "Here! He's shot." Ernie lay crumpled on the floor, as if he'd been on his knees when he he'd been shot in the back of the head. Part of his face was blown off where the bullet exited. Albert Tyrell stood immobilized by horror.

The first officer appeared. "Sir, you need to step out of here. Payne, go deal with the woman and the kid in the kitchen." Another pair of officers appeared and stopped at the sight of the corpse.

"Jeesus! Brutal."

"Yeah, go help Payne in the kitchen, and call the District and Homicide."

They heard a wail from the kitchen. "They've killed him! They've killed my husband."

Tyrell stumbled toward the kitchen. Claire and Little Ernie had been tied up and their mouths taped. Lengths of clothesline and duct tape lay on the floor where the officers had dropped them. Claire moaned softly and held Little Ernie to keep him from going to look in the living room. Albert's wife Evie slipped in the front door, ignoring the officer trying to block her way. She ran to Claire, asking in a trembling voice, "What happened?" Claire sobbed incoherently. Little Ernie answered.

"Two men, Mrs. Tyrell. They made us lie down. They had scarves over their faces. They were talking to Daddy. I heard them hit him."

Two homicide detectives arrived and took over. A small group of neighbors stood outside talking and shivering. The district commander arrived, and the detectives and uniformed officers fell silent. "What've we got?" he asked. They stood crowded in the hall looking into the living room. The answer seemed obvious.

"It looks like a hit, sir. The little boy says he heard them kosh his dad. The victim was shot in the back of the head at close range."

The district commander, a balding, weary-looking white man in his sixty's limped into the room. He shook his head and muttered, "A goddamn contract hit. That's not supposed to happen on the frigging Gold Coast." He turned toward the kitchen, saw the crowd around Claire and Ernie, shook his head again and walked out. He would let the homicide boys do their job.

As he left, he met Sergeant Larry Williams coming up the walk like a dark cloud portending ill. The Commander knew who he was and nodded. Williams paused. He was a big man, six feet six, bearded and broad shouldered, and he emanated power. He was dressed in "old clothes" from a night on duty in the city's red light district. He looked like a man in agony.

"Sarge, do know what this is about?"

Williams looked at him blankly, then put a big hand to the back of his neck and sighed.

"No Commander, I don't. But the dead man was my closest friend, and I'm gonna find out." He walked on, showed his badge at the door, and entered. The detectives recognized him and nodded in greeting. He took one glance at the body amid the swarm of technicians and asked, "Where's his family?"

"They're ok, Sarge. They're in the kitchen."

Williams turned and walked to the kitchen. Claire, wrapped in Evie's coat, was leaning against her, shivering and sobbing. Little Ernie was sitting forlornly at her feet. As soon as he saw Sergeant Williams, he leaped up and raced to the safety and comfort of his godfather's arms.

Williams had seen death in wartime, held men as they died, and caused the death of others. But he was utterly unprepared for what he felt in that moment. Horror, anger and a deep, disabling anguish. This family was where he had lodged his love and hope and belief. He wanted to roar, break things, escape from his useless, aching body. Instead, he held his godson, and wept silently.

"Uncle Sarge, is my daddy hurt a lot?"

"Yeah, man, he is."

Claire took an uneven gulp of air and said, "Larry, they called him Yellow Dog. I heard them. He let them in. He knew what was happening..." She broke down.

"Y-Dog? Somebody from our unit? No, no that must be wrong."

"Ernie said, 'Don't hurt my family,' and they said, 'You should know better' and something about him being 'Y-Dog'."

Detective Phillips, who had been sitting quietly by, asked, "Mrs. Hills, do you feel up to giving us a statement?" and then looking up said, "Sarge, you're welcome to stay. What do you know about Y-Dog?"

"Ernie was in my unit in Vietnam. A real light-skin smartass. 'High Yellow' they say in this town. His nickname was Y-Dog. Yellow Dog. Shit, man, no way anyone outside our unit would know that, and we were close, the ones that made it home. Real close."

"You ever get together?"

"We talked about it. Ernie wanted to make it happen."

They walked Claire through what she had heard and seen. She struggled to respond; she had not seen much. Little Ernie remembered more and more clearly. He seemed impatient with his mother's confusion. Williams was relieved to hear that neither of them had seen the men's faces or recognized their voices. No reason for the bastards to come back.

One of the neighbors arrived with a huge pot of coffee and filled cups for everyone. Claire had stopped weeping and stared at Williams in anguished silence. "Larry, what did they want? Was something going on?"

He shook his head. He didn't know. It had seemed like everything in his friend's life was on a solid footing at last. Evie stood up and said, "It's nearly two a.m., Claire. You and Little Ernie should stay with us tonight."

Williams looked at Detective Phillips, who nodded his agreement, and then carried Little Ernie next door. Claire, Evie, and Albert followed in sad procession. After putting the boy to bed, Williams sat with them for a long while as they talked about Ernie. Later he walked back to the crime scene. He felt cold, which never happened to him, and bone weary. The body was gone, the crime scene guys were finishing up. The little groups of neighbors who had stood shivering and watching the proceedings had gone back into their houses. Phillips was getting ready to leave.

Williams asked, "Pete, you got anything."

"Not much, Sarge. One lady thought she saw a dark colored car pull off after the shots, but she doesn't know the make and didn't see the plates or who was driving. The crime scene guys didn't get anything either. The best lead is that he knew them, and they called him Y-Dog. Will you give me a list of the men in your unit?"

"Yeah."

"I guess we're going to have to dig through his life."

"Sure, but Pete—he was a good man. And that family—we gotta protect them."

*****

The following night Williams and his partners Lieutenant Alan Dixon and Detective Amel Smallwood cruised slowly up 14th Street, watching the usual population of dealers and hookers with little interest except to find some of their 'friends'. When they did, a short conversation ensued.

"A couple of dudes shot a very good buddy of ours up on the Gold Coast last night. We gonna remember the guy who gives us a tip about who did it—big time."

Williams, Dixon, and then Corporal Ernie Hills had served together in Vietnam, and while they drove, Williams and Dixon talked about every man in their unit who might have had a grudge against Ernie. There'd been assholes, but they hadn't come home.

Dixon shook his head and said, "No, man, it can't be. We knew those guys. Shit, Sarge, you're the reason most of 'em made it back." Williams looked at Dixon, his jaw tight, stopped the car, and beat his head against the steering wheel cursing.

Chapter 4
The Judge

Paul Brown was engaged with a pot of coffee. It was 6:00 a.m. Outside the narrow kitchen window, he saw faint light spreading in the eastern sky. He knew the coffee wasn't up to his housemate's epicurean standards, but he'd heard McFarland come in around 4:00 a.m., and he figured even what he brewed would be welcome.

Tall, lanky, and easy going, with wild hair and a quick smile, Brown was a science teacher at the St. Albans School, one of the places that educated Washington's elite. McFarland, who had known him since rooming with him at college, needled him often about wasting his talent and education on spoiled school kids. He speculated aloud whether Paul was too lazy, or too scared to go back and finish his dissertation. Brown, in return, his blue eyes smiling, wondered how his old friend had decided to become a prosecutor. Why had the sincere idealist chosen to confront the grubby underbelly of society in the Superior Court of the District of Columbia. Why had this legal intellectual chosen a job that involved a lot less law than human combat. He knew perfectly well why. McFarland believed he could change things.

James Henry McFarland was an unlikely prosecutor. His friends knew him as serious, upright, and smart. The older of two brothers born to Dana Forbes McFarland, an art professor, and Joseph Egan McFarland, a Boston attorney, James Henry had grown up in a big house with a wraparound porch a mile from Harvard Square. Slightly built and frail looking, he had dark, straight hair, warm hazel eyes, and an open and expressive countenance. When he got arrested at an anti-war demonstration, his parents had been proud, but his father had still managed to get all record of the arrest expunged.

McFarland did very well at law school, got a good judicial clerkship, and then decided he had better find out more about the real world, and applied to the U.S. Attorney's Office in D.C., specifically because, unlike other U.S. attorney's offices, they handled street crime and D.C. had a reputation for crime that was out of control. Nixon had launched 'War on Drugs' in 1971 and D.C. had become a major battleground since then. McFarland had arrived imbued with the belief that the job was about justice.

This particular morning Paul sat at the kitchen table, long legs extended in front of him, and watched his bleary-eyed friend wolfing down a bowl of cereal. He grinned and asked, "You have any adventures out on the streets with those cowboys?"

"I'm not sure I'd call them that. They work in a world that seems to have its own rules. It felt like they're trying to do the job society's telling them to do any way that works. And none of us care much how they get it done."

Paul raised his eyebrows. "So you'd give them a pass on obeying the law?"

"No, no, they need to know the boundaries…"

"But what?"

"I like them—and I kind of admire them."

Paul pursed his lips and narrowed his eyes. "Hmm, tough, violent, lawless—just your kind of guys."

"Oh, screw you, Paul, I'm just saying I learned something. Give me some of that swill you've brewed. I've got to get downtown to prepare for another day of jousting with the judge. And, by the way, the evening did end with gunfire."

"McFarland, you're fucking nuts."

*****

McFarland knew—or thought he knew—what he was in for when he surprised his friends and his lawyer father by accepting a job as an assistant U.S. attorney in Washington, D.C.; a city that had its own police force, the Metropolitan Police Department, but not its own courts or prosecutors. Even after Congress had enacted so-called 'home rule' legislation, Superior Court judges were still nominated by the president, and everyday street crime was handled not by local DA's but by federal prosecutors. McFarland and his colleagues worked for the U.S. Department of Justice but practiced in the D.C. Superior Court as well as the federal courts. His case load was assaults, robberies, burglaries, rapes, and murders. He thought of it as a calling.

It was a ten-minute walk to catch the D-2 bus that carried him down Massachusetts Avenue and across the city to Judiciary Square. Another short walk took him to the ninety-year-old Pension Building, built after the Civil War to house the fifteen hundred civil servants hired to administer pensions to veterans of the Civil War. McFarland loved the building. It had been designed by General Montgomery Meigs, the same army engineer who'd built the U.S. Capitol Dome, but it departed from the Greco-Roman style of earlier government building. Instead, the Pension Building evoked a roman palazzo. A twelve-hundred-foot frieze of trudging Union soldiers ran around the outside, including an African American teamster, perhaps the first black man ever portrayed in a Washington, D.C. sculpture.

The building occupied an entire city block. The tall doorway opened into an atrium three hundred and fifty feet long and four stories high surrounded by arcaded galleries that provided access to scores of offices. The ground floor was lined with heavy padded doors with narrow windows that lead into courtrooms.

At 7:10 a.m., when McFarland hurried across the huge atrium, it was nearly empty. He loped up the wide stairs on the north side of the building and turned left to suite 237. The other two AUSAs on his team were already at their desks. Katharine Abbott, 'KA', a former lieutenant in the MPD, was laying out trial notes. Dennis Bartolo, the pugnacious loudmouth of the group, was ranting about the rat droppings he'd found when he arrived in the morning. "On my desk! Jeezus H. Christ, we need to get a cat—no, a terrier." His eyes gleamed, "Or maybe a twelve-foot Anaconda. I am a federal fucking prosecutor," he yelled, "I represent the people of the United States, and I have little pellets of rodent poop rolling around on my desk." He stormed out of the office looking for Clorox and a brush.

*****

All three members of the team were assigned to handle cases before Judge Frank Stanley, an assignment that, of late, had been a bitter challenge. After the *Washington Star* named him the 'laziest judge on the bench', Judge Stanley had gone berserk. Grumpy, red-faced, and irascible at the best of times, after the article appeared he became a blustery petty tyrant. Previously, he had been known throughout the shabby offices and dreary courtrooms of the Pension

Building as a connoisseur of delay, the King of Continuances, Judge Done-By-Lunch (and unpredictable afterward), but now he bullied and bellowed, hectoring any lawyer who asked to have a hearing continued or a trial postponed. "You aren't ready? Isn't that a shame? It's not my problem if you have deadbeat witnesses that don't show. I'm not going to be called lazy because some incompetent hack decided to go get drunk last night instead of preparing."

"Your Honor, I—"

"Don't argue with me counselor or you'll end up in jail with your client." The judge hated the world, and more than anyone else, he seemed to blame the three assistant U.S. attorneys assigned to his courtroom, believing their office had been the source for the story. After weeks of harassment, the three of them had gone to ask for help from their supervisor, the Chief of the Felony Trial Division. He was not sympathetic. "You represent the United States. You stand up to him. You need to look like you're in charge and act like you're in charge."

So they refused to be silenced. If he threatened them, they made a public show of asking that the record reflect what he had said. If he issued illegal edicts, they argued with him. When he glowered menacingly, they stood right before the bench and looked him in the eye. McFarland and Bartolo wore starched white shirts and kept their suit jackets buttoned. KA, naturally sober and just a bit frumpy, wore somber dress suits and had her hair done up in a tight bun. While other lawyers did their best to avoid Courtroom 7, or to let the DA's take the heat, the three young prosecutors were there every day.

*****

Late the evening of the Wednesday before Thanksgiving McFarland sat in his office in his underwear. He was exhausted after a difficult trial before Judge Stanley during which his pants had split and the judge had refused to take a recess for McFarland to make repairs. Now the jury was deliberating, and KA had handed him a cold hamburger, greasy fries, and a needle and thread. She asked, "Did you see Donatelli in the back of the courtroom?"

"Oh no, KA, you're shitting me? He's going to flay me."

"I don't think so. He hates Stanley more than we do. I think he was there getting evidence against the judge."

McFarland imagined what Donatelli might say about his exhausted closing argument. The bald, fire-plug senior prosecutor observed young AUSAs and provided 'helpful' feedback, usually scathing. He was rumored to do the dirty work for the 'Boss', United States Attorney George Rosen and reveled in his tough guy reputation. God help the assistant U.S. Attorney he saw in court with his suit coat not buttoned. Women he left alone. Contemptuous? Afraid?

Donatelli strode into the office while McFarland was sitting in his underwear stitching his pants. He rose, shaking his head and grinning sheepishly. "Vic, I…"

"That was a ridiculous situation. You handled it fine. The jury was on your side. They respect that you just did what you had to do. They'll sympathize and convict."

McFarland shook his head in disbelief, "You think so?"

Donatelli snorted, "They ought to convict that pathetic excuse for a judge. Do you know why he hates us?"

"I thought it was about who gave the *Washington Star* the story?"

"Yeah, well sure, that was me, but it started long before that. When he was in his 30s, he wanted to work for us and pulled all kinds of strings. We never even gave him an interview. He had a terrible reputation even then. That was nineteen years ago. Then his friends got him a judgeship. President Johnson owed somebody something and we got the turkey prize. The Chief Judge tried to keep him on the civil side doing landlord tenant stuff, but he wanted to get to the 'glamorous' criminal cases. We need to get rid of him."

Donatelli sat on the corner of Bartolo's desk and accepted a beer from KA. He told them the whole team had done a good job and he was proud of them standing up to the judge, hinting it wouldn't be too much longer.

By 8:45 p.m., there was a call from Courtroom 7, "They're coming back in with a verdict."

McFarland put on his pants, buttoned his coat, and walked down with Vic and KA. Two jurors smiled at him as they filed in behind the clerk. One winked.

"All rise."

The judge came in, flushed and wobbly. He scanned his domain and endeavored to look magisterial. "Ladies and gentlemen, have you reached a verdict?"

"Yes, Your Honor."

"Are you unanimous?"

"Yes, Your Honor."

"Have you elected a foreman?"

An elderly black woman stood up and peered at him over her reading glasses.

"I am the fore*woman*, Your Honor."

"How do you, the jury, find the defendant, Terrance Stanhope, on the first count of robbery while armed with a dangerous weapon?"

"We find him guilty on *all* counts, Your Honor."

McFarland stood. "Step him back, Your Honor, he's been on bail."

"We'd have to wait for the Marshals."

"Yes, we will. He belongs in prison. This is his third conviction."

The Judged nodded unhappily, "Ladies and gentlemen of the jury, you are excused. Thank you for your service. And have a happy Thanksgiving. Mr. Stanhope, you will be remanded and can see what they serve for Thanksgiving dinner in the D.C. Jail. Counsel will remain in case there is any difficulty. I'll be in my chambers."

He rose unsteadily and Donatelli followed him, his face screwed up in a brutal scowl.

The jurors stood saying goodbye to each other. Slocum, the detective who'd handled the case, came in to shake hands with McFarland. The forewoman approached him, a grandmotherly smile on her face. "Young man, the jurors asked me to thank you for putting up with that monster. We were on your side from the beginning."

"I am very glad you convicted the defendant."

"Oh, him, a couple of the jurors knew all about him from the neighborhood. Good riddance. No, we mean that judge. We'd of told him the verdict before we left the courtroom, but we figured we'd earned our dinner and you needed time to stitch up your pants."

McFarland looked at her thoughtfully. So much for his prosecutorial skills. The jury convicted because they knew the defendant was a bad dude and they felt sorry for the prosecutor. As he stood there trying to decide how he felt about getting the sympathy vote, Donatelli came back looking smug. "Well. That's done. Jimmy, your friends in 3D Vice have done us a real favor."

"My friends?"

"Oh, yeah, the sergeant's team has been letting people know you're their man."

"I spent one night completely confused in a prowl car, and they got a great story about me asking for salad at Mama's, and now I'm a mascot?"

"Mama likes you. And that crew knows what's going on."

*****

The following Monday, when the court returned from the short Thanksgiving break, the team learned that Judge Stanley had taken early retirement and Courtroom 7 had a new presiding judge, the no-nonsense Elena Raymond, the first Black woman on the court. It wasn't until later that week that McFarland spotted Detective Smallwood scurrying across the vast atrium toward Courtroom 3. "Amel, what the hell happened to Judge Stanley?"

"Yeah, man, I heard you had an equipment failure in your trial. Slocum thought it was pretty funny."

"Funny? It didn't feel funny. First Momma's, now this. I'm going to keep the whole court system laughing for weeks. But what went down with the judge? One night he's abusing us, the next thing he's gone. Donatelli said you guys had something to do with it…?"

"Us? Nah, not me. We jus' advised."

"Advised who?"

"Well, Counselor, you remember those extremely lovely police officers you met?"

"Oh, jeez, no…"

"Yup, his Honor comes cruisin' down 14th in a blue Chrysler with his judge plates on it. He pulls up in front of the ladies an' asks are they busy. One of 'em eases over and asks what she can do for him. She doesn't want to get in the car 'cause he's blasted an' his face is flushed like he's about to have some sort of attack, but she gets him to turn off the engine an' she climbs in. An' he asks for a blow job. She asks for the money, an' he pulls out a roll and says I'm good for it and starts undoing his pants. She pulls out her credentials an' says, 'I'm a cop an' you're busted,' and signals for backup."

"He's getting real obstreperous 'til Lieutenant Dixon gets there. Then he starts whining about how it's all a 'misunderstanding'. Dixon says, 'Yeah, tell it to the judge,' and he says 'I am a judge, and you need to forget about this.'

So they hold him in the car and Dixon calls the Commander and the Commander calls the Chief, and *he* calls the U.S. Attorney and wakes him up. The U.S. Attorney says, 'Take him in, but no paperwork, yet. Come to my office to paper it.' The next morning Dixon polishes his badge and goes to the U.S. Attorney's office and Donatelli is there. Vic says, 'Let him know the U.S. Attorney's gonna deal with this, and let him go.'"

"Holy shit."

"You gonna thank me?"

Chapter 5
Fraud

A week after Judge Stanley resigned, McFarland settled into a seat on the D-2 bus. He was impatient and wondered whether to get off downtown and switch to the little section of the new Metro system that was finally open. It would take him only three stops to Judiciary Square, but the Metro was quiet, clean, and magnificent. He loved the vaulted ceilings above the stations, indirect lighting, and rubber wheeled cars. It made him feel hopeful to ride it. His reverie was broken by a well-dressed young man he'd exchanged nods with on previous mornings. Sitting down next to him, the man smiled and said, "You're a fellow early rider. Do you work on the Hill?"

McFarland grinned and shook his head. "No, Superior Court, the seething heart of city justice. I'm an assistant U.S. attorney. How about you?"

"I work in the D.C. General Counsel's office."

"What does that mean exactly?"

"Everything from analyzing legislation that's moving through the city council to reviewing contracts." He paused and then said, "It's not a glamour job." McFarland looked at him, puzzled, and he added, "My wife's dad is a big wheel at Hogan and Hartson. He can't believe his daughter married a minor city bureaucrat."

McFarland laughed at the self-deprecation. "Yeah, well my hippie friends think I've sold out."

"How's that?"

McFarland chuckled, "You know, representing the tyrants against the people."

"So have you?"

"What?"

"Sold out?"

McFarland smiled again. "No, not yet. It's important to do this job with integrity and a commitment to justice."

"Hear, hear. I wish the White House lived by that credo."

McFarland shrugged. "Well, Nixon's gone, we're out of Viet Nam, and in a few more weeks we'll have a preacher president and a new Congress."

They talked on, and McFarland decided to stay on the bus. As they neared the District Building his seat mate introduced himself. "I'm Joel Garabedian, by the way."

"I'm Jimmy McFarland. It was good talking to you."

"Yeah, it was..." Garabedian hesitated, "Why don't you come over for a drink some time—with me and my wife?"

"Sure, sounds good. When?"

"Friday evening? Want to bring someone?"

McFarland shrugged, "I'll see if she's free. She works on the Hill. Her schedule's not predictable."

*****

Friday afternoon, not unexpectedly, Rachel called to back out. "I can't get away. The senator needs some stuff faxed out to Seattle tonight."

"On a Friday? When they're not in session?"

"That's the way it is, Jimmy, I'm really sorry."

McFarland ambled over to Paul lounging on the sofa, legs and arms dangling over the edge.

"*Stuff*," said McFarland, "she said he needs 'stuff'. The chairman of the Senate Armed Services Committee, the silver-haired senator from Boeing, needs 'stuff'."

Paul laughed, "Yeah, man, you better watch it."

McFarland grimaced and muttered, "Actually, I'm not even sure I care."

"No?"

"No. Like you said the other day, I don't really look forward to spending time with Rachel anymore."

Paul grinned, and asked, "Why don't you take Sal?"

"Your little sister? Miss Punk? Is she here?"

A voice from upstairs broke in. "I'm not a punk!"

"Well, who the hell put shaving cream in my coffee?" McFarland shouted.

"You had it coming."

"You want to come to cocktails with me?"

"Where?"

"A couple named Garabedian. I met him on the bus to work, and he seemed interesting. I think his wife writes for the *Post*. They live over by the Cathedral."

"Ooh, Chic! Yes, I'd love to Jimmy, thank you. Just give me a minute to get dressed."

McFarland had known Paul's little sister since she was thirteen. Now twenty-three and about to get her MFA in performance as a classical violist, she had arrived from Philadelphia to stay with her big brother while in town to audition for the Fairfax Symphony. She was as sprightly as Paul was languid, as graceful as he was gangly. She had short blond hair, large green eyes, a quick smile, and an irrepressible pixie quality. She appeared in a little black dress, boots and a purple scarf.

McFarland gaped. "Who the hell are you?"

"Sally's stylish twin," she responded.

"Maybe I better dress up," he said holding the lapel of his old sport coat between two fingers. She blushed and shook her head.

*****

The Tudor-style stucco house was on a quiet corner a few blocks from the National Cathedral. Stately old rhododendrons and azaleas loomed in the darkness beside the door. McFarland rang the bell. Joel welcomed them in. Jimmy introduced Sally. Joel raised his eyebrows and pursed his lips.

"Oh, no, *she* couldn't come. Sally's just my roommate's little sister."

"*Just his little sister?* I'm your date tonight," Sally murmured. She had always had a crush on her brother's friend McFarland and longed to get him to think of her as something other than a kid sister.

Joel led them into a warmly lit living room where two fat armchairs and a handsome regency sofa faced a blazing fire in a painted brick hearth. A grand piano dominated the rest of the room. Joel gestured elaborately, "This is the lovely Mariana, my wife." An elegant figure in a fitted green wool dress, shawl, and tall soft leather boots, Mariana had strikingly fair skin, defiant eyes, thick dark hair and thin lips. She looked faintly dangerous. This was interesting; not what Jimmy had expected. She seemed like a woman who might be high maintenance.

Mariana looked at him intently and said, "Jimmy McFarland, youthful federal prosecutor. Hmm. You don't *look* arrogant and cruel. More boyish and sweet."

"Why, Yes, Ma'am," he drawled, "I'm just a simple, small-town lawyer trying to do what's just and true here in the heart of Sodom and Gomorrah."

"Ah, the Twin Cities. And have you found truth and justice?"

"No, not so much, but I believe it is here."

"Where? The White House? Capitol Hill? Surely not the Superior Court?"

McFarland shook his head sadly. "No, not there, Ma'am. In the hearts of the people."

"Oh, help me before I swoon. Abe Lincoln walks among us spouting nonsense."

Joel, wondering why his wife had decided to play the role of the cynical big city reporter, intervened to offer drinks. Jimmy went with him to help get them. As they left, Sally perched on the arm of a red plush armchair, and Mariana came over and stood, bending slightly toward her.

"Who are you, besides someone's little sister?"

"A grad student, and, I hope, a violist."

"You play viola? Oh, dear, the most benighted of strings."

"Oh, not at all, the viola is just misunderstood. Mozart played viola. He loved the range of moods and being in the middle of the harmony. Orchestras always need violas; just like choruses always need tenors." She smiled sheepishly, "I'm here for an audition."

"You're here to audition? My, how exciting. Where, if I may ask?"

"The Fairfax Symphony."

"The symphony of the suburbs," Mariana said, "always in the NSO's shadow." Sally thrust her chin out. "They have a good reputation, and they do adventuresome programming. They performed Phillip Glass and Gyorgy Kurtag in a concert this fall."

"Ah, yes Minimalism meets Modernism. I'm afraid Glass bores me. I don't think repetition enhances the musical experience. However, I'll have to ask my editor to let me go see if the FSO has improved."

Sally was wide-eyed, chagrinned that Mariana had so casually brushed aside her obscure name dropping. Had she mentioned her 'editor'? Oh, God, was this the *Post*'s music critic? Had she already found a way to get crosswise with the Washington music establishment?

"Are you a music critic?"

"Critic? No, not really. They don't like us to criticize the home team. We're all for the proliferation of orchestras of any stripe so long as they're ours. I'm more of a Jill of all trades. I write for the Style Section. I go whither I am directed."

Joel and Jimmy arrived with the drinks. "A G and T, a Campari and soda, and whiskey for the counselor. Sally, did I hear you're a musician?"

"I hope so," she said, glancing at Mariana.

"Alas, the poor child aspires to be a violist."

"Any other instruments besides the viola?"

"Yes, the right question, Joel my love. Have you a life raft? An exit strategy? The music world is so dreadfully exacting."

"I play a little jazz guitar. And I sing for fun."

"My husband composes. It's something he's actually quite good at."

"Do you, Joel? Oh, play us something, please!"

Joel, obviously delighted, sat down at the piano, leaned back for a moment, became serious, and began to play and sing a slow ballad about the death of a friend. It was mellow and sad. McFarland listened in awe. It was lovely.

You said goodbye that foggy dawn
We all knew we'd live forever
Now dear friend forever gone
Always changed to never.

"Bravo, Joel. That was beautiful. Do another."

"Why don't you sing something with me, Sally." She hesitated. He pointed to a stack of music on the piano. "Find something you know." She leafed through *One Hundred Hits of the 60s.*

"Oh, wow, this is great stuff. John Denver? Nah, he's already a cliché. Oh, this, now, this I can do." She held the book open to *The Tracks of My Tears.*

"Didn't Ronstadt just cover this? Let's do it," he said, hoping it wouldn't be a case of a titmouse trying to be a lark.

Sally stood behind Joel, reading the score over his shoulder. Mariana sat in one of the armchairs looking bored. Her husband was at it again with a pretty, young thing. Sally put down her drink and started to sing. Joel smiled widely. It wasn't a little girl's voice; she sang with throaty ease, a very sexy sound. This would be an interesting evening. He could already see the annoyance on Mariana's face, and the beginnings of calculation.

People say I'm the life of the party
Because I tell a joke or two
Although I might be laughing loud and hearty
Deep inside I'm blue
So take a good look at my face
You'll see my smile looks out of place
If you look closer, it's easy to trace
The tracks of my tears

Sally nodded to Joel and eased into the final verse, looking sadly at Jimmy.

He's just a substitute
Because you're the permanent one,
If you look closer, it's easy to trace
The tracks of my tears...

Joel held the last melancholy chord, and Sally offered a little curtsey.

"Awwwriiight, little lady, way to sing that thing," said Joel.

Mariana lifted a long-fingered hand, holding it still while she clapped daintily with the other. "Oh my, yes, that was *something*. Foreswear the dreary viola; you have a bright future as a lounge singer."

Sally looked at her, puzzled. To hell with restraint. "Don't you think *Tracks* is more kinda Motown? Though, I suppose, considering the lyrics, it's actually *Vesti La Giubba* in modern dress."

Joel watched happily as Mariana tried to decide whether to cede the round. McFarland wondered who this woman masquerading as Paul's bratty little sister really was? Did little sisters sing like that? And one-up the Dragon Lady with Motown and Pagliacci allusions in the same sentence?

"Joel, dear, shouldn't you refill our glasses? Or shall we go out and get some dinner?"

"Jimmy, Sally, what's your pleasure?"

"Well, we hadn't planned…"

"Come on, Jimmy, I'm famished. How about that Cuban place where we went with Paul last year."

"The Omega?"

Mariana looked horrified. "Good Lord, wasn't there a murder there a few months ago?"

"Mmmhmm, a couple was cutting through the alley after dinner, and a group of kids robbed and then shot them," answered McFarland.

"Kids?"

"Yeah, twelve, thirteen, and fifteen. The twelve-year-old was the shooter."

"Oh, my God. A child?"

"Yup, too young to charge as an adult. He'll spend a few years getting toughened up at the D.C. Youth facility."

"So they were caught?" Joel asked.

"Sure. They were on a spree. Two more robberies that night. There were about twenty cops out after them, and they were caught breaking into one kid's grandmother's house."

"His grandmother? What were they on?"

"Crack. The new plague on the DC streets. The robbery rate for the Columbia Road area went practically to zero once those kids were locked up." McFarland looked around at his horrified audience and thought he was starting to sound like an arrogant prosecutor. Everything simple. Get the thugs off the street. Who cares if they're children? "We can," he added, "go to the Omega. It's heavily patrolled, and they have their own security now, but we should probably take a cab."

*****

The Omega had the best Cuban food in DC, maybe the best North of Miami. Steaming *Sancocho de Siete Carnes, Lechon Asado, Moros y Cristianos, Tostones, and Casco de Guyaba con Queso Blanco*. When they arrived, there was a trio with guitar and percussion playing, and the place was full of happy noise. Joel overruled Jimmy's request for a beer and ordered *Mojitos*. He knew Mariana would be seething and wondered where she'd direct her acid attention next. Or would she turn on the charm? She seemed to have decided on McFarland and turned toward him saying, "You know, Jimmy, that story of the murder spree…"

"Robbery. Only one incident involved killing."

"Oh, well then, it's ok. That story is why people fear for this city and wonder about its government."

McFarland stared back at her and said, "You mean home rule?"

Mariana scoffed. "We're still defined by what happened to the city in '68. The city burning. Tanks on the streets. We barely have a downtown. We *wouldn't* have one if it weren't for the federal government presence. People at the *Post* are moving their families to the suburbs."

McFarland wondered whether she baiting him? Almost certainly, but this was the kind of fear and suspicion that was dividing the city. He put down his glass, sat up, and said, "This is a majority Black city that's been run like a plantation for a century. No voice, no vote. Are you surprised the transition to some kind of home rule is difficult? Did *Congress* do a good job running the city? We had lousy services, cash starved schools, people living in shacks, and a mostly white police force that was like an occupying army."

Mariana sighed. "How can the most powerful nation in the world have a capital where it's dangerous to walk the streets at night?"

The food arrived along with a second round of drinks. Mariana reached across the table and put her hand on McFarland's arm. "I'm really not a redneck, Jimmy, but it's scary not knowing which way we're going."

Everyone mellowed. Joel described his total humiliation when he approached a band leader at a club and asked the man to listen to some of his songs. "He looked disgusted. As if I'd offered him a big juicy cow pie. He sniffed at me and said he wasn't about to listen to every white boy in town who thought he could sing." Joel shook his head and turned to McFarland. "Can I ask you a serious question?"

McFarland looked at him, unsure if this was some new game this couple liked to play. "Sure."

"How do you feel about fraud?"

McFarland looked at him, puzzled. "As a way of life? A political strategy?"

"Unemployment compensation fraud."

"I'm feeling like the answer may get me in trouble."

“It’s not a trap—well it is, but it’s one you can walk out of. One of the duties of my job is to sign off on unemployment compensation fraud settlements.”

Mariana groaned.

“Mariana hates this rant, but this is something that bugs the hell out of me. We catch people all the time working while they’re collecting unemployment compensation. Some of them are poor jerks who don’t know any better, but we get middle-class professionals who’re just ripping off the system. I can’t prosecute them—only you guys can do that, and you won’t. You never have. I don’t even have the resources to sue them to get the money back. So we settle for a small fine. A glorified parking ticket, and word gets around. In the last few months, we’ve caught a bunch of white hats working on the Metro and collecting unemployment, and even a guy who worked on Carter’s campaign.”

“You’re serious?”

“He’s in line for a West Wing job.”

“Jesus. That’s obscene. What is it, a misdemeanor?”

“Nope. Felony. It’s fraud, dammit. The money’s put in by employers so it’ll be there if there’s a slowdown and a lot of people get laid off.”

Mariana purred, “Who’s the Carter guy?”

Joel looked at Mariana and smiled. He shook his head. He lived with a reporter, but she wasn’t getting this story.

“Why don’t you convince your office to take a few of these cases and send a message?” he asked McFarland.

Mariana rolled her eyes and said, “Oh, the one time I might score something juicy you get all cutesy.”

McFarland looked at Joel dubiously. “You guys don’t have some kind of pillow talk ground rules?”

“Ah, those sweet pillows, they swear they’ll never tell. But I don’t usually have anything that Mariana would care about.”

Chapter 6
Junk

McFarland and Garabedian met over the weekend to select five egregious cases of unemployment compensation fraud for McFarland to ask the front office to let him bring to the grand jury. He was not optimistic. When he showed them to KA and Bartolo, they groaned.

"What the hell's the point, Jimmy?"

"I don't think we should let middle-class white guys rip off a fund that's supposed to rescue unemployed people in emergencies."

Bartolo laughed. "You are such a fucking Boston puritan, McFarland. Get over it. We're living in murder city."

*****

On Monday, December 6, McFarland went to the front office to argue for indicting a few fraud cases as a warning. He expected to find Donatelli, and maybe Hooker, the chief of felony trial. He was surprised to find the Great Man himself, George Rosen, a hero of Watergate, a man whose hand he'd shaken briefly when he was sworn in, and whom he'd never seen again. To everyone in the office he was simply 'the Boss'.

"Mr. McFarland, how'd you come by this unusual fascination with junk cases?"

McFarland winced and explained the meeting on the bus and his growing indignation when he looked at the cases.

The Boss said, "A lot of people steal from the government in this town, my friend."

McFarland took a breath, and soldiered on, "We don't have to condone it."

The Boss smiled ruefully. "True enough, but we have to decide where to use our ammunition."

McFarland had expected this. He pushed forward the file of the campaign aide. "We can't let this guy work in the White House. He's a sleaze."

The Boss rolled his eyes and muttered, "He wouldn't be the first."

Donatelli shook his shiny head. "Boss, people suspect you're a Democrat because you went after Nixon. That's a good thing right now, but if it somehow gets out that you let this turkey off the hook, Carter's going to have to replace you."

The Boss grinned. "See now, Mr. McFarland, that's how it's done. This is a political city, not an ethical one. You have me pinned. Move these cases. No more. And for Christ's sake, don't take them to trial. When you move against the Carter guy, all hell's going to break lose. Very smart and persuasive reporters are going to call. You have no comment. None. Not a word. They can call me."

*****

It was eye opening. The lawyers for the four defendants other than the one from the Carter campaign were indignant.

"Jeezus, Jimmy, what's going on? Why are you messing with this poor schmuck? Everybody does it."

"That's why."

They threatened to sue for selective prosecution. They said McFarland would look like an over-zealous asshole when this stuff hit the papers, as it soon did. The *Post* broke the Carter aide story first, on December 10th. All hell did break lose. A sad human story that struck close to the pious new president. A young man he had come to love almost as a son, destined for a West Wing job that took him in and out of the Oval Office every day, was caught up in common venality. McFarland got calls from the *Post*, the *Times*, CBS, and a very charming woman from *Newsweek*. He respectfully referred them to the Boss, who noted solemnly that these defendants had stolen funds meant for people who were really suffering because they had been laid off. The new administration hung the young campaign aide out to dry.

When Judge Raymond took the young aide's plea his lawyer, John Cartwright, a fixture of the Democratic establishment and a close friend of

McFarland's favorite professor in law school, looked at McFarland sadly. "He's just your age, you know. He *was* unemployed, and when his volunteer job for Carter turned into a real job, he just didn't get around to stopping the unemployment comp."

"John, he didn't stop until we indicted him."

Cartwright sighed. "Yes, stupid, very stupid. He was riding high, and now it's all down around his ears. But don't assume it could never happen to you, Jimmy. Don't let righteous arrogance kill your humanity."

Curiously, in several stories McFarland was portrayed as an unbending, stone-faced, silent prosecutor whom defense attorneys feared and hated. Paul guffawed and asked whether Jimmy would like his housemate to call the *Post* and correct this gross mis-portrayal of his bleeding-heart liberal housemate.

"At least it offsets the stories that are going around the courthouse about the split pants and ordering salad at Momma's," McFarland responded.

"Yeah, but those stories were true, man. This is fiction."

He had guilty pleas in each of the cases before Christmas. One defense counsel turned to him as his client entered his guilty plea and said quietly, "Merry Christmas, prick."

Garabedian was elated. He took McFarland out for coffee and told him that people throughout the district government had come to say thanks for getting the U.S. Attorney to take district laws seriously.

"For them, it seems like a mark of respect."

"Joel, you put together five iron-clad cases, tied them up with a bow, and I took five guilty pleas. It wasn't hard." Joel looked at McFarland, and smirked. "Now I have something else."

"No, no, no. I can't do any more. The Boss is still pissed that I leveraged him with the Carter aide."

"Nope, not more of those. Related, but different."

"No, Joel. Not going to happen."

"You remember William Minot?"

"Yeah, the head of the division that brought us those cases?"

"Him. So far as he's concerned, you are a hero."

"And?"

"And he trusts you to take him seriously."

McFarland frowned and shook his head. The Boss had told him to do those five cases and no more. This was exactly what he'd meant, but McFarland was curious and rather flattered.

"What's he got?"

"Can I bring him over to tell you himself?"

"Why not just tell me?"

"It'll mean a lot to him."

"Okay, okay."

"This afternoon?"

McFarland looked at his friend skeptically. "What the hell…?"

"Look, I'll get him out of there in thirty minutes or less. If you think we've wasted your time, I'll owe you a bottle of good wine."

"I have a motion to argue this afternoon, but the defendant may take the chance to plead out. If he does, I'll call."

*****

Garabedian brought a small man in his sixties with brush cut white hair, thick black rimmed glasses, and watery blue eyes, to meet McFarland that afternoon. He wore a plaid sport coat, narrow dark tie, neatly pressed slacks, and brightly polished shoes. He almost bowed when he shook Jimmy's hand.

"I want to thank you, Mr. McFarland. You've no idea what it means to have you prosecute those cases, and have your boss say what he did."

"You're welcome, Bill. Thank *you* for doing a thankless job."

"Yes, sometimes it seems that way."

"Joel said you'd discovered something."

"Yes, it was because of the indictments and the news coverage. A man came forward, an older man, an engineer. He wanted to turn himself in before we indicted him. It wasn't a case we'd ever have moved on. He said he'd pay the money back. We were working out a settlement when he asked if it would help if he gave us some information on a much bigger fraud."

"A lot of people try to weasel out of it when we catch them by telling us they'll give us information on someone worse than them, but this guy had turned himself in. And he was working for Conway Corporation on the Metro construction. You remember when they were doing the tunnels through downtown and things were a complete mess?"

McFarland shook his head. “I wasn’t here yet.”

“Well, it was a major cock-up. They had to shore up a bunch of buildings they’d already dug under, and they got way behind schedule. They were already behind, but this was a big deal. So, the contractors and WMATA agreed they’d work round the clock, seven days a week, whatever it cost, and they’d get paid on a cost-plus basis. The unions loved it—lots of overtime. The contractors loved it—it was extra money for the work they’d already contracted to do.”

“This engineer, the one who turned himself in, he was the ‘Acceleration Coordinator’. The whole scheme was called an Acceleration Contract. He gathered the information about the costs of accelerating the contract for the company to submit to the WMATA. Pretty quick, he saw that the contract was a license to print money. They were paying workers who never showed up, ordering materials they didn’t use. The prime contractor, Conway, made a profit on everything. The subs were skimming like crazy. And then as our guy started to get to know people, he got the impression that Conway knew and didn’t want to know.”

“So, Mr. McFarland, I thought I’d let you know in case you wanted to try to investigate this.”

“Bill, that’s a helluva story. Do you think it’s true?”

“I don’t know, sir. It certainly could be. The man seems believable, and this Metro contract is the biggest thing the city has ever tried to manage.”

“Did this engineer have any idea how big the fraud might be overall?”

“He guessed several million dollars a month.”

McFarland was aghast. A multi-million-dollar fraud. He couldn’t ignore it. This wasn’t junk. At the least, he should meet the man.

“Bring him to see me.”

“He’s waiting at my office. I’ll bring him over.”

*****

The man Minot brought, Aubrey Douglas, was hunched and saggy, his mouth drooped sadly, his eyes were half shut, and his jowls hung loosely beneath his chin. Even his clothes hung loosely, as if he’d been a bigger man not so long ago. His glasses were smudged and dusted with dandruff. He shook McFarland’s hand limply and looked around the crowded office uneasily. KA and Bartolo were both at their desks. A government chemist was sitting next to Bartolo's desk looking bored. Douglas backed away.

"I'd prefer to talk in private," he said in a near whisper, "I don't think it would be good if they found out I was talking to you. I'd rather talk where there aren't so many people."

McFarland looked at Douglas and saw fear. Did that make him more credible? It was late afternoon. Judge Raymond was done for the day. McFarland buzzed the clerk.

"Smitty, her Honor is done for the day, isn't she?"

"Why, you got something else?"

"No, I need to interview a witness where he feels safe."

"No problem, man, just turn the lights off when you leave."

McFarland took Douglas and Minot down to courtroom 7. Douglas sat in silence looking dazed.

"Mr. Douglas, what's on your mind?"

Douglas looked at him with near panic, and then stared at Minot.

"Go ahead, Aubrey, you wanted to talk. This is what you said you wanted."

"Maybe I made a mistake. I'm interfering where I don't belong. Why should I mess up people's lives? The job's getting done. It's not my business how they're doing it."

Minot put his hand on Douglas' shoulder and said, "Because you see something that's all wrong, and it bothers you."

Douglas took a breath, looked at Minot and then at McFarland and finally said, "A lot of guys are just doing their jobs and they see the stealing and nothing happens. And then little guys get caught for doing stuff that doesn't amount to much."

McFarland nodded and asked, "What did you see?"

Douglas stared at the floor. "A mess. Starting with the tunnel collapse downtown, and then what happened with the National Portrait Gallery." He glanced at McFarland who offered no response. "You know they were pushing right under that building, and it started to crumble. General Grisham wanted to tear it down and just keep going, but there was all kinds of fuss. They say the Portrait Gallery is one of the oldest buildings in the city. Congress really got on them. WMATA had to tell Conway to underpin the building and fix the walls where they'd cracked. Then the hurricane hit and flooded the downtown tunnels."

"Who's General Grisham?"

Douglas stared at McFarland in disbelief. "He runs the WMATA. He's as straight as a T-Square, but he's old style. He goes nuts about delays and screw-ups. He knew the delays would drive up costs and give ammunition to the people who want to cut back on the system and build roads."

Douglas went on to tell the story that Minot had summarized. How the acceleration contract made any expense profitable for the contractor, Conway. He held out his hands and said, "That acceleration contract pretty much took away the need to control expenditures. They were going to get a profit anyway. So why get in a fight with the unions?"

McFarland frowned. "What made you believe there were ghost workers? How do you count what isn't there?"

"It was my job. It wasn't very complicated. I visited the work sites to see what work was getting done. Since they were working twenty-four-seven, I'd go at night sometimes, or five in the morning. I'd count how many men were working and compare it with the time sheets I received."

"Did you ask the foremen about it?"

Douglas sighed and said, "Oh, sure. First, they said I must have made a mistake. Then they told me that maybe some of the men were at another site and they'd mis-recorded it. Then my boss told me to stop bothering them."

McFarland imagined trying to persuade the Boss they should investigate whether there really was a fraud. The city desperately needed public transit and the Metro was getting built. It was a seven-billion-dollar project. Who cared if laborers were stealing when they got the chance? No, that was wrong. He was prosecuting kids for armed robbery when they waved a knife at an old lady and stole her purse with thirteen dollars in it. These guys were skimming millions assuming no one would care.

McFarland refocused on Douglas.

"Mr. Douglas, people are going to say that you made this up to cover for your own fraud, and that you don't know what you're talking about."

"I'm not making it up. I told the company, and I told the WMATA, but I never saw anything change."

"Who'd you tell?"

"My boss at the company, Mr. Taylor, and a lawyer at the WMATA, a young Black man. I forget his name. I haven't heard from him in a while."

“Do you have proof?” McFarland meant proof that he’d spoken to his boss. The answer startled him.

“I started copying documents. I gave a bunch of them to the guy at the WMATA, but I still have three or four boxes.”

“You have documents that show what was happening?”

“They sure show something was going on.”

“I need to see them.”

Two days later McFarland was again seated at the big, polished table in the Boss’s office. He wasn’t sure what to make of the absence of Donatelli. It was just him and the Boss, who sat peering at him over the reading glasses perched on his long narrow nose, apparently deciding what to do with the young troublemaker now. There was a silence, then the Boss asked quietly, “You have found another case?”

McFarland nodded. “I believe so.”

“You believe so? What does that mean?”

“A whistle blower came to me to complain about pervasive fraud in the construction of the Metro.”

“And?”

“And I think he’s credible, and what he’s describing is serious.”

“Why you, Mr. McFarland?”

McFarland explained about Douglas turning himself in and offering to tell Minot about the graft in the acceleration contract. He described the documents, which were admittedly suggestive rather than probative, and how Douglas had left the strongest of the documents with a young lawyer at WMATA.

“Have you spoken to the young lawyer?”

“No sir. I didn’t think I should investigate on my own.”

“Well, that, at least, makes sense. Why did Minot bring Douglas to you rather than the police or the FBI?”

“I believe he trusts me—or…”

“Or?”

“Or he thinks I’m a softer touch.”

The Boss nodded. “Okay, Mr. McFarland, leave it with me, and I’ll get someone to take a look.”

McFarland’s face fell, and the Boss saw his disappointment. “You think you should be involved?” McFarland started to answer, but the Boss interrupted, “You think you did a pretty good job with those unemployment cases, and you deserve a role in investigating this one?" Again, he started to answer and was interrupted. "Listen my friend, you are a very junior assistant U.S. attorney. You have a job to do, and this isn't it. I let you file those unemployment cases against my better judgment. This is what I worried would happen, not that you'd screw up, but that you wouldn't, and you'd think you were special."

"No, I—"

"Get some experience. See what can happen when you believe that you can tell whether someone is telling the truth. Have some cases crumble because witnesses let you down. And get tougher, Mr. McFarland, get tougher."

McFarland got up to leave, jaw clenched.

"And Mr. McFarland."

"Yes sir?"

"Bring the documents over and leave them with my secretary."

"Yes sir."

"Now."

"Yes sir."

He should have known. No, he did know, and he should have paid attention to what he knew. They were never going to let him pursue this case. They were right. When Minot came to talk to him, it wasn't complicated. This was a case to take to the bureau. Experienced investigators who knew where to start, how to build or drop a case. They knew what fraud looked like.

When he arrived back half an hour later wheeling a cart with the boxes of documents that Douglas had given him, he found Gareth Olsen an AUSA from Major Crimes chatting with one of the women who worked in the front office.

"Well, give me the stuff. The Boss has asked me to see if there is a case here that belongs in Major Crimes."

"Let me know if I can be of any help. I'm happy to fill you in on the background."

Olsen recoiled and wrinkled his nose. "Why would I need that? You've already wasted the Boss's time, and mine. Don't make it worse."

Chapter 7
As a Friend

After Ernie Hills was shot, Detective Amel Smallwood watched Williams sink into grim fury; a silent, smoldering rage. It scared him. He had worked with Sarge for almost three years. He knew that though he cultivated an image of dangerousness, he was, in fact, a man of superbly calibrated self-control. Smallwood trusted him, relied on him. But now Smallwood thought Williams's anger was beyond his control. If he thought he knew who'd killed Ernie Hills, he would find and kill them. Then he would turn himself in and go to jail, which would be wrong in every way. Sergeant Williams was one of the best men Smallwood had ever known, so he decided he had to find a way to damp the fire and focus Sarge on helping to bring the killers to justice. The only plan he could think of to do this depended on Jimmy McFarland. A week or so after the shooting, Detective Smallwood caught McFarland outside of Courtroom 7.

"Hey man, long time no see. You got a minute?"

"I have a scheduling conference with Judge Raymond. It won't take long."

Smallwood raised his eyebrows, and McFarland laughed. "No, truly, this woman is all business, and she knows how to run a courtroom. So long as you're straight with her, she's totally practical."

Smallwood laughed. "Ooh, you in love, man?"

"It sure is a big change."

A few minutes later Smallwood led McFarland to a corner of the bustling atrium and said, "I'm worried about Sarge. You know his best friend was murdered? Right at home in front of his wife and kid."

"I heard. My housemate has the kid in his class at St. Albans School. Sarge brought him to school after the murder."

"Yeah, I knew the kid was in some sort of fancy white school. Sarge is his godfather. He dotes on that little boy and worships the mom. He's taken it real hard."

"I'm sorry."

"I think he plans to find the guys that did it and kill them."

"Oh, no. No, he can't!"

"Yeah, man, you know he can."

"No, I mean, it would be terrible for him to go vigilante."

Smallwood shrugged, "Not surprising."

"That he'd want revenge?"

"Well, that, but no, I meant I knew you'd react that way."

McFarland took a deep breath, and asked, "Did you talk to him about it?"

"He just looks at me like I'm speaking in tongues."

"Is he getting close to finding the guys?"

"You need to talk to him Jimmy."

"What about?"

"What you believe—about the law. If he crosses the line, a lot of people gonna notice."

"Me? Lecture Sarge about obeying the law? The young, white, Vietnam-protesting prosecutor who's spent one night on the streets with you guys? You gotta be kidding me."

"No, man, I'm not. The thing is you are who you are. You don't even know to hide it. He'll trust where you're coming from."

"And he'll tell me to fuck off."

"Even if he does, he'll hear what you say."

"Amel, you're serious?"

"Yeah, I'm serious. I'll set up for us to have a drink with him."

"When?"

"This evening."

"What will you tell him?"

"That I asked you to talk to him about the Ernie Hills case."

"And he'll agree to come?"

"Shit, yes. You haven't seen him. He's all torn up."

*****

McFarland met Williams and Smallwood at a bar a few blocks east of the Capitol. They were seated in a booth at the back when he arrived. There was a mixed crowd. Hard hats and grungy coats hung on the coat rack. At the bar, guys who'd been working outside all day sat swathed in multiple layers of sweatshirts next to young white staffers from the Hill in suits.

McFarland squeezed past the crowd at the bar and reached out to shake Williams's hand. He looked awful. The power he usually exuded was diminished. His eyes were dull and red; his shoulders sagged.

"Counselor."

"Sarge. I'm so sorry about your friend."

"I guess you heard what happened?"

"Tell me."

"He's there at home with his family. Claire, his wife, doing the dishes, Little Ernie doing his homework, and a couple of guys come, ring the bell. Ernie lets them in. They pull guns, tie up Claire and Little Ernie, pistol whip Ernie, then the bastards kill him. A bullet in the back of the head. Then they walk out the door and drive away."

"Homicide is on it?"

"Yeah, good guys. Pete Phillips and Donnie Blake. They got nothing."

McFarland waited, then said, "I think I had a case with Blake. That fourteen year-old who killed a kid for his Lakers Jacket?"

Williams answered so quietly that McFarland could barely hear, "Darius Jenkins."

"He ended up in Oak Hill didn't he? Juvie detention."

"A bad, bad place, Counselor."

Smallwood, who'd elbowed his way to the bar to get a round of beers, came back, spilling suds, and set the mugs down, pushing one to McFarland. "Well, here's to law and order."

They drank, and Sarge fell silent. McFarland looked at Smallwood and saw cool calculation in his eyes. He was watching Sarge, who seemed lost in despair, and waiting, his right hand gently tapping his beer in time to the loud music. The song changed, and Sarge turned back to them, his eyes blank.

"Sarge, you should tell Jimmy what you're thinking. You see me an' Dixon all the time. You know we're gonna be with you."

Williams almost sneered. "Yeah, I tell him so the U.S. Attorney Office can tell me what I can and can't do?" He glared at McFarland. "You here keeping an eye on the cowboys from 3D Vice, Counselor?"

McFarland sat silently, letting the question hang.

"Well?"

McFarland held Williams's hard stare. "I'm here because Amel asked me to come. I'm here as a friend."

"Whose friend?"

"His—yours."

"How'd you get to be *my* friend?"

That, thought McFarland, was a fair question. He barely knew Sergeant Larry

Williams. Barely knew him but admired and for some reason cared about the man.

"I don't know, Sarge, I guess I'm offering to be a friend. We both care about what's going on out there—and we both believe in right and wrong."

"Right and wrong? You think you know which is which?"

"Yeah, mostly. And I think you do too."

There was a long silence between them while Lou Rawls crooned, "You'll never find another love like mine," and someone at the bar laughed unpleasantly. McFarland looked at his glass, and then at Smallwood, who seemed imperturbable. Sarge pushed his glass away as if he was going to get up and then turned to McFarland, focused and present.

"As a friend, then, what the hell are you here for?"

McFarland thought, *There's no sense in tiptoeing around it, I got to lay it out there.* He grimaced, looked hard at Sarge, and said, "I'm hearing that you're going to kill the guys that killed your friend—if you can find them."

"If I can find them—yeah, that's about right."

"I think that would be wrong—wrong for you, bad for the city, and no help to the family you care about."

"And you think the Homicide Squad, and the US Attorney, and the courts will do the job?"

"They have to."

Williams shook his head and said quietly, "In your world, maybe, but not in mine. I don't believe it's gonna be alright, Jimmy, and I'm not letting it go. Most of your life you been able to feel things would work out ok. You been safe. Cops were there mostly to protect you. The courts were fair. You don't even know that if you are Black you grow up different. None of that is true."

McFarland drew a breath. He didn't know, could never know. He based his moral understanding on not knowing.

"You're right, Sarge. I don't know. I'll never *know.* There is a lot that's easy for me because I'm white, and there's a lot that happens to you because you're Black. Still, I believe we can fix the laws and the legal system and create a better society." It sounded lame to him as he said it. He was surprised by the response.

"Mm-hmm. You gotta believe that. It'd be scary if you didn't. It's your job—and it's who you are. But that doesn't mean you're right."

McFarland closed his eyes and sighed, then looked hard at Sarge. "Do you like the alternative where the law is just a tool of the powerful and anyone with a badge can take the law into his own hands?"

Williams grinned, the first time that evening he had done so. "Aww, Jimmy, you think I do that anyway."

"No, no, I don't. You want people to wonder what you'll do. You're scary, but you aren't dirty."

Smallwood got up quietly and came back with a bottle of Jack Daniels and three glasses. McFarland raised his eyebrows. Amel smiled. "This is getting real. We may as well drink the real stuff."

They talked about growing up in Wilmington, Boston, and Philadelphia. They talked about school and what happened to their hopes—realized for McFarland, defeated for Smallwood and Williams. They talked about opportunity and fear, the Civil Rights Movement, Dr. King and the riots, and what Sarge felt waiting to head home from Saigon at the end of his tour and seeing pictures of tanks rolling up 14th Street.

"I wondered what the fuck I was going home to, and why I'd lived through it all."

McFarland, floating in a whisky glow, said with earnest passion, "But that was *it*, man, that's *why* I was fucking protesting. The whole thing was a stupid waste, a dumbass stupid…" He shook his head, tears coming to his eyes.

Smallwood chuckled. "We gonna have to get you home."

McFarland held up his hand. "What are we doing about this murder?"

Williams put a big hand on McFarland's shoulder. "You tellin' me I can trust you, dude?"

"Yeah, you can."

"You dick around telling me the law this and the law that, I'm stickin your underwear in your mouth and tapin' it."

"While I'm still wearing it?"

"Yeah, you better believe it."

"Sounds like police brutality, Sarge, I may have to report you."

There was a long pause, Williams staring into space, McFarland nodding to the music, and Smallwood quietly watching. Williams turned toward McFarland, took a breath, and said quietly, "You're a ridiculous boy scout, but you're real."

McFarland didn't answer.

Sarge downed his drink and said, "Why don't you come with me to meet Claire and Little Ernie."

"Yeah, Sarge, I'd like to do that."

They wobbled out the door and walked slowly to the cab stand in front of Union Station where the two cops solicitously helped McFarland into a cab. He wondered blearily whether his friends would have trouble getting a cab to take them home, and then thought, *Shit, they're cops.*

He asked the driver to take Pennsylvania Avenue from the Capitol past the White House so he could see the National Christmas Tree, and then out Massachusetts Avenue and up Embassy Row with its grand mansions turned embassies. Christmas lights glittered from within the glass walls of the new Brazilian Chancery and restrained displays lit many of the European embassies.

He tried to make himself think about what had happened in the two hours he'd spent in the bar. He'd agreed—no, he'd asked to get involved in a murder investigation he had no business interfering with, working with a rogue cop planning an extra-legal revenge killing. He couldn't justify it, but at the same time he felt elated. He had to do it.

The cab pulled up in front of the row house he and Paul rented in Glover Park, a neighborhood just North of Georgetown that had been built rapidly when the government grew during the New Deal. Quiet, tree-lined streets nestled up against nearby parkland. Safe and privileged. An enclave.

McFarland paid the driver and walked unsteadily to the door, thinking he'd just about make it up the stairs to his room. As he turned the key, he heard a Christmas carol and loud happy laughter. The house was full of people and noise and the smell of food. He tried, unsuccessfully, to hang his coat, left it in the bottom of the closet, and peered into the living room. He saw Paul talking animatedly to a man holding a lute. Had he known there was going to be some sort of party? The smell of food made him aware that he felt mildly nauseous and the noise…

"Why are you frowning, McFarland? It's Christmas."

He turned and saw Sally, viola in hand, grinning at him.

"Um, not frowning, wincing."

She looked at him quizzically and giggled. "You're drunk. That's really funny."

"Like hell, it's funny. Who are all these people?"

"This—*we* are the Curtis Christmas Camerata. Everybody! Yo! This is Jimmy."

"*The* Jimmy? Do we have to hide our weed?"

McFarland closed his eyes and groaned softly. Sally grabbed his arm and guided him to a sofa.

"Can't you see the poor man's in pain? And he's misplaced the Christmas Spirit. Let's sing something for him."

They did. It was beautiful. He fell asleep.

*****

McFarland woke in a silent room, needing desperately to pee, his head throbbing, and his neck stiff from sleeping awkwardly. From across the room, out of the darkness, Sally asked, "Can I get you something? Coffee? Cocoa? Hair of the dog?"

"Oh, no, not that. Maybe just some water."

He staggered to the bathroom. When he came out, Sally handed him water and a couple of aspirin. He took them, and rolled his head to loosen his neck.

"I'm sorry you came home to an unexpected party. You probably just wanted to go to bed."

"Yeah, I did, but I seem to have crashed anyway. What are you all doing here?"

"We have some gigs doing Christmas concerts at fancy stores and Christmas parties."

That was true, but it was also true that she had spent hours on the phone arranging those gigs so she could come to Washington to see Jimmy and impress him with her talented friends. She had imagined him coming home at dinner time before they all came over and was distraught when she asked Paul, "Where's Jimmy?" and he smiled and told her he had no idea.

"Might be working, Sal, or," he whispered, "out with Rachel."

"Is that still going on?"

"Who knows?"

Then, three hours later, McFarland had staggered in bleary-eyed and far from delighted to see her or anyone else.

"Were you at a Christmas party?"

"No, not exactly a party. Work—sort of." He smiled ruefully. "I was in a noisy, smoky bar with a couple of detectives from the Third District Vice Squad."

"Surveillance?" she asked, eyes wide.

McFarland laughed, and then grimaced. "No. More like getting myself in trouble, I think. I was trying to persuade one of them not to kill a couple of guys."

She looked aghast. "What do you mean?"

"There's a sergeant I've gotten to know, a big bear of a man. Someone murdered his closest friend. Paul's met him. Paul's got the victim's son in class and Sarge brought the kid to school for a couple of days after the murder. Anyway, the murder looks like a 'hit' and Sarge has gone a bit crazy. He wants to make sure the shooters pay for what they did."

"He's going to hunt them down?"

McFarland looked at her uneasily. He wondered whether he wanted to try to explain.

"That's the way it looks."

"And you're going to help him?"

"No. Well, yes, I'm going to help him, but not to kill them." Although, he thought, it could look that way. "I want to convince him we can get the bastards legally."

"Why? I mean how come you're getting involved. Is he a good friend?"

"Not exactly. Not yet. But I think he is a good man. Honest. Wise. Somehow, it's really important to me not to—lose him. You know, I'm here doing this job because I believe it's possible to do justice. If a guy like Sarge loses faith that would bother me a lot."

She looked at him, not horrified, but thoughtful.

"He was willing to team up with a naive preppy?"

"It took us a while to get there."

"And a lot of whiskey apparently."

She looked at him severely, but her eyes twinkled, and he thought how very pretty they were.

"Did I—I mean I was completely out of it—did I do anything embarrassing?"

"Other than vomiting on the lutenist?"

"Oh, no!"

"No, Jimmy, you just passed out in the middle of an exquisite performance of *Lo, How a Rose E'er Blooming.* But you don't look that great right now. Sort of green."

"I think I need to sleep it off. Will you still be here tomorrow?"

"I was thinking of doing some Christmas shopping."

"Can I join you? I've hardly started."

"I'd like that."

Chapter 8
The Green Shawl

McFarland woke to the sound of Sally shouting at Paul.

"He's a sanctimonious Southern Baptist, for Chrissake! He got elected because Ford pardoned Nixon; it's like electing Mr. Rogers president."

He shuffled into the bathroom rubbing his eyes and hoping a hot shower would ease the throbbing in his head and the churning in his stomach. As the water pulsed on his back and the steam loosened the concrete in his head, he thought about how sweet Sally had been the night before when he'd woken from his coma.

Half an hour later he wandered into the little kitchen where the siblings' conversation had shifted to their parents' plans for Christmas. Their mom was a Jew turned atheist, and their dad, a mathematician, claimed to be a 'quasi-Buddhist'.

"What a heritage," Sally complained, "the Buddhists moan, and there aren't that many great pieces of atheist music."

"Sally, give it up. You aren't going to get them to do Christmas."

"I can try. I'm going to be like Scrooge's nephew and try every year. Why don't we conjure up some ghosts to persuade them, Pauli? You could do the ghost of Christmas Present." She knitted her eyebrows and spoke in a deep voice, "Come here and know me better, Man."

They saw McFarland and smiled. Paul spread his arms and announced, "He's alive! Get the man some coffee."

An hour later, the three of them were walking down the long Wisconsin Avenue hill into Georgetown. It was a cold, bright, Saturday morning a week before Christmas. The air felt clean. The sun glinted on parked cars, and they could see sparkling patches of the Potomac River and the towers of Rosslyn on the other side of the Key Bridge. The windows of the haphazard rows of low buildings lining the Avenue were filled with color. They ambled down gradually acquiring shopping bags full of packages. They went past M street to the canal, searching for a shop Paul remembered but could not find. At McFarland's insistence, they stopped at Jour et Nuit for lunch. "Wc can sit in front of the fire. My treat." They had *Soupe a l'Oignon, quiche, Salade Vert,* and *Mousse au Chocolate* and happily finished a bottle of white wine. McFarland, who knew nothing about wine, made a show of knitting his brows as he studied the wine list while the waiter nodded respectfully and guided him to a very expensive bottle.

Paul guffawed. "JHM, are you showing off?"

Laden with shopping bags and suffused with mellow goodwill, they started back up the hill, no one willing to suggest a taxi. Near the top of Georgetown, as Paul and Jimmy reminisced about a Christmas ski trip years earlier, Sally caught the glint of brightly painted tin in a window across the street and scampered across the busy street calling, "One more stop!"

The Phoenix was filled with fanciful and colorful Mexican crafts, tin figures, lamps, serapes, candlesticks, dolls and masks. McFarland was enchanted. He bought Christmas ornaments for his team members: a strutting peacock for Bartolo, an angel for KA, and a bird festooned Christmas tree for their assistant, Janice. Even Paul bought an embroidered bag for his favorite niece.

Wandering through the backroom, Sally suddenly cried out, "Oh, this is beautiful! Jimmy, you need to get this for your mom." Wistfully, she held out a soft, green woolen shawl with richly embroidered edges. He took it, nodding in agreement, and bought it without even looking at the price. He felt quite pleased with himself. By the time they'd trudged back up the hill, it was past four o'clock, and the December day was fading. They lugged their bags into the house, glowing from the long walk.

McFarland took the shawl to his room and wrote a label for it: "To my favorite brat, keep warm." He was cozy, happy, and tired. He grabbed the *Post* from the kitchen table where it had lain unread and settled into an armchair in the living room to read the latest about the incoming administration. Carter's choice for Attorney General, Judge Griffen Bell was already announcing his top deputies at Justice. Former prosecutors. Twenty or thirty years older than McFarland. Straight arrows. They probably hadn't run freelance investigations in their twenties.

Sally appeared arrayed in striped tunic, tights, floppy velvet hat, pointy-toed red slippers, and fur trimmed cape.

"Are you coming?"

He looked up puzzled. "Coming to what."

"Our performance. We have a gig on the Mall."

"No, I wasn't planning to. I'm meeting Rachel at a club."

She looked completely crestfallen.

"Sally, I didn't know you had a performance."

"No, I suppose not. Could you come before you meet Rachel?"

"No, that won't work. I was supposed to meet her last night, but I stood her up to go get wasted with Williams and Smallwood." Why was he explaining himself to an unhappy troubadour? Given the choice, he would not spend Saturday evening at the Gandy Dancer, but Rachel would kill him if he canceled. Sally couldn't just expect him to drop everything. Why did she look so—it wasn't annoyance—disappointed—defeated?

"Do you have another concert tomorrow?"

"No. We're going back. I couldn't get anything for Sunday."

"You arranged all this?"

"Uhhuh."

"Wow. You're an impresario as well as a troubadour."

"*Trobairitz.*"

"What?"

"The feminine of *troubadour* is *trobairitz.*" She smirked and doffed her hat.

"Why here?"

She looked at him evenly, shook her head, and said casually, "Oh, the nation's capital at Christmas, a chance to visit my big bro' and his roomie. All good," and turned away. "See ya."

She walked down the steps feeling she ought to go back and tell the moron the truth, but what if he just looked horrified and told her she was a really nice kid and he loved her—like a sister? He was going off on a date with the dreaded Rachel. Sally had never met her, but she had answered the phone once when Rachel had called for Jimmy. She had a gross Baltimore accent and a metallic voice. Sally imagined her as small, with dark hair, hard eyes, and lots of make-up. Rings, she'd definitely wear rings. Jimmy was way too sensitive and whimsical for a hard top like her.

Chapter 9
Something She Didn't Mention

Sergeant Williams was apprehensive. He was not a man who worried. He met life head on. He'd seen a lot of death. He'd let a lot of hate roll off him. To the extent he thought about it, he considered himself a realist. Those around him thought him fearless and powerful in a way that went far beyond his physical strength. On Monday evening, December 20th, he was having doubts as he waited for Assistant United States Attorney James Henry McFarland to come out of the Pension Building. Williams was on a mission of his own, going beyond his orders and authority. Somehow, he'd agreed to bring along a naïve, white, liberal federal prosecutor. He had to be crazy. Smallwood had played them both, the sonofabitch. What the crap was *he* up to? How could McFarland help Williams discover who had killed Ernie? It was like taking a boy scout on recon in the rice paddies.

But Williams knew perfectly well why he'd agreed. He had a suspicion about what had happened to Ernie, and he was hoping McFarland would help him snuff that suspicion before it ate him alive.

"Sarge, good evening."

"Counselor, you set?"

"Set."

"My car's on G street."

McFarland looked surprised. Williams smiled innocently and said, "Police plates." They walked in silence. McFarland asked about the Hills family and got the story of the two men meeting in basic training at Fort Bragg, the friendship that grew in the incomprehensible horror of Viet Nam, and Williams's determination to get Ernie back safely after learning that Claire was pregnant. Williams had introduced her to Hills when they were on leave, and there had been an immediate connection. They had married as soon as Ernie got back to the States and had later asked Williams to be Little Ernie's godfather.

"That little boy is the smartest kid I've ever met. He makes everything…"

Williams stopped and coughed to cover a sudden surge of emotion.

"What, Sarge?"

"He makes it feel like all this stuff is worth it. Now he doesn't have a dad. I grew up that way. I want to make sure things are better for him."

"My housemate, Paul Brown, has him in class."

"Yeah, the tall hippie."

McFarland smiled. "That's Paul. He says the kid is interested in everything."

"He is. He still believes he can do *any*thing."

They turned onto Varney Street. McFarland had never been in this peaceful neighborhood of curving streets and towering trees before. He knew almost nothing of the city east of the park. A few houses had Christmas lights strung on azaleas. They stopped in front of a house with a wreath on the door. McFarland saw Sarge take a deep breath.

"I'll follow you, Sarge, I'll just listen 'til you let me know it's ok."

Williams looked at him uneasily. McFarland felt completely out of place, uncertain why he was there, and what he was doing. Prosecutor? Friend? Looking at Williams he guessed that he was wondering the same thing.

They rang the bell and a graying man in a dark suit opened the door. "Hello Sergeant, Claire said you were coming by. Evie's with her in the kitchen. Is this your—friend?"

"Yes, I'm Jimmy McFarland."

"Jimmy, I'm Al. My wife Evie and I live next door."

"Professor Tyrell, isn't it? I'm glad to meet you."

They walked toward the kitchen past the wide entrance to the dining room on the right. There was a mahogany table with eight matching chairs, a tall glass-fronted cabinet filled with glasses and china, and heavy damask curtains on the windows. Opposite the dining room was the entrance to the living room with a big soft looking sofa and two deep armchairs. It seemed cold and dark. There were no holiday decorations. The floor was strangely naked. The murder room. A vision flashed through his head. A body crumpled on the floor, face down, two dark figures standing over it, blood spreading across the rug.

Williams was struggled, thinking of the two of them sitting, surrounded by cops and police brass the night of the murder. He was uneasy, wanting just to gather them up and hold them both, but unsure of himself with Al, Evie, and Jimmy there. Little Ernie, with no such doubts, raced over to him and climbed into his arms. Claire rose and gave him an awkward hug and a light kiss on the cheek, her eyes gleaming.

"Claire, Evie, this is my friend Jimmy McFarland."

"He's Mr. Brown's housemate and he helps put people in jail." Ernie said with excitement. "You're a lawyer like my dad, aren't you?"

"Yes, I am."

"I don't think I want to be a lawyer and my mom won't let me play football, so I'm going to be a scientist."

"What kind of science do you like?"

"Figuring out what's in space. We looked through a telescope, but there's too much light in Washington."

Williams wondered how this child could be full of life so soon after his father's violent death? Claire, knowing what he went through when they were alone, looked sternly at her son. "Ernie, you have homework, and Uncle Sarge and Mr. McFarland want to talk with me."

McFarland smiled and said, "If it's okay, Mrs. Hills, we'd like to talk to Ernie too."

She looked unhappily at Williams. Albert Tyrell said, "They've been through it all with the detectives. What's the point of going through it again?"

McFarland saw Williams's face tighten, and Claire leaned forward and put a hand on Tyrell's arm. "They're trying to help, Albert. It's ok. I think about it all the time anyway, and Ernie remembers things better than I do." Claire looked over at Evie and then Albert. "I am so very grateful to you both for taking such good care of us."

It was a dismissal. They hugged her and Ernie, said their goodbyes, and left.

Williams sat down in a small chair at the kitchen table, and McFarland thought about the way his bulk had dwarfed the chair in the little office the first time they'd met. Tonight, he seemed more blurred than dangerous, and Little Ernie leaned against him like a puppy.

Williams asked, "Albert thinks you should move out?"

"He's just trying to take care of us."

"Is it his business? I'll take care of you."

"You always have."

Williams watched out the kitchen window as the Tyrells climbed the steps to their house, apparently disagreeing about something. Albert Tyrell was a handsome, dignified, educated man, a professor at the Howard Medical School. He was part of the Black elite in Washington, and his calm self-importance rankled with Williams. Big Ernie had been perfectly a Williams of the tension between the two men and had teased his friend about it. He had said, "Yes siree, we are 'high yellow' here. This is the *Gold* Coast." Williams knew Claire could handle Tyrell, but still he felt the man was on his turf. He caught himself getting angry and dragged himself back.

He said, "Go ahead, Jimmy."

"Mrs. Hills, can you bear to just tell me the story of that evening?"

She smiled at him and said, "It almost makes it easier, Mr. McFarland."

"It's Jimmy. How easier?"

"That night is in my head all the time, like a song I can't stop hearing. We were sitting right here, and my husband was in the living room."

"What was he doing?"

"Reading the paper, *The Star*. They have better coverage of the district—well, of our community."

"Typical evening?"

"Yes, mostly. Sometimes he would come and talk to Little Ernie about school or sports, but not if he was wound up about work."

"Why was he wound up?"

"The General—General Grisham, he's the director at the WMTA—was pushing everyone to move faster and faster."

"What was he worried about?"

"He thought—well they were way behind."

McFarland watched her intently. Williams saw it too, the hesitation. McFarland asked, "Did he talk about papers that someone from the construction firm gave him?" She looked at him uncertainly, then looked down.

"No, he didn't talk about that." Little Ernie looked at his mother in confusion.

She shook her head and said sadly, "He was just reading the paper. We were here, in the kitchen. We heard the bell, Ernie went and said—well I couldn't hear what he said—something—then one of them came in here with a gun. He had his face covered with a mask or something."

Ernie shook his head. "No, Momma, it was a scarf. A blue scarf."

"He told us to lie down and shut up," she continued.

McFarland asked, "Was he white or Black?"

"I told the detective, I'm not sure. He didn't say much, and I couldn't tell by the way he talked."

Little Ernie interjected, "One of them had shiny shoes, real shiny black shoes." McFarland asked, "What did he do?"

"He tied our feet and hands with some rope…clothes line, and taped our mouths. He told us to stay quiet and we'd be ok. Then he left, and we could hear them with Ernie in the living room."

"What did they sound like? Angry? Threatening?"

It was Little Ernie who answered, "They sounded mean."

Claire added, "That's when one of them called him Yellow Dog."

McFarland looked at her intently. "What were they saying?"

"They said he'd messed up and he knew it."

He turned to the small boy standing by his godfather and holding his leg. "Did you hear that, Ernie?"

Ernie nodded solemnly. "They said he'd messed up."

"And called him Yellow Dog?"

Little Ernie shrugged.

Claire looked sadly at McFarland, "His dad never talked about the war."

Williams shook his head and said, "No one who wasn't in the unit with us, or real close—no one would know that name."

McFarland asked, "Is it possible they said something else?"

Claire looked at him blankly. "I don't know. It was just before they…"

Williams asked softly, "Claire, was it 'Yellow Dog' or 'Y-Dog'?"

"It could have been Y-Dog. Is that what I said that night, Larry?"

"Yeah, it was."

McFarland was alert. This was how memory got distorted. He asked, "Could it have been something that sounded like 'Y'? Like 'cry' or 'lie' or 'die'?" Little Ernie nodded his head "Yes."

Claire said softly, "I don't know. I'm not sure."

McFarland slogged on. "What happened next?"

Claire looked miserable and seemed on the edge of collapsing into her grief.

Little Ernie answered, "We heard them hit him, and a loud sound when he fell down, and then two shots. I—I—hoped it was Uncle Sarge coming and shooting them for hurting my dad."

Williams looked like he was about to lose it, and McFarland quickly broke in. "Thank you for taking me through that Mrs. Hills—and Ernie. There are a lot of people in the city trying to find out who did this."

Claire took a breath, looked at Williams and said, "Thank you, Mr. McFarland. I know you'll do your best."

McFarland's chest tightened. He obviously wasn't cut out for this. He was transfixed by the little boy. He blurted out, "Mrs. Hills, I'm wondering—I'm thinking that maybe Mr. Brown and I could take Ernie to the planetarium—as a Christmas treat."

Ernie jumped up. "Yesss!" but his mother shook her head.

"Thank you for the wonderful offer, but I think it's best if he stays around home."

Both Ernie and McFarland looked crestfallen.

Ernie wailed, "But Momma…"

Williams smiled more happily than he had all evening, took Claire's hand and said, "I'll go along to chaperone. It'll be ok."

Ernie danced, and Claire looked at Williams affectionately and nodded yes.

McFarland, surprised at himself, said, "Tomorrow? Can you make it tomorrow, Sarge? I don't have to be in court. We could pick him up around ten, go to the planetarium, then catch a bite of lunch?"

Williams looked at his godson, "How does that sound to you, Little E?"

"Cool, Uncle Sarge."

As they were driving back downtown Williams said, "You're a good man, McFarland. That was really nice."

"It'll make me happier than it does him."

"Yeah, yeah, that boy is special."

"Did you notice that Claire seemed to…maybe leave something unsaid?"

"We both loved Ernie and would maybe rather not know who killed him if it pulls him into the mud."

"How?"

"Yeah, that's what I keep asking," Williams said.

"Could it have been drugs?"

Williams reacted angrily. "No! I'd have known. And I'd have heard on the street. No, man, don't go down that path."

"My girlfriend knew him," said McFarland, "Her boss chairs the Senate District subcommittee and Ernie met with them to work on the budget. She said he was supposed to come meet with the staff director the week he was killed. He wouldn't tell them what it was about."

A deep crease spread across Williams's brow. "So, something to do with the big Metro contract?" He seemed both interested and relieved.

"Possibly, but the thing is she also said she'd seen him several times at the Gandy Dancer—sitting with Councilman Barry."

"Son of a bitch. He's a smooth-talking liar. He hates cops and white people until he doesn't."

"And it seems like drugs change hands at his table."

"Damn. Oh, man, I hope this ain't what Claire was worried about. Damn it if he was in trouble, he knew he could talk to me."

"What do we do?"

"We gotta pass this on to the homicide guys. Pete Phillips is real straight. He won't make something of it if it ain't there."

McFarland was relieved. He had feared that Williams would just put him off.

"You call him, Jimmy, I can't stand to do it. I wouldn't be able to face Claire."

"Okay. I guess it'll be natural for me to pass on something like this that I picked up in a bar."

"What're you doin' in that place, anyway?"

"My girlfriend loves it. I get the sense she's pretty interested in Mr. Barry."

Williams roared with laughter. "Don't take it personal. Seems to happen a lot."

McFarland thought, *I don't even care, and I need to think about that.* But his heart told him, you already know. You're only seeing Rachel because you're afraid to break up with her.

"Jimmy, there's another problem."

"Huh?"

"You know that I don't believe that anyone could have called Ernie 'Y-Dog' who wasn't in our unit." McFarland stayed silent while Williams drove, streetlights occasionally lighting his agonized face. He started again, "Ernie and Al Dixon had history. Dixon was our lieutenant. Him and one other guy were the only white boys in the unit, and neither of them was cool. Dixon was friggin' terrified all the time and stoned most of the time he was awake. He wasn't just scared of the Cong, he was scared that one of the guys would frag him."

"Why?"

"Cause he was a fuckin' racist and we all knew it, racist *and* chicken shit, and that put us all in danger."

"But he's your partner now?"

Williams ignored the question. "One night the whole unit had a meeting, and the guys demanded two things: that he agree that when he pulled racist shit we could call him on it, and when we were in the field I'd be in command."

"Whoa. Harsh."

"No, he was relieved. A few weeks later we had a New Year's party with a show that the guys put together. Ernie was behind it. He was always good at that kind of stuff—he could sing, play guitar, imitate people. So, he played a yellow dog, of course, and he had Dixon play a little red hen the dog chased around the rich folk's yard, a little red hen wearing a dress. It was funny, but Dixon, man, he hated it."

"I guess he must have."

"The three of us, we all got home. Dixon helped me get this job, and he even got his uncle to help Ernie and Claire get a mortgage—since the riots the banks in town don't like to do deals east of the park. But Ernie, he's been trying to pull together a reunion, and I think it's reopened the wound for Dixon."

Williams had not said any of this aloud before to anyone, though Smallwood seemed to have guessed. Now he found himself shaking. Dixon couldn't do it. He'd saved that man's life more than once. He knew him in ways you only could if you'd hunkered down in the jungle mud getting shot at. Dixon couldn't have done it.

"Do you want me to talk to Dixon?"

"Maybe, sometime Jimmy, but not now. I need to work with him and watch him, and if you talk to him, he's gonna know it came from me anyway. He's likely to get real pissed. He might let people know you were working on this case on your own."

"Not good."

"No. We got some other things to do first."

*****

The next morning Williams picked up McFarland and Paul at their house. It was the Christmas season, but McFarland had been able to get KA to cover for him. Paul had been touched and delighted when he heard the plan. He told McFarland he might grow up into a human being after all. McFarland had already reached out to Det. Phillips at homicide and passed on his tip about the Gandy Dancer. Phillips had expressed neither surprise nor skepticism.

He just chuckled and said, "I suppose I am going to have to interview the man himself."

Williams appeared dressed in a jacket and tie, and McFarland tried not to laugh. "What you grinning at?" he growled.

"Well, Sarge, this isn't your usual get up."

"I want Ernie to know this is a big deal. I want to be there for him in every way I can and I figure this is a good place to start." McFarland wondered whether it also had something to do with going west of the park with a couple of white guys.

They made their way up Wisconsin Avenue, and then east on East-West Highway. Paul was in rare form, telling stories about the kids in his class and their ideas about science. He talked about Little Ernie helping other kids.

"He gets everything before I finish saying it, and he has to sit on his hands to keep from waving them in the air to get me to let him talk. That kid is a Boy Wonder."

They collected Little Ernie and arrived at the Arlington Planetarium for the 10:30 session, parking right in front as Sarge, smirking, put down the visor with his MPD shield on it. "Hey, it's Christmas. The Arlington cops come into the city all the time to shop and do the same."

Paul was in full science teacher mode, explaining what a planetarium was, and questioning Ernie about what he thought he might see. It was Christmas vacation, and there were a lot of families seated in the auditorium. The noisy room went quiet when the lights went down and the night sky appeared above them. For the next hour, Ernie sat on the edge of his chair immobile except when he raised his hand in response to questions asked by the docent, a tiny gnomish man wearing a bow tie and thick glasses.

He got his audience involved from the start asking, "Well, my young friends—and I do mean my *young* friends. All you parents and old folks, I'm afraid I don't want to hear from you. Astronomy is exploding, and these kids, some of them, are going to discover and understand things neither you nor I can imagine. So, my *young* friends, what is that above us."

There was a roar: "The sky!"

"Good, good. But I'll let you in on a secret. Shhhh. It's actually just the ceiling of this room that we've made to look like the sky—but don't tell." There were shouts of laughter, and the exploration of the universe began.

"Does the sun move?" Some voices shouted yes.

"It looks like it, doesn't it? Does anyone think it doesn't move?" Hands shot up. Ernie's had already been up waving urgently like a reed in a storm.

"Yes, young man. Does the Sun move?"

"No sir, it looks like it moves because the earth is rotating on its axis."

"How fast?"

"Once around every 24 hours. And it orbits around the sun every year."

"You are exactly right."

When the session ended, Ernie looked around wide-eyed and said, "That was the most interestingest thing I've ever done."

Paul took his hand and led him to the front of the room. The docent came over and Paul reached out to shake his hand.

"Dr. Praeger, that was wonderful, as always."

"Thank you, Paul. And who is this young astronomer?"

"This is a student of mine, Ernie Hills. This is his Christmas present."

"Well, Ernie, having you here was a Christmas present for me. I hope you'll come back with Mr. Brown so we can discuss what's going on in astronomy. And Mr. Brown, you need to finish that dissertation."

As they worked their way toward the exit McFarland heard a parent say to his spouse, "—yeah, just cause he's a black kid." Williams stiffened. It was nothing new to him, but he wondered whether Little Ernie would ever be allowed to become what he could become, and how long he could be kept innocent of what was around him. He left the building aching with sadness.

"Where shall we have lunch, Jimmy? I saw a McDonalds down the block."

McFarland stopped on the crowded sidewalk and held up his hands saying, "No way. It's Christmas, and we're not going to feed that poison to a future astronomer. I made a reservation at the Old Ebbitt Grille."

"You what? That's uptown, man."

"Mm-hmm. Really good. Best hamburger in the city. It's on me."

"You tryin' to bribe a cop?"

"Oh, yeah, that is exactly what I'm doing. Look, Sarge, you're wearing a tie. It's a special occasion. You might as well enjoy it."

The Old Ebbitt was a Washington landmark, a saloon dating from before the Civil War, where senators, justices, and sometimes presidents rubbed shoulders with grifters, scoundrels, and lobbyists. When they arrived, it was crowded with lawyers, and pols out for long pre-Christmas lunches. Jimmy had called on a friend to get them a reservation, implying that a young African Royal would be among the party. The *Maitre'd* groveled wonderfully, and assuming Williams was the royal bodyguard, played up to the supposed princeling. Ernie and Williams were the only non-whites in the room, and they created a stir as the *Maitre'd* conducted them to their table.

Paul was chortling with pleasure. "Oh, man, I don't know what this cost you, McFarland, but it was worth it. You see that guy over there? That is the next head of the National Academy of Sciences trying to figure out who the fuck we are. Oh, I'm going to remember this forever."

The show was lost on Ernie, who was swept up watching the stupendous plates of burgers, fries, fried oysters, and onion rings sailing by above his head. An hour later, they sat marveling at what a small boy could consume and enjoying the complimentary brandies that had appeared on the table along with Ernie's chocolate sundae. It had been a good day.

Ernie looked at Williams, suddenly serious. "Uncle Sarge, there's something I need to tell you—about my dad. Something you don't know."

"What's that?"

"No, just you. It's something my mom didn't say."

Williams nodded and put his hand on Ernie's shoulder. "Yeah, it seemed like your mom was worried she needed to protect your dad."

"But not from you."

"No, not from me, and not from Mr. McFarland."

Williams looked at McFarland and told Little Ernie, "We'll talk later, kiddo, now finish that thing before it melts." And being eight years old he did.

The three men dropped their charge off, receiving thanks from Claire and Little Ernie who could not wait to tell her about the planets, Dr. Praeger, and fried oysters. As they drove off, Paul asked, "What're you getting him for Christmas, Sarge?"

"I was thinking of a helmet and pads, but Claire hates football."

McFarland, thinking about the little boys he knew, suggested a GI Joe.

"Oh shit, man, you are so clueless. You ever seen one that was black? My sister tried to color one with a marker and her son was embarrassed. An' I tell you this, I ain't bringing no war into that boy's life."

Paul waved his hands. "No, no, no. Don't you see? The kid's in love with astronomy. Get him a science present."

"Me? Where do I do that?"

"Let's go right now. There's a great store called Sullivan's just down on Wisconsin Avenue. They've got all kinds of science stuff. It's what I'd want for Christmas."

Sarge groaned, "Man, you guys are just dragging me from one white hangout to another. They gonna throw me out."

"Naw, they're all white liberals. They'll be way too polite." And so it was. Scientist, prosecutor, and burly cop, prowled through the narrow aisles filled with small people full of excitement. McFarland and Paul were picking up rocket ships, junior microscopes, and chemistry kits while Williams watched uneasily, his hands in his pockets.

"What's the matter, Sarge, look at this stuff. Ernie would love it."

Williams wasn't sure whether he was embarrassed, or mad. "If I start handling this stuff, they'll think I'm stealing it."

Jimmy was chagrinned.

Paul said, "Screw that." He threw a long arm around Williams's shoulder and led him to the front of the store to a round man in a shabby tweed coat. "Gene, this is my friend, Larry Williams. His godson is in my class, and he's about the brightest thing I've seen come through those doors. He wants to be an astronomer. Could you help us figure out the right thing for a Christmas present?"

Gene emerged from behind the counter smiling and curious. "I think half the parents of kids in your class have been in this Christmas, Paul. Now, Mr. Williams, tell me about this young genius."

They ended up buying a lighted globe of the heavens, Williams saying, "Yeah, I do believe his mom will like this is better than a helmet and pads."

As they pushed out the door onto the twilit street a portly man in dark camelhair coat and black fedora hat was coming in.

Williams stiffened. "Good evening, Chief."

The man nodded affably. "Sargent, Merry Christmas. I was sorry to hear about your friend."

The man looked curiously at McFarland and Paul.

"Ahh, Chief, these are my friends Paul Brown and Jimmy McFarland."

The man continued to look at them with interest.

"They, ah, Paul is a teacher where my friend's son goes to school, and Jimmy is an assistant U.S. Attorney. Jimmy, Paul, this is Deputy Chief Dixon." Dixon extended a small, gloved hand and stared intently at McFarland as he shook his hand.

Chapter 10
Olsen

Gareth Olsen's resentment of Jimmy McFarland was visceral, bitter, and since it was based on imagined slights, entirely beyond reason. Olsen lived in a perpetual state of frustrated self-importance that he mostly covered beneath a veneer of cool arrogance. He thought of himself as charming but came across as vain and disingenuous. Olsen and McFarland had met at a party early in McFarland's tenure in the U.S. Attorney's office. Olsen, tall, balding, and hawk faced, his small eyes darting nervously behind wire rimmed spectacles, had leaned over McFarland to warn him about the office in conspiratorial terms.

"I've been here eight years, Jimmy. Now I'm one of the senior trial attorneys they turn to for tough cases, but it wasn't easy, even for someone who's as naturally good in a courtroom as I am. The politics are vicious. Rushford's a bastard and Donatelli's a spy. Take it from me, keep your head down."

Olsen was enjoying this. Jimmy was attentive. A protégé.

Then a young woman had yelled from across the room, "Jimmy McFarland, what're you doing here?"

McFarland had spun around, grinned, and said, "Excuse me, Gareth, Nancy's a classmate from law school," and walked off. Disrespectful snot. Olsen knew the type.

Several months later, Olsen had joined a group of colleagues sharing lunch in Donatelli's office. He didn't trust any of the AUSA's there. They were jealous of him, he knew, but if he didn't join them, they'd talk about him. Donatelli was holding forth, telling the story of McFarland's trial before Judge Stanley.

"Here he is trying an armed robbery before a judge who hates everyone, and especially the U.S Attorney's Office. His pants split—rrrrrip—and the judge looks at him—nasty as the Devil in Hell, and says, 'Mr. McFarland, we're waiting for your opening statement.' McFarland, he plays it cool. Tries the goddamned case with his legs locked together. The jury loved him. It was brilliant."

Olsen recoiled. "What's brilliant about wearing pants that are too tight and provoking a judge?"

"Worst judge in the city. We got rid of him that night, Gareth, and Jimmy just handled it."

There it was, Olsen thought, *they all love him because he puts on this innocent boy act.* Donatelli wouldn't know a trial lawyer if he saw one. McFarland was riding for a fall.

Then, a few weeks later, the little shit somehow got a big story in the *Post* for prosecuting a few unlucky bastards who were unemployed. The cases were a ridiculous waste of time. No work. No legal questions. He just took pleas and got ink. Olsen and his colleagues sneered at the idea of going after poor suckers who'd lost their jobs when there was an epidemic of crack cocaine and murder on the streets. It wasn't just Olsen who thought kid was getting way too big for his tight britches.

The evening of December 22nd, the day the Boss sent him the fraud case to review, Olsen had taken his girlfriend, Kelsey Darrin, to dinner at The Occidental Grill. He was in a good mood. He liked being seen by the K Street lawyers and lobbyists who went to the Occidental to be seen. And he liked being seen with Kelsey, a sleek, good-looking woman who was pleased to be dating a glamorous big-time prosecutor and showed it. Kelsey was assistant to the manager of the Conway office handling the huge Metro construction contract, and she loved to talk to her boss and the other women in the office about her tough DA boyfriend.

This particular evening, Olsen vented his indignation about McFarland to Kelsey. McFarland, he said, was a stumbling beginner, a sweet-talking charmer who'd wheedled the Boss into letting him indict a bunch of garbage cases and had made the most out of a silly connection to the White House. Now he'd let some old loser trying to get out of trouble for his own fraud sell a cooked-up story of fraud on the Metro job. Kelsey nodded agreement, put her hand on Olsen's arm, the bright red nails decorating the sleeve of his blue pinstripe suit, and said, "He sounds like a jerk."

"Well, he's blown it now. He's blundered. Thinking he can spin a bunch of self-serving allegations by a broken-down civil engineer into a high-profile investigation. I'm going to crush him. I've looked at the stuff. There's nothing there."

When the Boss had asked him to review the fraud case, Olsen knew he had been vindicated in his dislike of McFarland. His job now was to get rid of this mess, and he would do his job. He had skimmed through the notes of McFarland's interview with Douglas, highlighting the most preposterous assertions that McFarland had naively credited. He'd write a scathing memo pulling the story apart. Here was a conspiracy that supposedly involved scores, perhaps hundreds, of people discovered by some doddering engineer with a clipboard. It was going to be very satisfying.

Olsen signaled the waiter to come pour more wine and told Kelsey, "The Boss gave me this case to review because he trusts me. The whole thing is based on a fantastic story made up by an engineer named Douglas who works for you guys, but you can tell Mr. Taylor he doesn't need to worry, it's going nowhere." Olsen felt a slight twinge of unease as he said this. He'd been indiscreet. But then, he told himself, the case was a non-case, so it didn't matter.

When she got to work the next morning, Kelsey told her boss what Gareth had said. He was interested, he said, and grateful. He told her to thank her friend and to urge him to let them know if anything changed.

Chapter 11
Twin Sources

Claire pleaded with Williams to join her and Little Ernie at her parents' house for Christmas dinner. He thanked her but declined. "I'll be out on duty all night Christmas Eve. I'm covering for guys who have families."

"We *are* your family, Larry."

"You are. But your parents are doing Christmas dinner for their own people, not me. I don't belong there."

"You do belong. You're my friend and Ernie's godfather."

Claire had seen that on the few occasions when Ernie had dragged Williams along to an event with her family he sensed her parents' quiet snobbery, but he never saw that they were awed by his huge calm presence. Dark, blue collar, and from the South, he didn't belong. They had focused all their effort on making sure each of their five children became a professional. And this powerful, charismatic man, afraid of nothing on the battlefield or the streets thought himself inadequate in a roomful of teachers, doctors, and businesspeople.

He interrupted her thoughts: "Maybe we'll do something for Watch Night."

"If you wake up Christmas morning and change your mind, you'll be welcome. My mom's is cooking turkey *and* ham and Louisa is doing crab cakes."

"Well, save me some leftovers." How could he have a place at that table, a vice cop whose job is busting junkies and street thugs?

*****

It was Christmas Eve. Dixon and Smallwood were with their families. Rose Abrams—one of the rookies who'd been assigned hooker duty the night McFarland rode with Smallwood—had volunteered for the shift, so Williams took her on as a partner for the night. The sin market didn't close for holidays, but it was a bitterly cold night and Williams doesn't foresee much excitement, other than the driving.

The storm that passed through earlier, dumping snow, sleet, and freezing rain on the city, had left ragged corrugations of frozen slush interspersed with sheets of black ice. Everything—ice, pavement, the facades of the boarded-up storefronts—seemed cold and hard. Only the twenty-four-hour liquor store behind its battered steel lattice was open. A little crowd had gathered outside the store's armored door, as if the light filtering out might keep them warm. Two tall women dressed in tight satin dresses, one light blue the other pink, wearing fake fur jackets, feather boas, and spike heeled boots, gesticulated as they argued with a ratty looking white man with a scraggly beard, dirty pea coat, and watch cap.

"Looks like the Twins got a date," Rose observed. "Lots of little guys got a thing for big women."

"Mmm, if they *were* women."

Chloe and her sister Daphne were the twin drag queens of 14th Street, loud, colorful, and well-liked by the entire cast of the venality play that ran there nightly. The Twins always worked together, plying the sex trade as a package. They strutted off north on 14th Street with the little rat man walking between them. Williams and Officer Abrams drove the other way. Williams saw two bent figures scurrying from the light onto a side street.

"We may need to arrest those SOBs just to keep 'em from freezin' to death. It's fuckin' cold." He dreads going into some shooting gallery and finding a bunch of junkies frozen stiff. He remembers the rigid bodies they found his first winter in the Third District. He and Abrams checked a half a dozen crumbling houses without finding anyone and then cruised all the way down to Pennsylvania Avenue. Brightly lit, empty and still; Christmas lights gleamed wanly on a few storefronts.

"There's a bunch over there, Sarge." She points to three mounds of cardboard and homeless shelter issue felt blankets on top of a vent from the Metro tunnel. They stopped and walked over. Rose pulled back the cardboard from one bundle.

"What the fuck? Get off me."

"Are you gonna be ok, sir?"

"If the fuckin' police stop harassin' me."

"We can take you someplace warm."

"Leave me alone."

"It's not a good night to be on the streets, it's gonna be awful cold."

"You're a cold bitch, an' I can be here if I want."

"Well, merry Christmas."

She tried the other two. They too were alive enough to spew insults. Like a mother with teenagers, she remained stoic. Williams approved. Anyone who could survive on the streets on a night like this deserved some respect.

They drove slowly back up 14th Street. A small crowd had gathered in front of the liquor store. The cops heard shrieks as they approached.

"You ain't never said you was payin' for pussy."

"You fuckers ain't real. You fuckin' wi' me."

"Man gets the city's best head and he's sooo pissed… Ooh watch out, Sis, he's got a knife."

"Gonna cut those fuckin' balls right off you, bitch."

Williams and Abrams pulled onto the sidewalk. Williams stepped out, looking dangerous.

Abrams stood behind him. She drew her weapon, her heart pounding. She had never used her weapon on duty. Williams walked over calmly, telling the Twins to back off. He showed his badge to the blurry eyed rat man and told him to give up the knife. The man staggered toward Williams and managed to slur, "Don't screw around wi' me sucker!"

There was a chorus of excited "Ooohs" and "Uh-ohs" from the spectators. Williams extended a big hand wrapped in a scarf. Rat man slashed at it ineffectually. Abrams shouted, "Drop the knife, mother, or I'm gonna blow your sorry head off!"

Rat man looked confused. Williams winced. "Easy, Officer Abrams, I got this."

Rat man staggered toward him slashing. Williams grabbed his arm, twisted, kicked his knee, and slammed him to the icy sidewalk. More "Ooohs" and a delighted cry of, "Oh, yeah, that do it for him."

Abrams called for backup and stowed rat man, now somewhere between surly and comatose in the back of a squad car. Williams invited the Twins to sit and talk in the old Ford.

"He *never* pay for no pussy, Sarge."

"You know we never try to sell no pussy. We ain't got none to sell." They tittered. "They's plenty of regular street meat for that."

"Girls, I don't care what you sold him. Doesn't matter. Slashin' ain't the way. But why the hell you out here on a freezing night?"

"It's what we do, Sarge."

"We are performers."

"Divas of the down low."

Williams shook his head. "Some sucker's gonna kill you one day."

"They get mad 'cause they embarrassed."

"Uh huh."

They sat and smoked. Abrams asked them how long they'd been in the business.

They cackled merrily.

"The 'business'? Ooh that sounds official. Girl, we born with pricks, but that just ain't who we are."

The blue-clad Twin looked at her. "You play the cards you dealt, honey. You, pretty girl, you got dealt real nice cards." Abrams wondered whether she should say, "Thank you," but decided against it.

Sarge asked, "You ready to pack it in for the night?"

"Sarge. We maybe got something for you."

"Yeah?"

"Mm-hmm, Honey, we know something."

Williams waited, looking at them. People tell him things. Sometimes to try to get on his good side, sometimes to exact revenge. What they tell him isn't usually much use, even if it's true. Street talk. Still, it helps him keep the map in his head up to date. He's gotten tips from the Twins before, usually with a grain of truth in them. He sat quietly and waited.

"You know, we don't jes' do street work, do we Sis?" Chloe spun one end of her boa, brushing Williams's arm hanging over the seat.

Daphne slapped her sister's arm. "Don't you play up to Sarge. We are serious, Sarge, we got a nice client up town, *Gold Coast* up town."

Williams grinned and asked, "What the hell you doin' up there, ladies?"

"Ooooh, nothin' bad. No, no, honey we jes' entertaining…"

"Man has a poker night and wants to have some entertainment."

"Aw Jeez, you gonna tell me some respectable citizen has a taste for a little smut?"

The Twins shrieked with laughter, kicking the seats in front of them.

"Oh, sweetie, you ought to know…"

"You the Man on the Third District Vice Squad. You know there ain't no such thing as a respectable citizen."

Williams frowned, impatient.

Then Chloe said, "This client lives on Varney Street."

Williams looked at them sharply, eyes narrowed.

"We was coming out after our gig."

"The customer don't like us to hang around in front of his house…"

"And we ain't allowed to show our pretty dresses…"

"That's right, so we put on ugly raincoats and walk right on and he picks us up on Sixteenth Street to run us home."

"But this night, well it was a couple weeks ago, we *saw* something."

"Someone."

"Yeah, someone we knew."

"Didn't think much of it 'til we hear there's been a murder across the street the next night."

"Right in front of his family."

"Terrible."

"Then we hear Sarge has the word out for anyone who knows anything. Victim is a friend of his."

"Who'd you see?"

"White dude."

"That lieutenant that rides with you. He was sittin' across the street in his car, watchin' and smoking."

Williams closed his eyes for a moment. This was what he feared.

"Did he see you?"

"Honey, what he was doing was watching."

"Just him?"

"Mmmhmm…"

"Unless, you know, someone had their head in his lap."

"Why you just tellin' me this now?"

"We was thinkin' about it, wasn't we, Sis."

"An' it's Christmas."

They dropped the Twins at the little townhouse on W Street where they lived with their mom. It had Christmas lights on the porch; the only house for blocks with any light at all.

Abrams was incredulous. "With their mom?"

"They take good care of her, an' the whole street knows not to touch her." They drove in silence, then Williams pulled over and gave her an intense stare. "Two things, Officer Abrams. Don't ever pull your gun just 'cause you're scared. You gotta learn to tell the difference between real danger and a situation that can be eased back down."

"But he was going for you."

"Did I look like I was in trouble?"

"No. I got it."

"And another thing."

"Yes, Sarge."

"What the Twins told me?"

"Yeah, about Dixon?"

"You didn't hear it. You don't know it, an' if word gets around, I'm gonna know it came from you."

"Can I help?" He glares at her and says nothing.

The rest of the night not much went down. They stopped two groups of kids cruising 14th Street, "looking for Santa Claus," they said. Williams took names and registration numbers and sent them home, saying, "I see you again I'm calling your parents."

They picked up a semi-corpse, a drunk who's half dead of exposure. They ran him to D.C. General, getting dirty looks from the ER staff who were enjoying a slow Christmas Eve and look skeptically on the stinking bundle they deliver.

"Alive?"

"More or less," responded Abrams. She actually felt good about saving this life.

Near dawn they headed back in. Shit, Williams thought, *What the hell do I do?* He realized what he should do was talk to McFarland. But not on Christmas. He imagined McFarland with his family in a big house full of warmth and color—a scene out of a movie. A White movie. He didn't want to sit alone in his apartment and think about Dixon—or about his family. He decided to accept Claire's offer after all.

Chapter 12
Dixon's Story

McFarland had driven through the snowstorm to visit his family for Christmas. The day after Christmas he and his little brother, Miggy, had gone to Vermont to ski. Now on the morning of the twenty-seventh he made his excuses and said he had to get back to work. Next to him on the passenger seat was a red, yellow, and green woven basket filled with carefully wrapped turkey sandwiches, fruit, heart shaped, pink-frosted lebkuchen, and two thermoses, one filled with coffee and the other with a rich broth (his mother's remedy for everything). His legs and shoulders ached from a ridiculous day of chasing his brother down lumpy ski slopes, but he was eager to be back. He'd spoken to Williams the evening before, and while the sergeant hadn't said much his tone was anguished. "I heard something. I'll tell you when you get back."

McFarland needed to be in DC. He ignored pleas to stay.

"At least for the Smiths' annual brunch."

"No," he insisted, "I really gotta get back."

His mother looked hurt. Miggy watched, smirking. "You got a date?"

"Yeah, yeah, that's it."

There was no snow this time. He was in DC by late afternoon and met Williams for beer and burgers. The sergeant was grim-faced.

"What'd you hear, Sarge?"

"Dixon was staking out Ernie's house."

"Staking out?"

"He was sitting in his car across the street the night before the shooting."

"Crap. Was he alone?"

"He was alone. The mother fucker was just sittin' there in the dark. No reason he's there except to watch the Hills' house. And why the hell would he do that? And why the hell wouldn't he tell me?"

"Where'd you hear that?"

"You remember Chloe and Daphne?"

"The Twins?"

"Yeah, they had a gig up there."

"They what?"

"Dirty dancing for a poker night."

McFarland shook his head in disbelief, then asked, "Have you talked to Dixon?"

"I can't, Jimmy, I'm so mad and disgusted—I don't know, I might just go off."

"I understand."

"And I heard something else. Pete Phillips told me the slugs are from a Smith and Wesson 38. A cop's gun."

"There are a lot of those around. Could you let Detective Phillips know what you've heard and let him question Dixon? You trust him."

"Pete would have to take it to Internal Affairs. Those bastards—I wouldn't trust them to carry shit from a cow barn."

"Why?"

"Lazy, goddamned mean, and bent. The Deputy Chief pretty much owns them."

They sat in silence, burgers untouched, McFarland trying to think what to say. Finally he asked, "You have the papers?"

Williams nodded "Yeah, in my car. I haven't looked at them."

"How'd you find them?"

"Little Ernie told me on Christmas that his daddy had some papers that he hid, but not in the house."

"That's what Claire didn't tell us."

"Yeah, I guess."

"But you think it's just coincidence that Ernie was shot just as he was getting ready to hand that information to the Senate Committee?"

"How the hell should I know? I just can't think of any reason for Dixon to be there. He's not a man to socialize with folks up on the Gold Coast. He sure as hell wasn't paying a social call on Ernie."

"So what do we do?"

"We talk to him."

"And...?"

"And I'll keep my cool and let you lead. I know the sonofabitch too well. I'd jump to answers. You can just go step-by-step. He'll freak seeing you there."

"Will he tell us the truth?"

"Nobody tells the truth."

*****

They were to meet at Williams's apartment in Anacostia, the sprawling southeast corner of the city. McFarland had never even been east of the Anacostia River. Williams's neighbors staring openly as he got out of his car.

The fourth-floor apartment was small and sparsely furnished, but the living room windows looked west toward the city. There was a low sofa, an armchair, and a leather covered recliner facing a large TV. Williams turned the recliner to face the sofa and slumped down. He watched McFarland who stared out the window at the lights of the city and the last of the December twilight.

"How long have you lived here, Sarge?"

"A little over a year. It's a friend's apartment, I rent it from him."

McFarland looked askance at his colleague.

"No, man, it's cool. All on the up and up. He moved in with his fiancé and didn't want to let this place go. I pay what it costs him."

"Quite a view."

Dixon arrived twenty minutes later, sober, alert and fidgety. A colorless man with a weak chin and skin that this night seemed too big for his face. Despite the cold, he was dressed only in jeans, a Redskins sweatshirt, and old loafers. His eyes shifted and blinked too often. He looked miserable, as if he was trying not to cry. Williams sat back in silence.

Dixon said, "Mr. McFarland."

"Lieutenant Dixon."

"Did you have a good Christmas?"

"Yeah, I did. And you?"

"With my wife and kids. You know, noisy." He tried to smile but manages only a grimace. McFarland saw no point in the small talk.

"Lieutenant, we want to ask you some questions about Ernie Hills' murder."

"Yeah, yeah, Sarge told me. Are you investigating that?"

McFarland ignored the question and felt himself slip into courtroom mode. "Do you know the neighborhood where Mr. Hills lived?"

"Uh, sure, the Gold Coast, yeah."

"Varney Street. Do you know Varney Street?"

Dixon, sitting on the sofa, tried to sit straight, but the sofa was too low and soft, so he just squirmed. "Varney Street?"

"Uh huh. Do you know it? That's the street Ernie lived on."

"I'm not sure. Me an' Ernie didn't socialize."

Williams started to lean forward, then sat back.

"Yes, Lieutenant, yes, you do know it. There are witnesses who saw you there." Dixon managed a look of disgust that barely concealed his terror. "Witnesses?"

"Yeah, individuals who know you."

"Fucking faggots."

"You *were* there?"

Dixon looked at Williams, nodded yes, and once again rearranged himself on the sofa. McFarland wondered whether he might bolt.

"In your car parked across from the Hills house?"

"Yes, but…"

"But?"

"I wasn't doing anything."

"You were sitting in your car?"

"Yes."

"In the dark?"

"Yes."

"At about ten p.m. on a winter night?"

"Fuck, I don't know, I guess—yes."

McFarland stared at him with an expression close to a sneer. "Why would you do that?"

Dixon's misery increased. He looked at Williams, then McFarland, then at his hands. His eyes seemed too heavy to keep open. McFarland was sure Dixon must have come fearing these exact questions. How can he not have given some thought to what he would say? But he stumbled on.

"I—I was going to talk to Ernie."

Williams sat forward again shaking his head. "That's bull shit!" McFarland looked at him in warning.

"No, Sarge. It's true," Dixon said, pleading, "I wanted to ask him not to do the skit at the reunion."

McFarland nodded and asked, "Why were you sitting in the car then?"

"I couldn't get up my nerve to do it."

"Do what?"

"To go in and talk to him."

"What were you afraid of?"

As Dixon responded, Williams flashed back to a patrol crossing through an expanse of rice paddies. Wisps of mist rising in the early morning air. They could smell cooking from the village to their right. It would have been beautiful if they weren't slogging through the water and mud of the paddy laden with weapons and gear and scared shitless. He had led the patrol. Dixon trailed at the end of the column. Williams had heard a dog barking and someone shouting, then rifle fire from behind him. He, and the rest of the column hit the mud, but it was just Dixon firing at the village in panic. Ernie had stood up, covered in mud, screaming at Dixon that he was going to get them all killed. That was the thing with cowards. They were dangerous.

McFarland waited for an answer. Dixon breathed heavily, his eyes flitting from Williams to McFarland. "I didn't want to look like a pitiful jerk."

McFarland leaned toward him, "You never went into the house?"

"No."

"What happened the next night?"

"I don't know. I wasn't there."

"Where were you?"

"Jimmy, you can't think I'd kill Ernie."

"Did you?"

"Shit no. We might have killed each other when we were in 'Nam, but if it didn't happen there…"

"Where were you the night he was killed?"

"At my uncle's house." Dixon winced, eyes turned down, eyebrows pressed together, as if he'd said something he wished he hadn't. Williams was seething and both McFarland and Dixon saw it.

Dixon asked, "You gonna offer me a drink, Sarge?"

Williams rose wordlessly and brought out a bottle, placing the bottle and three glasses on the coffee table. He remained standing. It was a small space for such a big man. Dixon poured three shots and held his up as if to offer a toast.

Williams said, "I don't believe you, Al. I don't believe you go up there and sit outside and can't go knock on the door. No, man, that didn't happen. What the fuck was going on?"

Dixon objected. The conversation went nowhere. Dixon, McFarland thought, was pathetic. Did pathetic men like this coolly execute their foes? Why did Williams still work with him? *If he were Dixon*, McFarland thought, *he'd be very uneasy the next night they were out on the street. But he was probably always uneasy.*

Dixon rose, pulled at his belt, looked back and forth at the two men across from him: McFarland gazing intently, Williams looking at the bourbon in his untouched glass. "I'm not lying," he insists.

McFarland wondered why he didn't just say he was telling the truth?

Dixon picked up his coat from the back of the sofa and stood uneasily, seeming to wait for permission to leave or a command to sit back down. Instead, there was silence. Finally, he twitched, as if in response to some stab of pain, or fear, walked to the door, paused, turned, and said defiantly, "Ernie and I didn't get along. He rode me any chance he got, but I knew he was a good man, and I didn't kill him." With that, he left.

Williams, like McFarland, thought that this man, this redneck whom he covered for and protected, was pathetic. But Williams knew something McFarland did not. Weak, pathetic, fearful men given power can be vicious. He saw it in the brutality of what they did to unarmed villagers after ambushes. And yet the picture wasn't right. He envisioned two men in Ernie's house that night: both cold and calm, clad in overcoats, faces covered, polished shoes, saying little. An execution.

He looked at McFarland and said, "Dude don't polish his shoes."

"Huh?"

"I've known that sonofabitch five, six years. He ain't one to polish his boots, his shoes, whatever. General Westmoreland came to inspect, we had to polish his boots *for* him so we didn't get busted on review."

McFarland looked puzzled, "Yeah?"

"Little Ernie said the guys had polished shoes. I know the bastard's lying. But he don't never polish his shoes. And you saw him, he wouldn't be able to just walk in and kill someone."

McFarland asked, "What do you think he was doing there?"

Williams shook his head slowly. "Nothin' good. He was there for a while, and it was the night before the murder. And I know he's lying about trying to get Ernie not to do the skit. He must have been involved."

Williams's phone rang. He answered, grunted, and thanked the caller. He looked grimly at McFarland. "That was Amel. Word is out that *we*'re hunting the killer, and *we*'re questioning Dixon."

"Shit."

McFarland realized the talk would get back to his office and to the Boss. There were plenty of people who'd be gleeful about bringing him down. *I'm an idiot*, he thought, *I shouldn't be doing stuff I don't want people to know about.*

Williams stared out the dark windows toward the lights of the city twinkling in the bitter cold of the winter night.

"Counselor, you need to drop this. It's my problem, and I got to go about it my own way."

"What way is that Sarge? An eye for an eye? You don't know what happened that night."

Williams tensed. "Are you fuckin' lecturing me? What are you doing here all this way from the courthouse? I don't see how havin' you along is helping, and you getting fired for screwing around on your own ain't gonna help me."

"Mm-hmm, but that is *my* problem." McFarland was trying to act nonchalant, but he knew Sarge would see through it. Bravado was not his strength.

"Sarge, I don't think Dixon did this. The documents you found in Ernie's car, they're a bombshell. Douglas kept meticulous notes of the discrepancies between what he saw and what was reported on the time sheets. I'm guessing that Conway decided the worst thing that could happen would be a work stoppage or, you know, some kind of slowdown. Letting the union report whatever they wanted kept them happy, and it didn't cost Conway anything since WMATA paid whatever they billed."

Williams turned to stare at McFarland in comical disbelief. "Crap. That's a better racket than selling drugs. We need to talk to Douglas."

"We really do. This just doesn't smell like a grudge killing. It was business."

As if you'd know, he thought.

Chapter 13
Douglas

The cold had deepened. It was a vicious, bitter, clawing cold. The temperature hadn't been above freezing since the pre-Christmas storm. People on McFarland's bus were complaining—except for a disdainful Minnesotan who called them sissies and said this would be spring weather in Minneapolis. The Pension Building was quiet, the great central atrium chill, drafty, and empty. Judge Raymond had taken the week off. Bartolo was in Florida with his latest woman. KA was at her desk. She looked up when McFarland came in and before he had his coat off, she asked, "Jimmy what are you doing?"

He didn't bother to pretend he didn't know what she meant. "I'm trying to help Williams figure out who killed his friend."

She gave him a disappointed look. "You're asking for trouble. I know you're friends with Williams, but he's not a homicide detective. You're off on your own going behind everyone's back. Pete Phillips and Donnie Blake are good detectives. Leave it to them."

McFarland felt scolded and embarrassed. He told her how he'd gotten involved and about Williams's fear that Dixon was the killer.

"I don't want Dixon to turn up dead."

"Do you have another theory?"

"Yeah. Ernie was getting ready to go to the Senate with evidence—documents and a witness—showing corruption in the Metro construction. It was the same corruption I heard about from the old engineer."

"And you think he was silenced?" She looked skeptical.

"It makes more sense than an old grudge from Viet Nam." McFarland didn't mention the papers they'd recovered, though he figured he'd have to tell Olsen. He called and learned Olsen taken the week off. McFarland sat at his desk and wondered whether to call Olsen at home. If it were him, he'd want the call.

"KA, do you have the DC phone directory?"

"It'll be in Janice's lower left-hand desk drawer. Are you going to call Gareth at home?"

McFarland nodded. Since their desks were all jammed into a single office, they didn't have much choice but to eavesdrop on each other's calls.

KA grimaced, "You trying to piss him off?"

McFarland grinned and dialed. "Gareth? It's Jimmy McFarland, sorry to bother you at home." He waited, but getting no response he went on, "I was wondering where things stand with the Metro construction fraud case?"

He heard a long sigh, and Olsen said, "There is no case. There never was. I sent the boss a memo before Christmas recommending no action, and he agreed. There was nothing there. A waste of time. When you've had a little more experience, you'll learn to know the difference between a real case and a collection of self-serving lies."

McFarland clenched his jaw. "You didn't find Douglas credible?"

"No."

"I wish you'd let me know. We found..."

"Why? They assigned it to me. Go back to trying robbery cases in Superior Court." He hung up before McFarland had a chance to describe Douglas' notes and the carefully highlighted supporting documents Williams had found in Ernie's car. Condescending sonofabitch! McFarland wondered whether Olsen had actually spoken with Douglas at all.

"He hung up?" KA asked.

"The bastard sent a no action memo to the boss a week ago."

"Yup. Olsen's a lazy self-important prick. But, Jimmy, don't let it get personal."

"The thing is, I was going to tell him about this." He pointed to the carton of papers he'd brought in and told her what it was and how Williams had found it.

"You need to tell Donatelli what you've got and how you got it. Now, so the front office hears what's going on from you. Donatelli really likes you. He'll manage the Boss. And I'll ask David to poke around a bit and see what's stirring." McFarland saw that KA's disapproval had evaporated. Her eyes were full of warmth, even affection.

McFarland made the call to Donatelli, who, judging by his grunted reactions, had already heard much of what he had to say. Olsen, Donatelli said, had said he would pass the memo on to McFarland.

"Well he didn't. I don't have it, and I haven't seen it."

Donatelli responded as if to himself, "That could be just as well." Then coughed loudly.

Half an hour later, McFarland was sitting at his desk, tapping a pencil on a yellow pad and brooding about what he should have said to Olsen when Joel Garabedian called. He suggested they meet at the venerable Mozart Café for knackwurst, sauerkraut and a stein.

"Good idea, I'll see you at one."

McFarland decided to walk the nine blocks, and set out bundled up in his parka, red toque, muffler and ski gloves. Overkill, it turned out. The weather was finally warming. The walk through Washington's little Chinatown and past the run down Art Deco bus station helped ease the rage seething inside him. By the time he got to the Café Mozart, he was looking forward to seeing Joel, giving him a scathing rendition of the conversation with Olsen, and eating heavy German food.

They were not the only people who'd decided a long lunch hour was acceptable the day before New Year's Eve. The café was steamy and noisy. Joel, dressed in an exquisite camel's hair coat, cashmere scarf, and astrakhan hat drew immediate greetings from behind the long glass cabinet filled at one end with meats, salads and pickles, and at the other end with gleaming pastries. He seemed to know the entire staff, and he and McFarland were quickly situated in a booth in the little room around the corner.

"Oh, Mr. Garabedian, we haven't seen you in ages. How are you?"

"I'm well, Annika. Happy New Year to you. Can you just bring us each the Munich Platter—and two drafts. And I think we'll need a nice assortment of mustards."

"Of course, and a pickle plate while you wait?"

"Perfect."

McFarland watched in awe as both the chef and manager came to fawn, and Garabedian dispensed noblesse and easy charm.

"Did I miss something? Are you some sort of celebrity? It's like you own the place. I mean, Garabedian isn't a German name."

"Isn't it nice? My curious moment of importance." He smiled slyly, his eyes shifting around the room. "Actually, it's all a case of mistaken identity. I came here one day to meet Mariana for lunch on our anniversary—you know the *Post* is just around the corner—and she brought her editor. He's a lovely guy and was making a big deal of our anniversary and treated us. The folks here know him, and they figured if he was taking me out, I must be a be a big deal. I've just kinda gone with it."

"It doesn't hurt that you're such a goddamn fashion plate."

"Ahh, style speaks."

They ate pickles, drank beer, and talked about Christmas. Annika brought a tray with four crocks of mustard and then two oblong plates each with fat *weisswurst, knackwurst,* and *bratwurst* stacked at one end, steaming sauerkraut and braised red cabbage at the other end, and a garnish of potato salad.

"Anything else, Mr. Garabedian?"

He smiled benevolently, thanked her, and said, "We'll see what we feel like after we have dealt with these magnificent plates." Turning to McFarland, who was examining his plate with wide-eyed awe, Garabedian asked, "What? Intimidated by a light German lunch?"

"Good Lord, Joel, if I eat this, I'll need an ambulance."

"Aye, laddie, life was austere for your people up there in the Highlands eating haggis. Ye canna abide a wee wurst?"

As they ate, their talk finally turned to the Metro Fraud case. Garabedian asked where things stood. McFarland told him about his call with Olsen: "You know, Olsen said he'd spoken to Douglass, but I don't think he ever did."

Joel tutted, "Millions of dollars stolen from the government with impunity because—why?"

"Olsen doesn't like me, and I don't think he likes to work. The thing is—you remember Douglas said he'd given some documents to a lawyer at WMATA?" Joel nodded. "Well, we found them."

"No shit. What did the lawyer say about the case?"

"He was murdered a few weeks ago."

"Are you serious? He was murdered?"

"Yeah, and he was supposed to go meet with the Senate District Committee's staff the next day."

Garabedian was wide-eyed. "Jeezus. Someone didn't want this coming out."

"It's possible. No proof—yet."

"What do the papers show?"

"That there was systematic, large-scale fraud run by the union and overlooked by the contractor."

Garabedian shook his head, "And your office is going to sit on it?"

"I don't know. It looks that way." McFarland, having kept it quiet for two weeks, went on to tell Garabedian the whole story, enjoying his friend's excitement. What the hell! He'd told KA and Donatelli that morning and apparently half of the MPD was already gossiping about him and Williams as some kind of death squad.

"Can't you do something?" Garabedian asked.

"I'm already in hot water for getting too involved. They may fire me, Joel. My actions make me look like an arrogant brat who does whatever he wants for—attention."

"Oh, sure, that's you alright," Joel said, "Stuck up and self-absorbed. You found crucial evidence and told your boss. The scandal isn't that you're digging, it's that your office is ignoring it. Someone needs to do something about it."

Garabedian's eyes were blazing. McFarland was startled by the passion. Joel always seemed smooth and in control.

*****

By New Year's Eve, the weather had turned completely. Congress was in recess. Work on the inaugural viewing stands had stopped. The quiet streets were bathed in warm, milky sunlight. It was the smell that had led to discovery of the body. Before 6:00 am, in the half-light on New Year's Eve morning, construction foreman Jason Browning unlocked the gate and pulled his truck into the site of what would be the Brookland—Catholic University Metro Station, part of the above-ground line toward Fort Totten and Silver Spring. Work had been stopped for a week, held up by the Christmas holiday and then by the bitter cold. Now the cold had let up and the front office was desperate to show progress before New Year's Day shut them down again. His guys straggled in, hard hats jammed over the hoods of grubby sweatshirts, heavy boots still muddy from a week before. He got them working on staging for the concrete pour. The trucks would begin to roll in by 8:00.

When the big backhoe lifted the steel plates off the footing holes, a thick almost liquid putrescent smell washed over them.

"Jeezzzus Christ," Browning said choking, "what the hell is that?"

"Gas leak?" asked the backhoe operator.

"Are you kidding? Something's dead." Browning put his arm across his face and leaned over the shaft trying to see down into the darkness, but he drew back, retching, and waved away the small crowd that was gathering. "Get some lights over here."

They wheeled over a stand of flood lights and cranked up the generator. The lights surged on. Twenty-five feet below, at the bottom of the six-foot by six-foot hole, crumpled face down on the matrix of rebar, one arm skewed awkwardly to the side, was a body. Browning backed away, nauseous, thinking, 'Another damn delay. They're gonna be all over me.' He wondered how the poor bastard had fallen in. The steel plates weighed close to four hundred pounds and had been in place since the evening before Christmas Eve.

"Ok, guys, back to work. Carl, you better put up a barrier. I'm going to the trailer."

"You gonna leave him there?"

"No, I'm gonna call the cops and let them deal with it."

He let himself into the warm construction trailer. The place reeked comfortingly of cigarettes and grease. He took a deep breath to clear his lungs of the putrid stench of the body, but he didn't call the police immediately. Instead, he called the office. As he expected, his boss yelled at him. As if it was his fault.

"You're supposed to cover the goddamned holes, Jason, and secure the site."

"Yeah, well I did. I checked it all myself before I left when we shut down before Christmas, and we ain't opened it since. The gate was locked, and the hole was covered when I arrived this morning."

"How the Christ did he get there? It's not one of your crew is it?"

"No, looks like an older white guy—in business clothes and a leather overcoat."

"How long's he been there? Did you go down and check him?"

"No, no way. Smells like two hundred pounds of rotting chicken guts. You can't get close without puking."

"Did anybody else—you know—see what was there?"

"Yeah, the whole crew."

"Shit. How soon can you get him out and start up again?"

"I'm not getting him. I'm calling the cops. I think we're done for the day."

A couple of cops and an ambulance arrived about ten minutes later. The EMTs took one whiff and went back to their vehicle to get respirators. The cops called for backup. It was past ten when they got a crane and rigged a pallet on a cable and slowly lowered two crime scene officers in full hazmat suits with cameras and a body bag into the deep narrow hole.

By noon when they pulled the body up in the bag, maneuvering it so it rose diagonal to the rebar lined walls, a crowd of cops, technicians, white hats from the front office, and a couple of reporters were standing around the tapes blocking access to the top of the shaft. A guy from the Conway front office was explaining to the reporters that it appeared the victim was a wino who'd somehow gotten onto the fenced site and fallen in. Hearing that, Jason Browning shook his head in disbelief, and one of the crime scene officers standing nearby turned aside in disgust. It wasn't a wino, and he very much doubted the man had fallen in. They'd found the decomposing body face down, but it was obvious that the back of his head had been bashed in. Papers in his pocket identified him as Aubrey Douglas, an employee of Conway Corp. Near him, amid the heavy mesh of rebar, they'd pulled out a three-foot-long piece of pipe stained at one end with what the crime scene officer was pretty sure would turn out to be blood. The man had been killed and thrown into the dark, narrow shaft to be entombed in cement. Only the snowstorm, Christmas, and the cold snap had defeated the killer's plan to bury the crime.

Chapter 14
Front Page

Not having partied the night before, McFarland rose clear-headed early on New Year's Day. He stood up, stretched, and wondered what the year would bring. What the hell, if he was about to lose his job, it would be for doing something he thought was right. The sun was still a glow in the east, and the neighborhood was barely lit by the thin winter light. What would happen if they fired him. He imagined Williams's anger and cynicism. The case would go nowhere, and the world would go on.

He shook himself. Coffee, breakfast, the paper, call home. Write thank you notes. Watch some bowl games. All good.

He tossed the paper onto the kitchen table, put water in the espresso machine, ground coffee, packed it into the little cup, put the machine on the stove, and poured milk into a small pot. He wandered over to the table to pull out the sports section, and his eye fell on the headline in the lower left-hand corner: 'Massive Fraud in Metro Project'. His stomach tightened. The story cited sources who alleged millions of dollars in false billing on the largest construction project in the city's history. An internal prosecution memo obtained by the *Post*, the story went on, conceded there was likely to be some fraud, but concluded it was inevitable, difficult to prove, and not worth pursuing. The author of the memo, assistant U.S. attorney Gareth Olsen declined to comment. Transit Authority officials could not be reached for comment.

Oh, God, McFarland thought, *now I am totally screwed. They'll never believe it wasn't me. Who the hell had leaked it?* All he could think was that it must have been Joel. They'd had lunch two blocks from the *Post*'s building. McFarland had trustingly told him the story. And the next day it was on page one. That, he muttered to himself, is what you get for trusting a Washington friend. There's no such thing. It's an oxymoron.

The phone rang. He answered it full of dread. Would they summon him to be fired on New Year's Day?

"Jimmy, it's Joel."

"You bastard."

"What?"

"You leaked that story as soon as I told you, and it's going to get me fired. They'll think it was me. What did you do, just pass it on to Mariana?"

Joel, sounding defensive, said, "I thought it was *you*. But that's not what I'm calling about."

McFarland shouted, "You thought it was *me*? That's bullshit! I told you at lunch, and the next thing I know the *Post* has it. Who else could have given it to them? Did you talk to them?"

"Yeah, I did—when they called and read me the memo and said sources in the U.S. Attorney's office confirmed it. I thought that was you serving it up to me."

McFarland said, "No, no, it wasn't me. Are you being straight with me?"

"Look, Jimmy, I didn't leak it. I'm not an operator. I'm a bystander. I can probably get Anderson to call you and tell you he didn't get it from me, but that's not what I called about."

"Who's Anderson?"

McFarland heard Garabedian groan. He answered with exasperated clarity, "The reporter. If you want to understand what's going on in this city, the first thing you read is the byline, so you can guess who's leaking what to whom."

McFarland stammered, "He'd call me…I thought…"

"Jimmy, shut up for a minute. Douglas is dead."

"Douglas?"

"They found his body yesterday at the bottom of a footing shaft up at the Brooklands station construction site. He'd been dead a while."

McFarland whistled, "That's why we couldn't reach him."

"The police think he was murdered and dumped. If it hadn't been for the snowstorm and the cold, he'd have been buried under fresh concrete by now."

McFarland's thoughts raced through the implications: If Douglas had been dead for more than a week, then Olsen had almost certainly lied when he said he'd spoken with him. If Douglas had been murdered, it suggested that his allegations were real and the two deaths, his and Ernie's were connected.

"Jimmy? You there?" asked Garabedian.

"Yeah, I'm here. And it sure seems like someone's trying to bury something."

"You mean other than whoever was trying to bury Douglas? Will this get your office to investigate, or will they just leave Douglas' murder to the MPD?"

"Two murders, a multi-million-dollar fraud, and the *Post* all over it. I expect they'll go after it right after they fire me."

"Jimmy, I didn't leak the story, but I'm glad someone did, and I don't think they're going to fire you."

"Why not?"

"Because you're smart, decent, charismatic, and as I keep telling you, you're right."

After the call, McFarland sat at the kitchen table with his coffee and an aging sweet roll, trying to concentrate on the Rose Bowl hype in the sports section. The pundits liked Michigan after their 22-0 beat down of Ohio State. McFarland didn't think so, not at all. USC was too fast, too creative, and Ricky Bell would run all over Michigan. He put the paper down. Did he believe Joel's denials? All that treacle about his decency and intelligence was just flattery.

He knew he was a good lawyer, but the morass he'd wandered into wasn't made up of legal issues. Ethical maybe, and political. He felt lost trying to understand who was doing what. If Joel hadn't leaked the story, then who? KA? Never. Someone from the MPD? They didn't have Olsen's memo. Nor did Joel. Donatelli? Sonofabitch, it must have been Donatelli. Why? His speculation was interrupted by a shout from Paul.

"Hey, McFarland, my kid sister wants to wish you happy New Year!"

His heart raced and he looked accusingly at his coffee cup. He grabbed the phone that hung on the kitchen wall next to the refrigerator.

"I've got it, Paul!"

"Hi Jimmy, happy New Year."

"Thanks, and happy New Year to you Ms. Brown."

"Did you have a wild New Year's Eve?"

"Sure, I stayed in."

"With Rachel?" There was a pause. She thought, *Oh, damn, too pushy.*

He thought, *why's she interrogating me?* "I—ah—I think we've broken up. She wanted to go to a big party out in Maryland somewhere and I didn't. I'd had a shitty day."

"And you broke up?"

"Yeah, I guess so."

"You guess so?"

"Well, she hung up on me, and I was relieved. That seems like a sign that we're done." There was another pause. "In fact, she was the second person who hung up on me in the last couple of days. I guess it's some sort of pattern."

Sally was not focused on what he was saying. He'd broken up with Rachel, and he was relieved. Maybe she should head for Washington. A concert? She'd travel down for a concert. McFarland, oblivious, was recounting his call with Olsen and wondering whether Sally thought he was a total loser. There was an awkward silence. He asked what she had done for New Year's Eve.

"We had a gig at a fancy party."

McFarland imagined elegant people waltzing; Sally recalled loud drunks spilling things while superbly trained young musicians tried to play tangoes, waltzes and foxtrots.

"It was awful. I'd rather have been there playing Scrabble with you."

"That would," he said, "have been fun." How, he wondered, did she know he loved word games. *Aha,* she thought, *good use of intelligence from older brother.*

*****

On Monday morning, January 3rd, McFarland showed up at the office dressed for a funeral. Charcoal gray suit, black tie, white shirt, shiny black shoes. He was not surprised when Janice said he was expected at the Boss's office.

"I'll just have to wait until the judge takes the bench so I can ask for time."

"No, Mr. McFarland, they told me to tell you they've already contacted her."

"Oh—crap."

He had prepared himself. He looked at KA and said, "Wish me luck."

Bartolo looked at him blankly. "What's up."

McFarland shook his head, grabbed his dark tweed overcoat, no parka today, and headed out the door. The offices of the United States Attorney, his top aides, and senior prosecutors were in the United States District Court building, a squat, gray Depression-era structure on the south end of Judiciary Square. He noticed the Art Deco influence as he walked over, perhaps for the last time. He would accept his fate with dignity and tell the Boss that he'd felt honored to work for him. If they asked, he would say it was not he who leaked the memorandum, but he wouldn't try to defend his conduct.

The reception area was spacious, quiet, and windowless. The Boss' assistant, Mrs. Thomas, looked at him disapprovingly, and said, "Mr. McFarland, the U.S. attorney will see you soon." She went back to her work. He sat uncomfortably on the huge, slippery leather sofa. He glanced at the perfectly arranged ranks of magazines and newspapers on the coffee table. He considered glancing at the *Post*, but looked at Mrs. Thomas and thought better of it.

The heavy door behind Mrs. Thomas opened. Donatelli emerged and waved McFarland in, looking at him soberly. The spacious office was finished in dark wood and furnished with a stolid government desk, a brown leather sofa, two armchairs, and a large conference table surrounded by upholstered chairs. A large window looked over Judiciary Square behind the Boss's desk. A thick blue and white carpet with an enormous eagle clutching a sheaf of arrows and a golden shield woven in the center covered much of the floor.

Donatelli sat in one of the big armchairs facing a sad looking man with drooping eyes and a younger woman with the same hard, tight look that KA often wore. The Boss gestured for McFarland to sit, not with Donatelli and the two strangers, but at the long, polished conference table on the other side of the office where the deputy, John Rushford, was already seated and staring at McFarland through small, steel rimmed glasses. The Boss stood. He was in his sixties, fit and deceptively drab. His face was impassive except for his eyes, which seemed at times to gleam with reptilian malevolence. His ability to hold the attention of a courtroom while he stood entirely still, like a coiled serpent, was legendary. At this moment, McFarland felt like the serpent's prey but willed himself to hold those eyes without wavering.

"Well, Mr. McFarland, you seem to be on the path to a certain notoriety."

McFarland sat as still as he was able, waiting, not breathing. The Boss turned away, looked out the window, and continued, "We generally do not expect young prosecutors to generate news, and we emphatically disapprove of them going off on their own, in secret, to investigate murders with Vice Squad detectives."

"I understand, sir."

"Do you? It isn't evident." It took all McFarland's strength to keep his head up. The Boss continued, "That story in the *Post*—it made for an interesting New Year's morning."

"It wasn't me, sir."

The Boss turned back toward McFarland, nodding, though McFarland couldn't tell whether he was agreeing or acknowledging that he had heard what he expected.

"You've been here, how long?"

Oh, God, thought McFarland, *here it comes.* "Thirteen months."

"Thirteen very eventful months: you've been involved in two front page stories in the *Post*, indicted a future Presidential staffer, formed an alliance with a notorious tough guy cop. What are you doing, gathering material for a book? Getting ready to run for something?"

"No, sir."

The Boss turned the gleaming eyes away and sighed elaborately. He gestured toward the little group seated around the coffee table. "These are people I'd like you to meet. Agent Smith," the man with the white shirt and narrow black tie looked at him expressionlessly, "and Agent Farwell."

Panic swept over McFarland as the female agent nodded to him. *Oh no*, he thought, *they're going to do a full-blown investigation. They'll nail me to the wall publicly. He'd flaunted his disregard for the rules, and they were going to make an example of him. He should just offer to resign immediately.*

The Boss looked at him intently. A small smile crossed his face, moving the wrinkles around his eyes and creating a look of weary understanding. Was that the look of the executioner?

"Be careful," the Boss said, still smiling, "be careful what you wish for, Mr. McFarland. You wanted to be involved. We are going to give you this case." McFarland gaped stupidly, like an infant hearing the sounds adults make, but not understanding them. Rushford was chuckling. Donatelli had his hands laced across his vest, his bald head gleaming, an angelic expression on his round face.

The Boss said, "You can breathe now, Mr. McFarland. You're going to work with Agents Smith and Farwell, rip the cover off this fraud, and find the bastards that murdered Hills and Douglas. Agents, Vic, come join us, we have an investigation to plan."

He sat down. Smith slipped into a chair on his right without moving it or making a sound. Donatelli sat next to Rushford, took a yellow pad from the pile in the middle of the table, and pushed it at McFarland. The Boss went out and asked Ms. Blake to bring coffee. Then he sat silently long enough for McFarland to wonder, uncomfortably, whether he was supposed to lead the discussion.

"Mr. McFarland, I want you to understand why you have this case, and what I expect going forward. You took naïve risks. You blundered around not knowing what you were doing, driven by sentiment more than strategy. You sure as hell stretched the rules. But, my friend, your instincts were spot on, and ultimately, when the thing got too big, you didn't try to cover up what you'd been doing, you told Vic the whole story. Sometimes passion counts more than experience."

He nodded to Rushford who said softly, "I'd have fired you, Jimmy. You're supposed to represent the United States Government. That means playing it very straight. No points for creativity."

The weary smile crept back over the Boss's face. "Agent Smith," he said, nodding at the sad-faced man, "is an old friend." The smile warmed. "He knows how to keep aggressive young prosecutors out of trouble." He looked at Smith and then back at McFarland. "I want a by-the-book investigation. These agents know how to dig deep. When you're ready, impanel a grand jury. Listen, watch, and let us know what you're doing. Don't talk, don't explain. Make the others figure you out. Someone has stolen a lot of money, and they probably killed two men to cover it up. They aren't going to be happy you're going after them." He turned back to Smith. "Hank, we probably need to move fast on some search warrants before stuff disappears."

"Yup."

"Well, Mr. McFarland, let's get this moving."

McFarland assumed he was dismissed. He needed time to absorb what had just happened. He stood and looked at the two FBI agents.

“Shall we meet at my office in half an hour? Pension Building, 307.”

They looked at him without moving.

Donatelli shook his head. “No, Jimmy, you work over here now. District court side. I’ll show you your new office. We’ve had your stuff brought over.”

Chapter 15
The Team

Half an hour after Donatelli had led him four doors down the hall to his new office, McFarland was seated at the small conference table with Smith and Farwell, trying to get his bearings. Somehow, he had gone from prosecuting street crime in the raucous precincts of the Superior Court to investigating a major fraud with an office in the District Court Building. He had a window and a conference table—and no rats.

He looked at the two agents, took a deep breath, and began, "The only way this is going to work is as a partnership. I need your help." To his surprise Smith smiled, a laconic smile that crinkled the corners of his Marlboro Man face.

"Mr. McFarland, if the Boss and Donatelli gave you this case, it's because they think you're going to get it done. That's good enough for me. Let's just get to work. Why don't you give us the whole story? Vic told us the essence, but we need the details."

For nearly an hour, McFarland talked and the agents questioned him, probing his acquaintance with Sergeant Williams, Lieutenant Dixon, and Detective Smallwood; the origins of the unemployment cases; Douglas' story, Ernie's murder; and right through to questioning of Dixon and the phone call with Olsen, an episode that elicited grins from both agents. They had, they told him, their own history with Olsen.

McFarland was unsurprised when Smith told him he'd been a fool to question Dixon on his own at Williams's apartment. "You have no record of what was said. It was completely *ultra vires* and obviously calculated to intimidate. Defense counsel would make it look like a conspiracy."

"I didn't know what might happen if Sarge just confronted him some night on the street, and I thought we were more likely to get the truth than the guys from homicide. Since it was 'unofficial,' I couldn't question him at my office."

Smith just looked at him and McFarland felt ridiculous.

McFarland recounted his call to Donatelli and his puzzlement at his lack of reaction. "It was like he knew already. Then when I saw the story in the *Post* on New Year's Day, I was pretty sure they were going to fire me anyway."

Smith stared at him with an ironic smile and said, "It was discussed when the Boss got us all in here that afternoon. I missed the damn Rose Bowl. Though that may be just as well. I'm a Michigan State alum. Donatelli reminded us that you had tried to get them to go after the fraud case as soon as you saw it, and we could have interviewed both Douglas and Hills if we had moved fast. You got that right. Do you have copies of all the documents Douglas passed on?"

McFarland pointed to one of the boxes that someone had brought over from his old office and said sheepishly, "I guess it should all be under lock and key."

"Yup," said Smith, "and we need to put a forensic accountant on it."

"Do you think we need a full analysis to get a warrant?"

"I doubt it. Don't you think you can make a probable cause without relying on those papers?"

Yeah, McFarland thought, *this is what I went to law school for,* and said, "Yes, I can."

"Then no use disclosing more than we have to."

McFarland nodded. That made sense. "Uh—is there…"

"Sure," said Farwell, "there's a form. You'll need one of us to sign an affidavit of probable cause. It goes to the magistrate's office on the ground floor. And we, ah, we also brought an example of an affidavit and a warrant from another case—if you want to see it."

McFarland laughed. "Okay, so you know what you're dealing with here. Rule forty-one for beginners."

They spent another half hour discussing the specifics of the search. There would be two searches: one of the Union offices, the other of the Conway office. As they were wrapping up, McFarland asked what they would do about the homicide detectives on the two murder cases.

"I think," Smith said, "That Farwell and I will pay them a call while you're getting the applications for the warrants ready. They have jurisdiction of the murders—for now, so we'll try to cooperate."

"What about Williams?" The two agents looked at him without answering. "He has a stake in this case."

"He does," answered Smith, "but it's personal, not professional. He's a friend of one of the victims—and of one of the suspects. You need to detach now. Your interest is professional. You represent the United States of America."

Farwell had been watching impassively. Now she said, "Mr. McFarland, I sure hope you don't play poker. You do not have a poker face, and your face says you aren't sure about this."

He had been taut with excitement and a sense of power, like sitting behind the wheel of a muscle car. Now he felt anguish. "Dumping Sarge feels like a betrayal, Agent Farwell. He trusts me. He brought me to meet Hills' family, and they opened up because he was there. He found the documents. He shares what he hears on the street. Hasn't he earned, I don't know, me keeping him informed? Involved?"

Smith shook his head. "No. Forget the sentiment. Do your job."

"I've got to at least tell him where things stand."

The two agents took their leave. McFarland moved to his desk and started unpacking boxes. He needed to call Sarge and tell him—what? What could he tell him? The phone rang. He jumped, startled, and answered just as someone else was answering.

"Assistant United States Attorney McFarland's Office."

"It's okay, I have it."

"Jimmy, it's KA. Congratulations. It sounds like you've been promoted."

"It's bizarre! I thought I was coming over here to get fired, and the next thing I know I'm running an investigation and have a couple of FBI agents working for me."

She chuckled, "Pushing the boundaries paid off."

"I think calling Donatelli when you told me to is what paid off."

"Nah. You are who you are. Listen, Jimmy, my husband, David, picked up some rumors you should be aware of. He has no idea whether they're true, but he wanted me to tell you."

"What?"

"Not on the phone. Can you meet me after work?"

"Yeah—latish?"

"Sure, seven-thirty. How about the Ruby?"

"Chinatown? I'll be there. Mai Tai's on me."

Since when had KA gone in for secret meetings in Chinese restaurants? For that matter, since when had MPD District Commanders passed on gossip to assistant U.S. attorneys? There was a knock at the door, and Donatelli burst in, looking pleased with himself.

"Jimmy, I want to introduce you to your assistant, Mrs. Bynum." A stocky black woman with thick glasses and a sour expression followed him in. "Mrs. Bynum is knowledgeable, discrete, and implacable. She's kept me in line, and she'll do the same for you. She knows more about the rules of Civil Procedure than you do, and Jimmy, you better not swear in her presence."

Assistant? McFarland was speechless. He had an assistant? That must have been who answered the phone.

"I'm very pleased to meet you, Mrs. Bynum, I'm Jimmy McFarland."

She looked at him critically and asked, "Do you need some lunch, Mr. McFarland?" Donatelli handed her a twenty and asked her to bring a couple of subs.

"Mr. Donatelli always has cream soda," she said, "what will you have Mr. McFarland?"

"A Coke, thanks, Mrs. Bynum. Where do you go to get a cream soda around here?"

"The Italian sandwich shop in the basement over on G Street. They know Mr. Donatelli, and they know he likes cream soda." She looked at her watch with disapproval. "Well, it's after one now. The jurors will be back in court and the line won't be bad." She turned back to McFarland and asked gravely, "Do you like pickles?" before turning and leaving the office.

Donatelli seated himself comfortably with his shiny shoes up on the table, and McFarland stood leaning against his desk.

"I think I owe you a big debt of gratitude, Vic."

"So, Smith told you about the New Year's afternoon meeting? The Boss knew what he was going to do before we met, but he needed someone who'd duke it out with Rushford. I reminded him of what he already knew. You were right. He was wrong. That's what he keeps me around for."

"Well, thank you. Halfway through that meeting I still thought I was done."

"Uh huh. We were all enjoying watching you wait for the axe to fall. But listen, you need to watch yourself. There are people who'd like you to fail. The story about you and Sergeant Williams working together as vigilantes didn't just get out. Someone put it out there."

"Why?"

Donatelli looked at him skeptically, as if wondering how naïve he really was, but McFarland wanted to hear what Donatelli would say.

"To stop you, Jimmy, to get you off the case, or to squash you because you haven't done your time."

There was a silence. McFarland wondered whether Donatelli was really a friend or simply trying to protect his investment, making sure McFarland didn't make them both look bad.

There was a knock, and Mrs. Bynum came in with the sandwiches and sodas. "I forgot to ask whether you take chips, Mr. McFarland. Mr. Donatelli doesn't eat them since his doctor told him to cut way down on salt and fat."

"But he eats Italian subs?"

Donatelli raised his chin defiantly. Cutting out chips and not putting salt in his soda, he said, was enough. They sat at the table and unwrapped the big sandwiches. Two kinds of salami, Parma ham, provolone, peppers, shredded lettuce, dripping with oil and balsamic vinegar. They hung their jackets on the backs of their chairs and ate in silence for a while.

Then Donatelli put his sandwich down, leaned back contentedly, and said, "She's gonna keep an eye on you for me."

"What, who?"

He knew very well what and who. Mrs. Bynum would let Vic know what her young boss was up to.

"Cora. She's an old friend."

McFarland wondered why Vic was telling him he had a spy. He may have read McFarland's mind, because he said, "You can trust her, and you can trust me. Just be aware that she'll let me know how things are going."

"Ohhhkaay."

Donatelli was chuckling. He daintily rewrapped the uneaten half of his sandwich, raised his eyebrows, puckered his mouth, and said, "Mmm, for teatime, maybe."

"Vic, what about Sarge?"

"What about him?"

"If the long knives are out for me, they're out for him. What do I tell him?"

Donatelli smoothed out the crumpled bag and put the rewrapped sandwich back in, folded the top, placed it precisely in front of himself, and examined it, as if judging the quality of his work. McFarland noticed he had manicured hands, a Masonic ring, and large lion's head cufflinks. Donatelli looked up.

"What do *you* think?"

So, thought McFarland, *the instruction is over and the mentoring has begun.* "I know he can take care of himself. He survived Tet. People on the street fear him, but they respect him, and he really cared for Ernie Hills and his family. I'm, well—I'm fond of him."

"And—what?"

"He trusts me, and I don't want to screw him over."

"Uh huh."

"He's got great sources."

"He does. I work with him on a lot of stuff. He's the one who told me you were worth watching."

McFarland digested that. The ride-along was a damned screen test?

Donatelli stroked his chin and asked, "So what's the problem?"

McFarland, still holding the end of his sandwich over his shiny government issue desk, looked down at the crumbs and drips of oil.

"Smith and Farwell think I need to drop him. It's not his case, and he's more interested in avenging a death than solving a major fraud case."

"Are they right?"

"No, damn it. They're not." He was surprised at his own vehemence. "He's not a cool buttoned up FBI agent, but he's a good cop."

There was a silence, then Donatelli said, "You're in charge, Jimmy."

The older man collected his coat and bag of leftovers, looked at McFarland, and told him, "The question about you is whether you are tough enough."

By the time Mrs. Bynum left for the evening, they had the application for the warrants and the supporting affidavits ready, and he had finally seen her smile when he'd imitated an imagined magistrate asking in a deep voice, "Mr. McFarland, do you know what you're doing?" and he had answered in a small squeak, "No, Your Honor, I do not."

She had responded, "When he sees Agent Smith's name on the affidavit, he's just going to get out his fancy pen and sign it."

"He's a legend, huh?"

"He and the Boss went toe-to-toe with a crooked president, Mr. McFarland. I'll let the FBI know that Agent Smith needs to come sign this."

McFarland spent the next two hours rereading Douglas' documents and making sure he read the recent probable cause cases in the D.C Circuit. Then he locked the papers in his drab green file cabinet, grabbed his coat, and headed for Chinatown.

*****

The Ruby was dim and mostly empty. By day, it was a thriving lunch spot. One of McFarland's former supervisors, an enormous man with a booming laugh, an infamous capacity for Mai Tai's, and a taste for Moo Shoo pork, held court there most Fridays, but people didn't hang around Washington's two block Chinatown at night. Although that might change if the rumored venue for Washington's hockey and basketball teams was ever built.

The dining room was suffused with red light, lit by dusty red paper lanterns, the walls papered with figured faux red velvet. McFarland saw KA and her husband sitting at the back. It was hard to miss Commander David Abbott in his impeccable uniform. He was a long, lean man who looked tall even folded up on a high-backed chair with his legs hidden under the table. He greeted McFarland warmly, and congratulated him on 'graduating' from street crime to white-collar fraud. McFarland thought his smile as he said that looked faintly sardonic.

"Thanks, David, I owe it all to KA's savvy advice."

"Yeah, me too, man. Sounds like you got a tiger by the tail."

"Umm, maybe something slimier than a tiger."

KA looked at him ruefully, as if to say they were all deep in the slime, though she didn't look it. She was crisp and prim at the end of a long day. She suggested they order drinks and a platter of pot stickers. They chatted about the Red Skins' upcoming playoff game, and the department's preparations for the inaugural ceremonies.

"Word is that Carter's determined to walk a big part of the parade route," Abbott said. "The Secret Service are having conniptions."

McFarland nodded. "He wants to show accessibility and openness to contrast with Nixon."

Abbott scoffed. “Nah, that’s a crock and we all know it. Where you walk doesn’t necessarily say where you’ll stand. Anyway, every cop in the city is going to be on duty trying to keep him safe.”

The Mai Tai’s arrived in big martini glasses with small paper umbrellas sticking out over the edge. They held their glasses up.

“To better times!”

KA put her hand on her husband’s arm. “David, I told Jimmy you’d picked up some gossip he should hear.”

David examined the class ring on his right hand as if reading an omen. He was something of a golden boy, the youngest district commander in the MPD, an affable man with a big warm smile and a Texas accent whom others underestimated at their peril. As KA told it, he was both astute and ruthless at navigating the seething politics of a department with a redneck DNA that was suddenly trying to adapt to a Black city and a Black city government.

“What have you been hearing, David?”

“You need to take this for what it is, gossip. I don’t know if it’s true or if I’m being spun, and I can’t really follow up without setting off alarms.” He fell silent, and then looked hard at McFarland and said, “Word is that Lieutenant Dixon’s Uncle Herman, the Deputy Chief, was steamed when he found out that his nephew let you and Williams question him about Ernie Hills’ murder. The Deputy Chief had his nephew over to headquarters and reamed him out so loud they could hear it in the hallway. He asked what you were up to—’What the hell’s that goddamn smartass boy prosecutor doing messing with a police investigation that isn’t assigned to him and never will be?’ He said he was going to put a stop to it and told the lieutenant to remember he was Williams’s superior, and it was time Williams got a lesson.”

“I don’t understand. What’s it to him?”

“I don’t know. Maybe he’s trying to protect his nephew—or the department’s jurisdiction.” Abbot rolled his eyes toward the ceiling as if to assure McFarland he didn’t believe a word of it.

“Is Herman Dixon bent?”

“I couldn’t say, but he’s got expensive taste in clothes, cars, and cigars.”

KA looked askance at her husband who was laughing. She scoffed, “David, you know that man is a crook and a bully.” Abbott nodded and said softly, “There’s something weird going on with the Deputy Chief. He’s been the real power in the department for more than a decade. He’s ruled with an iron fist, but I don't know, maybe he's tired—or too comfortable. The iron fist is getting rusty and loose I think—I hope."

He held up his glass to his wife, pursed his lips, blew the umbrella out of his glass, and drained what was left.

*****

Early the next morning, Agent Smith showed up to sign the affidavits. McFarland asked him to sit and told him about his conversation with David Abbott. To his surprise Smith grinned broadly.

"That figures. I'd love to nail the Deputy Chief. He's a crooked sonofabitch." Smith told McFarland that Deputy Chief Dixon had tried to put pressure on the Boss get rid of McFarland. "It wasn't a wise strategy. The Boss doesn't like to be pushed."

"What do you think is going on?" asked McFarland.

"Maybe a favor for a friend," Smith answered flippantly. "Who knows? We may find out more when we execute these warrants."

"Agent Smith?"

"Mr. McFarland?"

"I'm not going to freeze Williams out. I think he has a role to play, and I trust him."

"Okay."

"I just thought I should be straight with you."

"Got it."

McFarland had expected an argument. An explosion. Instead, Smith turned in his chair and said, "Let's think about what we ask him to do."

The magistrate signed the warrants that afternoon, and Smith and Farwell began organizing teams to execute the searches. They phoned McFarland and asked him to come to the FBI office the following morning to participate in the team briefings. He arrived early and brought pastries. Farwell was introducing him to the team when Smith came in, looking grim, and pulled him aside. McFarland thought perhaps he'd breached etiquette by bringing food.

"Lieutenant Dixon was shot and killed in his vehicle last night," Smith told him.

"Oh, God, no. Where were Amel and Sarge?"

"I don't know. Apparently not there."

"It can't have been Sarge. I don't believe it."

"Yeah, but the case has been assigned to Internal Affairs. Someone thinks it was him, or…"

"Or wants to put it on him?"

"It's not impossible. But let's not rush in and start messing with their investigation. If this is someone's play, they may expect you to try to protect Sarge."

"But I've got to talk to him."

"No, Jimmy, no you don't. Leave it to me."

McFarland was startled, both that Smith had called him 'Jimmy' and that he had said he would talk to Sarge. He saw Smith was watching him closely. He returned the gaze for a long moment. He wasn't sure he was any good at reading what was in someone's eyes, but Smith's look was very steady.

"They'll be watching him, and I don't mind them seeing him coming to the FBI," said Smith.

"Makes sense."

"You should assume they've tapped your phone."

"In the office?"

"Not in the District Court Building. The Marshals sweep the phones. The judges are pretty sensitive about that. At home." McFarland wondered what he'd said on the phone that he'd be embarrassed by.

"And, Jimmy, you may as well call me Hank, and Agent Farwell is Nora. We should get back in there before they finish all those pastries."

It was a long day. There was a forensic accountant, Agent Rohrig, who went through the documents that Williams had copied and the information he'd recorded in excruciating detail. He described the types of records that would reveal more of the scheme and who knew about it.

"Mr. Douglas's notes show that more paychecks were issued than there were people working. We're pretty sure those checks weren't being cashed by the workers whose names were on them. We need bank statements and payroll records that enable us to track that."

How, McFarland wondered, would this come across in a trial? Rohrig sounded like he was reading from a textbook. How would he make it a story for the jurors? And who would the defendants be? McFarland looked around the table. The agents looked, well, fascinated. A practiced response to tedious briefings? McFarland decided he had to interrupt.

“Agent Rohrig? Can I break in?” The man looked annoyed but stopped and waited for his question. “I assume from what we already have that we’ll find further evidence of ghost workers and materials that disappear. Surely money was going to senior people in both the union and the company. They won’t have recorded that as illegal payoffs.” There was muffled laughter around the table. “Where do we look for it?”

“You would be surprised, Mr. McFarland, how artless and obvious some of our fellow accountants can be.”

McFarland caught Smith looking intently at a ceiling fixture.

“There may be obvious payments, or there may be accounts of payments with totally ridiculous explanations, or there may be discrepancies—lines that simply don’t add up. That stuff drives people like me crazy. We’ll seize the documents and figure it out later.”

*****

Thursday morning, January 6th, it had turned cold again. Each of the FBI teams arrived at their target office as workers bundled in heavy coats hurried through the weak light. They had determined that both offices would be occupied by 8:00 am and timed their arrival accordingly. Smith had been clear this was an FBI operation and McFarland was not welcome. McFarland sat by his phone like an anxious parent in case any legal issue might arise.

The agents had decided Farwell should handle the search of the Union offices, a role she relished since there were few women in the union, and none in leadership. When she and her team of six agents arrived in two black vans and parked illegally in front of the drab four-story building that housed the Union offices, they attracted a crowd of gawkers. Inside, a small group of staffers standing around a gurgling coffee machine were visibly startled when the team in dark suits and FBI jackets entered. Farwell introduced herself and presented the warrant. An older white woman held up her hand as if to ward off a blow.

“I’m Marie Drayton. I am the office manager. We need to call our boss and ask him what to do.”

“Yes, Ma’am, but we are going execute this warrant.”

Farwell saw panic in the woman’s eyes and nodded to her team to get started. Panic was manageable.

"You have to let us contact our lawyer."

"Yes, Ma'am, you can call from here if you stay out of our way, but this warrant is a court order. It gives us full legal authority to search these premises and seize any evidence we may find."

Twenty minutes later a bulky, red-haired man in a wrinkled gray suit came to the door and demanded to be let in. One of the agents blocked his way.

"It's my goddamned office. Let me in. You have no right to keep me out."

"Who are you?"

"I'm Dan Adams. I run this office. Let me in."

"Mr. Adams, we have a warrant to search these premises."

"This is ridiculous, flagrant union busting. You can't just come in here and say you have a warrant and take over."

He turned to an athletic looking man with short hair, a heavy mustache and cold, blank eyes who was standing behind him. The man gave the slightest shake of his head. Farwell walked over to the door and said pleasantly, "Mr. Adams, I'm Agent Farwell, the agent in charge. I can show you a copy of the warrant, and you can stay in the reception area if you don't get in our way, but your companion—I didn't get your name?"

"No, you didn't."

"Who are you?" She looked hard, trying to recall where she had seen this dark, malevolent face.

"My name is none of your business."

"Do you work here?"

"No."

He turned and walked away. She thought to follow him, but decided she was there to execute a search warrant and she'd be asking for trouble if she went beyond that authority. She turned back to Adams.

"Who's your associate?"

"No idea. He doesn't work for me."

She smiled at him, shook her head, and walked away as her colleagues began to wheel boxes of documents out of the building. One of the agents pulled her aside and said something to her. She turned back to Adams. He was sweating, and his eyes were darting from one face to another. She wondered how far she could push him without causing a heart attack.

"Mr. Adams, we need the keys to your desk and the locked file cabinet in your office."

"I don't have them."

"Who does?"

"Ah, I'm not sure."

"Oh, I'm sorry, then we'll have to break the locks."

"I, uh, I'll find them."

"Just tell me where they are, sir."

"In a box on my desk, under my cigars."

"Yes sir, and is there a safe?" He closed his eyes.

"Yes."

The older woman called Adams to the phone. He held one hand over his mouth and the phone as he spoke, shaking his head in disagreement, but then seeming to subside into misery. When the call ended, he sent the staff away, except the older woman, Mrs. Drayton, who was the office manager. He strode up to Farwell, trying his best to look confident.

"I'm leaving. You'll hear from our lawyers. Mrs. Drayton will wait for the inventory of what you take." He scurried out.

One of the agents came to Farwell with a green ledger. He shook his head in amazement. Almost too obvious to believe. It contained a list of dates, funds received, and payments made with initials.

"It was in the safe. There's about $8,000 in cash and what might be a list of names in some sort of code. It's like they didn't think anyone would care."

Chapter 16
Who They Think You Are

Sergeant Williams was in uniform, not his working costume. He had just left a second grilling by three Internal Affairs investigators. They knew, they told him, that he had killed Dixon. He was a dirty cop and a violent bully. They had leaned close to his face and shouted. They were going to nail him, they screamed, breath stinking of coffee, cigarettes, and corruption. He had remained still, and silent. He had been yelled at by coaches, drill sergeants, and any white cop in Wilmington who thought he looked too big and sure of himself. He had walked out of the interview room still not facing charges.

Now he was summoned to the FBI Washington field office. He wondered what the hell was going on. He wanted to call McFarland and ask whether he knew, but he hadn't heard from him since the New Year. Maybe Jimmy had decided that his Vice Squad sergeant friend was a liability. That was what he'd told Jimmy the day they'd questioned Dixon. Things had gotten crazy in the weeks since they'd started working together.

The FBI receptionist told him an agent would be out to get him in a moment, and he could put his coat on the rack. The place made him uncomfortable. Awed. None of the stories about corruption and abuse of power that had come out after J. Edgar Hoover's death changed that. Like the doctor's office. He didn't know what was going to happen and didn't feel he had any control. Why would the FBI be interested in him or Dixon? He was surprised when a small, trim woman with short dark hair, piercing eyes, and a look of coiled energy entered from the door at the back of the reception area.

"Sergeant Williams? I'm Agent Farwell. Thank you for coming. We thought our offices might be the best place to meet in light of the circumstances."

What circumstances, Williams wondered, and why was this agent making it sound as if this were a business meeting? It made him even more uncomfortable. Agent Farwell led him down a featureless hall to a plain, windowless conference room. There was a picture of Director Kelley on one wall, a picture of President Ford facing it on the opposite one. Williams wondered whether the FBI would substitute Jimmy Carter at the precise moment he took the oath of office a few blocks away. Agent Farwell told him her partner would be joining them, and as she spoke a middle-aged man in a dark suit came in. He looked just as Williams thought an FBI agent should look. He was erect, wiry, with close-cropped gray hair, and wary eyes behind glasses in black frames. He crossed the room with an eerie economy of motion. He was impossible for Williams to read, his thoughts seemed protected behind a baleful mask.

He held out his hand, "Sergeant, I'm Hank Smith." He gestured for Williams to have a seat.

Williams sat across from the two agents, waiting silently. He heard Nana in his head saying, "If you don't know what to say, Lawrence, you don't never get in trouble by just listening." Nine years old. Bruised after his first real fist fight. She had told him he was going to be big, and he didn't need to fight to prove anything. He needed to be smart.

Smith put his fingers together under his chin and caught Williams's gaze for a long moment. "Sergeant, Agent Farwell and I are working with Mr. McFarland investigating fraud in the construction of the Metro. He speaks highly of you."

What kind of trick was this? He hadn't heard from Jimmy and didn't know anything about any FBI investigation.

Smith looked at him calmly and asked, "Sergeant, did you kill Al Dixon?"

"No."

"Do you know who did?"

"No."

"The boys over in Internal Affairs think you killed him."

"I know. They told me that."

"And?"

"If they had the evidence, they'd have arrested me."

Smith nodded slowly as if to say that made sense to him. He said, "Dixon was shot at close range. He must have known whoever shot him. You could have done that. You had evidence he might have killed your friend."

Williams struggled to stay calm, to not let them get in his head. "If I knew Al had killed Ernie, I might have killed him, but Jimmy convinced me there were too many questions."

"Like what?"

"Like if Dixon was there, why Ernie's wife didn't recognize his voice. Like how a guy who never shined his shoes could have had bright shiny black shoes. Like why there were two guys who carried it out with complete efficiency, when Al is—was a slob and a coward."

"Will you tell us what you know about what happened the night Dixon was killed?"

"Is the FBI investigating the murder of Lt. Dixon?"

"We might be."

Williams raised his eyebrows, "Might be?"

"If it's related to our fraud case."

Williams was taken aback, struggling to understand this, trying to piece together what he knew. Why would they think Dixon's death had anything to do with the fraud case? Smith seemed to read the question in his face. He responded, counting off his observations on the fingers of his right hand.

"First, as you know, an engineer named Douglas started handing over documents to your friend Ernie Hills, and Douglas was killed. Second, your friend was going to take those documents to the Senate District Committee, and he was killed. Your informants made Dixon watching Hills' house, you found the documents, and you and Mr. McFarland questioned him about it, and then Dixon was shot. Someone wants you in the frame for that killing. What do you think is going on?"

"Shit. I'm no risk. I'm just a big, dumb, Vice Squad guy."

"Big for sure."

"But I guess they need to stop McFarland?"

"He's a problem for someone, isn't he?" Williams stared at Smith.

"And you're telling me it's someone in the MPD?" Smith sat in silence. "What do you want from me?"

Farwell responded, "We want to know what happened Tuesday night. We want to know what you saw when you arrived at Hills' house the night he was killed. We want to know why Phillips and Blake are getting nowhere? Is somebody screwing with them?"

"Oh, shit, I don't believe that. Pete Phillips is too experienced to get pulled into that crap."

Farwell nodded and asked, "What about Tuesday night? What happened?"

Williams gathered his thoughts. He'd been through this with the Internal Affairs guys multiple times.

"The three of us were out on old clothes detail."

"Three?"

"Dixon, me, and Detective Amel Smallwood. We work together most nights. We usually go out in a couple of cars."

"And do what?"

"We try to keep the streets under control, keep a lid on the drug trade, and keep the idiots from the suburbs from getting themselves killed."

"And Tuesday night?"

"Dixon radioed us that something was going down in an abandoned building at fourteen-thirty-five U street."

"Where'd he get that information?"

"I don't know, but that's a house we've been in before. We agreed he'd stay out front and me and Smallwood would come in the back."

"His idea, or yours?"

"His call."

"And…?"

"Nothin'. Dixon was the senior officer. Me and Detective Smallwood… looked around. There was no one there and it didn't seem like anyone had been there in a while."

"Was that unusual?"

"No. It happens all the time. People give us bad information just to get us out of the way. Usually you can tell, you know, by the source, but not always."

"How long were you in there?"

"Less than five minutes. We heard a shot, couldn't raise Dixon, and went out to see what was going on. He was there in his car, parked across the street, slumped over the wheel, shot in the back of the head, blood and brains spattered on the dashboard. I sent Detective Smallwood to get our car. I radioed it in."

"Smallwood was with you the whole time before that?"

Williams looked at her and nodded. The Internal Affairs guys had assumed Smallwood was covering for him. They'd spent hours trying to convince him to save his ass and turn on his sergeant, because they were going to get Williams anyway and Smallwood would go down with him. Williams had wondered whether Smallwood would crack.

Smith who had been watching in silence broke in.

"The car window was open?"

"Yes, but he can't have been shot from there. The blood was all splattered forward. It looked to me like the slug must be in the dashboard."

"Is it a four-door car?"

"Mm-hmm. '69 Ford LTD. The back door wasn't locked. We're supposed to keep them locked."

"Could someone have reached in the driver's side window and unlocked the back door?"

"Yes. If it was one shooter, he could have had the gun in his right hand and reached around with his left hand to pull up the lock."

"Were you wearing gloves, Sergeant?"

"Yes. It was goddamned cold."

"The crime scene unit pulled prints off the outside door handle."

Williams looked at Smith in surprise. Not that there were prints, but that these agents had obviously read the crime scene report, and they were disclosing it to him.

"Seems like they weren't mine, or they'd have charged me." He hesitated, then went on. "I can't use my weapon with my gloves on, not with these big paws." He held out his hands.

"You didn't draw your weapon coming out of the house?"

"No. Detective Smallwood had his weapon out, but I've learned that holding a weapon narrows your thinking."

"Was it unusual for one of the team to stay in the car that way?"

"If we don't know what's going on, two go in, and one stays out on the other side to watch for runners. If it was me, I'd have stood outside of the car."

Smith cocked his head to one side and asked, "Was the engine of the car running?"

Williams allowed himself a wry smile, "Yeah, Agent Smith, it was, and the heater was cranked up. Son of a bitch could have been just keeping his ass warm while we checked out a bad tip."

"Or he could have been waiting for someone."

"Or that."

Williams had the sense these agents were filling in a mental picture, not like the Internal Affairs guys who were working from the theory that he'd shot Dixon and were trying to trip him up. Smith looked at Farwell. She nodded as if agreeing to some shared conclusion and Smith turned back to Williams.

"Sergeant, the evidence doesn't tell us much one way or the other. You could have killed Dixon, but I don't think it's likely. For one thing, you and Smallwood would have had to plan it together, and I don't think you would have involved him if you were taking vengeance on Dixon. And if you had killed him, I think you'd admit it."

Williams could hear his heart pounding. He found it difficult to breathe. Like he was dead scared, but it wasn't fear. He was stunned that these two buttoned-up, unsmiling agents saw him as he saw himself—honorable.

"We have a proposition for you."

Williams was jolted back to guarded alertness. They were spinning him to sell him some sort of deal. He waited in blank silence. Smith continued, the shadow of a smile in the wrinkles at the corners of his mouth.

"If someone is using you to get at McFarland, that's a federal offense, and we'd like to know what the hell is going on. Even if they're not after McFarland, we need to know. You can help."

Williams warned himself to be cautious, but he relaxed. He had wondered the same thing. What the hell.

"What do you want me to do?"

"Act like you *are* who they think you are."

*****

Later Williams, still trying to understand what the FBI might be up to, searched out Officer Abrams in her dress uniform waiting to testify in Superior Court. Williams, too, was still in uniform—dark blue, polished black leather, bright silver badge, weapon on his hip, and deep dark eyes that this morning looked like windows on the pit of hell.

"Abrams, I need to talk to you." She saw he was angry but didn't know what was wrong.

"Sure, Sarge."

They stood in a grimy hallway. He leaned in so they won't be overheard.

"I told you not to talk about what we heard from the Twins, but you been talking."

"No, Sarge, not to anybody."

"Yeah, you did. Within a couple of days, it's all over the department."

"It wasn't from me. I heard the talk, but it didn't come from me. And I didn't know anything about that DA they say you're working with." He stared hard at the young face filled with misery and supplication. If not her, then who?

Chapter 17
Cooked and Scrubbed

Agents Smith, Farwell, and Rohrig, the forensic accountant who'd been at the briefing, filed into McFarland's office late Friday afternoon. Each lugged a briefcase. McFarland watched with excitement. Was this a selection of the evidence they'd seized? The fraud case in three bags? Smith put his big, black attaché case on the conference table, looked at Jimmy solemnly, unlocked it, and pulled out a sixpack, moisture beaded on the cold bottles, and a couple of bags of chips.

"Just returning the favor, Jimmy." He laughed.

Farwell said, "You should have seen how you looked Wednesday morning."

"I was just trying to figure out…"

"Naw, when Hank came and pulled you out of the room, you thought you'd stepped in it."

"Well, I did wonder whether you guys are even allowed to enjoy a sweet roll at work."

Jimmy McFarland, left wing intellectual, bleeding heart liberal, erstwhile protester, hanging out with FBI agents. No, in awe of them. Depending on them. Despite the spying, dirty tricks, and malfeasance, he still thought of them as hard edged and upright crime fighters, not the bearers of a Friday afternoon sixpack. Smith handed around the bottles and chips. The cold bottle felt real and familiar.

"Hank, have you talked to Sergeant Williams?"

"This morning."

"How'd that go?"

"Well given that the MPD Internal Affairs Division is working pretty hard to prove that he killed Dixon, we had an interesting discussion. We'll talk more about that later."

There was a knock, and Mrs. Bynum appeared with napkins and a bowl of some sort of dip. She explained to McFarland, "Agent Smith has his Friday afternoon traditions."

Smith saluted her and asked, "Whoever said the FBI is no fun? Mrs. Bynum, is Mr. Donatelli still here?"

"I believe he is. Shall I get him."

"Jimmy are you okay with having Vic sit in?"

"Sure. He'd be down here soon anyway, wanting to know what we found."

Ten minutes later the three agents, McFarland, and Donatelli crowded around the small conference table by the window in McFarland's office. Farwell and Rohrig opened their cases and began to spread thick folders across the table. Each folder had a grid printed on the front which had spaces for dates, times, and agents' names. Chips and dip were moved to McFarland's desk, more folders were laid out on the floor, Rohrig fussing to keep them in proper order.

Donatelli watched happily. "Oh," he sighed, "the smell of raw evidence. Like the rich manure smell of a barn in the morning."

"You saying we're full of shit, Vic?"

"Certainly, and I'm ready to dig in. Like they say, with all this horse shit there's got to be a pony here somewhere."

He draped his perfectly pressed suit coat over the back of a chair, held up his bottle, and saluted McFarland. "Jimmy, my friend, we are going to ferret out some wrong-doing and bring the perpetrators to justice."

McFarland watched Donatelli prowl around the table, reading the fronts of the folders. The man really got off on this stuff. He looked around. The table was filled with crimefighters. What the hell was he doing here, and why did he feel elated?

"Okay, Counselor, how do you want to do this?" Smith asked. "We've taken a quick look through the stuff. This is what seemed relevant at first glance. Shall we brief you on what we've got?"

It had been their search, but it was his case. He needed to assert control and form his own opinions.

"No. Let's go through it, piece by piece."

"It could be a long night..."

"Yup," said Donatelli dryly, "for the Union and Conway too, I imagine." He tapped a finger on one of the folders. His bald head was glistening as if he'd polished it for the occasion. Farwell picked up the first folder of evidence seized from the union offices.

"These are membership records for the past three years. They're a mess, but they do detail who's paying dues, what job they're on, and who has died or resigned. The local tracks that carefully. That's their base, and they pay the national union based on their membership. Metro construction is a union job. The number of laborers on the Conway payroll should match the number shown here as working on that job. Just to end the suspense, it doesn't. Douglas was right. There are at least ninety workers being paid who aren't active members of the union, probably more. They're earning six hundred to twelve hundred dollars a week plus time and a half for overtime. That's over a hundred thousand a week."

"Jeezus, that's brazen," McFarland exclaimed, "who's getting the money? And how're they cashing the checks?"

Farwell looked at Rohrig, who frowned. "We can answer the second question pretty easily, sir. We've got the canceled checks. We'll look at where each ghost worker cashed his checks."

"And...?"

"So far it looks like it all went through one bank——Washington Commerce and Trade. Same branch the union uses. You'll have to subpoena their records to confirm it. We'll see whether it was just one teller. Maybe we can figure out who authorized it, and who they dealt with at the union."

"And who got the money once the checks were cashed?"

Farwell held up her hands. "Whoa. That's a couple of folders down the table."

McFarland looked at the mass of paper uneasily, wondering whether his indignation was naïve. "Is this what happens on every big construction site?"

Donatelli shook his refulgent head. "No way. There might be a couple of no shows getting paid on any big job, but nothing on this scale. Usually, the contractor has a strong incentive to get what he's paying for. Ghost workers come out of his pocket. But after WMATA signed the acceleration contract with Conway, they got paid to work around the clock on a cost-plus basis. They got their percentage on *every* cost, whether the work was done or not. The General's a tough, upright, sonofabitch. He has to have known what was going to happen, and I'm betting he doesn't care. The thing is getting built. The corruption is just collateral damage."

McFarland watched Smith, sitting across the table from him, as he slowly finished his beer and then adjusted his deadpan expression with a slight lift of his eyebrows.

"General Grisham might just think we ought to leave this investigation where it is. Seems like we'll have stopped the fraud, why disrupt the project with a big noisy prosecution?"

McFarland's face reddened; his lips compressed and his brows knitted. "Screw that, Hank, I can't believe what I'm hearing."

Farwell was laughing. "I keep telling you, McFarland, you gotta work on your poker face. *And* do a better job watching Hank's face. His eyes move when he's jerking your chain."

Donatelli put a hand on McFarland's arm. "Jimmy, the thing is, the Boss is going to get that call from the General, or the AG is. He'll say that this is the nation's capital, and there are millions of people waiting to ride this subway. No one's going to look good when you tear the cover off this scheme."

"Oh, crap. That argument applies to any kind of public wrong-doing or corruption." Smith nodded sadly and said, "Yeah, even corruption at the FBI. I'm just telling you to be ready."

Mrs. Bynum knocked and stuck her head around the door to say she was getting ready to leave. Donatelli smiled at her, she nodded and asked, "Pizzas or chicken?" Donatelli and Smith both said, "Pizza," and started to list the toppings they wanted. She told them to hush, she'd gotten them enough pizzas to know what they wanted.

After she'd left, McFarland asked, "Is that fair? It's Friday evening, and she should have left half an hour ago."

"I'll sign an overtime slip for her. She's as committed to this work as you are."

"It seems like we're taking advantage."

Donatelli rolled his eyes. "This is what happens when you start hiring goddamned liberals in a prosecutor's office. Why don't you ask her how she feels about it?"

An hour later they spread copies of the *Post* and the *Star* over the folders and took a dinner break. They had looked at the records of the union's operating accounts, and Rohrig had told them they looked messy, but routine.

"They have a part-time book-keeper who does a good job tracking income and expenses, or at least what's on the books. They seem to have kept the ghost workers entirely separate. They're recorded, sort of, in a set of files that were in Adams' safe. Sloppy, not consistent, and not the same handwriting as the formal accounts. The records in the safe seem to roughly correspond with the ghost workers, but the names are coded, and there are fewer than there should be."

McFarland asked whether that looked to be an error.

Rohrig shook his head. "I doubt it. Someone was probably skimming."

"Oh good," exclaimed Donatelli, "crooks stealing from crooks. That's rich with possibilities for turning them against each other."

"So, do we know where the money was going?"

"No, not yet. We found a notebook in Adams' safe that is probably his record of what was paid out, but the numbers look weird, and the names, if that's what they are, are coded. Then there are some sheets of paper, maybe transactions, that hadn't yet gone in the book. Those might help us break the code."

Farwell was thinking about Dan Adams. Pudgy, panicky, out of his depth. She couldn't picture him creating a sophisticated code, let alone managing a complex fraud.

"I wonder," she said slowly, "whether someone else has another set of records? What do you think, Jim? Adams didn't seem like the mastermind type."

"Maybe not."

Rohrig laid his hand on the first folder of documents from Conway and said, "The ghost workers' case is all here. Between these files, the canceled checks, and the records from the union office, we have a solid case."

McFarland imagined himself going in to brief the Boss, telling him that he was ready to take the case to a grand jury, but he saw Smith's skepticism.

"But what, Hank?"

"I think those files have been scrubbed. Douglas's notes say the fraud was bigger than these records show and it was growing. Plus, they claimed there was no index of what was there. Bullshit."

"How do we figure out what was going on?"

Rohrig answered, "Gotta follow the money." He looked positively animated. "We have to compare their cash accounts with the records of what came onto and went off the sites. The records of those accounts are not here, they're at corporate headquarters. The job will be tedious, but very doable." He paused and with a smug smile continued, "It would be way harder for them to falsify their basic accounts than to scrub a few files."

McFarland tapped the file and said, "So, Conway isn't a victim. They know and they're hiding it?" *If that was true*, he thought, *then the question was, how high did the rot go.* He found it hard to believe that senior executives would be involved in this kind of crude corruption. He turned to Donatelli: "Vic, does this make sense to you? Have you seen big companies—well, stealing from the public like this?"

"Oh, come on, Jimmy. Do you imagine they see money lying around and just turn up their noses? They rig bids, they inflate prices, they do deals with generals, and then hire them when they retire. This scam is crude, but it's what they do."

McFarland winced. He felt naïve, a kid trying to masquerade as a prosecutor. He was taken aback by Donatelli's angry scorn for corporate ethics.

Farwell broke in, pointing at Donatelli. "Vic, that's a huge generalization. We don't know yet just what they were doing or who was doing it. Jimmy is right to ask whether the whole thing is plausible before we form a posse and gallop off after them."

Smith watched his partner with interest. He had never heard her so outspoken. Donatelli laughed and held up his hands. "Okay, okay."

It was past eleven. The building and the streets outside were still. Donatelli rose to leave, but Smith stopped him. "We need to talk about where the boundaries are. Are we investigating a fraud case, or a fraud and three murders? And what are we going to do about Jimmy's friend, Sergeant Williams?"

McFarland winced. He had not been thinking about Sarge, but he belonged in this room. He stared hard at Smith and said, "Wait, Hank, you think the three murders are connected?"

Smith looked at him, bemused, "Don't you?"

"What did Sarge tell you?"

Smith took a breath and said, "That he didn't kill Dixon, that he might have, but you convinced him there were too many inconsistencies in the evidence. He told us that Internal Affairs has him for killing Dixon, which is what they told us as well. But so far as I can tell, they don't actually have any evidence. You gotta wonder why they have him down for it without doing any investigation? Whose instructions are they following?"

McFarland started to speak, but Donatelli, his face as tight and cold as it had been when he had showed up to 'talk' with Judge Stanley, held up a hand.

"Do *you* have evidence, Agent Smith, or is this your gut speaking?" Smith stroked his chin, narrowed his eyes, and nodded to Farwell. "Nora, you sum it up. Vic knows how I feel about some of the folks at MPD Headquarters."

She stood up; hands clasped behind her as if she were reciting.

"The first two murders happened fast after Douglas began raising questions and Hills arranged to brief the Senate Committee staff. Both murders look like hits. We don't have physical evidence that we know of. We need to get the evidence in both cases sent to our lab for testing. The MPD lab is a decade behind the times, under-resourced, and, in our experience, tends to go where headquarters wants them to go."

"Then there's Dixon. Sergeant Williams could have killed him, but it seems more likely that if Williams was going to avenge Hills, it would have happened sooner, and we don't think he would have involved Smallwood. So, we have the question: Why was Dixon parked in front of Hills' house just before he was killed? It's an unlikely coincidence. More likely, his visit was connected to the murder and someone killed him before he told Sarge what he knew. Admittedly it's circumstantial, but that's a lot of circumstances." She stopped speaking, watching Donatelli and McFarland.

Smith cleared his throat. "There's something else we need to think about. Conway cleaned up their files before we got there. Someone told them we were coming. There wasn't much time, and not many people besides the five of us knew."

McFarland recoiled and said, "They could have acted as soon as they knew Douglas was raising questions. He'd gone to his supervisor, Elliott Taylor, first. When Bill Minot brought Douglas to talk to me, he was scared. He didn't want to be seen."

"Yeah, that's possible, but I'm worried we have a leak."

Smith and Farwell looked at each other and turned to McFarland. Smith said, "Jimmy, one way to look at the focus on Williams for the Dixon killing is that someone is going to considerable lengths to make this investigation go away. One way to throw the investigation off the tracks is to discredit you."

"With the help of the MPD? That's farfetched."

Smith frowned. "You think so? To me it makes sense. Metro is the biggest public project ever built in this city. There's a river of money and a lot of people trying to dip their buckets into it. Wouldn't there be folks in the MPD looking for their cut? There's an old guard that's been there a long time and feels like greasing the wheels is just how it's done."

"Who?"

"Ask your friend KA who actually runs the MPD…"

Donatelli had been silent, leaning his chin on his folded hands. Now he stood up and walked around the table to face Smith.

"Hank, you've been looking for this for a while."

"Uh huh. You too."

"I don't know what you're planning, but you need to read Jimmy in."

Smith turned toward McFarland, let out a long breath, scratched his head, and began to speak slowly and very carefully. "Whoever is Chief of Police in Washington, D.C., Herman Dixon runs the MPD. That's the way it is, and that's the way it's been for a long time, ten years maybe. He controls promotions. He controls assignments. He's got his guys in Internal Affairs, so he controls discipline, and if there's something going on, he gets his cut. You'd think we could nail the SOB, but he's been there too long, knows too much, and done too many favors. He takes care of a lot of people."

"But Hank," McFarland said, "Do you have evidence he's a crook."

"Well, that's a bit of a story…"

Donatelli, still standing across the table, snorted, and responded, "Yeah, a short and sad story. Hank and his old partner had a case, and I screwed it up."

"Mmm, well, we all did. We got the Deputy Chief on a wiretap that had been approved for a different case, and we didn't do the paperwork to pursue Dixon, so the wiretap evidence got suppressed. Then we had a couple of witnesses we didn't stay close enough to and he got to them…"

"And the over-zealous assistant DA—that would be me—didn't follow the rules on disclosing exculpatory evidence to the defense team. The judge found out and dismissed the case." McFarland tried to keep his expression neutral but abashed by this tale of over-zealous prosecution and really dumb screw-ups.

Hank smiled and winked. "Never happens nowadays."

Donatelli said almost to himself, "Not in any case I'm involved with." In that moment, he was recalling the excruciating session when the then U.S. Attorney had strode into his office the afternoon the case was dismissed to tell him he didn't need prosecutors who couldn't tell right from wrong and sent him home to think about it and come back with an argument for why he should keep his job.

"Vic, how'd Dixon keep his job?"

Vic, who'd been thinking how he kept *his* job, stared at McFarland wordlessly, and Smith answered.

"Oh, his lawyer argued that the dismissal of the case made it improper for any action to be taken against him. Really, I'd guess he'd solved problems for a couple of the District Commissioners—that was before home rule—you know a drunk driving charge that turned out to be a mistake, or evidence in a pot case against a commissioner's son that went missing."

McFarland thought about David Abbott's suspicion that something had slipped with the Deputy Chief, and said, "Ok, he's a tyrant and a crook, and you'd like to nail him, but what's the evidence that he's involved in this fraud or these murders?"

Donatelli went back to his chair. A slight smile flitted across his face. That was the right question. Most of what they had was hearsay or supposition. They started to catalog what they knew. Conway officials had met with Deputy Chief Dixon as the project was getting underway to assure smooth communication about street closings and site security. They knew that after the meeting the Deputy Chief had told the district commanders he would review and approve all assignments relating to Metro construction. Lt. Dixon had staked out Ernie's house just before Ernie was killed, and later the Deputy Chief had been heard screaming at his nephew about getting McFarland and Williams under control. They knew the Deputy Chief had called the Boss to try to get McFarland off the case.

"What's with that?" McFarland asked, "The Deputy Chief sounds smarter than that."

Donatelli answered, "I would guess he was probing for information."

"Did he get any?"

“Not much, but he confirmed that we were pursuing it and you were in charge.”

“And then Lt. Dixon was shot.”

“And then Lt Dixon was shot, and the case went straight to Internal Affairs, not Homicide.”

Rohrig, who had been taking notes as they ‘built their case’, observed that nothing he’d written down so far other than the payroll records would be admissible in a trial.

Smith nodded sadly. “Yes, true, but there is one thing more. Nora?”

She looked up, and said, “When we were executing the warrant at the Union offices, Dan Adams showed up, spouting indignation and looking like he might have a stroke. He had a guy with him I thought I recognized. Big guy, dark mustache, hard eyes. He refused to give his name and walked off, but later I remembered who he was. When I met him, he was an Army Ranger. He came down to teach a class on sniper tactics at Quantico when I was an FBI trainee.”

“Who does he work for now?”

“Well, I had a hunch, which turned out to be pretty good. He works for the MPD, in the Deputy Chief’s office.”

Smith gave a grim chuckle. “The Deputy Chief has a kind of Palace Guard. They’re enforcers and bag men.”

McFarland was dumfounded.

“How the hell…?”

“He had on really brightly polished shoes. His name is Caleb Ransome, Detective Caleb Ransome.”

Chapter 18
If a Guy Saves Your Life

It was past one when Donatelli dropped McFarland at his house. Tired as he was, he noticed the old Ford with someone sitting inside smoking, the tip of the cigarette glowing when the smoker took a drag. Sarge. He suspected Donatelli had noticed too, but nothing was said. Donatelli just muttered, "Good night. Get some sleep." McFarland walked over to the car. The driver cranked down the window. Smoke drifted out into the glow of the streetlight.

"Sarge, I'm really glad to see you."

"You been out late man. You have a date?"

"I did. It was quite an evening. Me, three FBI agents, and Donatelli. We ate pizza, drank beer, and reviewed documents. Why don't you come on in?"

"It's late for someone that doesn't work nights."

"Uh huh, but we need to talk, and you must have been waiting a while."

McFarland felt relieved, almost as if he'd been expecting to find Sarge, certainly hoping he'd show up. Williams looked dubious.

"I think your housemate, Professor Brown—Paul, may have a young lady visiting. I saw her go in."

McFarland squinted at the house. "Nah, I really don't think so."

"Young lady. Short blond hair. A lot of energy. When he came to the door, she kind of jumped into his arms."

McFarland laughed. "That would be his little sister, Sally."

Williams stared at him, nodded as if to say he got it, opened the car door, and got out, stretching elaborately. They climbed the steps onto the porch. As Jimmy got his keys out, Williams turned and looked carefully up and down the street. The door swung open as McFarland pushed his key in the lock, and he shook his head. Paul was not good about locking up. He entered the dark foyer and held the door open behind him for Sarge, tripping over a pair of boots lying by the radiator as he felt his way to the hall light.

"What can I offer you, Sarge? Whisky? Beer—I'm pretty sure there's beer unless Paul and Sally drank it all."

A voice from the second-floor landing called, "I didn't drink your beer, and I brought some good wine." Sally came down the stairs wearing a robe and looking with bleary-eyed curiosity at Sarge.

"Sally, this is Sergeant Larry Williams. Sarge, this is Paul's little sister, Sally."

She shook Williams's hand and gave McFarland a kiss on the cheek.

"I was asking Sarge what I can get him to drink."

"How about some of that coffee of yours?"

McFarland wondered how to gently encourage Sally to go back to bed so he and Sarge could talk. He muttered something about how late it was and left to make espressos.

Sally turned to Williams with a wan smile and said, "I'd like to get to know you, Sarge. Jimmy speaks so highly of you, but I'm getting looks that give me the sense you've got business to talk about, so I'll go back up to bed. Nice to meet you." She turned to the kitchen door and said, "Jimmy, I brought some good bread and cheese, you may as well get it out," turned, and went back upstairs.

"You like her, counselor?"

"Sure."

"No, I mean, you really like her?"

McFarland mumbled something about Sally being a lot of fun to spend time with.

"Mmmhmm, well she really likes you."

The espresso maker bubbled and hissed. McFarland gathered up cups and sugar, trying to focus his thoughts. He did like Sally, but she was like an exotic bird who appeared mysteriously in his life and left while he was still wondering what he'd seen. She was creative, funny, unpredictable, and full of fun. He was serious, straightlaced, and cautious. He always had been. But then, what was he doing making coffee for Sergeant Williams at two in the morning?

"Jimmy, why do you drink this stuff?"

"Wait, wait, give it a chance, Sarge, let the taste spread through your mouth and then take a second sip. It's bitter, but incredibly rich and pure. The essence of coffee."

They sat quietly sipping, like a pair of monks McFarland thought. Finally, he asked, "How're you holding up? It sounds like it's been rough since Dixon was shot."

"Rough? Yeah. I feel like all my life I been controlling my temper so I don't hurt somebody and I don't give them an excuse to take me down. It's hard. It locks you up, makes you hate yourself. It's making me tired. I didn't shoot the sonofabitch. He was a weak, scared man, and I never liked him. If I was sure he'd killed Ernie, I don't know, I might have killed him, but you convinced me there's too much that doesn't fit. Justice would be sweeter than vengeance."

Once again, as on the night he, Amel, and Sarge met at the bar, McFarland had no idea what to say, or how to acknowledge what he'd just heard.

"I know you didn't shoot Dixon, Sarge. If you had, you would have stood there called Homicide and asked them to arrest you."

Williams smiled and nodded agreement. The two agents had said the same thing. For a long moment, he held McFarland's eyes, then McFarland looked away and asked, "Sarge, do you buy Agent Smith's theory that this is all connected back to the fraud case through Deputy Chief Dixon? It seems like Smith hates the guy and might be seeing everything through his hatred. They've got history."

"You think? Agent Smith seems like he calculates everything. You and I already figured Ernie and Douglas were killed because of what they knew and what they were doing about it. And Dixon—there's what you heard from Commander Abbott. Amel thought that Dixon was trying to get up the courage to tell us the truth about why he was at Ernie's house."

"What did he say?"

"Dixon told Amel, 'If a guy saves your life, no matter what else they do, you owe them, you can't screw around with them.' Amel said he seemed like he was about to cry. That'd be Al Dixon."

"What do you think he was going to say?"

"Christ, I don't know, but the man didn't do stuff on his own. He got drafted 'cause he couldn't figure out what to do next. His dad and his uncle pulled strings to get him into officer school and tried to get him a Pentagon job. He blew that and ended up in 'Nam with us. Like I told you, he was outta his head most of the time. We took care of him, and weirdly, the Cong didn't kill him, and we didn't either. Next thing you know he's in the MPD and somehow, he's fast-tracked to Lieutenant."

McFarland remembered Dixon slouching behind Sarge that first morning, and lurking at the edges of the action the night they were out on the street. He thought about the afternoon they had questioned him.

"If he didn't kill Ernie, and neither one of us thinks he did, then what the hell was he doing there?"

Williams grunted and said, "Damned if I know. He lied to us about wanting to talk things over with Ernie, and he knew I'd know he was lying."

"He must have been scared. More scared of someone than he was of you."

Williams grinned. "And I'm scary."

"Yeah, you are. But do we know if it was his uncle he was scared of?"

Williams smiled again and said, "Besides the fact that his uncle is a mean bent cop and controls the department?"

"Yeah, besides that. We got that covered."

"The Deputy Chief also controls Internal Affairs. Those are his guys. That's a part of how he controls the department. If they're after me for shooting Dixon, it's because he sent them."

"Smith seems to want to send you right into his hands."

"I don't think the Deputy Chief gives a rat's ass about finding the guy who killed his nephew. Maybe it was someone he sent. I think Smith may be right, and they want you out of the picture and the case discredited."

"It seems like a stretch to me, but if it's true we must be getting close to something."

They fell into silence. It was nearing three in the morning. The house was quiet. The street outside was still. McFarland was starting to feel cold. He went and got Sally's cheese and bread, a knife, and a couple of plates, and then climbed the stairs to get a sweater. He passed the little guest room where Sally was sleeping and felt something he would have recognized as an ache of longing if he had let himself. His life had become a strange and confusing battle. Things might move fast and violently. He was apprehensive that he wouldn't know how to handle it and would make a fool of himself. He came back down to find Sarge eating a piece of bread and cheese. He could hear the crunch of the crusty bread. The sound was real and mundane. He felt reassured.

"If we're going to do this, Sarge, how do we keep in touch?"

"We don't. Not unless they send me. They won't trust me, and you're the enemy. Smith and Farwell will be running the show. We gotta trust them."

"Do you?"

"Uh huh, I do."

For a moment, McFarland wondered who was entrapping whom. Could Williams already be working for the Deputy Chief? Or the FBI? He looked with horror at his friend, who laughed, and had obviously read his mind—or his face.

"No, man, I ain't. We cool."

Williams stood up and asked, "Is there a window upstairs where I can get a look at the street?"

McFarland was incredulous. "You think someone might be watching the house?"

Williams shrugged. "You can look out my bedroom window. The door's open."

Williams went quietly upstairs and took a long look from the darkened room. Satisfied, he slipped out, leaving McFarland shaken.

Chapter 19
Hurt Feelings

McFarland was exhausted, but slept poorly, awakened frequently by dreams in which he struggled vainly with problems he could not resolve but knew he should. Half-awake his thoughts churned. By seven, as the gray winter morning filtered in through the curtains, he heard Sally stirring, and gave up the struggle to sleep. He put on a robe and went downstairs. Might as well let Sally have first shot at the one bathroom. He was ready for coffee. He opened the front door to retrieve the *Post* and caught himself looking warily up and down the street, and then felt silly. He had no idea what he was looking for. He sat down, unfolded the paper, scanned the front page, took a quick look at the Metro Section, and pulled out the sports section.

Sally appeared and asked, "Anything about you in there?"

"Not that I can see. That's not unusual."

"What's not?"

"That the *Post* somehow left me out of their coverage."

"You want to take a shower? I'll make some breakfast. You can't have had much sleep."

"Thanks, Sal, I'll be right back down."

He ran up the stairs faster than he'd come down, slipped into the bathroom, and then luxuriated in a very hot shower, letting it wash away the detritus of his fitful night. Why was Sally visiting? Just her being there seemed to lift his mood. What did Williams mean, about her "really" liking him. She was just a warm, free spirit. He thought about the expression on her face when she'd said she'd like to get to know Williams, open and interested. Not guarded or afraid. With a suddenness that made him gasp, he thought, *She's special. I really like her*. His reverie was shattered when Paul pounded on the door.

"McFarland, stop basking in the shower, I need the bathroom."

"Oh, sorry."

He turned off the shower, decided to forget about shaving, and wrapped himself in a towel. As he opened the door Paul groaned.

"Christ, it's like a steam bath in here."

"Don't bother to thank me."

He grabbed a pair of jeans and searched in his bureau for his favorite turtleneck. *Crap,* he thought, *it's in the laundry basket with everything else I own.* He pulled it out, sniffed, and recoiled. I really need to do the wash. He took out a T shirt and the black cashmere turtleneck his mother had given him for Christmas, which he had thought too precious to wear. *What the hell*, he thought, *I'm just going down to breakfast on a Saturday morning.* The smell of something that involved cinnamon and nutmeg drifted up the stairs along with the wonderful aroma of coffee. He pulled on wool socks and old loafers and went back down. The table was set in the little dining room. Where had she found that fruit? Sally smiled and gave a little curtsy.

"Breakfast is served, sir."

She pulled plates of French toast and bacon from the oven and took hot milk and a fresh pot of espresso from the hot plate.

"Would you bring the pitcher of juice from the fridge, Jimmy."

"Wow, Sally, this is amazing. I…" He was going to say he thought she was amazing, but instead said lamely, "I didn't even know we had all this stuff in the house."

"Yeah, I had to do some scrounging. I threw out anything that had major mold." Paul appeared from the hallway and looked at her in horror.

"What the hell, Sis, are you going domestic? What happened to the Rebel Elf?"

Sally swung at him with her dish towel, and he held her off with one long arm, both choking with laughter.

They sat down for breakfast and ate hungrily for a while. Finally, McFarland asked. "What brings you south, Sal?"

"My future employers, the Fairfax Symphony, are performing the Hindemith Viola Concerto with Walter Trampler, who is a certified demigod for us violists. You want to come along?"

"OK, sure…"

"You sound dubious?"

"I'm not sure I like Hindemith."

She scowled. "Of course, you don't, but you will after I instruct you."

"That sounds ominous."

"It is necessary to fill the appalling gap in your education. You'll thank me in the end."

Paul watched, dark eyes twinkling. He thought to himself, *Jimmy, you are doomed.* He was delighted. He got up to clear the plates and pushed his friend back into his seat.

"Finish your coffee, Jimmy. I'll just throw these in the washer."

Sally looked at McFarland earnestly and asked what he and Williams had been up to. He started to give a non-committal answer and then thought, *It's my goddamned case and I can decide what I say to whom.* He told her about Douglas's body found at a Metro construction site and the *Post* story and the miserable morning he'd spent—just a week ago—sure he was finished. He recounted the meeting in the Boss's office when he'd realized he was going to be fired, and then he wasn't. He described Smith and Farwell, and how they'd been utterly different from his expectations.

"At least, these two agents are smart and dedicated—and Smith has a droll low-key sense of humor. Farwell is tough and kinda sassy."

"What did you expect?"

"Law and order robots who treat anyone who isn't pro-war as a dangerous traitor."

"And?"

"Right now, they're my team and, to be honest, they're carrying me."

*****

That evening, Sally having instructed both McFarland and her brother on Stamitz and Hindemith, all three piled into Paul's car and rode through the Saturday traffic to the other side of the Potomac. They'd decided on pre-concert burgers and fries. Sally was more amped up than usual, cracking jokes, teasing her brother, and speaking in silly voices. McFarland, watching with a certain awe, put it down to her excitement at seeing her future colleagues in action, but that wasn't it at all. She was wondering about him. They had had a wonderful day. She trusted her instincts, and her instincts told her he had enjoyed it as much as she had. But he seemed to regard her as a pal. Still Paul's little sister. What did she have to do, leap on him? An image of Jimmy pinned wide-eyed and helpless on the sofa, flashed through her mind. She'd be wearing a Barbarella costume.

Paul, too, thought he knew what was going on. He had watched his friend's diffidence with women sow confusion before. Too bad Jimmy had never had a sister. His sense of women had been shaped by his brilliant and formidable space cadet of a mother. The story was that his father had never actually proposed to his mother, she had just taken him out to look at some particularly beautiful rings she'd found. The night before, as he and Sally had sat drinking wine and waiting for Jimmy to get home, Paul had assured Sally that Jimmy would eventually realize that he adored her, but he worried that some fatal misunderstanding would creep into the silences created by Jimmy's befuddlement. He was tempted to take them by the hand, tell them, "You two were made for each other," and lock them in a room with the Lovin' Spoonful singing 'Did You Ever Have To Make Up Your Mind?' Life would have been simpler if by some sort of comic book voodoo wavy balloons containing their thoughts appeared above their heads. But each of them sat thinking one thing and saying another.

They arrived in the packed foyer of the concert hall and while Sally pushed through the crowd to get the tickets the orchestra's manager had promised to hold for her McFarland felt a hand on his shoulder and turned to find Mariana smiling conspiratorially.

"I have come to see what's happening with Viola Child's future employer. Is she here?"

"Yes, fetching our tickets. Is Joel with you?"

"He's dealing with the car. We need to get that Metro built. It's impossible to get here. I hope you're not going to bring the whole thing to a screeching halt."

"Just the criminal part. Mariana, this is my housemate, Paul Brown."

"Ahh, Viola Child's older brother?"

"Yes, pleased to meet you," said, Paul, thinking, *So this is the Dragon Lady*.

Sally appeared and was visibly startled to see Mariana.

"Mariana? I thought the FSO was too far off the beaten track for you."

"Well, you piqued my interest dear. I thought with Trampler playing you might come."

Joel arrived flushed from walking fast in the cold. He doffed a broad brimmed black fedora with an elaborate sweep of his arm and kissed Sally on the cheek.

"Wonderful to see you, Sally. Jimmy, I am eager to hear the latest on your adventures in crime. Notwithstanding your fears, they don't seem to have fired you. More promoted, as I hear it."

McFarland looked at Joel sheepishly and nodded. "Yes, I was lucky."

A gong sounded. They turned to head for their seats.

Mariana pulled McFarland toward her and whispered, "I need to talk to you." McFarland was puzzled.

"Sure," he answered, "At intermission?"

"No, I have to schmooze. After the second half. I'm sure Sally will take you backstage after the second half. I'll find you there."

Two hours later they found their way backstage through the chaos of musicians packing up and surly stagehands putting away chairs and music stands. The Maestro was in the corner amid a small cluster of fans. The orchestra manager spotted Sally and almost danced over to her.

"Hello Miss Brown. What a fabulous evening. Sold out. A smashing success, don't you think? I'm so glad you could come. Is this your brother? He seems to have taken all the tall genes before you came along." There was a deep chuckle before he went on. "And this must be your friend." He arched an eyebrow and sighed. "Ah, well. Now, dear, you have to let me introduce you to Walter. He's such a marvelous man."

He led her off, and Paul released the rich chortle he had been attempting to suppress. Mariana, who had been in a corner chatting with the conductor, freed herself with a flirtatious smile and found McFarland, who was watching as Sally spoke animatedly to Trampler, to his obvious delight.

"Jimmy, I have a message for you."

"A message?"

"You need to get in touch with my colleague, David Anderson."

Anderson had written the New Year's Day story that disclosed that the U.S. Attorney's Office had declined to prosecute a major fraud. Apparently, he was still working the story.

"No, Mariana. I don't have to get in touch with him, and I won't. I'm not playing that game. He can call the Boss."

"Jimmy, you don't understand…"

"Yeah, I do. Everyone in this city leaks stuff. Everybody plays both sides. I don't."

It pissed him off. She was trying to take advantage of his friendship with Joel to get him talking about the case. She grabbed his arm, gripping hard. "Listen, you self-righteous twerp, David isn't trying to get information *from* you, he wants to *give* you some. The long knives are out, and he might help you protect yourself."

She dropped his arm and stalked away. McFarland noticed she went straight for Trampler, and in thirty seconds the Great Man's attention had shifted from Sally to Mariana.

*****

The following morning the three of them sat lazily pawing through the Sunday paper, occasionally reading a sentence from an opinion piece aloud and agreeing or shrieking with derision.

McFarland, trying to sound casual, said, "Listen, Sally, my dad gave a bunch of money to the Carter campaign, and he got tickets to the Inaugural Ball. Would you like to go—as my date?"

"Oh, wow, yeah—when is it?"

"A week from Thursday, January 20."

Her face fell. "I can't. I…uh…agreed to go to a concert with a guy from school." So, there it was. She might flirt with him, but her interests lay elsewhere.

"Oh, okay."

"I'm really sorry."

"Sure, right."

"Maybe I could…"

The phone rang. McFarland welcomed the excuse to get up and hide his humiliation. It was David Anderson, Mariana's colleague.

"Our mutual friend suggested I call. Maybe we could have coffee?"

McFarland was about to demand to know what this was about when he thought about Smith's warning. No telling who might be listening. Anderson had covered Watergate and had a healthy fear of malicious eavesdroppers. McFarland felt a little silly slipping into this cloak and dagger style of exchange, but at the same time he felt a thrill of excitement and self-importance.

"Yeah, sure, where shall we meet?"

"There's a bookstore near DuPont Circle, Kramer Books. They've opened a cafe."

"I know it. I'll see you there in half an hour."

He found his shoes and a jacket, waved goodbye, and headed out.

Chapter 20
Spin

Riding the early bus down Massachusetts Avenue, slumped in his seat staring unseeingly out the window McFarland struggled with what he'd heard from Anderson the day before. They had sat at a small table in the Kramer Books café called Afterwords. Anderson had been there when McFarland arrived, still feeling bruised by his exchange with Sally. The place was crowded, but he saw a guy in jeans, a ratty tweed jacket, and a ponytail waving to him. He wondered whether he had 'prosecutor' written all over him.

Anderson got up, stuck out his hand, and smiled.

"Ah, just as Mariana described you."

"How's that?"

"Dark hair, dark eyes, handsome, and intense."

"So, not just the guy who looks like a Fed?"

"Oh, that too."

Anderson ordered café au lait in a bowl-like cup with crisp chocolate coated biscotti. McFarland had a double espresso, which arrived, to his delight, with a twist of lemon peel, a cube of sugar, and a plate of tiny macaroons.

Anderson looked around appreciatively. "This place is going to take off. Really good pastries, snobby coffee, serious books we're glad to be seen with, and just off DuPont Circle. It's an amazing idea."

McFarland tried not to be charmed by the big-time investigative reporter talking earnestly to him about a coffee shop. It made him feel like a Washington insider. Federal Prosecutor. *Washington Post* reporter. Sizing each other up. He had to keep his mouth shut. Then he heard a shout from several tables away.

"Jimmy! I figured you were Anderson's source."

He looked up to see the Public Defender, Marilyn Burke, standing and waving, dressed in a long, embroidered wool overcoat with a faux sheepskin lining, a neon blue silk scarf around her neck, her unkempt golden hair streaming out of a creamy white cap. She was smirking.

"Are you and that thuggish sergeant of yours going to indict some people who matter this time?"

He felt his face getting hot. *What a pile of crap*, he thought, *Williams's not my sergeant. He's my friend.* To his relief, Anderson answered.

"Oh, beware, it's Burkle, the sexiest lawyer in Superior Court, on the prowl. Have a care, Jimmy, she's a mantis. She eats her mates for nourishment."

"You survived, Anderson. Why do you always screw around with my name?"

"Just affection. McFarland is not my source for anything. Maybe someday he'll play by Washington Rules, but right now he's a ridiculous close-mouthed good boy."

"Right, and Rosemary Woods really did accidentally erase seventeen minutes of Nixon conspiring to cover up Watergate."

"Yup, she sure did. Now leave us alone so *I* can leak some information to *him*." She was caught off guard and looked sharply at him.

"Shit, you're serious, aren't you?"

"Always."

"Screw you."

"Just give me a call."

Feeling like a child watching his parents argue, McFarland wondered whether he really was an innocent in a land of Visigoths. Maybe it was just performance art? Sally would know. Would she? How? He needed to remember she was just a pal, Paul's little sister.

"You and Burke have history?"

"History? What an idea. We dated. We even earned a little notoriety for some loud disagreements at parties. Not historic though. I'd say she has her eye on you."

The infernal blush betrayed McFarland before he could adopt a show of casual disdain. Farwell claimed she could read him, but the color of his cheeks had been like a poster of what he was thinking since he was a kid. His parents had tried to contain their laughter when their little boy told a solemn fib and instantly turned deep crimson. He'd learned not to lie. It was humiliating. But blushing because he was the target of a notorious vamp was doubly embarrassing. He wanted to control this conversation. Instead he looked totally uncool. Two tables away, under a window, Marilyn Burke and the two women she was with erupted in laughter. McFarland cringed. He wanted to grab the furry overcoat that hung off the back of Burke's chair and throw it over her head to snuff out the hilarity.

Anderson watched his companion with interest, wondering whether he could possibly be as much of a straight arrow as he seemed? Heart-warming, but how in hell would he survive prosecuting the powerful? He lit a cigarette and pitched the match hissing into the dregs of his coffee.

"Listen, Jimmy, did Mariana tell you what I want to talk about?"

"No, nothing, but it's going to be a one-way conversation. Ms. Burke really does have it wrong. I'm not going to be a source."

"Yeah, you can just listen. I've got some information you should know."

"Why?"

Anderson looked puzzled. "Why should you know it?"

"No, why would you tell me? You're press. I'm a prosecutor. We may investigate the same things, but for different purposes."

Anderson laughed. "Are you trying to talk me out of helping you? It's partly that the long knives are out, and it pisses me off. And your investigation turns up stuff that I can feast on. You've already got the evidence to indict a dozen people for fraud, but I believe, and I'm pretty sure you believe, there's more."

"How do you know what evidence we've got?"

"C'mon, Jimmy. You guys executed two warrants. The affidavits are accessible. So are the terrified folks who stood around in those offices watching and wondering whether they're going to jail. That story is written, but so long as you and your FBI friends keep digging, some of the people you're after are going to talk to me to try to shape the story, shift the blame, and protect themselves."

"I get it. You want to feed me some stuff so we use the power of the government to get you your story."

"Jeezus, McFarland, stop being a fucking jerk! Why don't you just shut up and listen, and then you can do whatever the hell you want with what I give you."

Anderson was scowling, looking ready to get up and leave. What, McFarland asked himself, was he doing? He felt petulant, wondering whether he was being played, a credulous innocent, a lamb getting advice from a wolf. But then, so what? He didn't have to believe what he heard, or act on what he believed.

"OK, I'm listening," he said finally.

"You've got a leak in your office. Conway knew you were coming the day before you executed the warrant."

"Yeah, we figured…"

"It's Gareth Olsen."

"Oh, hell. That doesn't seem—how do you know?"

"Have you met his girlfriend, Kelsey Darrin?"

"Yeah, to say hello to at a couple of parties."

"She works for Elliott Taylor…" McFarland looked at Anderson blankly. "He's the VP who runs the Conway office here in D.C. Thinks of himself as a player."

"So, Olsen let something slip and she passed it on?"

"No, he told her about the load of crap you'd brought him and bragged to her about killing it. He told her to take it to Taylor. Later, he heard from someone in the magistrate's office that the notorious Agent Smith was on the prowl again and had gotten a couple of warrants that were going to create a stir and he managed to get a copy."

"How did you get this?"

"Kelsey is not discreet. She couldn't wait to tell her friends about her big-time boyfriend and what he could do."

Anderson watched the anger rise in McFarland's face, and then pugnacity. He shook his head and said, "Jimmy, Olsen is a self-important creep, and I hope you nail the SOB, but I'm not giving you the names of my sources."

McFarland looked sheepish, and then smiled. "You read my mind."

"You law enforcement guys are all alike. You really don't believe in the First Amendment."

"What's that?"

Anderson looked at him sharply and then laughed.

McFarland said, "I appreciate the tip."

"Hold on, I've got more. It looks like Conway is really concerned about this investigation. As I said, Taylor thinks of himself as a player, and Conway has always managed to connect with sixteen hundred Pennsylvania Avenue, no matter who was living there. They are warning the White House and the new AG not to let some out-of-control young DA wreck Carter's opportunity to take credit for completing Metro and opening up the city."

"The Boss isn't going to give in to that."

"No? Ask your friend Vic how the Boss's deputy, Rushford, feels about this case. Watch your back."

McFarland didn't go straight home. He was staggered. Anderson knew more than he did and understood what it meant. He needed to walk and think. When he did get home, Sally was gone and Paul seemed distant, though McFarland had no idea why.

He had slept poorly, dreaming that he was in a dark wood following a trail, or maybe fleeing a pursuer.

That Monday morning on the bus, he was still brooding. Charging another AUSA with malfeasance was a big deal. He had to report what he'd heard, but he had no idea if it was true. Anderson had told a believable story, but that didn't make it something other than hearsay. Just the fact of an investigation would be devastating to Olsen even if nothing was proven in the end. Could he, Smith and Farwell quietly check at least some of the facts before taking it. to the Boss? And what about Vic? If he couldn't trust Vic, he was screwed anyway. If Vic found he'd concealed something like this, McFarland figured, he'd never regain the man's trust. Without Vic, he knew he'd be job hunting now, not running this investigation. Hadn't he leaked information himself? He had told Joel much of the story. But that was before there was a case.

Chapter 21
Traitor?

When Farwell and Smith arrived at McFarland's office that morning in response to an abrupt early summons, they wondered what was up. McFarland asked the agents to wait and walked down the hall, past Olsen's still locked office to the one marked Assistant United States Attorney Vincenzo Donatelli. He knocked and entered, knowing he would find his friend sitting bolt upright at his desk reading the *Times*. What was the use, he said, of having two competing great newspapers unless you read them both?

"Vic, could you join me and Smith and Farwell to talk something through?"

Donatelli was about to ask what was going on and whether it could wait until he'd finished his coffee, but seeing his grim faced protégé, he stood, pulled on his jacket, grabbed a yellow pad, and followed McFarland down the hall.

Mrs. Bynum appeared with donuts and coffee, and McFarland asked her to make sure they weren't interrupted. He got everyone seated, took a deep breath, and started a speech he had been rehearsing in his head most of the night.

"I have received some very troubling allegations about a colleague. I don't know if they are true, and I have been agonizing about what to do. I need you to help me figure it out and perhaps help me gather some information, but I ask that, for now, you agree not to act until we're all in agreement."

McFarland watched them carefully. He was going to do this right. Donatelli sat motionless and deadpan. Smith's face had hardened almost imperceptibly. Farwell just looked worried. "Are we all in agreement?" There was silence. "Hank and Nora, I'm not going to ask you to cover something up. I'm just asking you to wait to take action 'til we've all worked it through."

The corners of Smith's mouth twitched slightly, and he nodded. So far, so good.

"You all know Dave Anderson of the *Post*?" Smith looked at Donatelli, who stared innocently at his donut. "Despite what a lot of people around here think, I had never met him. He asked to meet with me yesterday, even though I told him I wasn't giving him anything. He knew way more than I would have thought possible about our investigation, but that's not the main point." He stopped, took a breath, and continued, "Anderson told me Gareth Olsen is leaking stuff through his girlfriend, Kelsey, to her boss, the guy who runs the Conway office in Washington, Elliott Taylor. That's why they knew we were coming and scrubbed their files."

Smith and Donatelli both reacted. Donatelli slammed his fist on the table so hard his coffee spilled. Smith, uttered a *sotto voce*, "Dirty bastard."

McFarland held his hand up, "I don't know Anderson, and I don't know whether what he told me is true. He could be playing me, or he could be getting played himself by someone looking to discredit this office. But, again, according to Anderson, it wasn't just the warrants. Before that, when Olsen wrote the memo to the Boss telling him there was no case, he bragged about it to Kelsey, gave her a copy of the memo, and told her to tell Taylor there wouldn't be an investigation."

There was a seething silence. Farwell leaned forward with a bird dog expression.

"Vic, when did he send that memo to the Boss?"

"I dunno, sometime just before Christmas."

McFarland nodded, looking grim, knowing what she was thinking. He said, "He sent it December twenty-second."

Farwell looked at McFarland. "Douglas," she said, "was killed just before Christmas, probably late on the twenty-fourth." The air thickened in the room. Farwell articulated what all were thinking. "Olsen gave Kelsey the memo, she gave it to Taylor, and they got rid of Douglas."

Donatelli got to his feet and paced, then turned to them as if arguing to a jury. He mopped his face with a big white handkerchief before tucking it neatly into his pocket. He looked not angry, but as if he were fighting back tears.

"We absolutely have to involve the Boss and the guys across the street at Main Justice. Anything less than that is the beginning of a cover-up."

McFarland gripped the edge of the table. "Vic, we don't know that any of it is true."

"No, Jimmy, we know a lot. We know Olsen is a puffed up, self-important asshole. We know he tried to kill this investigation, at least partly because he is jealous of you. We know someone leaked the information that we were coming with a warrant."

McFarland had thought about this moment a dozen times. He was going to stand his ground. "We should bring the Boss something concrete. Let's do what we can to confirm what Anderson told me. Look, if we go to the Boss, if we just walk down there now, he absolutely has to go to the Acting Attorney General. They'll put a battalion of agents on it because they don't want to be seen as covering up. Every person in the Conway office will be questioned, they'll haul Anderson in front of a grand jury. Since this courthouse is full of people who detest Olsen, it'll all play out publicly. And, if they don't find the evidence, people will think we covered it up anyway. Who knows what the hell will happen to the fraud case. Is it just possible that someone thought all this through and planted the story with Anderson for just this purpose?"

Donatelli started to speak, then decided not to and went back to pacing. Smith licked his lips, drummed his fingers, looked approvingly at McFarland, and pointed at Donatelli.

"He's right, you know, Vic. That is just what will happen, although I think we'll get the evidence. Why don't we try a careful approach? Nora can go to Conway to do some warrant follow-up and chat with the ladies. You can drop in on the Boss and give him a 'know' but not 'know' heads-up. If he raises hell, we'll just hand it over. But give us a few hours."

Donatelli glanced at McFarland, turned to Smith, nodded 'yes', and left the room without a word.

McFarland said nothing about the second part of Anderson's warning.

Chapter 22
Asking for Help

The squat gray building at 300 Indiana Avenue, Northwest, was never intended to be beautiful. One of the last products of the Art Moderne style of construction in New Deal Washington, the Henry J. Daly building was intended to be the southern face of a complex of monumental buildings symbolizing the solidity of the rule of law. The whole project was bitterly opposed by conservatives in Congress. The first few buildings had gone up just before Pearl Harbor shifted all attention to the war. The rest were never built.

The Daly building had not aged gracefully. Grander and more elegant structures had grown around it. No tree or shrub softened its hard lines. Wide stone steps spanned the front of the building looking north over Judiciary Square. Hot in the summer and harsh in the winter, these steps were too big, a barrier rather than a welcome. The building, after trying on a variety of identities had finally become firmly established as Police Headquarters. It was a dreary, daunting, dingy place. No one ascended those steps with joy. Certainly not Sergeant Lawrence Williams. He appeared diminished as he wearily made his way upward, willing himself small and weak, summoning all the ways of compliant deference he had learned in order to survive. It was Monday morning, and he had an appointment to see the Deputy Chief.

The main entrance opened into a wide, high-ceilinged hall. Dirt covered the Depression-era mosaics that spread unremarked on the walls. The hall was populated by extraordinary characters—pimps in floor length fur overcoats and broad brimmed hats, women in minimal outfits that identified them as practitioners of the world's oldest trade, garishly suited bail bondsmen—all milling together, they looked like a collection of exotic sea creatures lurking around the face of a coral reef. Williams knew many of them but today walked by them stone-faced.

The Chief's office was at the top of the stairs, Suite 400. Across the hall and a little to the West was Suite 401, the office of the Deputy Chief, his name emblazoned on the clouded glass panel. Behind that window panel was a different world. Richly appointed. Immaculate. Imposing. Two polished wood desks dominated the reception area, one occupied by a white woman with hair piled high on her head, glossy red lips, and jeweled kittycat eyeglasses. Her desk stood in front of a heavy set of double doors. At the east end of the room, a broad man with short cut blond hair, blank eyes, and a dark suit sat impassively behind a desk with only a pen and pencil set, a lamp, and a blotter on it. He looked like a high-end bouncer attending a funeral. At the other end of the room, were a large, low sofa, an armchair, and a coffee table with copies of the *Washington Star* but not the *Post*.

Williams entered quietly, his uniform spotless, his coat folded over one arm. The man at the desk remained motionless, but his predator eyes fixed on Williams and narrowed when he nervously stood in front of the secretary's desk, a deferential supplicant. The woman at the desk, Mrs. Marsden, carefully reviewed a set of notes on a steno pad, then looked up with annoyance.

"Can I help you?"

"Yes, Ma'am. I'm Sergeant Larry Williams."

"Yes, Sergeant?"

"I have an appointment to see Deputy Chief Dixon at ten."

"It's not ten yet, and the Chief is very busy."

"Yes, Ma'am."

"You'll have to wait."

She looked back to the notes, and Williams edged over to the corner but did not sit. To Mrs. Marsden's obvious disappointment, it was only moments before a beefy man in a beautifully tailored pinstripe suit emerged through the heavy doors, a broad toothy smile stretching across his florid face. He motioned Williams into his office, saying, "Sergeant Williams. It's good to see you. I don't think I've seen you since I pinned those stripes on your shoulder." He closed the door and sat down behind his desk, motioning Williams to the seat in front of him.

"You had a friend who was in your unit with my nephew. I heard he was murdered. Have they made any progress investigating?"

"No sir, not that I know of, but Pete Phillips is a real good man."

"Yes, he is. I'd have promoted him, but he claims he was born to be a detective. Well, Sargent, what can I do for you?"

"I need your help sir."

The Deputy Chief put his hands on the desk in front of him, his eyes narrowed, and the jolly mask fell away revealing a hard, aging face.

"My help, Sergeant?"

"Yes sir."

"Regarding what?"

"The murder of your nephew, sir. I didn't do it. I thought about it when I thought he may have been the one to kill my friend Ernie, but I'm pretty sure he didn't. I didn't kill him, and I don't know who did."

"So, you say you had nothing to do with his death?"

"No sir, nothing at all."

"Why did you suspect him of killing your friend?"

"Because I know he was staking out Ernie's place the night before the shooting."

"How?"

"Huh?"

"How do you know that?"

"A source of mine saw him, and he admitted it when I called him on it."

"What did he tell you?"

"That he was planning to talk to Ernie—about a skit we did in 'Nam that Al didn't want Ernie to run again at a reunion he was planning."

"A skit?"

"Ernie and Al hated each other, and Ernie looked for opportunities to get at him. In this skit, Al had to—well, admit he was chicken."

The Deputy Chief's face softened for a moment, and he sighed. He said, half to himself, "Yeah, he was a weak man." He looked up at the sergeant and said, "He was a wimp at school. We hoped the Service would toughen him up, but I guess you just had to cover for him."

"I kept that man alive for two years in the rice paddies and the jungle. His own guys woulda fragged him, but they knew I'd kill them if they did."

"I believe you, Sergeant. Did you believe Alan when he told you he was there to talk to Ernie?"

"No sir, I didn't."

"What did you figure he was doing?"

"I was hoping he would tell me—eventually."

"And?"

"I think he'd have talked to me if it was about that skit. He knew I thought Ernie had crossed the line."

The Deputy Chief nodded, leaned back in his big chair, and asked, "And what made you believe he didn't kill the man?"

"Well, sir, a couple of things. I don't think he had the balls to walk in, look Ernie in the eye, and shoot him. And there were two shooters. It doesn't make sense that Al would take someone with him. The clincher for me was that Little Ernie said the shooters had very shiny shoes. Your nephew ain't never shined his shoes."

There was a deep chuckle from across the desk.

"No, Sergeant, no he didn't. Not even when we had a special promotion ceremony for him. So, what is it you want help with?"

"The guys in IAD got me picked for this, and they won't let go."

"If you didn't do it, they won't find the evidence."

There was a long silence. Williams just looked at Dixon, careful to keep the anger and defiance he felt out of his eyes. Finally, he drew a deep breath, and answered quietly, "By the time they are finished, sir, I won't have a career, whether they manage to hang it on me or not."

"And you'd like me to ask them to back off?"

"Chief, you are the man they answer to. You run this department, and we all know that you do. Around here people listen when you speak."

There was another silence. Williams sat still, imagining himself in an ambush, controlling his breathing and quieting his thoughts. His face was blank. The Deputy Chief was also waiting. Considering? Calculating? He had his man. He knew how to bend people to his will, and the question was how to use this big naïve sergeant.

"Sergeant Williams, you're a good man. I see why Alan trusted you." *And,* he thought, *why the sonofabitch wanted to square things with you.* "If I were to find a way to help you out, Sergeant, I wouldn't want it to be just charity. I'd need to know that if I needed help, you'd, well, you'd return the favor."

"Yes sir, I understand that. It's not a one-way street. Is there something you need me to do now?"

The Deputy Chief looked at him sharply, and Williams wondered whether he'd pushed too far, too fast. He looked at his big hands clasped in front of him, grateful and submissive. The Deputy Chief, who knew that he was a master of men, saw that Williams's question was simply a sign that he'd already handed over his balls. Williams saw the Deputy Chief's pleasure in his submission, but thought he also saw concern, or perhaps perplexity.

Chapter 23
The Ladies' Evidence

Agent Farwell had shown up in the Conway offices offering friendly smiles and appreciative chuckles. She was there, she said, to verify which files had come from which cabinets and to take pictures of where they were located. The women sitting in the back office where the files were located tried to watch her surreptitiously. She grinned sheepishly and raised her eyebrows.

"Yup," she said, "female agents are still pretty unusual." Someone asked what it was like for a woman working at the FBI? She laughed. "There's never a crowd in the ladies' room."

Then, turning serious, she said she'd always wanted to work in law enforcement, and she appreciated the people she worked with. One of the women lowered her voice and said, "There's a girl who works here who's dating a prosecutor. He's some sort of big cheese over there. He was working on the same case you are."

This, Farwell thought, isn't even going to be hard. She drew her eyebrows together quizzically and said, "Huh, that's an amazing coincidence. Who is he?" The women looked at each and shrugged.

"Gareth Olsen," said the young woman. Farwell remained silent. "He was," the young woman added, "going to get rid of the case, but I guess some young creep went behind his back and showed their boss stuff Gareth hadn't had a chance to investigate."

Farwell perched on the edge of the woman's desk. She nodded sympathetically: "And now, here we all are. But it's nothing for you girls to worry about so long as you don't get involved." She paused. "But let me give you some advice. Don't let the guys put you in the position of covering for them. Then you get in trouble for things you didn't do." She looked at them sternly and left it at that, knowing they'd be talking about what she meant, and perhaps about what she knew.

Farwell returned to the FBI office feeling almost as if she had acted immorally. The young women seemed eager to trust her, and she'd used that trust to get the information she wanted. She and Smith would, she knew, have the chance to interview them under less sociable conditions, and they would confirm that the files had been purged in anticipation of the execution of the search warrant. But even before that, they'd likely have a frightening session with an independent team investigating Olsen.

Farwell and Smith talked about what she'd found, and she called McFarland to say they'd confirmed Anderson's story.

"Okay, it's time. I'm going to the Boss, and I imagine he'll go nuts."

He didn't. Donatelli's unofficial conversation had given the Boss time to think it through, and when McFarland went to his office, Mrs. Thomas told him to wait, knocked, went in, spoke briefly, and McFarland heard him say, "Gentlemen, you'll have to go. I've got a crisis to deal with."

Three men in dark suits, white shirts, and conservative ties came out looking disgruntled and stared at McFarland with annoyance and curiosity. Mrs. Thomas waved him in. The Boss was direct.

"Mr. McFarland, you keep bringing me problems, but this one is a bitch."

"Yes sir. I wish I weren't here to tell you this, but we've gotten corroboration of what Dave Anderson told me."

"I'm not surprised. Anderson is a straight shooter. He's been spun by the best. Tell me what you've got—from the beginning."

McFarland went through the story carefully, watching the figure before him take in what he said. One of his employees, an officer of the law, was providing information to a possible defendant. It was a violation of the law and the cherished values of the office. McFarland waited for questions. There were none. "Boss, I don't know why Anderson came to me with this. I don't know him, and I swear I haven't given him anything. The wife of the guy who brought me the unemployment compensation cases is a colleague of his."

The Boss looked at him in silence for a long time.

"He came to you because he thinks you're upright and idealistic, and what Olsen is doing pisses him off as much as it does you and me—well maybe not me."

McFarland wanted to say "upright?" but instead asked, "What happens to the fraud investigation—and the murders—while they go after Olsen?"

"They? There is no 'they.' You, me, Olsen, Smith, we all work for the Attorney General in service of the people of the United States. Justice might handle it through the Office of Professional Responsibility, or they might assign it to another U.S. Attorney's office, or—well, we'll see how it plays out."

"In either case, they'll have another set of agents gathering evidence, right?" McFarland said, "They'll want control of all the Conway witnesses, and maybe the Douglas evidence."

There was another silence. The Boss swiveled his chair to look out the window behind his desk, then rotated slowly back, his fingertips touching in a steeple before his face. He began to speak, not to McFarland, but as if thinking aloud.

"Olsen is a weak man, puffed up and full of grievances. He didn't think this out. Now he's screwed. He may already have heard about Farwell's visit, but when the FBI shows up at his apartment tonight, and they are going to move quickly before he has time to organize a story with his girlfriend, he's going to weasel, and then he's going to crack. At that point, he might be useful to us—to you. Taylor will be getting very uneasy, and the DOJ team might be willing to leave Olsen in place for a few weeks to feed whatever we want to Taylor."

McFarland tried and failed to suppress a grin. The Boss saw it and chuckled.

"Yes, delicious, isn't it? Olsen gets to work on the case he sneered at. He can be the worm on the hook of the angler he hates. Sometimes fate does seem to have an ironic sense of humor. Now, Mr. McFarland, I have an appointment to see the Acting Attorney General to explain what the hell you've been doing."

"What do I say to Vic and Hank and Nora, sir?"

"Tell 'em the whole thing. Tell 'em I said, 'well done', and then get back to your investigation as if nothing has changed. And once you've told them, don't talk about it. We'll see what the AG says."

Chapter 24
Atonement

Assistant United States Attorney Gareth Olsen had a one-bedroom condominium apartment on the sixth floor of an elegant old building on Connecticut Avenue just north of the National Zoo. The apartment looked over Rock Creek Park and had a small balcony with space for a couple of chairs and a little table. Soon the Metro Red Line would open to Bethesda and his trip to work would become swift and easy. Five stops to Judiciary Square. The Woodley Park neighborhood would take off and the value of his little apartment would sky-rocket. He was set.

On this Monday evening, however, he was uneasy. Kelsey had called to let him know that one of the FBI agents had returned to the Conway office.

"It was that lady agent, the nice one."

"What did she want?"

"She was just following up on the warrant, taking some pictures and stuff."

"Yeah?"

"She asked the girls some questions about you. They didn't say anything."

"They don't know anything, right?"

"Well, they know we're dating."

"What did the agent say?"

"Not much, I guess, just that the girls needed to be careful not to get involved covering for anybody."

"Did you tell Taylor?"

"No, not yet. I wanted to talk to you first."

"That's smart, Kelsey. Let me think about it."

And he was thinking about it. He had thought about nothing else for the past couple of hours, trying to work out what the FBI and that vindictive prick McFarland were after. He was having trouble considering all the options.

Surely, they were after Taylor. Would Taylor try to use what he knew about Olsen as a bargaining chip? It had been a mistake to give Taylor the memo. Not that he'd done anything that bad. He'd just let a top business leader know where things stood in an investigation that affected his business. He had thought the case was over. It should have been. He wouldn't be surprised if McFarland had invented evidence to keep the case going. That's what he would say if he was asked. Sure, he had spoken to Kelsey about a case that was not going forward, and he would just hint at the possibility that he had reason to believe McFarland made stuff up. He hadn't wanted to rat on a fellow AUSA, he'd explain, but when McFarland had called him after Christmas, he had spun all kinds of fantastic stories.

When the agents knocked on his door at 9:00 that evening, he felt his legs fill with lead. We are, he told himself, on the same side. He welcomed them in and offered coffee. They shook their heads, and when he said he would go get himself some they told him politely, "We'd prefer that you stay here, sir." When they began to question him, it was clear what they were after. Not Taylor. They were focused on him. He told them, oh yes, he had spoken to his girlfriend about recommending that the U.S. Attorney not pursue the case, and he stood by that recommendation.

"Perhaps," he admitted, "I shouldn't have spoken to her about the case, but I thought it was over."

"Did you know she had passed that information to her boss, Elliott Taylor?"

"Yes, I did. I wish she hadn't, but again the case was over."

"Did you know she had passed your confidential memo on the case to Taylor?"

Olsen tried to keep the mask of his face independent of the terror he felt. He needed to answer calmly. He hadn't done anything wrong.

"No, I didn't know that."

"Did you give her the memo?"

Oh shit, he thought, *they have the memo and it'll have my prints on it.*

"I showed it to her. She's my fiancé. I was proud of it."

"Did you give her the memo?"

"Well, I guess so."

"You guess so? What's that mean?"

"I gave it to her to show her my work, but I didn't intend her to pass it on. It was a memo about a non-case."

"And when you passed on the copy of the search warrant for the Conway office, was that a non-case?"

That was it. They had everything. He hadn't even covered his tracks. He wondered whether Kelsey, and maybe Taylor, had already given him up and told the FBI everything. Kelsey had sounded squirrelly when she called. He thought, *My God, I'm going to jail.* Could he bargain? He was trying to figure out how to raise that possibility with the agents when he realized one of them was speaking to him and holding out a paper. A search warrant for his apartment.

He sat in the living room in silent misery while the agents searched the condo. They took all his files, including a copy of the Conway office warrant that he had kept with the warm note of thanks he had gotten from Taylor. And when the agents finished searching, they took him. He asked whether he was under arrest, and they answered grimly, "Not yet."

Olsen slouched despondently in the back of the big black car. He was surprised when they drove down Pennsylvania Avenue past the FBI Building and turned right down a side street and into the basement of the Department of Justice. Not the FBI office? The two agents led him to the Attorney General's elevator and from there to the Attorney General's conference room. Olsen was having difficulty walking. He couldn't think. He was sick with fear. Why here? He managed to swallow a sob, turning it into a sort of groan. He was abjectly terrified. They weren't going to buy the idea that he'd made a stupid mistake. They were treating it, he finally understood, as a big fucking deal.

And that was exactly what the Boss intended. He had planned this with care. He did not want Olsen seen in the hands of the FBI, and he wanted him terrified. Of all the venality he had confronted in a career as a government lawyer, the betrayal of trust angered him most. This man, an officer of the law entrusted with the power of the United States had abused that trust out of vanity. The Boss knew that he, himself, had helped create this situation by passing the evidence McFarland brought him to Olsen to review. He had wanted to teach McFarland a lesson, but he'd learned one instead. His gut had told him Olsen was a problem. He should have gone with his gut, but he had decided to exercise his power instead. He'd blundered, and that made him all the angrier. His anger, at that moment, was not fire, it was ice.

The room was grand. It was where the chief legal officer of the United States wielded the power of place. Like the conference rooms of the Secretary of State and the Secretary of Treasury, it was heavy with history. Portraits of Edmund Randolph and Harlan Stone looked down sternly from the wood paneled walls, seeming to watch Olsen from the shadows as he entered between the two agents. The big room was lit only by two brass lamps with green glass shades that stood on the long conference table. He saw the Boss and McFarland sitting on the far side of the wide conference table. Behind them, seated in the dim light against the wall, were two men and a woman he did not recognize. No one greeted him. The two agents who had brought their quarry in showed him a chair at the conference table across from the Boss and McFarland and then took seats with the others along the wall.

The Boss looked like some sort of atavistic monster, pale and cold. Whatever plans or artifice Olsen might have considered simply drained from his mind. He just wanted this over. He suddenly realized that he was in his usual blue pinstripe suit but had taken off his tie when he got home and had not retrieved it when the agents took him. Not dressed. He wanted to explain that he didn't mean to be disrespectful. He was still an Assistant United States Attorney.

The Boss began to speak.

"Mr. Olsen, you are not under arrest, but you are the target of a criminal investigation. You do not have to answer any questions, and anything you say may be used against you. You have the right to an attorney. Are you fully aware of your rights?"

For the first time, Olsen noticed there was a court stenographer in the corner.

"Yes sir, I know my rights."

"And do you freely consent to talk with us?"

"Yes."

McFarland watched Olsen waiving his rights. He looked barely sentient—the python's prey. He was doomed.

"Mr. Olsen, you have violated your oath of office. You have admitted to an appalling betrayal of trust. As an officer of the law, you have a higher obligation to integrity and you have manifestly failed to live up to that obligation. Do you understand that?"

"Yes."

"It appears that your betrayal may have led directly to the murder of a man who was a witness in a case I trusted you to review. Did you ever speak with Mr. Douglas?"

"I—I had Mr. McFarland's account of what he said."

"You rejected Mr. Douglas's evidence on the basis of Mr. McFarland's account, but then you disregarded McFarland's judgment of the credibility of the man that he but not you had met?"

"I didn't see why I should pay attention to what he thought, he doesn't have any experience."

"And you don't like him." Olsen looked down at his hands on the deeply polished table. The Boss continued, "You passed your memo to Miss Darrin to pass to Mr. Taylor?"

"Yes, I thought the case was over and he should be informed."

"That wasn't your decision, Mr. Olsen. Did you know that shortly after you passed your memo to Mr. Taylor, Mr. Douglas was murdered?"

"No, well yes, I know he was murdered. That was terrible."

"Do you understand that your action of leaking the memo may have led to his death?"

Olsen was silent. He should be figuring out how to defend himself, how to convince them a man like Taylor would never be involved in a murder, but his mind wouldn't work. He was desperate to know why he was in this awful cavernous space overhung by shadowed portraits of grim-faced men, and what they wanted from him. The Boss was leaning over the table. His face, lit by the lamp, was partly in shadow.

"Mr. Olsen, you will lose your job and your license to practice law. You will go to jail. You cannot avoid that. You may be able to atone somewhat for what you have done, and that may be considered in your sentencing. You will have to help us. Are you interested?"

Olsen was interested. He would have agreed to anything. 'Helping' would put him back on the right side.

Chapter 25
Shakedown

The Chief of the Washington Metropolitan Police Department had a driver who also served as his bodyguard and general factotum. In his office, he had a secretary and a special assistant. The Deputy Chief, however, had long ago realized that to build *his* power he should surround himself with the trappings of power. He had built up a formidable force of his own that had come to be known as the Palace Guard or just the Guard. The members of the Guard called their boss 'Chief', or 'the DC'. The Guard was a group in which that passed for an inside joke, a clever play on words. He was the DC both for Deputy Chief, and because they and he thought of themselves as protecting DC, the city, against crime, violence, and soft-headed liberal policies.

The leader of the Guard was Lt. Thompson 'Tommy' Rankin, a chunky man with dyed black hair, a droopy face, and hooded, staring eyes. Universally disliked and distrusted before he came to the DC's attention, now he was feared. The six men he commanded were big and hard and not especially articulate. Rankin was slow, ruthless, and mean to the point of sadism. He understood that the real mission of the DC's office was to keep the MPD out of the hands of the Black city government and its liberal allies. He was comfortable with the idea that every corrupt source of income to the department should be tithed to the men upholding the values of the department.

The newest recruit to the Guard was Detective Caleb Ransome, the man whom Agent Farwell had recognized as an instructor from when she was at FBI School in Quantico. Farwell had remembered him because he was humorless, dull, and quick to take offense, almost coming to blows with another instructor who had corrected him when he insisted the Hoover Dam was named after J. Edgar Hoover. Rankin liked this new recruit. He was easily manipulated and seemed to have few values other than obedience and loyalty. And he was a proficient killer.

The DC had personally designed and paid for special uniforms for the Guard, with a stripe of gold braid around the cuffs and collar and a unique golden eagle insignia that appeared over their heart, just below the American Flag. They were an elite unit. Each of them understood that the country, and particularly the city of Washington and its police force, were under threat from Black Power agitators and white liberals who had taken control of the Democratic Party, the courts, and the news media. The DC was holding the line, and they were his troops.

Rankin had grown uneasy, however. He saw the DC bending to pressure from the new Chief and the city council to promote Blacks and women. When Rankin demanded that he be promoted, the DC temporized. Not yet, he'd said. Rankin began looking for leverage to use against his boss. The DC thought he could use Sergeant Williams. Rankin had his own plans.

*****

When Williams's doorbell rang that night, he found Rankin and Ransome standing in the hall in uniform. Now he would get the real answer to his plea for help from the Deputy Chief. He wondered for a moment whether they had found out he was working for the FBI and had come to kill him. But that was unlikely. He had no doubt they would kill him if they knew he was working undercover, but they wouldn't show up in uniform at his apartment, two very noticeable white cops in Anacostia, to do it. They could shoot him in the back some night on the street or execute him as he thought they must have executed Alan Dixon. The answer to his plea must be 'yes', the deal was on, and he was about to learn the conditions.

He shrank himself. His shoulders drooped, his head hung, his face softened. He mumbled a welcome. They entered, unsmiling and unfriendly, peering around the small apartment as if it were a crime scene. He could feel they were tense—on guard. They were afraid. Not of him he guessed, but deeply uneasy to be in this place. He gestured to the two armchairs and offered to brew coffee or pour beers. Rankin shook his head, and Ransome didn't even respond. Williams pulled over a straight-backed chair and sat uncomfortably, looking from one to the other. Rankin finally spoke.

“Sergeant, you’re in a fix. Internal Affairs has you for killing a fellow officer. You say you didn’t, but the facts don’t look too good.”

“No sir. I never shot that man, but I know it don’t look good.”

“You asked the Deputy Chief for help. That’s a big favor you’re asking.”

“Yes sir, I know it is. He’s the only one can help me.”

“Uh huh. That is true. The Deputy Chief is a generous man. He knows that you’ve been a good officer, a tough officer. He wants to help. But we have to make sure people don’t take advantage of his generosity.”

Williams lowered his head and looked down at his hands. Rankin watched him and began again.

“We need to know you’re going to be helpful to him.”

“Yes sir.”

“He has a problem he wants you to help him solve. That pissant prosecutor you’re pals with is getting to be a real pain in the ass. The Chief wants to teach him a lesson.”

“I haven’t seen much of McFarland since he got all wound up in that fraud case.”

“But he’s your bro’. You can go see him and ask for help.”

“I can go see him, but I don’t know if he’ll mess with a murder investigation…?”

“Crap. He’s already messing with the investigation into the murder of that friend of yours up east of the park. You both been messing with that, Sergeant.”

“Well, yes sir, that’s a fact.”

“He doesn’t think you killed your partner, does he?”

“I don’t believe so, Lieutenant. No, I don’t think he does.”

“So, you can ask for his help, just like you’re asking the DC.”

“The who?”

“The Deputy Chief.”

Williams furrowed his brow and ran his fingers over his hair. “Can’t the Deputy Chief help me?”

“Mm-hmm. He can, but he’d like you to have your friend help too. That DA can go to the IA guys and ask why they’re looking at you. And he can go to the Deputy Chief and explain why a good man like you can’t have shot his partner.”

A slow light of understanding spread on Williams's face, as if the rules of a complicated game were finally being explained so he could understand. He nodded.

"Yeah, I see, Jimmy needs to learn how the world works."

"Something like that, yeah."

Rankin leaned back, yawned elaborately, and put his feet up on the coffee table in front of his chair.

"Now, how about that drink? You got something better than beer?"

Williams smiled gratefully and went to get the bottle of Wild Turkey he'd bought in case he had such a visit. Rankin looked at Ransome, chuckled, made a circle with the thumb and forefinger of his left hand, and jammed his right middle finger into the hole. They had their man. The DC had it figured. When Williams returned with the whiskey and poured, Rankin thought, *It's not just Williams who's fucked. I can screw with the DC and this DA too.*

"To your health, Sergeant."

"And back at you, sir."

"If you want to stay healthy, you need to deliver McFarland and then keep your fucking mouth shut."

Rankin finished his drink, put the glass on the floor beside the chair, stood up, took the bottle and walked out with Ransome behind him laughing.

Williams called the number Agent Smith had given him to use if he needed to talk. He left a message for his cousin Adele, as agreed. Twenty minutes later she returned the call and asked if he was too tired to come out for a drink, and he said that'd be fine. She named a bar, but he knew he had to find his way to Smith's office. He drove downtown, winding slowly along the back streets of Anacostia and then onto MLK Avenue. No one was following him. It was after one o'clock when he slipped in out of the cold. The guard just pointed at two men standing to one side. They stepped forward, showed him their IDs, and introduced themselves as Agents Gorham and Danforth.

"Hank asked us to bring you down to DOJ where we're meeting."

They didn't say and he didn't ask how they were involved. They took him in the same car they'd earlier used to transport Olsen into the same underground garage and up the same elevator.

The big room was better lit now than it had been earlier that evening. Williams was taken aback, startled to find not just Smith and Farwell, but McFarland and a weary-looking man he thought must be McFarland's boss.

He wasn't sure why he was in this big, formal space surrounded by people who, unlike him, seemed to know what was going on. The Boss looked up with an amused smile.

"Come in Sergeant Williams, this isn't an ambush." He looked over at the two agents who'd brought Williams in. "We did stage an ambush earlier this evening, but that part of our business is successfully concluded. These two gentlemen executed it with perfection. Agent Gorham, Agent Danforth, thank you for getting the notorious Sergeant Williams here safely. Sergeant, we are eager to hear about your evening, and hope it was as productive as ours."

Williams continued to stand by the door wondering what the hell was going on. McFarland looked at his friend and wondered what he felt about being brought unexpectedly into this intimidating room, the only 'outsider' and the only Black man. He didn't know what to say, so he stood and pulled out a chair for Williams.

"Sarge, come sit with me, we've been waiting for you." He looked at the Boss and asked, "Shall I fill him in?" The Boss nodded.

"Sarge, Gareth Olsen has admitted to passing his memo and the search warrant to Conway."

"Son of a bitch."

McFarland grinned. "Yes, he is that, and seemingly not very clever. Gorham and Danforth brought him here tonight and the Boss pretty much broke him."

The Boss interrupted to pick up the narrative.

"Olsen is a petty, jealous, insecure man, and now he is one screwed son of a bitch. He will be working for us… Well, he was supposed to be doing that before. Now, he's going to help us feed them some bad information."

Williams turned away from the Boss's intense stare and looked curiously at McFarland, who said, "It happened fast. I got a tip on Sunday, we corroborated it, and the Boss got the go ahead to handle it this way in the afternoon."

Williams shook his head. "There's a lot going on around this case. Seems like things are starting to boil."

"Sarge, tell us what happened tonight?"

"I had an unannounced visit from Lieutenant Rankin and Detective Ransome of the Deputy Chief's Palace Guard. They wanted me to know that you don't get something for nothing in the Deputy Chief's office, and the price of me not getting framed for Dixon's murder is bringing you to them—to plead for me." He went on to recount the whole visit.

When he finished, the Boss, who had been listening without expression shook his head and said, "Gutsy performance, Sergeant." Then he turned to Smith and asked, "Do you think we have enough to get authorization to tap their phones?"

"Rankin's and Ransome's? Sure. But not Taylor's, not yet." Smith turned to the other two agents and asked, "Did you get into Olsen's apartment while we had him?" They nodded. They would keep track of him.

The meeting did not break up until nearly 3:00 a.m. They had planned what they would ask Olsen to feed Taylor. He would say that yes, he'd been questioned, but only about the warrant, and he had handled it, convincing the FBI that he had nothing to do with the leak. He would suggest to Taylor that the agents were still searching for Douglas's papers and that they were struggling to connect the three murders. He would try to draw Taylor into talking about his concerns. The Boss reluctantly agreed that McFarland, too would visit the Deputy Chief to ask for help for Williams in order to see what the 'price' would be for that help.

The Boss rolled his eyes and observed, "Now I have two assistant U.S. attorneys who are bait in stings. I don't like it. They're attorneys, not investigators. McFarland, it seems like rules bend and boundaries crumble wherever you go."

Everyone was tired. But Williams cleared his throat and said he had one more thing. He pulled out a pink message slip that Claire had found in the pocket of one of Ernie's suits. A message from Douglas to Ernie. "New evidence," it said, "Cover up," and "Safety warning." Ernie had written "12/10/76—10:00 am," but by the morning of December 10, he was dead.

He handed it to the Boss. "It seems like Ernie must have been killed because he was poking around into a mess of corruption." He grinned sadly. "That was Ernie, he couldn't leave it alone."

Smith got up and looked over the Boss' shoulder and said, "Well, shit, that confirms there's more to this than padded payrolls."

Williams offered to drive McFarland home. It had been agreed they could be seen together now, and Williams wanted to talk. They walked from the DOJ through streets bathed in the lurid blue-green glare of mercury vapor streetlights. The neon sign outside Flo and Andy's was flickering and buzzing erratically. This was a downtown that went to sleep at night.

"Sarge, I've gotten you in pretty deep."

"Other way around, man"

"How do you figure that?"

"I was getting crazy trying to figure out what had happened to Ernie. You pulled me back, Jimmy. Now we're pulling on that string and it's attached to all kinds of shit."

"That message Claire found gives us a new way to think of this case."

"Claire wants you and me to come have dinner with them."

"That would be really nice."

"I'm thinking not. Those guys that work for the Deputy Chief are mean SOBs and not too bright. I don't want to draw their attention to Claire and Little Ernie. Pretty soon we're going to make them mad and they're going to be looking for people to hurt."

Chapter 26
Crab Whisperer

Dr. George Griswold was a notorious curmudgeon. He looked as if the chemicals he worked with had had eaten him away leaving him shriveled and stooped. He had bushy eyebrows over small dark eyes and a hooked nose. Almost everyone he encountered was either dead or an FBI agent, so there wasn't much to cheer him in his day-to-day routine in the FBI Crime Lab—and the crime lab was his life. If he'd ever had a sense of humor, it had died of loneliness, its corpse pickled in formaldehyde on a dusty shelf.

Griswold had left a message for Agent Smith on Saturday afternoon, saying that he had completed his review of the Douglas evidence. He was irked that it had taken the agent three days to respond. Dr. Griswold was in his lab six days a week, pausing only on Sunday to go to Mass, do the crossword, and visit his mother. He saw no reason why Agent Smith should take time off when there was work to do. Now Smith and Farwell waited respectfully in the gleaming reception area as Dr. Griswold scuttled through the heavy metal door. Smith knew the routine.

He stuck out his hand and said, "Good morning, Doctor," getting a growl in response. "I don't believe you've met Agent Farwell, my new partner."

Farwell, who had been warned about the doctor's prickly character—the agents referred to him as "Grizzley Griz" behind his back—looked at him directly, held his gaze while she shook his hand and told him she was honored to meet him. She meant it. Griswold turned abruptly and led them into the lab.

"The DC Medical Examiner concluded that this man was killed by a single blow to the head with that steel reinforcing bar and then thrown into the excavation where he was found. Here is the bar." He held out the three-foot length of rough and rusted steel in its exhibit bag. "The ME could be correct; the body was significantly decomposed when it reached the ME. But from what

I can see, and from the ME's documentation, I'd say it was more likely that he was unconscious, but not dead, when he was thrown in, and that he died of exposure. Before he was killed, however, I am quite certain the subject was beaten. His legs and torso show signs of heavy blows from a hard object."

Farwell cocked her head to one side and asked, "With the state of the corpse, how can you tell the injuries weren't just a result of the fall?"

"Yes, yes, Agent, a good question. How, indeed? The ME concluded exactly that. But he was rushing and making assumptions. The man landed on his back. His legs and chest were beaten on his front—two ribs broken, a knee shattered, and I'm pretty sure he was held from behind."

"Could he have been beaten with that piece of rebar?"

As he listened, Smith was trying his best to keep a straight face. You weren't allowed to interrupt the doctor, let alone question how he might have reached his conclusions, but Farwell was getting away with it.

"No, Agent Farwell, he could not. Look at the subject's clothes. The bar is rough and dirty, but there are no marks on his clothes. More consistent with a truncheon I would say. And something else..."

"Fingerprints?"

"Yes, exactly, fingerprints. The subject was wearing a leather overcoat. I had hoped there would be usable prints on the arms, but whoever did this must have been wearing gloves. We did, however, find usable prints on the lapel, and a very clear thumb print on the subject's belt." This time Farwell knew better than to interrupt. The doctor clearly had more to say and was enjoying the moment in his own way. "The thumb print, as I say, was a clear impression, and we found a match for it in the data base." He paused. "An employee of the Metropolitan Police. Silas Blackstone, Sergeant Silas Blackstone, formerly Sergeant Silas Blackstone of the United States Army."

Smith punched the air, nodded, and whispered, "Yes!" He turned to Griswold with a grin. "Doctor, thank you, that's brilliant. You don't think Sgt. Blackstone could have been one of the crime scene officers?"

"You'll have to check that Agent Smith, but I doubt it. They know to wear gloves."

"And the other two cases, anything there?"

"No. I have confirmed the ME's findings. You've had your quotient of joy for today."

Farwell smiled and said, “Doctor, may I ask a hypothetical question?” Griswold looked as if he might snap at her, but then smiled indulgently and nodded. “Lieutenant Dixon was shot at close range, less than three feet I believe the ME said.”

“Yes, that’s right.”

“It was a cold night. Let’s say the shooter was wearing a coat and gloves and did his best to clean them afterward. Would you still be able to find blood and powder residues on them?”

“Unless they were washed repeatedly with bleach, I think so, yes.”

“Has the MPD submitted any material for testing in that case?”

“No. They processed the victim’s clothes and the car. No surprises there.”

They thanked the doctor profusely and left. Once they were out of the building Smith turned to his partner laughing. “Damn, Nora, you are some sort of crab whisperer.”

“What?”

“I’ve never seen an agent get away with interrupting Dr. Griswold, let alone questioning him. You had him charmed.”

“Yeah, well, I was just respectful. I like him. He gave us a goldmine.”

“It sounds like there were two killers in the Douglas case as well as the Hills case. And they were trying to get information from Douglas before they disposed of him.”

“I wonder,” Farwell asked, “where Sergeant Blackstone works? For the Deputy Chief?”

“Uh huh.”

“And Internal Affairs never swabbed Sarge’s hands, and they never got his clothes for testing.”

“Inept, or they didn’t want to take the risk of a negative result. We could try the clothes even now.”

They discovered that they were wrong about Sergeant Blackstone. Checking with the MPD, they learned he had never worked for the Deputy Chief. The FBI data base was out of date. Sergeant Blackstone had left the MPD six months earlier, under a cloud. He had been accused of stealing and selling seized drugs, although he was never formally charged.

Chapter 27
Lawyers

While Smith and Farwell visited Dr Griswold, McFarland was preparing to seek grand jury subpoenas for testimony from the union and Conway, along with additional documents from Conway. He brooded about the slow progress of the investigation. Three people were dead. At least two of them, apparently, because they were prepared to act against corruption they saw taking place. Now they were preparing to rely on a corrupt AUSA to find out who was involved.

His phone rang. Startled out of his reverie, he was relieved to have a distraction. He picked up the receiver.

"Yes?"

"Mr. McFarland, Attorney John Cartwright would like to speak with you."

"Oh, yes, thank you Mrs. Bynum. Please put him through."

Why would Cartwright be calling? A message from Professor Wandel? No, probably to give him a hard time for picking on working men and women.

"Jimmy?"

"John, how are you?"

"Busy. It's an exciting time just before a new Democratic president takes office."

"Yes, and not a bad time to be a superbly connected Democratic insider. Have you been in touch with my favorite law professor recently?"

"Yes, she and I are part of a group developing a criminal justice reform package. Want to join us?"

"You know I can't do that."

"Too bad. Listen, Jimmy, this isn't a social or a political call. I have a client I imagine you may be getting ready to indict."

"Who is that?"

"Dan Adams."

"Ah, the union boss at the heart of the ghost worker scam. First, I plan to subpoena him to testify before a grand jury."

"I'll advise him not to comply. But he knows you have a case against him."

"We do, and it wasn't just that he participated in a ghost worker scam. He was stealing from his co-conspirators."

"He doesn't see it that way."

"Of course, he doesn't, but I wonder how *they'll* see it?"

"He is very concerned about how it might look."

"I'll bet. What does he want and what's he offering?"

"Hypothetically, if he were to give you the whole story, including the names of other union officials getting a cut, would you consider a suspended sentence and witness protection?"

"Names and testimony?"

"Possibly. He knows once it comes out that he was skimming he's probably gonna get killed anyway."

"What about information on what was going on at Conway Corp?"

"I don't think he dealt with them at all. So far as he could tell, they just looked the other way to keep the union happy."

"And the MPD?"

"The MPD? What've they got to do with it?"

"When he showed up at Conway the other morning when the FBI was executing the search warrant, he had a guy with him who got out of there as soon as he realized it was the FBI. We have identified him as a police officer."

"Crap, I have no idea who that was."

"You need to find out."

"Yes."

"You can imagine we were intrigued."

"Yes—I'll get back to you."

"And I'll check in with my boss."

McFarland hung up, leaned back, and thought about how this might play out. Adams had gotten a top-flight, politically connected lawyer, and he was trying to cut a deal before they'd even had a chance to apply any pressure. He must be rattled. If the guy who showed up with Adams when Farwell was executing the warrant was really Caleb Ransome, then Adams had a lot more to give them than a few other union officials. And if it was true that he hadn't dealt with Conway, what the hell was Taylor up to?

The phone rang again, an annoyance this time.

"Yes, Mrs. Bynum?"

"It is attorney Jason Levy calling for you, Mr. McFarland."

"I don't think I know him, do you, Mrs. Bynum?"

"I believe he is a partner with one of the big firms, Arnold and Porter."

"Do you know whom he's representing?"

"He didn't say."

"Okay, thanks, put him through, please."

Perhaps, he thought, he should have asked Mrs. Bynum to take a message. A power move.

It turned out that Levy was representing Conway. Both the targets were sending lawyers to sniff around. Conway, Levy said, would cooperate fully, but hoped to avoid further disruption from searches or the FBI coming to the offices to question employees without advance notice.

"Is your client prepared to supply a witness who will tell us what the company knew about the ghost workers and stolen materials?"

"You have to understand, this is a multi-billion-dollar project moving ahead under enormous time pressure. There will always be some messiness."

"Just routine?"

"I'm afraid so."

"Your client accepts the theft of millions of dollars of taxpayer money as routine?"

"Oh, come on, Mr. McFarland."

"What action did your client take to investigate or stop the stealing? Did they audit the payroll or beef up security at the job sites?"

"They can't act on something they don't know about."

"But if they had known, they would have acted—or should have acted?"

"They would certainly act appropriately given all the circumstances. Listen, I called to make an offer of cooperation. If you will let us know what questions you have, and what information you need, we will endeavor to provide it."

"Fair enough. We believe that information was removed from the files before we executed our search warrant. We'd like to know what, and why, and who. Let's start there."

There was a long moment of silence.

"That's a very serious allegation. What evidence do you have?"

"I can arrange for you to be briefed by Agent Rohrig. He's an FBI forensic accountant. We'd also like to know who spoke with an engineer employed by the company, a Mr. Aubrey Douglas, who tried to report the fraud he saw going on."

Another pause.

"I understand Mr. Douglas died."

"He was murdered."

"How do you know he spoke to anyone in the company?"

"Because, Mr. Levy, he came to present his evidence to me when the company failed to take action."

"I see. I'll check into that."

"I'll have Agent Rohrig get in touch with you."

McFarland hung up, started to make notes of the two calls, but then sat drumming his fingers on the yellow legal pad. After a few minutes, he got up and left his office.

"Mrs. Bynum, I'm going to go bother Mr. Donatelli. Is he there?"

"Oh, yes, I think he's expecting you."

"How is it he always knows what I'm going to do before I do?"

She shrugged, the slightest hint of a smile raising the corners of her mouth, "He's been doing this for a long time."

McFarland found Donatelli standing at an antique lectern he used as a stand-up desk.

"Vic, do you have time to talk? There's a lot going on, and I feel like my head is about to burst."

"You had quite a night last night."

"Yes. I saw a side of the Boss I'd never seen, and then Williams came in and gave us more. It looks like the Deputy Chief is taking the bait."

Donatelli shook his head in a show of disbelief, drummed his fingers on the lectern, and said, "Just a couple of warrants and Hank and his partner poking around and they're all starting to squirm. Adams, the Deputy Chief, and, I would guess, Taylor. I understand why Adams is scared, but we don't know why the Deputy Chief is so concerned. Or Taylor. What was worth three murders?"

"Those are the questions. I was hoping you'd help me to sort it out."

Chapter 28
The Bait

Gareth Olsen sat in his office under the watchful eyes of Agent Gorham. He almost felt as if the terrible events of the previous night had never happened—a nightmare now fading back into his subconscious. He was on the phone with Kelsey Darrin, assuring her that he had no trouble with the FBI. "I work with them all the time," he told her, "I know how to handle them." Kelsey seemed surprised and relieved. She thought they were both in a lot of trouble.

Olsen found that the bleak dread that kept him awake the night before had been replaced by a strange kind of high. He was at the center of the investigation. They would have to trust him. He did not know they had tapped his phone and bugged his apartment. They didn't trust him at all. He was a dirty necessity. Olsen imagined he'd earn forgiveness, even admiration, by coolly playing the role of the corrupt prosecutor who brought dangerous criminals to justice. He also imagined his investigation would expose McFarland's incompetence and puerile vindictiveness.

Agent Gorham told Olsen to call Kelsey with a message for Taylor. Olsen had neither forgotten nor forgiven the fear and evasiveness in Kelsey's voice the evening before when she called to tell him the FBI had been asking the girls in the office about him. She wasn't straight with him. He realized he couldn't trust her. He told her to let Taylor know that everything was cool and that he had information Taylor might find useful. She said she would.

"Gareth, I'm so relieved that everything is ok. I hope you'll be really careful."

"Sure I will, darlin'. Now, how about dinner tonight?"

"Oh," she said, her voice doubtful, "yes, of course."

Olsen smiled to himself. *You*, he thought, *are done*.

Olsen spent the remainder of the day at the FBI offices. The two agents questioned him meticulously and repetitiously. It irked him. He'd admitted what he did and moved on. They went over and over every detail and then demanded a signed statement before moving forward. While the statement was being typed, a technician showed him how to use the recording device he would wear in some encounters and the transmitter he'd use in other settings. James Bond stuff. This he enjoyed. He wanted to ask whether he could have a small sidearm but decided to wait until he had proven his value.

His dinner with Kelsey would be at *Dominique*, an up-scale restaurant on Pennsylvania Avenue a few blocks from the White House. Popular with cabinet members and White House staffers, it was a place with personality. Wild boar and rattlesnake were on the menu. The agents had reconnoitered and found an inconspicuous table in the corner where they would sit and another table for Olsen and his date. Dominique, who presided over his establishment wearing a sash covered with medals he sometimes hinted were for his heroism in the 'Resistance', was excited to facilitate an FBI investigation. There would be a transmitter in the flowers. *So cool,* Olsen thought, as they did a practice run. Kelsey would sit with her back to the agents. Dominique himself will bring a bottle of very nice *Pouilly Fuisse* once they were seated.

The agents left to wait in their car, bored. Ten minutes before Kelsey was due, they quietly took their table. Olsen walked past the White House, intentionally arriving late. He greeted Kelsey graciously and joined her at their table. She exclaimed over the flowers, which to serve their purpose formed a centerpiece larger than those at other tables. Kelsey thought Gareth had taken trouble to make this a really special evening. Perhaps he was going to propose to her? She was flustered. Not ready. He would be angry if she said she needed time to consider his offer.

Their salads arrived—greens with pear and blue cheese. Kelsey orders crab cakes, but Gareth overruled her. They would have entrecote with sauce bearnaise, pommes frites, and epinard a la crème. A new bottle of wine arrived.

"Kelse, did you talk to Taylor?"

"Yes. He seemed relieved."

"He's naïve. The whole thing got blown out of proportion. It wasn't a problem." Kelsey looked frightened. He was enjoying this. He had forgotten his own fear.

"I want you to pass him a message."

"What? I mean, aren't you going to—I don't know—lie low?"

"No. You have to have nerve."

Across the room, in their corner, eating hamburgers and listening on tiny earphones, the agents rolled their eyes.

Olsen leaned over the table and almost hissed, "McFarland is a nasty, manipulative little sneak. I think he's out to get us, me and Taylor, to make himself look good. We need to stop him. We need to talk."

"OK, Gareth, I'll tell him, but…"

"But?"

"I don't know, shouldn't you—we—be careful?"

Olsen thought how weak she was, a timorous rabbit. He felt powerful. Provoked by her fear, he forgot that he was the bait and imagined instead he was the fisherman. He would take her back to his place after dinner and express his power and anger. He told her he would meet Taylor the following evening in the lot behind Saks in Bethesda. He was certain she'd do what he told her.

The entrecote was superb. The velvety bearnaise, rich with butter, shallots, and fresh tarragon, enveloped the tender aged beef. Olsen washed the earthy flavor of the wine around in his mouth. Not everyone could appreciate this as he did. He watched Kelsey cutting tiny pieces off the meat and taking demure forkfuls of spinach. There was so much she didn't know.

The next day she called and told him, "Everything is arranged." Of course, it was. Taylor was caught in his net. He would, Olsen thought, be grateful for the help Olsen offered. Another frightened man.

It was dark at 6:00 pm when they met, a dank Washington winter night. The lot was lit by harsh arc lights installed after several armed robberies frightened off the suburban clientele. Olsen found Taylor's car and got into the passenger seat. The two agents sat in their car on the other side of the lot. Olsen's task was to form a partnership with Taylor against McFarland and the investigation and to find out why Taylor was concerned about the investigation. Why was he even showing up for this obviously clandestine meeting? He worked for a company that had made its way in tougher places than this. Olsen smiled benignly.

"Good to see you, Elliott. Kelsey says you've been driving them pretty hard."

Taylor looked back, unsmiling and said, "We have a subway to build. The General doesn't take excuses."

"Yes, I understand he's a Tartar."

"He knows how to get results. We try to respond."

Taylor's face was lit by the glare of the light overhead. He looked impatient, not frightened. Olsen wondered whether he understood his peril.

"Elliott, I know you're just trying to get the job done, but we have a problem."

"*We* do?"

"I handled the questions from the FBI, no problem, but the guy who's leading the investigation, Jimmy McFarland, is a self-aggrandizing little shit. I think he's looking for scalps to promote himself—ours."

"Why would he be interested in me?"

Olsen looked at Taylor with an expression of exaggerated impatience.

"He knows you scrubbed the files before the FBI executed the warrant, and he's looking for someone to hang Douglas' murder on. You certainly had a motive."

Taylor's eyes remained hooded, his lips compressed. He looked stoned, not frightened. He slowly shook his head. "No, Gareth, I didn't have a motive. If there was corruption, I needed to know about it and stop it. That's what I told Douglas."

"Oh? What did you do to stop it?"

"Is this an official interrogation?"

"Bullshit. I'm trying to help you."

"Why would you do that? You're a prosecutor."

"I already helped you. You didn't ask a lot of questions when I gave you my memo, or when I passed on a copy of the warrant. You said, 'Thank you very much.' We have a common interest in blocking McFarland. We can do that better together than if he can play us off against each other."

Taylor continued to stare dully at Olsen who waited calmly. He knew he had the power in this conversation.

"Why," Taylor asks, "should I trust you? You've betrayed your office, and now you're asking me to conspire against another prosecutor."

"You don't have a choice, Elliott. Neither of us does. If I screw you, with what you know you can destroy me. And I can make your life pretty miserable."

They were at an impasse. Taylor had disclosed nothing. He didn't appear convinced that he needed Olsen's help. Olsen saw he needed to turn the conversation around and make Taylor show his hand. He put his hand on the door handle and said, "If you don't see that we can help each other there's nothing for us to talk about."

He opened the door. Taylor put a hand on his arm.

"Let's keep talking. Give me something. Show me that…"

"Prove my good faith?" The agents sitting in their car listening to this conversation lean forward. They had foreseen this moment and prepared Olsen for it.

"Yeah."

"That's a two-way street. I'll need something back." Taylor nodded. Olsen continued. "They have concluded that the fraud and the murders of Hills and Douglas are connected. They have the papers that Douglas gave Hills, the papers Hills was taking to the Senate Committee."

Olsen saw a flicker of discomfort, the beginnings of fear. Good.

Taylor arranged his expression.

"They're way off base."

"Oh?"

There was a silence. Olsen waited. Taylor knew what was expected, and Olsen would not ask again.

"The corporate guys are squirming. The big-time lawyer they hired went to see McFarland. He told the guy we'd scrubbed the files. The lawyer went screaming back to the guys who hired him and asked if they knew that. They said no, they were shocked. They would have just thrown me overboard then, except that I'd documented that I'd told them first that I had an inside source, there was a warrant, and I was going to take care they didn't discover too much."

"Smart."

This was pay dirt. Leverage. Olsen gave what he hoped was a cunning smile. He told Taylor he'd gather more information and they'd figure out how to feed information to the FBI that sent them in the wrong direction. They could discredit the investigation or at least assure that it focused on the wrong people. Taylor still looked blank. He didn't trust Olsen, and he didn't see how they'd throw the FBI off the trail. He had a vague sense that something was off. Olsen seemed too confident for a man in as much danger as he said he was—they both were. Where was the fear?

As Olsen left Taylor's car, the two agents looked at each other. Olsen had over-played the role and Taylor wasn't convinced. Taylor was surely lying, but he had conceded they scrubbed the files before the warrant was served, and that his superiors knew about it.

Chapter 29
Leads and Loose Ends

Donatelli, Smith, Farwell, and McFarland gathered Wednesday morning in McFarland's office for another coffee-and-Danish session. McFarland asked whether he should try to get the FBI agents handling Olsen to join them. Donatelli objected vehemently.

"They aren't part of this team. They work for the anti-corruption guys in Justice. They're handling Olsen while we try to get inside Taylor's head, but they're not committed to our case. They're committed to nailing Olsen. For all we know, they think we're suspects. They'd screw us in a second to build their case."

Smith agreed. McFarland did not yet understand the scale of the jealousy within and among law enforcement agencies.

"They're meeting with Olsen and his attorney this morning, and they're going to put Olsen in front of a grand jury this afternoon to lock him in. I have their transcript of the Olsen—Taylor meeting last night."

McFarland looked at Smith, aghast. "Olsen just got an attorney?"

"Uh huh, and he's cooperating without a written deal. The attorney is going to have a conniption."

Donatelli smiled happily. "Can we trust the attorney to keep his goddamned mouth shut?"

"They'll do their best to put the fear of God in him—or actually, I think it's a her."

"Who?"

"A woman named, Kirk, Noel Kirk."

McFarland chortled. "Christ, Olsen used to date her. She clerked for Justice Douglas. She's at Williams Connally. She's a very good lawyer."

"She's arriving late at the party."

"She'll raise hell about that."

"The Boss had a stenographer in the shadows the other night. It'll be ok."

Smith briefed them on the meeting the previous night between Olsen and Taylor, reading Olsen's comments about McFarland from the transcript.

Donatelli hooted. "At least, he got that right. But the man is a jackass. Taylor won't buy it."

Farwell broke in. "No, wait Vic, Taylor doesn't know Jimmy, and it could look like he'd managed to—well, get himself into the Boss's favor." She looked at McFarland and smiled.

He returned the smile and said, "Hell, yes! Ruthless, conniving and mean."

"That won't hurt your image in this city," she responded, "but look, Olsen tried to screw you, and it didn't turn out real good for him."

Donatelli stood up, tore a page off the easel, taped it to the wall, grabbed a marker, and wrote 'DOUGLAS' at the top of the page on the easel and 'HILLS' at the top of the one on the wall. He remained poised, marker in hand and nodded to McFarland.

"Jimmy?"

"We know Douglas didn't fall; he was thrown into that pit. Whoever did it expected him to be entombed in concrete the next morning. We know he had been investigating ghost workers and theft of materials at Metro construction sites and had told his boss at Conway about it. Then he told Ernie and later told me. And we know a former DC cop was involved in his killing."

Donatelli asked, "Who had an interest in Mr. Douglas's death? The tox screen on him was clean, so he wasn't buying drugs from Sergeant Blackstone."

Smith leaned back and began a slow list. "First, Dan Adams and the union leadership. They had a sweet deal with Conway turning a blind eye to the fraud. Second, Conway. They ignored him when he complained, and they purged their files when they heard we were coming. Taylor claims that he told them, in writing, what was going on. That takes away deniability for the top brass. And that phone message from Douglas to Hills suggests they had more at stake than just having ignored evidence of some ghost workers."

Donatelli looked at them happily. "That's a list that should make a lot of people uncomfortable. What about the Deputy Chief?"

Smith shook his head. "You know my feelings about the man, Vic, but we can't just put him in the frame because we know he's corrupt and we hate him."

Donatelli rubbed his hand over his bald head. "Hear me out. We know the Deputy Chief sent out a memo saying he'd coordinate MPD security for Metro construction. That surely meant he expected to get first cut of whatever protection money they collected. And we have Nora's evidence that Detective Ransome, a member of the Deputy Chief's Palace Guard, showed up with Dan Adams the morning she executed the warrant at Union Headquarters. He must have been the bag man. And now we know Sergeant Silas Blackstone was involved in the Douglas killing. He strangely escaped prosecution for selling seized drugs. Who else could have protected him?"

"Okay the guy runs the MPD as a criminal enterprise," said McFarland, "and he's maybe tithing the ghost workers' fraud, but do we have evidence to link him to Blackstone?"

Smith rubbed a hand across his face and said wearily, "Let's hold on that until we deal with the third killing. We don't yet have hard evidence that Dixon's killing is connected to the other two. Dixon was shot in his vehicle while he was waiting for his partners to follow up on what turned out to be a false tip on some action in a boarded-up house. Strangely, Internal Affairs focused on Sergeant Williams for the killing as soon as it was reported. They're trying to take down Williams, and IA is owned by the Deputy Chief."

Donatelli tapped his marker on the easel, like an orchestra conductor getting his players' attention.

"Let's get back to this. It should be interesting. Who wanted Dixon dead?" Farwell held up a hand and asked, "Are we assuming Sergeant Williams really believed Dixon didn't kill Hills?" McFarland nodded "Yes," and Farwell said, "Okay, so let's suppose someone sent Dixon to Hills' house the night before he was killed, and Dixon didn't do what he was supposed to do. Williams's informants placed him there, but you don't believe Dixon told you the real story of what was going on. Maybe he was scared and didn't feel good about it. Dixon told you he couldn't summon up the nerve to talk to Ernie. He claimed he wanted to talk about the reunion. But we don't credit that. What if someone sent him to warn Ernie off?"

McFarland had heard something like that from Detective Smallwood. He said, "Who? Whoever it was didn't know much about Ernie or his relationship to Dixon. According to Sarge, Ernie would have laughed in his face if Dixon tried to warn him."

Farwell nodded. "But what if Dixon was getting ready to tell Williams why he was really there. Whoever sent him to Hills' place would need to stop him."

McFarland leaned back and ran his hand through his hair. "I have an MPD source who says the Deputy Chief was heard screaming at his nephew about being a gutless screw-up, and he needed to get his sergeant and that smartass prosecutor under control, but it's just third hand gossip."

Donatelli looked at the paper on the easel and said, "If the Deputy Chief has told IA to put it on Williams, then it doesn't seem like he actually wants to find out who killed his nephew."

McFarland shook his head. "Suggestive, but still not evidence."

"Okay, okay, Jimmy," Donatelli said, "but there is a distinctly rotten smell." He put a thumb and forefinger to his small nose and grimaced. McFarland tried to keep a straight face, saw Farwell covering her mouth, and could not stop himself laughing.

Donatelli feigned injured pride. "Twenty-five years' experience and this is what I get? Laughed at?"

Farwell stood, bowed in his direction and said, "Begging your pardon sir, could you show us again what it smells like?" She walked over to pour another cup of coffee. Smith rose, walked to the easel and pointed to Dixon's name.

"We know Internal Affairs went after Williams for Dixon's killing pretty much as soon as they got the case, and they got the case almost as soon as it happened. Not normal. It looks like they began questioning Williams without bothering to look for evidence. Why Williams? Did they think they could turn his partner Smallwood? Was Williams just an excuse not to look anywhere else? How bad do they want to keep the focus on him? I wouldn't want those guys to have any room to manufacture something."

Donatelli looked at his watch.

"*Tempus fugit, memento mori* gentlemen—and Agent Farwell. Let's make a plan. We have too damn many loose ends and leads. Mr. McFarland, your call, how shall we proceed?"

McFarland knew Donatelli was right. It was his case and his call. He stared at Donatelli and said slowly, "We need to find Blackstone. He was a crooked cop who got let off. Now it looks like he's a hit man, involved at least in Douglas' murder. He was directed by someone. Whoever that was, they'd want him out of sight for a while. That news might spread among his acquaintances in the drug world. Williams has a lot of sources in that world. Let's enlist him and Smallwood in this."

McFarland stood for another moment looking at the easel and then suggested a break, saying sheepishly, "Too much coffee," and hoping Smith would see him gesture with his eyes for him to follow. Standing at the urinal, he said to Smith, "We've got three murders and millions of dollars of the public's money stolen, and it's starting to seem likely that the corruption and maybe the racism in the department are part of it. You seem to want to go after the whole thing. You and Vic have scores to settle. I'm wondering where to draw the line."

"Jimmy, you're the boss."

McFarland wondered silently as they walked back to his office why he was in charge. He felt as if he were playing gin rummy while everyone else was playing chess. He groaned and said, "Every hypothesis I can think of involves someone in all three institutions: the Union, Conway, and the MPD. Maybe they're all dirty."

Vic smiled wryly, looked at the ceiling and said, "It's like sorting the laundry. Pull a sock off a towel here, fish underwear out of a shirt sleeve there."

McFarland wrinkled his nose.

"Huh?"

"I dunno. It's a mess. Gotta sort it out piece by piece."

McFarland sighed elaborately. "Christ, Vic, stop mentoring and tell me what you think? We have corporate corruption, police corruption, a corrupt colleague a few doors down the hall. I thought Nixon was an aberration, but each line of inquiry we look at seems to lead into some dark putrefying abscess of corruption."

Smith clinked his pen against a coffee cup and cleared his throat.

"Listen, let's not get too worked up. This isn't Watergate. They aren't attacking the foundations of our government. They're just vicious crooks. Violent, greedy men, pursuing power and money. We know Adams was running a huge scam. We know Conway was ignoring the corruption, and maybe trying to hide something else. We have pretty good evidence the Deputy Chief's office was connected to the scam. They all had a motive to silence Hills and Douglas. And we can connect Blackstone to at least one killing. I think he's a weak spot. How did he escape prosecution when the department caught him stealing and selling drugs? The only person who could arrange that was the Deputy Chief. We need to find Blackstone and we need to explore his connection to the Deputy Chief. Let's go forward with the sting. The DC wants McFarland to ask him to help Williams. OK, we'll wire him up and send him in there to see what the Deputy Chief says."

McFarland looked at them uneasily and asked, "What's the deal I'm offering?"

"You beg him to protect Williams. The price is giving him information, maybe ignoring evidence."

"I become Olsen?"

"You play the role"

"No."

The room fell silent.

Smith waved his arms and said, "I thought we agreed on this."

"I hadn't thought it through."

"Well, think now, dammit. Sarge has taken a big fucking risk creating this opening. Now you suddenly back out when it's time to go meet the scary devil face-to-face."

McFarland could feel the heat prickling inside his collar. He allowed himself several breaths then said flatly, "Agent Smith, I infer that you think I am afraid of the Deputy Chief and his thugs. That is not the case…"

Smith started to interrupt, "No, Jimmy…"

McFarland ignored him. "I am afraid of something worse. I am afraid that if I act corrupt, I'll become corrupt."

"But it wouldn't be real."

"Not real? I'd be offering illegal acts to get improper assistance for a friend."

Donatelli exploded, "Ridiculous. It's a sting, police work."

McFarland bit his lip and looked at them, no longer angry, but uneasy. "I'll go see him. He can think whatever he wants to think about why I'm there and what I'm willing to do, but I'm playing it straight."

Hank laughed. "Maybe we'll get just as much this way."

Chapter 30
Meet the Devil

Sergeant Williams had apparently delivered. Deputy Chief Herman Dixon was surprised that the sergeant had so quickly prevailed on McFarland to ask to come see him on 'a confidential matter'. The young man was a fool, a white liberal with too much sentiment and no balls. The sergeant might be tough on the street, but he was a weak man. He could be used. The U.S. Attorney's Office had gone after Chief Dixon a decade earlier. They had screwed it up and only made him stronger. Now he saw an opportunity for revenge. Lieutenant Rankin had suggested it, and the Deputy Chief had seen a chance to solve a problem and get revenge at the same time. The Deputy Chief worried about how deep in Rankin was getting with that pissant union guy, Adams, but not knowing exactly what was going on had its advantages, and the money was good. Dixon was content to take his cut in ignorance. Hell, he didn't mind violence, but he wouldn't have done it that way. And his nephew—he didn't believe Williams had killed Alan. He had a sick feeling that Rankin had heard him screaming that afternoon and just decided to take care of it. Rankin was an angry man and he needed to be watched.

McFarland arrived exactly on time; his face flushed from walking in the cold. He greeted the Deputy Chief without smiling, declined coffee, and sat stiffly upright in the uncomfortable chair set before the shining expanse of desk. He stared at the Deputy Chief who was posed calmly in his throne-like desk chair. McFarland thought he looked ridiculous.

The Deputy Chief smiled. "I'm glad to have a chance to meet you, Jimmy. Sergeant Williams speaks well of you. How can I help you?"

"Why is Internal Affairs focusing on Sergeant Williams for Lieutenant Dixon's murder? He didn't do it."

The Chief nodded thoughtfully, as if he hadn't thought much about it, but was listening. He said, "Well, of course you know, as a senior officer I'm not involved in particular investigations. The men in Internal Affairs are some of the best in the force, and I let them do their work."

"They're not."

"Not what?"

"Not doing their work. They are focusing on one man against whom they have no evidence."

Dixon had expected a supplicant, not an argument. Not only a fool, but an arrogant fool.

"Oh come, Jimmy, the sergeant had motive and opportunity. He thought my nephew had killed his friend, and everyone knew he wanted revenge."

So much, McFarland thought, *for not being involved in particular investigations.*

"That's gossip. There is no evidence against Sergeant Williams. They didn't swab his hands. They didn't test his clothes. They didn't canvass the neighborhood. They have no prints, no ballistics, and no witnesses. This is an effort to smear a good officer."

"That's ridiculous. Why would they do that."

McFarland sat silent, glaring at the Deputy Chief. He waited, and Dixon asked, "Have your FBI friends got some sort of information you think clears the sergeant or implicates others?"

The question might be genuine. Was Dixon concerned there was something he didn't know. McFarland continued to stare:

"You need to tell Internal Affairs to produce evidence or back off."

"How could I do that?"

"Every one of them owes his job to you. They wouldn't be going after Sergeant Williams without your approval, and you can stop them."

This was not the conversation Dixon had planned. He looked uncomfortably at the cigar humidor on his desk.

"Now, now, Jimmy, you have a very distorted picture of my role in the MPD. You're new to this. Let me give you some advice: be careful of what Donatelli and Smith feed you."

McFarland sat motionless, staring at Dixon.

"Will you call them off?"

"Even if I could, why would I?"

"Because I'm investigating a fraud and extortion scheme, and some of the evidence leads to your office. The investigation may well implicate you. Don't add to your problems."

The Deputy Chief smiled, showing a gold tooth, but McFarland thought he saw worry in his eyes.

"What leads to my office?"

"Are you going to call off Internal Affairs?"

"If I did, then what?"

"Are you going to do it?"

"I'll expect some help in return."

McFarland knew there was a tape recorder in the Deputy Chief's desk and a microphone in the polished mahogany cigar box. The Deputy Chief did not know there was a small recording device in McFarland's pocket. McFarland didn't respond to the implied question.

Dixon started to rise from his heavy chair, but McFarland remained seated.

"Chief, do you know who killed your nephew, Hills, and Douglas?"

This was a crucial moment. He'd been instructed by Smith and Farwell to get the Chief off balance, and Farwell had said, "Watch his eyes. His eyes will shift if he's lying." The Chief's eyes flickered to his left. He answered, "No, do you?"

McFarland looked at him steadily and said, "No, but I think you do, and I will soon." He rose, leaned his fists on the desk and said, "I'll be waiting to see what happens."

He left. Lieutenant Rankin came in through a side door.

"Did he ask for help?"

"Yes."

"Then we've got him."

"I think they've got evidence on the money and the killings."

Rankin caught the fear in his boss's voice. Disgust and anger churned in his gut. The Chief had grown soft.

"They can't touch you. After the way they fucked up before, they won't mess with you, and if they did, you could take them apart. That's what we got this tape for."

The Deputy Chief took the tape from the machine in the humidor and locked it in his safe, although he was not sure that what was on it would be of much use.

Chapter 31
The Dog Might Turn on His Master

Williams was again waiting to be admitted to speak with the Deputy Chief. He fingered his hat nervously and cast furtive glances at Detective Ransome who seemed to have drawn office duty this day. Ransome was apparently reading the *Washington Star*. Williams tapped his foot restlessly. A phone buzzed. The woman with the high hair picked up the phone, nodded, and told Williams, "The Chief is ready for you." She did not say 'Deputy Chief'.

He entered carefully. Tentatively. Be who they think you are. He saw the Deputy Chief leaning back in his big swivel chair, looking out the window. Lieutenant Rankin was perched on the edge of the DC's huge desk, scowling at Williams as he came in.

Williams nodded. "Chief, Lieutenant Rankin."

The DC swiveled with an avuncular smile.

"Now, now," he said, "no need to promote me. Chiefs come and go."

Williams grinned. "Yes sir, they seem to."

Rankin looked at him coldly and said, "Maybe you're waiting for the first *negro* Chief, Sergeant Williams?"

"I can't say I've thought much about it, Lieutenant. I just do my job."

Rankin turned away, and Williams tried not to think about throwing the vicious little cockroach out of the big window behind the DC's desk. He was puzzled by Rankin's presence and by the sour dynamic between the two men.

The DC leaned forward, adjusted the blotter on the wide shiny surface of the empty desk, and asked, "Are we working together, Sergeant?"

"Yes sir. I have asked for your help, and I am grateful for anything you can do. I know that help goes both ways."

"So it does, Sergeant, so it does. What I need is information, and it seems like you might be able to help me with that."

Williams looked at him expectantly. It was not easy to maintain this look of subservience while he thought about what a venal fool this man was, but he had had long practice. Rankin moved away from his perch on the desk to watch Williams from the side. Williams ignored him.

The DC said, "Your friend McFarland did come to ask for my help, but he seemed to think he had evidence implicating this office. What can you tell me?"

"Well, there's one thing. Detective Ransome went to the Union offices while the FBI was executing their warrant, and—well—he was made. They know he was there, and they're wondering why."

Rankin's head jerked up and he hissed, "Fucking idiot!"

The DC listened unruffled. Puzzled. "What makes them think he was there?"

"One of the agents recognized him from a lecture he gave on sniper tactics to her training group at Quantico."

Rankin spoke softly, calmly. It wasn't clear whom he was speaking to, "Probably a mistake."

Sure it was, Williams thought. You admitted it. I heard. The DC heard.

The DC ignored the issue of Ransome's presence and said, "What we want to know is why those agents are poking around in the Internal Affairs investigation of my nephew's death?"

Williams was about to respond, but Rankin interrupted. "Sergeant, you had motive and opportunity. If it wasn't you who killed the lieutenant, who the fuck was it? And what's the lieutenant's death got to do with what they're investigating?"

Williams wrinkled his brow in confusion, and the DC said, "Tom we know it wasn't the sergeant."

"We don't know shit. It's gotta be someone."

Williams looked up at the DC expecting anger but saw fear instead. He waited to let the tension play out and then said, "Well, I guess they think the three killings are connected."

Rankin glared at him. "What three killings? A lotta people die in this city."

"My friend Ernie Hills, Lieutenant Dixon, and that engineer Douglas."

"He a friend of yours, too? Seems like there's a lot of killing going on around you, Sergeant."

"Yes, it does seem that way."

"A shooting on the Gold Coast—probably a drug deal gone bad—a pathetic old drunk of an engineer who falls in a hole, and both connected to a cop murdered on duty. Bullshit."

Williams thought it interesting that Lieutenant Rankin seemed to know a lot about the murders. He wrinkled his brow and said, uneasily, "They seem to think they have evidence that ties the killings to the fraud case."

The DC thanked him and bid him goodbye with candied friendliness, but his eyes were on Rankin, not on Williams.

Williams left and heard the door close hard behind him. He decided to head for McFarland's office. He wanted to talk about what he had heard, and he wondered where the rest of the investigation stood. He also wanted to see Jimmy without Smith present. He found the office and grinned when he saw 'James H. McFarland, Assistant United States Attorney' on a plaque beside the door. He walked in and smiled at Mrs. Bynum.

"I'm Sergeant Larry Williams."

"Oh," she replied, "I know who you are, Sergeant. Mr. McFarland is just down the hall delivering a memo to the front office. Will you wait?"

"Yes, ma'am, I will."

She poured him a cup of coffee and offered him a stale Danish from the morning meeting. He laughed and held up his hand as if to ward off a blow. He sat and looked around, thinking how weirdly quiet and serious the place seemed. The offices in the Pension Building were arrayed on the upper levels around the central atrium, above the court rooms. The din of voices was pervasive. It would drive him crazy, this quiet place with its wood paneled walls, carpeted floors, and leather sofas in muted tones. Mrs. Bynum watched him and smiled.

"It's not the MPD," she said.

"No, Ma'am, it surely is not. Does the—quiet bother you?"

She chuckled. "No, Sergeant, I've gotten used to it. I used to work over in Superior Court. *That* was chaos. That's how I know who you are; I saw you there in court. Mr. Donatelli brought me over here, and I like it."

"I kinda like the craziness over there."

"Well, to each his own. I also know about you from Claire Hills. She and I belong to the same church, and I know you are a good man the way you are taking care of that family."

Williams was amazed to meet a friend of Claire's, and even more to find she somehow knew about his efforts to support Claire and Little Ernie. He started to respond and then choked up.

"I—I'm Ernie's godfather. I need to be there."

"They care about you."

McFarland burst in through the door looking flushed and pleased with himself. He stopped, surprised and glad to see Williams, and then sensed the emotion in the room and stood, caught in a welter of conflicting feelings. Mrs. Bynum rescued him.

"Mr. McFarland, the sergeant and I were talking about the Hills family. I know Claire from church."

He took a breath. "Mrs. Bynum you are full of surprises."

Williams looked on, bewildered. McFarland saw his confusion and said, "This lady knows everyone and knows how everything works. Oh, and yes—by the way, I am really glad to see you, Sarge."

Williams shook his head and then reached out with a big hand to pat McFarland's shoulder. They went into McFarland's office. Sarge nodded and gave McFarland a sly smile.

"Man, I turn aroun', and next thing I know you're a player."

"I wish I understood the game. I've got a nice office, but the case is a mess."

"A mess?"

"We've got too many suspects, and too little evidence. We can prove the payroll fraud, but apart from the one fingerprint and what Ernie and Claire saw and heard, what we've got on the murders is supposition and circumstance. We don't have hard evidence."

There was a knock, which McFarland already recognized as Mrs. Bynum's, "It's time for lunch knock." She entered and looked at the two of them still standing by the door. Her face tightened in disapproval. Sergeant Williams looked worn and worried. McFarland needed to learn about taking care of his friends.

"Mr. McFarland, it is nearly one o'clock. The sergeant needs his lunch, and you need to stop imagining that you can run on coffee. Sergeant Williams, the beef sandwich?"

"Are you going to the Deli, Mrs. Bynum?"

"I am."

“I’d be grateful if you’d get me a steak sandwich, peppers, mushrooms, extra cheese.”

He reached for his wallet. She stopped him. “Mr. McFarland is buying. Do you want onions?” Both McFarland and Williams were smiling.

“No onions, but I’d like chips and a soda.”

“Shall we invite Mr. Donatelli?” asked McFarland.

“He’s gone to lunch. He’d never wait this late.”

She left. Williams was cracking up.

“She’s not your secretary, she’s your auntie. She’s gonna teach you manners.”

“She’ll teach me manners, Donatelli will toughen me up, and Smith will show me strategy—if I don’t screw it all up.”

They sat. McFarland asked how Williams was doing. He shook his head slowly and said people were being careful of him. Some thought he’d shot his partner, others suspected he’d sold out to the Deputy Chief. Williams explained he was back on duty and the IA investigation seemed to have gone quiet. McFarland nodded. That was consistent with their assumption that the focus on Williams was driven by the Deputy Chief. McFarland recounted his meeting with the Deputy Chief and Williams frowned.

“There was something weird going on when I went to see the DC today. His office called and said to get down there asap. When I arrived, Lieutenant Rankin was in the DC’s office, and the place felt hot—tense. Rankin seemed pissed. He doesn’t like me, and he didn’t seem pleased that the DC was talking to me. But it wasn’t just that. He wasn’t giving the DC much respect.”

“How do you mean?”

“Well, the DC was pushing me for information about the investigation and about you. That was the deal. And Smith and I had talked and agreed I’d tell them about Farwell recognizing Detective Ransome when he showed up with Dan Adams at the Union office. I did, and it was like Rankin had been hit. He said ‘fuckin’ idiot’ real sharp, and the DC looked at him confused, like he’d never heard any of this. Then Rankin changed the subject. The DC asked why you guys are interested in the Dixon case anyway, and Rankin broke in, real angry, and started saying I must have shot Dixon. The DC said, ‘no’, and Rankin kinda hissed ‘well someone has to have done it.’ It sounded to me like he was telling the DC they had to pin it on someone. I thought the DC would tell him to can it, but he looked scared.”

"What do you think is going on?"

"Rankin's guys were in on all three murders, and Rankin is going to protect them."

"And what about the Deputy Chief?"

"He's like a guy who keeps a vicious dog for protection and then begins to wonder whether the dog might turn on him?"

McFarland's stomach felt tight. He twisted on his chair and stared out the window at the gray afternoon. It had started to rain again. Damn the damp, raw, wimpy Washington winters. He pulled his thoughts back to Rankin, the Deputy Chief, and Sarge, and turned back to face his friend. Williams's face was still, his eyes wary.

"There's something else, Jimmy. I'm pretty sure Blackstone is working for Rankin, maybe in exchange for Rankin protecting him. The dude was using, and he was stealing narcotics evidence and selling it. Christ, he was killing junkies to get their shit so he could sell it. He's an evil son-of-bitch who likes to hurt people. We nailed him, and then the case just disappeared."

They sat in silence until Mrs. Bynum returned carrying multiple bags. McFarland watched her unpack the food and asked, "Why are you bringing me the *Washington Star*?"

Mrs. Bynum frowned at him, opened the paper, and pointed. There, on an inside page, was a story about Olsen being questioned by the FBI. McFarland's heart sank. Who the hell had leaked now? He grabbed the paper and skimmed the story as Williams and Mrs. Bynum watched. The reporter didn't seem to have any idea why Olsen was questioned, or that he was hauled away for further questioning. McFarland thought of that night in the AG's conference room. *That* would be a *helluva* story. He pushed the paper to Williams who read it slowly and carefully.

He grinned. "Christ, Jimmy, that's not a problem. Taylor knows Olsen was questioned, and that story coulda come from a desk clerk—or a neighbor. Doesn't even mention you."

"If it came from a desk clerk, the agents should have been more damn careful. This reporter didn't get the story, but what is Anderson going to make of it?" He gasped and turned to Mrs. Bynum, who was quietly on her way out the door.

"Cora—Mrs. Bynum, is that who Mr. Donatelli was having lunch with, David Anderson?"

"Yes, I believe that might be right."

McFarland leaned over and quietly beat his head against the table. "Damn, damn, damn it. This is a tough city. It just isn't possible to do anything without leaks and creeps."

Williams was silent. McFarland rolled back his head, groaned, took a slow, deep breath, and said, "Okay, I should know that by now."

"Look, Jimmy, the story's a pain, but I'm more worried about Rankin and what he'll do to stop the investigation."

"Yeah, nasty. You need to be careful, Sarge."

"No, man, *you* need to be careful. I still have friends in the department and on the street, and I carry a gun." He patted his side. "You think they'd never go after a prosecutor, but these guys don't care. You're annoying the hell out of them, and I'm pretty sure three people who annoyed them ended up dead."

They were interrupted by Donatelli who strolled in looking well-fed and satisfied. He saw Mrs. Bynum at the door, tight-lipped, Sarge staring grimly at McFarland, and the *Star* lying open on the table. He handed his hat, umbrella, and overcoat to Mrs. Bynum, carefully hung his suit jacket on the back of a chair and sat down. No one spoke. They could hear drifts of rain blown against the window and Metro buses pulling noisily away from the stop across the street. Donatelli ran his right hand over his gleaming head as if brushing back an invisible mop of hair.

"Anderson will give us a week, but then it's his story for the *Washington Post*. What else we got?"

Chapter 32
The Proffer

That same afternoon, as the day faded from the windows of McFarland's office and the lamp on his desk created a puddle of light, he called John Cartwright to discuss the terms of a deal for the testimony of his client Dan Adams. He was surprised when Cartwright expressed doubt that they could agree.

"What the hell, John? You told me your client was eager to get a deal done. Now he's not? Is this some sort of bargaining tactic?"

There was silence. McFarland waited, drawing multiple lines under Cartwright's name on his yellow pad and wondering what game he was playing. Cartwright responded slowly and carefully. His deep mellow voice always reminded McFarland of Robert J. Lurtsema easing Bostonians into their day on Public Radio's *Morning Pro Musica*—melodious and a little sad.

"Jimmy, I'm not screwing with you. The man is terrified."

"Of what?"

"Oh, come on, you already have a couple of dead witnesses."

"Have you found out more from your client about the guy who showed up with him?"

"Maybe."

"I'm not bluffing, John. He's a detective who is part of a special unit that reports to the Deputy Chief. Telling us about that connection gets Adams witness protection. Otherwise, no deal."

"He doesn't think you can protect him. You're asking him to talk about people who're way too well-connected. They'll find out he's talking to you. There's no way they'll let him testify."

"That's what witness protection is for."

McFarland heard the creak of Cartwright's desk chair as he leaned back. This didn't seem like a case that a Washington dealer like Cartwright would want to mess with.

"John, I have a question? Why are you involved? This is a grubby graft and corruption case. It doesn't seem like it's really on your beat?"

He heard a deep chuckle. "You're thinking how much easier it would be to deal with a hard eyed cynic who does criminal cases for a living instead of a bleeding heart like me?"

McFarland felt himself blushing and was glad this was a phone call. "More or less, yeah."

"Dan's a good labor Democrat. He's helped candidates I was supporting and he's a good guy. A charming Irishman who likes single-malt and good cigars. He's a friend, and I owe him."

"He was stealing money, John, and it sounds like he was paying off MPD officials."

"That's the culture he grew up in."

"You're offering the 'everybody does it' defense? I trust not with a straight face. I'll take a plea to one felony count and put him in front of the grand jury. If he declines to answer my questions about MPD involvement, he gets no witness protection and no favorable allocution."

"Jimmy, if you were me, you'd never advise your client to accept that deal. Let me suggest a different approach. You come meet with my client here in my office—meeting with his own lawyer isn't going to raise alarm bells if he's being watched. He'll tell you what he knows, but it's off the record. He won't testify about it, and you can't attribute it to him. It'll help you to know where to look and what to look for."

"What does he ask for in return?"

"The whole deal..."

"That's not gonna..."

"Wait, Jimmy. I'm not asking you to commit until you've heard what he's offering. We'll trust you. If you think it's worth it, then we complete the deal."

There was a long silence.

"He'll remain available to you—to talk—Jimmy."

"I'm trying to figure out what I'm missing here. He gives me the information, and then I decide whether to go forward, but I have the information either way?"

"Yeah, that's it. Just a proffer, but direct from the witness."

"Can I bring one of the FBI agents?" Another silence.

"Okay, but not the woman who served the warrant. They know her now. And you and the agent should arrive separately."

"Do we wear disguises?"

"Screw you, Jimmy. It isn't funny. My client's life is at stake, and you know damn well the folks you're after are killers."

McFarland hung up the phone and sat and stared at it for a while. Then he went and found Donatelli and the two of them walked down to the Boss's office. Mrs. Thomas nodded in greeting when she saw him. "Back so soon, Mr. McFarland?"

"Yes, ma'am."

"He's on the phone, but it shouldn't take long. He's just arranging hockey practice."

"He's what?"

"He plays in a senior league. His team is called the 'Geezers'. Go on in, he's done."

McFarland looked at Donatelli and shook his head in awe. As they entered the office, the Boss was scribbling a note. Donatelli pointed a thumb at McFarland and said, "The young man is surprised you play hockey."

The Boss beamed. "Oh, do we ever. We're old and achy and not very good, but boy do we know how to play dirty."

McFarland summarized his conversation with Cartwright, saying he didn't see that there was much to lose in listening to what Adams had to say. Donatelli agreed. The Boss smiled an evil smile. "No, indeed. Are they betting that with what he gives you we can find the evidence to bring down the Deputy Chief? He must figure that would make him a lot safer."

"But we'll need his testimony," McFarland said, "and if he suddenly disappears into witness protection, they'll know he's been helping us. He might as well testify."

They were interrupted by a call the Boss told them he had to take. They stepped out of the office and when they returned, he was rubbing his chin. He smiled ruefully and said, "The folks over at the Department of Justice want to be able to announce an indictment against Olsen before the inauguration. I said no, but they're pushing hard. The irony is that no one but them will even care. It's not as if prosecuting that sorry sonofabitch is going to clear the lingering reek of Watergate. Well, Jimmy, let's figure out what you're going to do tomorrow."

"Yes sir. I better establish from the outset that if we go for a warrant or a wiretap authorization, regardless of whether we reach a deal, we can use the information for probable cause attributed to a confidential source."

The Boss nodded and added, "And absolutely no agreement in the meeting. Leave open that you might need to talk again. And make Vic's point. Adams will be safer with the whole crew in jail."

McFarland got up to leave, and Donatelli waved him out, saying, "I need to talk to the Boss about what I had for lunch, and you need to remember we've got a deadline."

*****

The following morning Smith and McFarland arrived at Cartwright's Connecticut Avenue offices a few minutes apart. McFarland, in a dark blue overcoat, white scarf, and charcoal gray suit, looked like any other Washington lawyer. Smith, sidling in a few minutes later in a cheap suit and three-quarter length trench coat, and carrying a satchel, looked as if he'd come to repair a copying machine. He arrived at Cartwright's office to find McFarland sipping an espresso in a small conference room full of light and indoor plants. Democratic firm or not it was posh.

"Oh, man, can you believe it, Hank? They've got an espresso machine in the kitchen. It looks like a copper and brass calliope. Cartwright brought it home from a trip to Italy a few years ago and now how to use it is part of the training for secretaries here."

"Well, they've got your number. You gonna come work here?"

McFarland blushed. "You know, he did try to hire me. He's friends with a professor of mine."

"Yeah, but now he's the opposition."

Cartwright appeared with his client. Both men looked funereal. McFarland saw a flash of interest or perhaps awe cross Cartwright's face when he introduced Smith. Adams looked furtive, eyes shifting around the room, a failed smile turning to a grimace. McFarland felt like reassuring him but let the pall of fear sit. McFarland took a deep breath, reminding himself that he held all the cards here. He could put Adams in jail. He could accept or reject the deal they were offering. *He had bigger fish to fry,* he thought, *than Dan Adams—and he didn't need to impress John Cartwright.* Faced with Adams' obvious terror, McFarland struggled to remain cold and tough. He felt sorry for the man.

He looked at Cartwright and asked, "Where are we, John?"

"My client will tell you what he knows. He is staking his life on my assurance that you will not misuse the information. He is hoping you will understand that it is in the government's interest to protect him."

"We will not attribute the information he gives us to him, but we may use it to get authorization for wiretaps or searches based on information from a confidential source. We think that is in his interest too, because we have a shared interest in seeing the guilty parties locked up."

McFarland saw Adams roll his eyes. He sat quietly staring at him, wondering what sort of witness he would make. He waited. Adams coughed and began to speak in a soft, Boston monotone.

"Metro construction is a union job. The biggest in the country right now. There are laborers working on every station and stretch of tunnel. Once things began to go wrong and sections of tunnel started collapsing under buildings, all hell broke loose. The work didn't stop. They started working twenty-four/seven, and WMATA was pretty much only interested in getting tunnels dug, tracks laid, and stations built. It was chaos. We'd have guys disappear from the job and Conway would issue a paycheck. They didn't want to know if some of the guys they issued checks to weren't around. They just told us 'find 'em'. It was obvious they didn't give a fuck what we did with the checks. So we held 'em for a few weeks, and then we began to cash 'em at our bank. No one noticed, or if they did, they didn't care."

Adams stopped and sipped his coffee. He straightened a pad lying in front of him, laid the sharpened pencil neatly alongside it and said, "It started small—a few thousand dollars every two weeks—but the numbers just kept going up. We realized that every time a guy signed on and then went on a bender and stopped showing up for work it added to the skim. Well, we aren't stupid, and the company didn't care. We went out and found every useless wreck who'd ever held a union card, dragged him to the jobsite for a few weeks, paid him off, and went on collecting the paychecks."

Smith nodded in appreciation, and asked, "How many were there—guys who got paid but didn't actually work or collect their checks?"

Adams looked at him with a small smile. "At one point, the workforce count, our guys, was over twelve hundred, and about a third were ghosts."

Smith whistled and said, "Four hundred at, what, a thousand every two weeks, and nobody noticed?"

"It was way more than that when you included overtime. I don't know whether anyone noticed. No one said anything. Not until that guy Douglas started walking around with fucking charts on a clip board counting. Shaking his head, asking questions, making notes. I don't know why." Adams grew animated. "Conway had every reason to want not to know. When they started to run twenty-four/seven, WMATA put them on a cost-plus basis. Every dollar they paid out they charged WMATA and added their management fee. The more *we* stole, the more money *they* made. Why would they care? They needed us to keep the work going. Overtime was proof they were pushing hard to get the job done. No way they wanted to pick a fight with us about ghosts."

McFarland looked at Smith. He hardly knew where to begin.

"What about WMATA? Did they know?"

Adams shook his head. "I doubt it, Mr. McFarland, I wasn't out on the site that much recently, but when I saw engineers from WMATA, they'd be with a bunch of white hats from Conway checking construction details and pushing to move faster."

"How?"

"Doing a lot of stuff all at the same time. Electrical work, construction, tracks, stuff like that. The WMATA engineers were looking for structural issues or any foul up that might cause delays. They sure weren't counting noses."

"How'd you hear about Douglas?"

"A foreman saw what he was doing, got worried, and came to me."

"The foreman knew what was going on?"

Adams smirked. "Oh man, he just wanted his little cut. There was enough to keep everybody happy."

"Including the Union brass?"

There was a pause, but Adams nodded yes.

Smith asked, "So no one really wanted to hear what Douglas was digging up?"

"You got that right."

"What'd you do?"

Adams fell silent, looking down at the table, his lips compressed as if to assure he said nothing. They waited. Cartwright watched with concern finally placing a hand on his client's shoulder and reminding him that they'd discussed this and he needed to answer. Adams shook his head. "I can't do this. I shouldn't be here."

McFarland was surprised when Smith broke in.

"You *are* in a tough position, Mr. Adams, we understand that. You don't have any good options. We are closing in on some violent men. You are a risk to them. They already know that. Do you want to walk out of here to face them alone or with a bunch of FBI agents on your side?"

Adams closed his eyes for a moment, and then renewed his account. "I—well—I discussed it with Detective Ransome."

Smith nodded. "What did you discuss?"

"That Douglas was going to be a problem."

Smith nodded again as if this were obvious. Adams looked sick.

"Why did you go to him?" Smith asked. McFarland held his breath.

"We had a deal with the MPD. We called it 'paying the extra costs of jobsite security,' but we knew what it was. That was the way it was from the start. No big deal, just making sure they took care of our guys. You know, everything from parking tickets to fights. Ransome was our 'liaison'. He picked up our payments. And he was the one I talked to about any problems."

Smith's face, which had been bland for most of the conversation, took on a look of harsh intensity, but Adams wasn't looking at him. He was staring out the window as he spoke.

Smith asked, "Did the guys from the MPD get in on the ghost workers scheme?"

"No, not exactly. They knew what was going on. They seemed to think it was funny. Then at some point they suggested that since there was more at stake, it would be a good thing if we increased our payments to them."

"What did Ransome say when you told him about Douglas?"

"Ransome's not much of a talker. He just said, 'dumb fuck,' and I shouldn't worry about it."

"When was that?"

"It was just after the Skins beat the Eagles, early December, I think."

"Did you hear anything about what happened next?"

Adams glanced at Cartwright.

"I heard that Douglas's body had been found up at the Brooklands job site, and later Mr. Cartwright told me about Douglas being murdered and about the Black guy, the lawyer from WMATA."

"Did you know that the guy from WMATA had Douglas's evidence and was going to bring it to Congressional investigators?"

Adams pulled back looking shocked. "No!"

"How about Conway, did you talk to them?"

"Conway?"

"Do you know Elliott Taylor?"

Adams looked confused. "Who?"

"Elliot Taylor, the top guy at the Conway office."

Adams shook his head, "Nah, I don't hang out with management guys."

Cartwright leaned forward, looked at his client and then at McFarland. "That's the basic story, Jimmy. How are we going to proceed?"

"We may need to talk further, and I'll need a couple of days to discuss this with my office."

Adams shook his head sadly. Smith cleared his throat, and said, "Jimmy, I think we owe it to Mr. Adams to move faster than that. We need a few hours, not a few days."

McFarland was taken aback. Wasn't this his call? Smith knew it was, so was he up to something, or perhaps concerned about Adams' safety. McFarland nodded assent, said they'd better get to work, shook hands with Adams and Cartwright, nodded curtly to Smith, gathered his overcoat, and headed out. He walked the block to the Farragut North Metro station, one of the seven stations now open, and stopped to wait for Smith who appeared seemingly out of nowhere, grinning at him.

"I told Cartwright to keep his client there until we call."

Chapter 33
A Mess

McFarland and Smith went straight to the boss's office and found Mrs. Thomas's desk empty. They heard her grumbling in the Boss' office and went in. The long conference table was strewn with papers, half-filled coffee cups, and ashtrays. The chairs were in disorder, and an assortment of newspapers lay scattered on the floor. Mrs. Thomas peered disapprovingly at a gray overcoat. She turned and scowled at Smith and McFarland. Smith clucked and raised his eyebrows. She shook her head. "Budget meeting. They were in here all morning until he had to leave. They can't even keep track of their own clothing." She held out the coat with distaste. "Whoever it is will notice when he goes outside."

"Yes, indeed, Mrs. Thomas, he will."

"Are you gentlemen looking for the Boss?"

"Yes, ma'am, we are, and it is somewhat urgent."

"He's at a meeting on the Hill. He just left fifteen minutes ago. I think he plans to go straight from there to an appointment. Do you want me to try to get a message to him?" McFarland started to say no, but Smith said he would very much appreciate it and they would be in McFarland's office if she had any news.

She followed them out of the office, placed the coat on the rack, and shooed them out as she sat at her desk and picked up the phone. They walked down the hall in silence. As they entered McFarland's office, Mrs. Bynum handed McFarland a sheaf of messages, noting that a young lady, "a Ms. Brown," said it was important that she speak to him. McFarland's face reddened. Mrs. Bynum maintained a deadpan expression as she handed him the messages, but Smith chuckled, saying, "You'd better return that one Jimmy."

McFarland stuffed the messages in his pocket and snapped, "When I get a chance." He blushed again and decided to change the subject, closing the door after he and Smith walked into his office and saying, "Man, you got balls telling Mrs. Thomas to pull him out of a meeting on the Hill."

Smith looked at him with amusement. "I don't think he'll mind. For one thing, it's a sign of importance when you get urgent messages like that. Makes everyone wonder. And I've got a feeling," Smith tapped his stomach with his right fist, "I've got a feeling that our witness is in danger."

"You and Williams. You think Adams is in danger, Sarge thinks I'm in danger." Smith stared. "You didn't tell me that. Sarge has good instincts. Trust him. These guys would have to be incredibly stupid to go after you. But they certainly aren't showing signs of a lot of smarts."

Smith went out to use the phone extension on the small table between the two chairs facing Mrs. Bynum's desk. McFarland took the messages from his pocket, looked at the one from Sally, put it aside, and saw a message from Jason Levy, Conway's lawyer. He called him back. When Levy's secretary heard who it was, she said, "Oh, yes, he wants to speak with you."

She put him through, and Levy said, "McFarland, thanks for getting back to me. I wanted to let you know that I no longer represent the company."

"What?"

"You can deal with an in-house lawyer named Harry Maddox. He's at their San Francisco office."

"What's going on?"

"You'll have to speak to Mr. Maddox." The line went dead.

There was a knock on the door and Mrs. Bynum stuck her head in to tell him that he and Smith were to meet the Boss at the Senate Judiciary Committee offices in twenty minutes. She handed him his coat, saying they'd need to hurry. When they found their way to the Judiciary Committee, the receptionist looked at them curiously and called an intern to lead them down to a small conference room behind the Committee's big hearing room.

Smith frowned ruefully and said, "I spent some time in there a few years ago."

Almost immediately the Boss came in, sat them down, and said, "Tell me."

McFarland summarized what Adams had told them. The Boss listened without comment, his eyes half closed. When McFarland stopped, the Boss nodded slightly and asked quietly, "What do you recommend?"

McFarland wondered whether he should turn the question over to Smith, but he realized the Boss was telling him it was his call.

"We need to get Adams into protection. I believe we can get more from him if he feels safer, and I think it will also increase the pressure on—those involved."

Again, that slight nod. The Boss stood up and said, "Do it." He turned to leave, then turned back. "Good job."

They walked back to McFarland's office and he threw down his coat and called Cartwright, looking forward to conveying the news. But when Cartwright came to the phone, he was distraught, his deep voice raspy. He told McFarland that his client had disappeared.

"Shit, John, you were supposed to keep him there. What happened?"

"I've no idea. He grabbed his coat, told the receptionist he had to go to his office, and walked out. I called his office. They haven't seen him."

Smith, listening to McFarland's end of the call, muttered "Dammit." And then held out his hand for the phone. "John, are you willing to help us find him?"

"Were you going to accept the deal?"

"Yes."

"Then, yes."

"I need you to sit down right now and make a list of everyone you know he spends time with and every place you can think of that he has any kind of connection to. I'll be there in thirty minutes, just as soon as I get word out."

Smith hung up and looked at McFarland. "I screwed up. I didn't listen to my gut. If the man's alive, we'll find him. We need to find him before they do."

McFarland felt as if he'd fallen into someone else's story.

"How can I help?"

"Keep the case moving."

"I'll track Sarge down and let him know what's going on."

Smith thought for a moment, nodded, and left. McFarland sat, thinking uneasily about why Adams would have bolted when he knew they were trying to get approval to put him in protection. He tried to reach Williams at home without success, then called and woke Smallwood.

"Amel, I'm really sorry to wake you."

"Nah, no problem, I need to get out and do some stuff before my shift tonight. What's up?"

"I need to talk to Sarge—to bring him up to date on some stuff that's going on."

"You need to see him tonight?"

"Yeah, I do."

"I won't see him 'til our shift begins. Maybe we'll stop by your place?"

He looked at his watch and realized it was nearly three in the afternoon and he hadn't eaten. He told Mrs. Bynum he was going to get some lunch. She pointed to a bag on the corner of her desk. McFarland shook his finger at her and laughed.

"How much do I owe you?"

"Oh," she replied, "Agent Smith took care of it."

He took the bag, sat at his desk, and unwrapped a fragrant and messy pastrami and cheese sandwich with an extra pickle. But it lay there, untouched, while he brooded. A key witness was missing, probably dead, because he hadn't been experienced enough to know he had to keep the man in hand and safe while he had him. Without Adams' evidence he didn't have enough to go after the Deputy Chief, and Anderson's story on Olsen would run in a few days and blow their efforts to get admissions from Taylor. The Boss had taken a risk letting him run this case, and he'd screwed it up. He picked up the phone and buzzed Mrs. Bynum, asking her to call the front office and let them know he needed five minutes to update the Boss.

He turned back to the sandwich and saw the message from Sally. He dialed and got her roommate. He asked if Sally was there.

"Is that Jimmy? Oh, man, she's been waiting for you to call."

He heard her yell, "Sally! It's Jimmy!" *She'd been waiting,* he thought. Since ten that morning?

"Jimmy?"

"Yeah, hi, Sal—how are you?"

"I was worried you might not call."

He thought guiltily about pushing her message aside. "Why would I do that?"

"Well, you know, I thought you were mad at me."

He felt a pang of embarrassment. "No, I—well I was, but I got over it."

"Good. Listen, can you still get those tickets?"

"Tickets?"

"To the Inaugural Ball. Wasn't that what you were pissed about?"

"Oh, right. Yeah, they're around somewhere."

"Am I still invited?"

"I thought you couldn't do it?"

"I couldn't. I, well, I made an excuse. Well, actually I totally fabricated an excuse which the guy saw right through."

"Wasn't it some sort of concert you were really supposed to go to?"

"It was—is, but it was a professor taking me, and it was a little creepy. They're not going to flunk me."

There was a charged pause.

"Sally, I would be really happy if you could come. Really, really happy. It has been a bad day and you've—made me stop feeling sorry for myself."

There was another, even longer silence, then Sally coughed and asked in a muffled voice, "Is it black tie?"

"Yes, do you have a ball gown?"

"Ah, maybe my fairy godmother will come up with something."

When the Boss called him, Jimmy was able to convey the news about Adams' disappearance without drama.

The Boss seemed unsurprised. "Hank will find him."

Chapter 34
Gatorade

It is well past midnight. Sergeant Williams and Detective Smallwood cruise slowly up 13th Street. They ride in silence. They have been to McFarland's house where he gave Smallwood coffee and reheated pizza that he ate alone in the kitchen while Williams and McFarland talked quietly in the living room. Smallwood wants to know what the hell is going on, but he doesn't ask. They turn east on T Street. They are near where Dixon was shot, and the atmosphere in the old Ford gets heavier. A figure is sitting incongruously on the stoop of a boarded-up house with a collapsing porch. Smallwood points and says, "It just about looks like Gatorade's been waiting for us."

Williams pulls over, gets out, and tells Smallwood to wait. He stands very still looking slowly up and down the street before he walks over toward the seated figure.

Gatorade is, in fact, waiting for Sergeant Williams. He has one of the gray felt pads the shelter provides wrapped around his shoulders and over his head like a cowl. It is not a particularly cold night, but there is a raw, damp feel to the air.

Williams nods and asks, "Sup?"

"I hear you lookin' for some folks."

"Mm-hmm."

"One of 'em that bastard Blackstone?" Williams remains quiet and Gatorade continues, "He hurt people 'cause he can—'cause he en*joy* it. Killed a guy I knew, a junkie who was pretty far gone…" Williams waits. He knows this script and wonders what Gatorade wants. Gatorade is shaking. It might be the cold, or the amount of time since his last hit. "Sarge, you're a good man. You tough, not mean. Word on the street is your own people lookin' for someone to help them stitch you up for Dixon's murder. It ain't right, and I know you didn't do it."

"How do you know?"

"'Cause I saw Blackstone and another dude walkin' away from the car right after I heard the shot that night."

"You were there?"

"Right across the street, man, in the foyer, you know, of that house we use sometimes."

"How'd you recognize Blackstone?"

"You shittin' me? Big ugly nose and that nasty smile he gets when he hurts you? I know him. He busted my face and broke my hand with his stick when he was still a cop. He was around here some after he got run off the force. Seemed like he was tryin' to claim the turf."

"You know the other individual?"

"Nah, never seen him before."

"What'd he look like?"

"Big, white, an' mean. I stayed real quiet where I was."

"Gator, you seen a lot. Is there something you want from me?"

"I ain't done, Sarge."

Williams is amazed. He has never seen Gatorade like this, able to string together sentences into a coherent story, and without whining for help getting his next fix.

"What else?"

"I know what Blackstone did with the gun."

"The one he used that night?"

"Uh huh. He sold it to one of the Denhams, Bobby."

"Who told you that?"

"Bobby."

"Bobby did?"

"Uh huh. You know, Blackstone had his gun nickel-plated with some kinda fancy grips, right?"

Williams nods. He's seen Blackstone's gun. The man had showed off his gun and his custom baton whenever he got the chance—showed and used. Gatorade, rocked by tremors, continues, "I was tryin' to score from Bobby and he was wavin' *that* gun. I ask, 'Where in hell you get that, Bobby? I been slapped in the face with that gun.' An' he says he bought it off Blackstone."

A faint smile crosses Williams's face. He waves Smallwood over saying, "Amel, you gotta hear this."

He wants to make sure he isn't the only person who's heard a witness say Bobby Denham has an illegal weapon probably used in a murder. He has Gator repeat the story and then asks, "Gator, you know a lot tonight. What do you need?"

"No, Sarge, this isn't a trade. You just find the sonofabitch, hang him by his feet, and stuff his balls in his mouth so he chokes."

Williams smiles at the thought. "Maybe when we lock him up, he'll meet some of his old friends. If they're feeling merciful, they'll kill him that way."

Gator's shaking increases. Sarge realizes they're just about done. "Gator, you are on it tonight. I got one other question—no, a favor to ask." Gator looks skeptical. "You remember my friend, the white kid who came out to ride with us a couple of months ago?"

"Looked like a college kid tryin' to score?"

"Him, yeah. Well, he's lost a witness and we would like to find him. The witness's name is Dan Adams. Pudgy Irish dude. He runs the laborers' union."

Gatorade smiles, "I know him."

"You know him?"

"Yeah, he fixed me up with a job helpin' build the subway. Real good pay. But I only made it about a week. I couldn't stay straight enough to make it into work."

Williams puts a hand on Gatorade's shoulder so he can hold his gaze. "Adams is missing, and we need him. If you hear anything, find me."

Williams gives Gatorade ten dollars and tells him to get some food, take care of himself, and keep his mouth shut. Then he sees headlights turning onto T Street and whispers urgently, "We gonna rough you up a bit, man. Don't know who's in that vehicle, and best they don't think this is a friendly conversation."

Smallwood grabs Gator's arms and Williams makes a show of a blow to his gut. The car passes slowly by.

Williams and Smallwood return to their car. Williams wants to see if they can find the Denhams. Amel talks him out of it. Internal Affairs, he points out, will just say Williams planted the gun, and the Denhams will be happy to play along. Smallwood suggests they give the tip to the FBI. Then they can grab the Denhams and the evidence won't ever come into the possession of the MPD. Williams, convinced that this will prove to be the gun that killed Ernie, agrees.

Chapter 35
Ballistics

Saturday night. Smith didn't want to spend time on anything else until he had found Dan Adams. Farwell had been his partner for a little over a year. She had never seen him so driven. He was like a hot ember, radiating heat and intensity. He seemed to have little need of sleep and no interest in food. He ate if someone put a hamburger or a slice of pizza in his hand, but he didn't stop working. He had enlisted six other agents in the search full time and dragooned others for specific tasks. His superiors at the bureau, who had seen this mood before, had no appetite to rein him in. Colleagues shook their heads and tried to stay out of his way. Still, Farwell was not going to back down.

"Hank, that gun could be the linchpin of the case. We have to get it, and we have to get Bobby Denham in custody before someone else grabs him."

"It's the MPD's job."

"Sure it is. And if they seize that pistol and it goes into the MPD evidence cage, *we'll* never see it again. Not the gun or Bobby Denham. Williams is right. We need to go find him tonight."

"Christ, Nora, Adams' life is on the line. We need to find him if he's still alive."

"You've got half the bureau looking for him. If the other side got him, he's already dead. If they didn't get him, he's well-hidden and he'll keep."

He looked at her balefully, knowing she was right.

They met Williams and Smallwood near midnight on the 1300 block of S Street, Farwell driving with Smith slumped in the passenger seat. She pulled up next to Williams and Smallwood who had their old car parked facing the wrong way on the one-way street. They briefly rolled down their driver's side windows and Williams told them he'd put out the word there was a new cock on the Denhams' roost. He thought they would be out looking for the interloper. He suggested where to look and how to play it. Both Denhams, he said, were crazy and unpredictable. He and Smallwood would back them up.

Smith turned to his partner with a sour smile. "Twenty years at this. I investigate crooks in the White House, and now here I am on the street tangling with stoned hoodlums. What the hell?"

It didn't take long. They found the two men in front of an abandoned storefront on 14th Street transacting business with a couple of dark, bent figures. The older Denham, Ricky, was handling the money. The agents pulled over on the opposite side of the street and walked across slowly. The customers looked up like startled deer suddenly aware of a hunter and moved way. The two brothers stood still and defiant. Smith, unhurried, walked toward them while Farwell lagged off to the side, seemingly unimportant. Smith stopped a few feet away and stared in silence. Farwell eased further out of the way. The two brothers fidgeted, watching Smith. After a long moment, Smith asked, "Bobby Denham?"

"Who the fuck are you?"

"Hank Smith. I'm an FBI agent."

Bobby Denham sneered, "Bullshit."

His right hand went to his waist, and Farwell, whom they had ignored as she sidled up to them, grabbed his arm, spun it behind him, hooked his leg with hers and threw him to the ground, dislocating his shoulder. He screamed in pain. Ricky, momentarily distracted, moved to help his brother and found Smith's weapon in his ribs.

"Hands behind your head, Ricky."

Farwell released her grip on Bobby's arm and reached down to extract the gun from his waistband. She held the bright, nickel-plated, pearl-handled, police special saying, "Aha, the famous pistol," stuck it in *her* waistband and flicked handcuffs on him. She saw Smallwood and Williams emerge from the shadows and head for their car. The broad smile on Williams's face somehow felt like the biggest compliment she'd ever received.

Farwell and Smith moved their prisoners into the back of their car. Bobby groaned. Farwell turned to look back and asked, "Comfy?"

"Why are you messin' with us Mr. Fed?" asked Bobby, "What the hell do you want with us?"

"Where'd you boys get the gun, Bobby?"

"We bought it."

"From whom?"

"A guy who wanted to get rid of it."

"What's his name?"

Bobby responded with a moan and said they needed to get him to a hospital.

Smith repeated, "What's his name."

"How the hell would I know?"

"Because everyone on 14th Street knew who carried this gun, and you've been telling people where you got it, showing off."

Bobby Denham looked away. Farwell looked at him with a beatific smile. "You know, we've got you for armed assault on a federal officer, and when that goes to trial everyone's going to know you got beaten up by a girl, and then you'll go to jail and be laughed at for a decade or two. Or you could help us out, and maybe get a deal."

"Agent Farwell, let's get this guy to the hospital so he'll stop whining, and he and his brother can think how they want to spend the next ten years."

Once they had prevailed on the young intern at D.C. General to see that it was in his interest just to get the arm back in its socket without admitting the patient or getting involved with the FBI, they took the brothers back to their office, put them in separate rooms, fed them, and extracted full statements without too much difficulty. Bobby had indeed bought the gun from Blackstone, but hadn't seen him in a while.

"He said he was going to report it stolen, and I needed to lay low with it. That man's a bastard, a pig among pigs. He busted guys for drugs and then sold the shit himself. I hope he's dead."

Once they'd signed their statements, Smith asked both men whether they'd heard anything about Dan Adams.

"No, but you ain't the only ones looking for him."

"Oh, who else?"

"A detective and a lieutenant. I don't know them. The detective didn't talk, and the lieutenant just kind of hissed. The detective was dressed like he was goin' to a parade. He had real shiny shoes."

*****

The ballistics report came back the next day. The nickel-plated police .38 they had seized was the weapon that had killed both Ernie Hills and Lt. Alan Dixon. The evidence tied Blackstone to all three murders. They knew Maddox was tracking the case behind Taylor's back, and they knew the Deputy Chief's Palace Guard was hunting for Adams. Who was acting for whom?

Chapter 36
On Whose Orders?

McFarland woke in the early dark of Sunday morning and lay awake worrying. He had lost control of the case. It felt as if the investigation was going in a dozen directions at once. Dark thoughts circled in his half-conscious brain, orbiting the question of who conspired to kill Hills, Douglas, and Dixon, and why. He tried to turn his thoughts to happier images. When he had spoken to Sally the evening before to plan her visit, she was warbling with excitement. He wanted to suggest she come down Sunday and stay through the inaugural but worried it would distract him from the case. Before six a.m., he surrendered. Sleep was impossible.

He got out of bed thinking about a cup of coffee. He loved to sit in the quiet house sipping strong coffee and reading the morning paper before Paul was awake. This morning he told himself his coffee ritual was indulgent. He needed to clear his head. He pulled on running clothes and a knit hat. He opened the front door and then the creaky storm door and set out into the frigid dawn.

He tried to focus. They could prove that Blackstone was involved in all three murders, but who'd sent him? Who wanted them dead? Conway and the Union knew what was going on and, in different ways, benefited from it. Adams admitted he'd told Detective Ransome that Douglas was a problem. But that might be hard to prove without Adams or Blackstone. Put Lt. Ransome in front of a grand jury? He'd just refuse to answer.

He ran up 34th Street into the well-heeled precincts of Cleveland Park. Almost every house had a fat *Sunday Post* waiting on the porch. Some had an even heavier *New York Times* in its blue plastic bag as well. A few houses, he noticed, had lights on and the papers were gone. Some houses were awake. Perhaps they had young children. He imagined K Street lawyers trying to ignore squabbling siblings, combing the paper for gossip on appointments amid the aromas of coffee and bacon. That was how it had been when he was growing up, his father in robe and slippers immersed in the *Times* and then the *Globe*, his mother creating breakfast, singing to herself, and then taking her coffee, the Arts section, and the Book Review to an enormous wingback armchair where she sat, legs curled under her, wrapped in a beautiful red and orange cashmere blanket if it was cold.

He began to work his way back home, forcing his thoughts back to the case. When he and Smith met with Adams—a stab of anxiety tightened his stomach as he wondered whether Adams was still alive—it was clarifying. They learned a lot about the mechanics of the fraud, who was involved, and how such obvious and extensive theft had gone unchallenged. Each of the four institutions—Union, Conway, MPD, and WMATA—was getting something they wanted. But one plodding and honest engineer had been perplexed by the obvious disparities between written records and what he saw on the ground. When he'd documented rampant and unabashed corruption, he'd dutifully reported it to Taylor, the man in charge. When Taylor took no action, Douglas approached Hills, and then McFarland. He had been terrified. Soon after Adams mentioned Douglas to Ransome, he was killed. Had Adams told Ransome what he wanted, or did Taylor give the order?

McFarland had called Bill Minot on Friday afternoon to ask what he thought Douglas had been afraid of. Minot had been reserved. He told McFarland that when Douglas had met with Taylor to let him know what he had discovered Taylor had, at first, seemed interested and responsive. Douglas had grown concerned when Taylor questioned him closely about whom he had told about what he'd found but took no action. Then, Minot said, one of the construction engineers had asked Douglas what he'd done to upset Taylor and shocked him by saying, "Watch your back, Aubrey, he thinks you're a troublemaker."

The wind cut through McFarland's sweats. He picked up the pace, heading back down Wisconsin Avenue. No longer thinking, just running. He arrived home to find Paul in the living room, spread on the sofa in his robe, long legs in striped pajamas stretched over the coffee table, the Sunday paper scattered all around him. He looked up as McFarland came in breathing heavily.

"I'll pick it up. I'll pick it up."

"No problem," McFarland said, not meaning it. He hated having to find has way through a pawed over paper. Paul knew this, and did his best, but morning wasn't really his time.

"Long run, huh? You were up early."

"I didn't sleep well. I'm just trying to think out where this case is going."

"And…?"

"And—I don't know. But I should."

Half an hour later, showered and warm, McFarland made coffee, a familiar and reassuring ritual. He thought about eggs and bacon but decided not to take the time, toasting a bagel instead, loading it with cream cheese and jam. Coffee in one hand and bagel in the other, he made his way to the table. He gathered the news and sports sections and settled down to see what was going on.

Nope. That wasn't gonna happen. His mind raced off down the same winding paths of ambiguity. They'd lost Adams. They hadn't questioned Taylor, or the Deputy Chief. Why not? They hadn't found Blackstone.

He got up abruptly and called Smith, who he was pretty certain would be in his office. Farwell answered.

"Nora, it's Jimmy. I thought you guys might be working. Is Hank around?"

"He went out. He ought to be back soon."

"I'm worrying about a bunch of loose ends. I thought I might stop by."

"Sure. We can come to your office if you want?"

"No, I'll come there. I need the change of scenery."

"Yeah, this stage of a case can make you crazy. You get too close to it."

"I don't know about close, but crazy sounds right. I'll be there in half an hour."

He cleared up, threw away the uneaten bagel, took a swig of lukewarm coffee and poured out what was left. He started toward the door, stopped, turned, and sprinted up the stairs to his room and pulled on a ski sweater that always made him feel good. He hesitated, then took his car keys. It was Sunday. He'd be able to park somewhere near the FBI office.

*****

Smith was back by the time he reached the FBI office. He still smoldered with angry intensity, but he reported possible progress. They had found

Adams' car parked at a train station halfway between Washington and Baltimore.

"How long has it been there, Hank?"

"Since the day we lost him, we think. No signs of a struggle."

"So he might be alive and in New York or Boston—or anywhere?"

"Pretty much anywhere. It looks like he made a choice to disappear. We'll interview the conductors who were working the trains that afternoon and evening to see if anyone remembers him. We don't know that he got on a train. And we're processing the car to see if we find any interesting prints. Once we have those results, I'm going to talk to his ex-wife and the folks in his office again."

Smith stopped abruptly, took a deep breath, and smiled wryly, asking, "Well, Mr. McFarland, what brings you to the drab precincts of the FBI on this dreary winter Sunday? And would you like some stale coffee cake or cold pizza and coffee?"

McFarland felt the knot in his stomach loosen. He was among allies—friends. They were looking at him, expectantly.

"Oh, coffee cake sounds like breakfast."

Smith nodded. He understood. "Yeah, I've been having trouble eating. Nora damn near force-fed me yesterday."

McFarland expressed his frustration about their halting progress. Smith asked what he thought they were missing. McFarland started to answer, grimaced, stood up, and began to pace. Farwell watched. It looked like a Donatelli imitation. *He had no idea,* she thought, *how motivating his questioning and frustration were.*

McFarland stopped and said, "Blackstone was involved in all three killings. We have all kinds of circumstantial evidence that the killings are tied to the fraud. Why the hell can't we figure out who ordered them?"

"Well to start with," Smith responded, "We've lost Adams, we never found Blackstone, and we made the decision to use Olsen rather than question Taylor."

Farwell brought in the stale remains of a Sara Lee coffee cake, which McFarland devoured. She also brought a coffee, saying, "I don't ordinarily do this. The agents make assumptions, you know?"

"Thank you, Nora, I'm honored."

"You seem pretty low, Jimmy, what's going on?"

“I guess I need to toughen up, but I feel this huge sense of responsibility not to fuck this up.”

“To whom?”

McFarland stared at his hands and said, “To the Boss. He’s put a lot of trust in me. To Douglas and Hills—and to you guys.”

Chapter 37
Pressure

On Monday morning, January 17th, the city was beginning to hum with excitement. It was the week of the inauguration, the great tribal gathering, the quadrennial affirmation of what the capital city stood for; a moment of power, pomp, and politics all coming together in the person of a leader, democratically elected but preeminent even so. Restaurants were filled with happy out-of-town Democrats eager to celebrate. The Georgians especially, with their cowboy hats, peanut lapel pins and heavy drawls were eager to be seen and heard. Washington was their town now. Their pious peanut farmer, nuclear engineer, governor, had been chosen by the country to lead the world. Old guard step aside. Things are going to change.

McFarland was in his office by six, determined to make things happen. He, Smith, and Farwell had made a list of priorities and assignments the day before. Farwell had found Williams on duty Sunday night to ask him to come to an early meeting at his office. McFarland was writing key names on sheets of newsprint and taping them to the wall when there was a knock on the door. *Smith and Farwell,* he thought, *showing up early.* "Come on in," he yelled.

He was startled when the door opened and the Boss walked in—startled and briefly worried. What had he done? The Boss leaned against the desk and said, "At ease, Mr. McFarland. I figured you might be here, and I wanted to have a private conversation about a couple of things."

"Yes sir."

"Can you give me a two-minute summary of where you are?"

McFarland told him about the call from Taylor to Rankin and the discovery of Adams' car at the train station. The Boss listened, eyes locked on McFarland's. There was a silence, then he laughed and said, "It is encouraging when a new source of evidence independently supports your theory of the case…" He paused and seemed lost in some train of thought. At last, he looked at McFarland for a long moment and said, "I think it's time we closed Olsen down."

McFarland's brows knit in an almost comical expression of perplexity. "We still have a few more days before Anderson's deadline, and I was thinking he might extend it so his story doesn't get buried in inaugural coverage."

"You're starting to think like a Washingtonian, but we aren't getting much from Taylor. He obviously doesn't trust Olsen, and there's something else. The Deputy AG has pushed me hard on this. He and his boss want the Olsen story before they leave on Thursday. The deputy's someone I owe a lot to, personally and professionally."

McFarland was flabbergasted. They were going to shut Olsen down as a political favor? The Boss saw his consternation.

"Look, Jimmy, this whole operation is only possible because they were willing to go way out on a limb to support us, letting us use the AG's conference room, reining in an internal corruption investigation that ordinarily we'd have been shut out of."

McFarland grinned sheepishly, "And they left it all in the hands of a naïve beginner."

"We'd stonewall them if I thought we'd get more out of Taylor, but we won't. We can send Hank to go after him directly. But don't sneer at connections and politics. They make this city go. Think about building your own relationships over at Main Justice."

McFarland compressed his lips and bowed his head. Then he looked up. "You're the Boss. I know you understand stuff I don't even notice, but I have one request. Anderson won't publish until tomorrow. Let's move quietly until then and try for one more meeting to see what Taylor says before he knows for sure Olsen was acting for us."

The Boss nodded his head in agreement. McFarland thought they were done, but the Boss didn't move. He frowned and said quietly, "There is more politics to think about."

McFarland groaned inwardly, and said, "Uh oh."

"Maybe, but maybe not. Conway is famous—notorious—for working the White House, whoever is there. They're good at it, and they're tenacious. I've learned that they've reached out to the incoming White House staff to talk about the importance of the Metro project and the opportunities it offers for the new president. They came with a warning that there's an investigation of some serious, but pretty ordinary, fraud that should be resolved quickly and quietly or it'll screw the pooch. They told the incoming chief-of-staff that he should make sure somebody gets briefed and that Judge Bell knows what the president wants."

McFarland's heart sank. "I can't believe they would cut us off because it wouldn't look good if we uncovered serious corruption. It's all stuff that happened before they took office."

The Boss shook his head and waved his hand as if to say, "Slow down!"

"You're not thinking. I don't know that the White House is going to do anything, probably not. But if what I heard is true, what does it tell you?"

It felt like someone had turned on a light.

"Conway is worried about this case. They're worried at the highest levels of the company. Then there must be something to worry about, something more than some ghost workers."

The Boss smiled. "Uh huh. Now *we* know that, and we know senior managers were told, but they don't know we know. We've seen their cards. Let's not be afraid to bet."

"Will the White House help us?"

"That's above my pay grade my friend, and way above yours. But you need to get some arrest warrants and get that subpoena issued, a very broad subpoena. Today."

"Can I brief my team?"

"No. Not even Vic. Just let them know that Main Justice is shutting Olsen down. Nothing, not a frigging word about the second matter I mentioned to you. Not to your team, not to your girlfriend. Bring them in to meet with me. This morning."

McFarland was thinking, Do I have a girlfriend? Does he know about that too?

Chapter 38
Boy Wonder

McFarland assembled his team outside the Boss's office. Williams, who had arrived in his 'old clothes' uniform for a night on duty, uneasily tried to tuck in his shirt. McFarland saw him and laughed. "No worries, Sarge. This is a guy who plays hockey because he can hit people. You and he have a lot in common."

Williams was still trying to figure that out as Mrs. Thomas showed them in. The Boss looked at them for a long silent moment. Then he said, "So, this is the team that's going to break the biggest corruption case in this office's history? Sergeant Williams, I'm glad there's someone streetwise to take care of the Boy Wonder here. I need you to know I am still really pissed off that one of my own prosecutors was casually corrupt just to satisfy his vanity. I never saw it, and I'm embarrassed. We're going to bring down this whole crew."

McFarland was wide-eyed. It was like sitting in the locker room with coach Donnelly screaming at him. He'd been willing to eat nails for that man. But what was the 'Boy Wonder' stuff about? He didn't feel like a wonder—or a boy for that matter. The Boss went on to explain that Olsen would be shut down the following day. "When you found out what Olsen was doing, you gave me a chance to think it through before I started hurling thunderbolts, thank God. That enabled us to set him up to be used. Now he thinks he's a player. But I don't trust him, and I doubt Taylor does. Why would Taylor give him anything more?"

Surprised by the question, McFarland responded, "For the same reason, the Deputy Chief let me see what he was concerned about. They're desperate to know what we have."

Donatelli stopped pacing and began pointing at them one-by-one, as if they were jurors whose full attention he wanted. "We can tie all three murders to Blackstone, and we think we can tie Blackstone to Lieutenant Rankin and the Deputy Chief. We know the Deputy Chief is scared he's losing control. We know that Rankin is trying to find Adams. We know that a top lawyer for Conway is checking on Taylor behind his back. They are all scared. Why?"

Williams looked at Donatelli and said quietly, "If Taylor is connected with Douglas's or Ernie's murder, he must be real uneasy that someone's gonna get in a hole and try to buy their way out by giving him up."

The Boss nodded, "Yes. He must. Go on."

"If we let him know we have a fingerprint and ballistics evidence tying Blackstone to all three murders, maybe it'll convince him Olsen's giving him real stuff, and it might push him to take risks to put it all on Blackstone and the MPD."

The Boss looked at the others. "What do you think?"

Donatelli growled, "Too much. We should keep them wondering."

Smith shook his head. "No, Vic, I don't think we risk much. We already had Sarge tell the Deputy Chief about Ransome. They'll have heard we arrested Bobby Denham and got the gun. *Maybe* Taylor has heard from the Deputy Chief, but if he hasn't, he'll freak out. And if he *has* heard then we've got him. I like it."

The Boss turned to McFarland. "Jimmy, do you think we have enough evidence now to get the court to approve taps on Deputy Chief Dixon's phones, home and office?"

"Yes sir, I do."

Williams was visibly aghast.

"What's the matter, Sergeant?"

"Tapping the Chief's phones? It seems like a declaration of war."

"Uh huh. Not so different from you meeting with him wearing a wire, Sergeant. And I don't want any of you harmed. If the information Olsen gives Taylor stirs the pot, we might pick up some interesting chatter with the wiretaps. Let's get it done fast."

Williams let a sly smile cross his face before he controlled it. He said, "Yes sir. Then you better go after Lieutenant Rankin and Detective Ransome as well."

The Boss raised his eyebrows and cocked his head, and Williams continued. "That's where the violence comes from. If Taylor's gonna call someone, I'm guessing it'll be Rankin, and he won't be near as careful about what he says on the phone as the Chief."

"Yes, Sergeant, in fact we already have taps on the Palace Guard."

*****

Olsen was frustrated and bored. How was he supposed to prove himself if they didn't give him anything to do? Instead of espionage, he was sitting around pretending to work, wondering what was going on, and waiting to be included. He was pleased when his 'handler', Agent Gorham, appeared accompanied by Agent Farwell. They told him they were there to brief him for his next meeting with Taylor. *They're realizing how much they need me,* Olsen thought. *I need to exert more control of this process.*

He said, "Good. If I'm going to build a relationship with Elliott, the long lapse between meetings won't help."

The agents ignored him. They very much doubted there would be more meetings after this one, and they weren't interested in Olsen's advice.

"You need to contact Taylor through Kelsey," said Farwell. "Tell him you have some information he needs to be aware of before he gets questioned."

"You're going to interview him?"

Farwell ignored his question and continued with the instructions.

"Here's what you can tell him when you meet. We now have ballistics and fingerprint evidence to identify one of the killers. And we have two witnesses tying the Deputy Chief and his Palace Guard to the fraud."

Olsen was disbelieving. "You really have all that?"

Farwell gave him a thin smile. "Yes, Mr. Olsen, we do, and we want Taylor to know it. When you tell him that, we want you to watch how he reacts. Is he surprised, or does he know it already? Then you need to tell him he has to put the whole thing onto the Deputy Chief and his men. You can imply that we are hungry to nail the Deputy Chief."

"Are you?"

The two agents just looked at him, expressionless. Then Smith asked him to repeat what they'd told him.

When Olsen called Kelsey, she told him her boss was traveling.

"He needs to get back here. I need to talk to him, urgently."

"He's in San Francisco. He'll be back tomorrow afternoon."

"He needs to meet me tomorrow, then."

"He'll want to see his family."

"That will have to wait. This is important."

"Is something wrong, Gareth?"

"Tomorrow at five. Where we met before."

By Tuesday afternoon, the outbreak of polar air that had frozen the Midwest and ravaged the Florida citrus crop had reached Washington where it settled down to await the inaugural festivities. The Friendship Heights parking lot was filled with the cars of suburban shoppers. The two agents were again parked in the back corner with large coffees in paper cups. Taylor arrived late and Olsen was on edge as he left his car and walked over to Taylor's car.

"Elliott, greetings. I hope you had a good trip."

Taylor barely looked at him and did not smile.

"What's up, Gareth?"

"There are some developments I think you need to know about—to protect yourself."

"To protect myself? From what?"

"If I were running this case, I'd have you in front of a grand jury to testify under oath. It's just you and the prosecutor and the jurors. No lawyer for the witness. You need to know what they've got."

"What have they got?"

Now, Olsen thought, *he had Taylor's attention.* "They've identified at least one of the shooters in the Hills and Dixon murders, and they know that individual was involved in the Douglas killing and is linked to the Deputy Chief."

Olsen could see Taylor's mouth tighten and his eyes dart to the side. "What kind of evidence? Some junkie who heard something?"

Olsen stiffened, offended, as if he really were a member of the team. He took some pleasure in responding. "Witness testimony, ballistics, and fingerprints."

He could see this was news to Taylor and that it upset him. He tried to be nonchalant, saying he supposed that was good news, they could wrap up the case and move on, but he couldn't make it convincing, even to himself. Olsen was encouraged by Taylor's struggle to appear unconcerned. His own confidence waxed, and he decided to be more aggressive.

"When they close in on the Deputy Chief and his squad, you'll have plenty to worry about."

"What do you mean?"

"Don't bullshit me, Elliott. Your hands are plenty dirty."

Olsen was on thin ice. He had no idea how Taylor was involved but sensed from his reaction that he at least knew about the murders. Taylor stayed silent and Olsen was drawn into the space. "It isn't you they want, it's the Deputy Chief. He's been crooked for a long time, and this is a chance to take him down. You need to think about how you're going to put it on him if you're questioned."

Taylor's face seemed to sag, and he spoke quietly, as if to himself, "And get killed."

"What do you mean by that?"

Taylor just shook his head, put the car in gear, drove across the lot to Olsen's car, stopped, and waited silently for him to get out. Olsen worried that Taylor had admitted nothing. The agents, knowing about the wire taps wondered what they would harvest that night.

Chapter 39
Security

When Mrs. Bynum arrived the next morning, she found McFarland placing a series of notes with instructions on her desk. He appeared almost incandescent, as if he'd had too many of those weird coffees he made. He greeted her cheerfully, "Mrs. Bynum, we are going to have a busy day."

"Yes, Mr. McFarland, what do you need first?"

"The team will be here at nine. We'll need to feed them. And Sergeant Williams will be coming. He really loves apple Danishes. And I'll need some time with Mr. Donatelli. He needs to have lunch with his friend and get us one more day."

"I'll make sure you aren't bothered."

"Yes, and something personal."

She looked flustered. Something he had never seen.

"A friend of mine is coming from Philadelphia for the Inaugural Ball, and I'd like to get her some flowers, or a corsage, or something."

"I can do that."

"Oh, no, I don't think that would be right. But do you think I should get her a corsage?"

"No, Mr. McFarland, these balls are not like a prom. Maybe a bouquet to give her when she arrives?"

"I knew you'd know."

What was it? He had felt uncertain, but now he was focused. The Boss had given him the straight story. He was sure of that. He was filled with a sense of knowledge and power.

He asked Smith to review the last Olsen-Taylor conversation. "Do we have the wiretaps in place so we can see if he calls Rankin or the Deputy Chief?" Smith smiled, gave him a thumbs up and said he had more news. "We got a tip that Blackstone might be in Philadelphia. He had a girlfriend here in DC, and she's pretty pissed at him. She thinks he ran off with some woman from Philly. We're working on getting help finding him, but Commissioner Rizzo and his department like us even less than the MPD does."

McFarland chuckled and said, "I assume you'll win that one, Hank." Then he saw wrinkles of concern on Smith's usually calm face. McFarland asked, "Is there a real problem with the Philadelphia police? Should I Ask the Boss to call his counterpart in Philly?"

Smith got up, closed the door and said, "You know, we have taps on Ransome and Rankin as well as the Deputy Chief." Smith looked at Williams who just nodded. "Nora wasn't sure Ransome even knew how to use a phone, but yesterday evening, he got a call from another guy in the unit grousing about having to come in that evening for a meeting. One of them asked what was up, and Ransome told him they had to figure out what to do about that sonofabitch Williams and his little white lawyer." Williams grinned.

McFarland gaped, and asked, "Who was he talking to?"

Smith shook his head and said, "Wrong question."

Farwell was impatient. "Jimmy, don't be naïve. Pressure runs both ways. All the evidence we have suggests those guys have been involved in at least three killings in the last two months. They know we're pulling together a case and it points at them. Soon they'll read that we were running Olsen under cover."

McFarland responded defensively, "Sarge is in more danger than I am."

Smith slammed a hand on the table. "No, no he's not. Sarge can't indict anybody. He can't mobilize the FBI. He can't get search warrants. He's just a sergeant and he can be squashed. And Sarge has been under fire more than any of us ever will be. You, however, if you'll pardon the expression, don't know shit. You take chances you don't even know you're taking."

McFarland shook his head and said, "It just isn't credible. If they go after me. It wouldn't kill the investigation; it'd just call down the wrath of God on them."

Smith groaned and said with exasperation, "These are guys who thought the solution was to kill Hill and Douglas and Dixon. They've personalized this around you. You're what they hate—an arrogant, snotty liberal trying to interfere in their world."

"I'm not going to back off."

“No one’s asking you to, but I spoke to the Boss and we’re going to do some things to protect you. We’re going to replace some doors and windows at your house and put in an alarm system.”

“What? Wait, don’t I…?”

“The Boss authorized it this morning.”

“But he…”

“No, he thought, *I should tell you*.”

“Hank, I only rent the place. What about the landlord?”

“Oh, I imagine he’ll appreciate the free upgrade. The department will take care of it. And starting tonight you’ll have a driver who takes you to and from work. It’ll be like being a cabinet member, but more fun.”

“Oh, come on, this is weird.”

Smith ignored him and handed him a card.

“If you see trouble or think you might see trouble, call this number.”

*****

McFarland was barely in the front door when Paul yelled, “Jimmy what the fuck is going on?”

He hung up his coat, paused, took a breath, and went into the living room where his roommate lay sprawled on the sofa reading. He was indignant. “Man, I no sooner get home and light a joint than a couple of humorless guys in dark suits and narrow ties come and ring the bell and tell me not to be alarmed. Of course, I was alarmed. I thought they were probably Cosa Nostra, or narcs, or maybe the IRS. They tell me the place is going to be fortified. By the time you get home tomorrow, there’ll probably be a machine gun nest on the porch. Jesus, man, I’m just a humble schoolteacher.”

“I thought we had an agreement about dope.”

“We do. I never even mention it while you’re around.”

“Just when the FBI’s around?”

“They weren’t FBI. They said something about justice department internal security. What the hell have you done, McFarland?”

“The Boss is worried that the someone might try to intimidate me.”

“Is that ‘intimidate’ as in ‘kill’?”

“I doubt it.”

"Well, our visitors sure as hell didn't. They spent half an hour going over all the things to watch out for."

"Yeah, so did my driver."

"Your driver? Holy shit, my roommate has a driver. Does the car have a siren and stuff?"

"Paul, chill out. Listen, somebody killed Little Ernie's dad and a couple of other people. We think we're getting close to them. I very much doubt they're stupid enough to go after a federal prosecutor."

As he spoke, he pictured Blackstone on speed, his eyes like pinwheels, and wasn't so sure. On the ride from the office, his driver had introduced himself as Officer Ed Ross.

"Are you FBI?"

Ross chuckled. "No sir! I'm kind of a high-class rent-a-cop with security clearance and a license to carry a pistol. And I have to brief you before we get to your place." He then launched into a detailed set of instructions on how to keep safe. It did not make McFarland feel safe.

*****

The next morning McFarland arrived at his office with his briefcase in one hand and a warm bag with his breakfast in the other. He'd had Officer Ross stop at a diner. Mrs. Bynum had already laid the *Post* on his desk. Anderson's story on Olsen's arrest had been crowded off the front page by news of the record cold. Ice floes had clogged the cooling water intake of the Calvert Cliffs nuclear power station forcing it to stop generating and leaving hundreds of thousands of Marylanders without power in sub-zero cold. Anderson's story was on the front of the Metro Section.

Donatelli, Smith and Farwell appeared in McFarland's office before he even had his breakfast box open. Donatelli was grinning. "Anderson is mad as a wet hen. Some editor decided the Olsen story was just a local scandal, not a national scoop."

"I haven't had a chance to read it yet, Vic. Is it ok?"

"Well sure, he got it right. The Deputy AG has a really nice quote on the shameful betrayal of trust."

He asked Smith and Farwell about their interview with Taylor.

Smith sighed and said, "He had his lawyer with him and didn't answer questions."

"We should have talked to him sooner and gotten him on the record lying."

"Oh, I don't know, Jimmy. We thought Olsen would get more. We've got their attention for sure."

McFarland frowned and began pawing through the layers of greasy paper wrapping his breakfast. Farwell cleared her throat and said, "We didn't come away from Conway empty handed. We found the guy who'd warned Douglas he should watch his back. He was pretty upset about Douglas's death. He confirmed the conversation with Douglas. He said Taylor had asked him what the hell Douglas was doing and had urged this guy, Lamsen, to talk to Douglas."

"That's helpful."

"That's not all. Lamsen told them there had been rumors they'd all heard that there had been a consultant's report warning that several buildings could collapse if they dug under them, and that Taylor buried it. Then the buildings did collapse. Douglas told Lamsen he'd found evidence the safety report existed."

McFarland took a few moments to absorb what he'd heard.

"That would explain why Taylor has been so concerned. He doesn't give a shit about the ghost workers. He's guilty of criminal negligence."

Donatelli examined the beautifully trimmed nails on his right hand, and observed, "They just don't learn."

"Who?"

"Liars and crooks in Washington. You'd think that Watergate would have taught them that it's always the cover-up that brings you down."

*****

Very early that morning, with Smith in a surly mood about their lack of progress finding Adams. Farwell had pulled on her overcoat, wool hat, and mittens. She had a hunch, she told Smith, and headed for the Fort Totten Station construction site to interview the crew to see whether anyone remembered seeing anything unusual going on at the site just before Christmas. She knew she looked like a cute little girl, and she figured she'd play to their sympathy.

She found the foreman and introduced herself, expecting him to growl about delaying the work, but he just called the crew in. It was bitterly cold. Most of his crew were clad ineffectually in multiple sweatshirts. A few wore old army jackets. They were happy to talk with the cute agent if it meant they could stand amid the rubble by the empty oil drum in which a blazing fire had been built. They stamped their feet and tried to warm their hands on cups of coffee. Clouds of vapor rose from the cups and the men's breath. The winter sun was still low among pink and purple clouds in the eastern sky, and the reddish light, flaming can, and wisps of steam reminded Farwell of a picture of hell in the children's Bible the teacher used when she was a kid in Sunday school.

She passed pictures of Douglas around to the men, who handled them daintily in dirty gloved hands. Several recognized Douglas as the company engineer whose body they had found in a pit a month earlier. No one, however, recalled seeing him just before Christmas. He was, they said, quiet and respectful, occasionally asking questions about their work and how long they'd been on this job.

"Did you see anything at all unusual around that time?"

Heads shook. No. Then one heavyset man with two sweatshirt hoods pulled tight around his face under his hard hat said, "Unless you count our union local president showing up. That was unusual. We don't normally see much of him." There was laughter.

Farwell was alert. "You mean Dan Adams?"

"Yeah, that's him. Danny Boy."

"When did you see him?"

"It was that morning, just before it started snowing. Real cold then, too. Adams was walking around talking with a couple of guys I didn't recognize. I figured them for officials from the national union."

"Can you describe them?"

"Aww, it was a while ago, and they was wearing hats and scarves."

Another man, who was flapping his arms trying to stay warm, said, "The big one looked like he was worried about getting his shiny shoes dirty."

"Had you seen him before?"

"Mighta seen him. I'm not sure, but a guy like him was around the Union office one time when I went in to fill out some papers."

As McFarland stuffed the remnants of his breakfast in the grease-stained bag and tossed it in the trash Farwell told him there was more and reported her early morning expedition to the construction site.

“I think that ties Adams to Douglas’ death.”

“It does, but we need more of an ID than ‘mighta seen him.’”

Chapter 40
Jimmy in Love

When he got in the car that evening, McFarland barely greeted Officer Ross. He was brooding about the Conway subpoena that he and Donatelli had managed to get served on the Conway offices in Washington and San Francisco. He had gotten a satisfyingly quick call from Harry Maddox, the Conway lawyer, who had blustered about 'A fucking federal fishing expedition' and threatened to complain to the Attorney General. The subpoena, he'd told McFarland, was amateurish, ridiculously overbroad, and the U.S. Attorney's office would be embarrassed when he moved to get it quashed. "You're not," he growled, "dealing with a guy in a cheap suit defending a sleazy gang banger. You are harassing a company trying to do the work of the nation."

McFarland had just listened, but he wondered whether he wasn't being way to cerebral. Why not go ahead and indict Taylor and the company for criminal negligence, and as co-conspirators in the fraud? Their behavior was outrageous.

When he dragged himself through the door expecting razzing from his roommate, he found, instead, Paul's little sister in a slinky blue dress and an old gingham apron. She was cooking dinner.

*****

Sally had arrived that afternoon, a day early. Paul knew she was coming to surprise Jimmy and had a pretty good idea why. He had hugged her, looked at her meaningfully, and offered to get out of the way.

"Oh, sure, great."

"Poor guy doesn't know what he's in for."

“My cooking isn’t that bad. I’m making pasta with veal ragu and endive salad.”

“I don’t mean the food. Remember you’re still my little sister, and I can read your mind.”

She had blushed, giggled, and pushed him out of the door saying, “Don’t be smutty.” She had switched on *All Things Considered*, listened briefly, sighed, switched it off, and pawed through Paul’s jazz collection, smiling when she found an Edith Piaf album, which she put on. She finished the sauce, tasted, added more red wine, tasted, sorted through the fridge, found an aging half used tin of anchovies, chopped them up and put them in, made the salad dressing, flung off Paul’s ratty apron, and danced up the stairs to shower.

She’d brought her red underwear from the New Year’s party, and the blue dress. She smiled and dabbed on a little perfume. She came down to set the table, put on the water for the pasta, extracted the pastries she’d brought from their fancy pink box and put them on plates. She opened the good wine and swore. She’d forgotten to take out the cheese. She put it on top of the radiator and set the timer.

Okay, she was ready. It was time. He was usually home between seven and eight. What if he didn’t come? He and Rachel could have gotten back together. He could have decided to work late. Then she heard him at the door and her heart jumped so violently she gasped.

*****

When McFarland saw her, a look she could not interpret crossed his face. Was it horror? He laughed. “I sure am glad to see you!” He meant he might now be able to forget an appalling day, but Sally was sure he knew why she was there. She almost blurted out, “McFarland, I love you so much I’m not sure I can stand it.” But she couldn’t get the words—or any other words—out, which was probably just as well.

She finally managed, “Would you like a glass of wine and some cheese?”

“What is that fabulous smell?”

“That is your dinner, Jimmy, but it’s not quite ready.”

She sat him down and said she’d get the wine. But he didn’t want to sit and wait.

He followed her, noticing the sparkling wine glasses on the table, the candles, and the vase of hot house tulips. He ambled into the kitchen. The sight of Sally chopping parsley made his heart race.

"Shall I take the wine and cheese to the living room?"

"Yes, thanks, that would be great."

"Shall I use the glasses from the table?"

"No, they're for the red wine, there's a white in the fridge."

"You smell good."

"What?"

"Nothing," he replied reddening.

"It's Chanel, do you like it?"

Had he done what he was thinking at that moment, they might not have had dinner at all, but he just replied, "Mm-hmm" and went back to the living room, only to reappear moments later.

"Where's Paul?"

"He's out—all evening."

As they sipped the tingly wine, he finally thought to ask, "What are you doing here anyway? I didn't expect you until Thursday morning."

She smiled and recited a carefully rehearsed explanation. She talked fast. "I had to come down again to meet with the concertmaster at the FSO. I thought I could combine the trips. I decided to cook us some dinner."

She might as well have been speaking Russian. He didn't absorb a word she said.

Her explanation *was* half true. The FSO manager had said she *could* come meet with the concertmaster and the first chair violist before she signed the contract they'd offered, and she planned to go see them tomorrow.

The dinner was fabulous, but they never made it to the elegant little pastries. When Paul came back the next morning, having slept on a friend's sofa, the shiny gateaux au chocolate were sitting on the counter. Paul ate one for breakfast, made coffee, and yelled upstairs, "I'm home, so be discreet. And there's fresh coffee."

Jimmy came down wearing old jeans and a sweatshirt, a dazed smile on his face. Paul looked at him approvingly.

"I am—in love—madly in love—with your little sister."

"Jimmy, that's been obvious for a while."

"Really?"

"Ever since that night you took her to Joel and Mariana's house."

"You knew then?"

"Everybody knew but you."

"They did?"

"The only risk was that you'd screw it up. But my wonderful little sister seems to have decided to take things into her own hands."

Sally appeared in a pair of Jimmy's pajamas and his bath robe. "Sometimes," she said, "impulsive is good."

Jimmy walked over and put an arm around her shoulders. "Did you really have to come down to meet with the FSO manager?"

"Well, no, but I am meeting with him."

"Oh, Your Honor," he said in a tiny pleading voice, "my client didn't really lie, she just redecorated the truth."

He kissed her. Jimmy McFarland was in love. Taylor and Conway would get what they deserved when the time was right. Suddenly, for James Henry McFarland life was very, very good.

Chapter 41
Cop Killer

The night of McFarland's seduction, acting on a tip, six squad cars and a black Chevy Suburban scream up in front of Mick McSorley's Grill Room in Philadelphia. It was a little past 11:00 p.m. on Wednesday night. There was nothing unusual in this scene except that it was Wednesday night. The patrons came to MMGR as much for the fights as the cheap beer. The burly officers who piled out of the Suburban were not the usual cops who arrived to break up fights. Dressed in black uniforms, helmets, and flak jackets, they brandished automatic weapons. They had heard that a dirty cop who'd murdered a police lieutenant in D.C. was in MMGR. They had come to get him. When they burst in simultaneously through the battered front door and the greasy kitchen yelling for everyone to hit the floor face down, former Detective Silas Blackstone could barely stand anyway. He certainly couldn't run or fight. He was cuffed and dragged out of the now quiet bar into the cold night. The biting air woke him briefly to hear the captain who was leading the raid say he is a "fucking cop killer" and that cop killers didn't have any rights. By the third blow, he was unconscious.

Detective Pete Phillips heard from his Philadelphia cop brother-in-law the next morning. The Tactical Unit had found and arrested Blackstone, but he resisted arrest and was under guard in critical condition in Pennsylvania Hospital. Phillips called Agent Smith to tell him. Smith had already heard the same thing from the FBI field office in Philadelphia. Blackstone, they told him, had a fractured skull and severe withdrawal symptoms. It was touch and go whether he would live.

"It looks like the Tactical Squad had some fun with him," the agent on the phone observed neutrally.

Smith grunted. "Yeah, unfortunate. We really want to talk with him. Don't let our friends from Philadelphia finish the job."

Chapter 42
The Money

Inauguration morning. The Boss had asked McFarland for a briefing document to send to the incoming team at Justice. "I want the whole thing from Douglas coming to see you to the present. It should be a narrative, but I don't want an adventure story. Clear and simple—plodding wouldn't be bad." The prospect of trying to summarize it all was daunting, and he bridled at the idea of 'plodding'. He wrote a few pages and then wandered restlessly down the hall to Donatelli's office from which issued the sounds of the inauguration. Donatelli had brought in a television and a dozen or so attorneys and staff were gathered around it.

"Come on in, Jimmy, the other Jimmy is about to preach."

That proved to be prescient. From the cadence of the speech to the Bible quotes to the call to unify around shared moral values, the speech was more sermon than stemwinder.

"Oh dear," Donatelli moaned, "we have elected a pious Baptist and he is telling us all about right and wrong."

To McFarland's surprise, Mrs. Bynum objected. "No, Mr. Donatelli, he's a good man, and I'm glad he spoke out about justice."

"Point taken, Cora, but this is a political city. They'll scoff at the sanctimony and assume they can roll the man while he's contemplating love and morality. Jimmy, you're a morally driven young idealist, how'd it sound to you?"

McFarland felt the heat and color rise in his cheeks and saw his colleagues smiling. "He's our president, and I support him. He sure as hell is better than Tricky Dick."

McFarland stayed long enough to see the new President and First Lady climb out of their armor-plated limousine to walk the mile up Pennsylvania

Avenue to their new home. It was a new day, cold, bright, and hopeful. The television commentators were excited by the president's gesture, and the fact that he stopped here and there to shake a hand. The Secret Service was in a controlled frenzy. It was less than a decade-and-a-half since they had lost a president on the streets of Dallas.

By mid-afternoon, the happy crowds had mostly found refuge from the frigid streets. McFarland had finished his summary and heard from Smith that there was little change in Blackstone's condition, but the Philadelphia agents had found a wad of cash, nearly four thousand five hundred in new bills, in Blackstone's apartment.

"The money was drawn from a Washington bank. I'm working on a discreet way to identify the account, and maybe the name on it, but it's where Conway does its local banking."

McFarland did a little dance around the phone. "Man, if we can link Taylor and Blackstone that gives us all kinds of leverage."

Smith also told him that there had been a sudden decline in useful information from the wire taps. "I think maybe they know what's going on. The Deputy Chief must be having his phones scanned pretty regularly by people who know what they're doing. But before they got cautious we picked up Taylor calling Ransome asking how the hell he let the FBI spot him with Adams, and Ransome muttering he should shut the fuck up. Then there's a call where Ransome tells the caller he can't talk, 'they're listening.'"

"Just out of curiosity," McFarland asked, "who was Ransome talking to?" There was a long pause, then Smith said he'd see McFarland in a few minutes and hung up.

When he arrived, he came in, closed the door and sat down in silence. McFarland waited and then finally asked, "So, what's going on? Can you tell me what you and Sarge are up to?"

"Yeah, let me explain why I'm being cautious. That call to Ransome, it was from a Philadelphia police captain briefing him on Blackstone. Somebody in Philadelphia is linked with the guys around the Deputy Chief."

McFarland leaned back with his eyes closed and groaned. "Christ, Hank, are they all corrupt? Do you think the beating was planned?"

"I doubt it. The Philly police are notorious for their street justice. Let's see what my colleagues find."

"And Sarge?"

"He found Adams."

"No way!"

"Good news, huh? There are a bunch of crooks and misfits who owe Sarge one way or another, and they all hated Blackstone. When Sarge put out the word he wanted Adams, well, they found the SOB in under twenty-four hours. The FBI has been looking for over a week and got nothing. Adams was living with a girlfriend and wearing a false beard if you can believe it."

"Did Sarge have to—arrest him? Does Cartwright know?"

"No, and no. Sarge told Adams there was a warrant for him, but that he probably wouldn't want to be in the hands of the MPD. He suggested Adams might want to go with him to give himself up to the FBI and try to work something out."

"Damn. That's brilliant."

"Thank your friend Sarge."

"Where is he?"

"We have Adams someplace safe. Sarge and a couple of my colleagues are working on turning the sonofabitch. I want to know what's going on before anyone knows we have him."

"Hank, you can't just hold him without access to due process."

"He knows he's free to end the conversation, and then we'll arrest him. We even told him he could call his lawyer if he wanted."

"What'd he say?"

"Apparently he just snorted. I think Mr. Cartwright has served his purpose. You and I, it seems, got totally spun, and Adams figured Cartwright would help his credibility. He's not the fool he likes to pretend to be."

"What have we gotten from him?"

"Not much as of this morning. He was still trying to sell the victim story. We've told him we've got Blackstone and that we have witnesses that put him at the Douglas murder site with Blackstone and Ransome. Mr. Adams doesn't have a lot more cards to play and he knows it. He needs us."

"You sure?"

"He could have told the agents to arrest him last night. He wants to keep talking."

This felt like the crux of the case. McFarland wanted to be in on it. "I want to talk to him."

"You already are. Every time he asks for something or whines about how hard it is Sarge tells him, 'Oh that ain't gonna fly, dude. Mr. McFarland is rip shit. He fought to get you a deal and negotiated with you in good faith. Right now, he'd just as soon drop you off with the MPD.'"

McFarland laughed. "I get to play tough cop?"

"For now, you're the boogeyman. When he decides to cooperate, we'll need you to wrap up the deal."

"Hank, I want to see Adams soon. Tomorrow. I need to make my own judgment. And then let's tie Taylor to that money and see if we can turn *him*."

"Yes sir, Boss."

Chapter 43
Inaugural Ball

"Ed, would you take Pennsylvania Avenue on the way home. I want to see the where the first couple walked this morning."

As they drove west on the broad avenue that connected the Capitol to the White House, the sun had set but a few purple clouds caught the last of the day's light. Little knots of people left from the big crowds that had lined the parade route wandered slowly along the wide sidewalks, perhaps looking for a restaurant not already fully booked. It looked peaceful. McFarland asked, "Were you working on the parade route this morning? How was it?"

"You heard what happened?" Ross asked. "The Secret Service was going nuts." McFarland was incredulous. He leaned forward from the back seat and said, "You mean he hadn't warned them?"

"I dunno what he told them, but when he had that limo stop and he and the First Lady got out, man the radio was crackling. I think some of the commanders wanted to tackle him and put him back where he belonged."

"That would have created a stir."

"Those guys are absolutely responsible for the president's safety. They're deadly serious about it. But they sure didn't know how to handle an impromptu stroll."

"But there had been news stories that Carter planned to walk."

"I guess the Secret Service thought they'd convinced him to forget about it."

"New President. New style."

They rode in silence. McFarland was amazed he was part of all of this and on his way home to meet his girlfriend to take her to the Inaugural Ball. The invitation said, "black tie." He imagined a glittering scene. Would there be dancing? The president and his cabinet nominees hoofing it in triumph? Power personified. The invitation was for 9:00 p.m., so they'd have time for dinner.

"Sir?"

"Ed?"

"You're going out tonight?"

"Yes."

"I doubt there's any problem, but it'd be best if you stay in crowds. You know, don't wander around on dark streets."

"Got it."

McFarland discovered Paul, not Sally, at the stove, cooking crab cakes. Grease was spattered on the stove, the wall behind it, and the floor in front. The flowers McFarland had sent were on the kitchen table in a coffee can, empty beer bottles were in the sink among the dirty dishes. When Paul cooked, things got messy.

"Smells good."

"My specialty, Boyo." Paul looked down his long nose at his friend and added, "Baby sister is upstairs struggling with her dress. She may need help…"

"No," Sally yelled from the top of the stairs, "it's all under control."

Paul said in a stage whisper, "The friend who lent her the dress is bigger than Sal, and, well, whatever she's doing seems to require an awful lot of safety pins."

"Just a few adjustments," she yelled, and then, "Oh, damn, damn, damn!"

Paul gestured with his head for McFarland to go upstairs. He found Sally draped in stiff folds of blue satin.

"How can I help?"

"A seamstress, I need a seamstress—and don't say anything. I know I should have figured this out before I came."

Paul appeared smiling benignly and handed McFarland a spatula.

"Roommate, go fry some crab cakes. And make a salad. SalSal, my love, stand still. We'll get this thing fixed up—maybe."

He stood at arm's length from her. The dress hung loose like a bed spread toga at a fraternity party. His sister looked utterly forlorn and perhaps about to cry. Paul chuckled and then started laughing uproariously, leaning his head back, pointing at his sister, and braying.

"That thing was cut for a Valkyrie, you idiot. Who lent it to you, Anna Russell? This is impossible—OK, get your clothes on, we're going shopping."

Sally just stood there. Paul unzipped the dress. "This would have looked awful even if it did fit. Get your clothes." He turned to the door and shouted happily down the stairs, "James Henry McFarland, stop what you're doing. Turn off the stove. We're going to buy a dress."

Sally, still standing in her slip, said, "You're crazy."

Paul looked at her thoughtfully and said, "Something small, and exquisite."

"No, I mean, we can't. It's too late, and I'm broke."

Paul scoffed. "The hell with that. Garfinckel's is five minutes away. It's Thursday, they're open late. Your boyfriend is a big-time prosecutor. He has plenty of money."

"I can't ask him…"

"Doesn't matter. He adores you."

Paul led them out to McFarland's car, Sally alternating between hilarity and embarrassment, her brother singing merrily, "We're off to buy a dress, a dress, a dress, a beautiful sexy dress." And that is what they did. Paul hustled them past the post-Christmas bargain racks and the overwrought velvet and sequin gowns straight to an elegant, long-sleeved, fitted black dress, with delicate silver trim on the cuffs and the high neck. "That," he told her. She looked at the price tag and turned away, eyes wide. Paul grabbed McFarland's shoulder and directed him to Sally.

"Jimmy, take charge. Your beloved needs a dress. *This* dress. She's afraid you're too cheap to buy it."

McFarland smiled, found a well-dressed, heavily made-up sales lady, and said, "I think my girlfriend needs help with that dress."

Sally emerged from the dressing room. Paul had found a deep green and purple silk scarf and tossed it over her shoulders. McFarland gaped. His heart nearly stopped. Sally was wide-eyed, holding the dress's price tag out in awe and horror.

Her big brother danced around her chortling and intoning "Here comes the princess!"

The saleswoman said, "Honey, you look so good in that thing, we oughta give it to you free."

By the time Jimmy and Sally set out for the ball, every towel in the house was on the floor of the bathroom, clothes were strewn about Jimmy's room, and no one had eaten. The two of them got into McFarland's old car giggling about Paul's skill in getting the problem resolved. McFarland shook his head,

"He was amazing. He just knew how to make things right, and he managed us incredibly deftly. The only thing he didn't do was turn this junk heap into a limo."

"I'm so sorry I showed up with that awful sack. I thought I'd been really clever borrowing a ball gown."

"You just needed a fairy godmother to make it all work out."

The ball was at the Woodley Park Sheraton on Connecticut Avenue, less than a ten-minute drive from McFarland's house. They arrived at the sprawling hotel to find a line of cars waiting to get into the garage. McFarland snorted impatiently. "This is ridiculous. I should have called a cab. Are you willing to walk?"

She thought about her high-heeled, red boots, and said, "Um, sure."

He made a U-turn, swerved into the neighborhood behind the hotel, and found a spot a few blocks away, across the street from what, judging by the array of diplomatic plates parked around it, must have been the site of a diplomatic reception.

"Shall we try to crash that party? We wouldn't have to walk as far."

"It's just a couple of blocks."

The ball at the Sheraton Woodley Plaza was one of seven inaugural balls happening across northwest Washington. They were not equal. The Carter campaign graded their friends according to their wealth and power. The A list received tickets to events at downtown hotels. The Sheraton Woodley was C list. Carter supporters like Joe McFarland, who had assiduously raised money from his partners for the Carter campaign, knew none of this. He was delighted when he received his invitation and pleased to be able to pass on these tickets to an elite event on to his son, although it irked him that after all he had done, he still had to pay five hundred dollars for each.

Jimmy and Sally walked in through the hotel lobby, wondering whether they should feel important, and if so, how they should act. A doorman pointed to the escalator down to the ballroom. They surrendered their coats, showed their tickets, and entered the cavernous venue. More than a thousand Carter supporters were already there: a pulsing mass of gowns and tuxedos. There may have been music, but the efforts of a thousand people to make themselves heard obliterated all other sound.

Somewhere at the edges of the enormous room frazzled bartenders served drinks. Long tables were littered with platters that had once held shrimp cocktail, little hot dogs, and small slices of spanakopita. None of that mattered. Even the Redskins offensive line could not have opened a path to the bar. They stood, stunned, until new arrivals pushing in from behind swept them forward. McFarland was embarrassed. He'd invited Sally to a ball. This was a mob. Sally worried that it might occur to McFarland that buying her a dress for this was a fraud.

Jimmy gestured to Sally and with mutual relief they pushed their way back out of the crowd. They found the hotel coffee shop and ordered hamburgers and beer.

"So that's the Inaugural Ball?" McFarland asked. "More like a rock concert without the music or the acid. What a scam. I wonder whether Jimmy and Rosalyn will make it."

Sally smiled and said, "We can say people were fighting to get in. We don't have to explain the room was so full you couldn't move past the door."

McFarland squeezed her arm. "I'm sorry about the whole evening."

"I'm not. I get to spend it with you. You bought me the most beautiful dress I've ever owned, and now we get to go home and go to bed together."

They walked in silence along the quiet, dark streets. A car turned off Calvert Street and came slowly down Woodley Terrace. McFarland froze, then pushed Sally behind him. "Stay back," he hissed. The driver opened his window. McFarland's breathing stopped.

"Are you folks about to pull out of a space down here? The parking is impossible tonight."

McFarland looked at the friendly face blankly, took a breath, gasped, and then laughed. "We—We're just a half a block down. The space is all yours."

Chapter 44
Adams and Taylor

McFarland stood in the shower feeling sad and telling himself he wasn't. He shaved, wrapped himself in a towel, and went back to get dressed. Sally, who'd gone back to sleep, woke, and extended a hand to him. It was Friday morning. She needed to get back to Philadelphia for rehearsals. She was sad and said so.

"I don't want to leave. This stinks!"

"Can't you stay the weekend?"

"No, Jimmy, you know I can't. People are counting on me. These performances are part of our degree requirements. They're a big deal."

"Stay 'til tomorrow. You can still make your quartet rehearsal."

"It's my career. I'm a performer. I have to commit to it."

"We can leave really early. I promise, I'll get you there for breakfast."

She smiled and agreed.

Officer Ross collected McFarland and then swung by the FBI office to get Smith. They drove to a squat, stolid building on 16th Street set unremarkably among a row of drab apartment blocks. Adams and his minders were in 5E, a minimally furnished, one bedroom apartment that looked out onto an alleyway. The hall was dingy, and when Sarge let them in, there was a smell of bodies, bacon, and stale cigarette smoke. McFarland reached out to shake Williams's hand but was enveloped in a hug and a greeted with a broad smile that left him briefly overwhelmed. Adams watched with interest, but said nothing, and McFarland barely nodded to him. Smith introduced the two agents and asked how everyone was doing. There was a heavy silence. Finally, Adams said, "We have not made a lot of progress, Agent Smith."

Smith nodded, and asked, "Do you want to shut the conversation down? We can book you and call your lawyer."

Williams, the agents, and McFarland all stared at Adams, whose eyes briefly flickered from Smith to McFarland.

"Is the deal you offered me still on the table?"

"No."

"Why not?"

McFarland laughed. "Cut the crap, Dan. You spun us a story and then disappeared. I don't think we can believe anything you tell us."

"No, I didn't lie, I just left some stuff out—because I was scared."

McFarland turned to Smith and said, "We're done here. He's an idiot. Let's just arrest him."

Williams looked at Adams sadly, and said, "I told you not to fuck with him. You are about to blow your only chance for a deal that protects you. They know you're lying, man, they have more evidence than they did before."

McFarland listened without expression and then reached for his coat.

Adams said, "What are you offering?"

"Nothing. You talk. I'll listen. If you persuade me you're telling the whole story, then we can talk."

"How do I know you'll treat me fairly."

"You don't, but you don't have any choice."

The phone rang. Smith looked quickly at his colleagues. "It's gotta be the office." The younger of the two minders answered and passed the receiver to Smith who listened, grimaced and asked, "Do you know any more than that?"

He listened again and then hung up. He gestured to McFarland to follow him into the bedroom and closed the door.

"Taylor is dead."

"Elliott Taylor?"

"Killed by a train pulling into the Farragut North Station."

"How?"

"No information yet."

"Shit! Another dead witness…or defendant."

"Don't assume. We don't know anything yet."

McFarland stood and thought and then told Smith, "Let's go over there. What do we do with Adams?"

"My guys and Williams can continue the conversation and let him know they have to be able to convince you to go along. Seems like he's decided he has to deal on our—on your terms." McFarland flung open the bedroom door, stood in front of Adams, and said, "See if you can tell a story that Sarge believes enough to call me and tell me I need to come back."

Smith called his office from the phone in the bedroom and determined that the Metro Transit Police and safety officials were on the scene. McFarland took Williams aside and told him what had happened. Twenty minutes later a Metro official, John Reed, led McFarland and Smith in through a maze of yellow warning tape to the east bound platform. A train was stopped and dark. A team of federal safety officials and their Metro counterparts were taking measurements and talking animatedly.

Reed said, "It's the first death—the first serious accident in Metro operations. It's terrible, just shocking."

Smith asked, "When?"

"Excuse me?"

"When did it happen?"

Reed instinctively looked at his watch and said, "Nine fifty-two am. Just at the end of rush hour."

"Who was the first on the scene?"

"There was a crowd of passengers and the operator. Poor man, he's a mess. This is a safe system, you know. Look how the platforms are built with two feet of rough granite at the edge to warn people to stand back and lights that flash when a train is entering the station."

"Who was the first official on the scene?"

"The station manager heard screams and he…"

"Who did he call?"

"He called operations. They had to know there was an accident so they could divert trains and…"

"Did anyone call the police?"

"I think someone called nine-one-one and asked for an ambulance, although it was pretty obvious the man was dead."

"Mr. Reed, I need to know who called the police, when the police arrived, and who was first on the scene."

"Oh. I'm not sure. I think the station manager, Dante Anthony, would know."

"Get him."

"I'll have him find you as soon as I…"

"Go and get him and bring him here, now."

Reed started to say something, looked at Smith's grim face, and scurried off down the platform gesturing to several Metro police officials. Smith groaned. There had been dozens of witnesses. He wondered whether anyone had gotten their names let alone preliminary statements. A woman in a parka came toward them and introduced herself as a reporter from the *Star*. She'd heard, she said, that they were from the FBI, and she wondered why they were there.

"You'll need to talk to Metro, Ma'am. They're in charge." After a few more attempts, she wandered back to the harsh glare of TV lights.

It took ten minutes after Reed had returned with Station Manager Anthony to get the names of the MPD officers on the scene and to learn that Mr. Anthony had called the MPD. He had also thought it might be useful to have a list of the names and contact information for the people on the platform when the accident happened, so he had recorded the details in a notebook. Smith thanked him, took the notebook and handed it to Reed.

"You'll need to keep this in your incident file, but I need you to make a copy for me."

"I'll send you one."

Smith shook his head and told Reed he would not need to send it since he would make a copy immediately and bring it to them at the station.

They watched as the crime scene officers, Metro police, and two technicians from the Medical Examiner's Office debated who should remove the body. A young woman appeared with the copy of the witness list and said Mr. Reed had asked her to bring it since he was very busy.

"I'm sure he is busy. Just be sure to tell Mr. Reed he'll have to come to the FBI office this afternoon to give a statement."

She looked terrified. "Oh, but he can't, he'll be in meetings."

"Shall I send an agent to get him?"

The woman recoiled. Smith ignored her and turned to McFarland. "Let's go before the TV crews notice us. Once the body is gone, they'll start looking around."

"You need to take charge of this, Hank, before…"

"I'm on it. Even if we trusted the MPD, they'd fight with Metro over jurisdiction. I'd appreciate it if you'd brief the Boss so he can make sure DOJ will back me up. We need to get to those witnesses and the train operator before they hear so many versions of the story, they forget what they saw."

McFarland nodded and said, "I'm going to push the Conway counsel, Maddox. They have two dead employees. They need to stop stonewalling." McFarland paused, realizing they were standing at the entrance to the Farragut North Station where eight days before, they had stood discussing their first meeting with Adams. They'd let Adams get away from them, and Taylor was dead. If Sarge hadn't found Adams, they'd be nowhere. Smith saw that McFarland was distracted and edgy.

"And…?"

"We keep letting events get ahead of us. We need to push harder. Can you make sure we get to the Deputy Chief, Rankin, and Ransome? Today."

"With pleasure, Mr. McFarland."

McFarland hadn't even hung up his coat before Donatelli strolled in. It annoyed McFarland. How the hell did the man know?

Mrs. Bynum said, "They want you down the hall. You're not even to go to the Gents." Donatelli cracked up. McFarland didn't. The Boss had trusted him with this case. What did he have? A bunch of dead witnesses, another in a coma, and a scheming Irish huckster who would invent whatever got him a 'get out of jail free' card.

In the Boss's office, he found Rushford sitting at the conference table, obviously angry, the Boss looking, well what the hell did that look mean? Quizzical? And a twitchy looking guy in a three-piece suit whom the Boss introduced as the 'Chief-of-Staff'. Whose Chief-of-Staff? The twitchy man muttered, "Until Judge Bell is confirmed I'm just a designee."

The Boss smiled mildly—not an encouraging look for those who knew him—and said, "Designee Jefferson, this is assistant U.S. attorney McFarland who wrote that briefing memo sitting in front of you. It needs to be updated. Mr. McFarland, would you bring us up to date?"

McFarland tried to remember what had happened since he finished the memo.

"We've found Adams, Taylor is dead. We've tracked the money that was found in Blackstone's apartment in Philadelphia to a bank here in D.C. where Conway keeps its local accounts, but so far they are stonewalling."

"Admirably succinct. Now a little more context please."

He told them about finding and questioning Adams, the apparent compromise of the wiretaps, the circumstances of Taylor's death, and his concern that he had moved too slowly against the deputy chief and his guard.

The twitchy man seemed unsure of how to respond.

Rushford said, "Caution isn't foolish when you don't have the evidence. Will Adams give us Ransome and Taylor?"

"I think so."

"Will he testify?"

"That is the only circumstance under which I would recommend a deal. He certainly doesn't want to be on his own in the prison system."

McFarland was watching the Boss as he spoke, something Rushford noticed, amused. Rushford said, "After the Olsen story the press are sure to connect this death to the case, and someone will oblige them by spinning lurid stories of why Taylor wanted to die—or had to die."

The Boss smacked his lips and said, "Oh, good, a mini-feeding frenzy. It's been a while. Mr. Jefferson, Judge Bell is going to be sworn in as Attorney General, and he will walk into that building across the street almost naked. No deputy or assistant AG's will be confirmed, perhaps for weeks. And he's going to have other priorities than a bunch of sleazy grifters and crooked cops. I suggest you leave the press and the investigation to us. We'll keep you discretely in the loop. If the need arises, you can blame us for screwing up." The twitchy face froze, and then Jefferson almost smiled.

There was a knock. Mrs. Thomas came in and handed a note to Jefferson, who read it and did, in fact, smile. "Gentlemen, Judge Bell was confirmed unanimously by the Senate twenty minutes ago. The president wants to swear in his attorney general this afternoon, and I need to go organize the event. Thank you for the briefing. I'll bring the judge up to date. I am quite sure he will agree that it is your case, and we will back you up."

After Jefferson had hastened out, Rushford shook with mirth. "He ain't coming back here if he can avoid it."

The Boss sat still and unsmiling. It was rumored he had wanted to head the Criminal Division, but Judge Bell had passed him over for a protégé of the senior senator from New York. He glanced around the room, and said, "Jimmy, it's time to question the principals and then get arrest warrants. Smith and his partner can question the Deputy Chief, but don't go after him, not yet, not unless you have to. Let's see if he'll come to us. You go to the bank for the information you want and let Conway try to block you if they can stand the heat. Vic, let's get ahead of the story. Work with your friends to warn them off anything too bizarre."

“I think Jimmy should call Anderson,” Vic responded. “Anderson’s tip got us started on Olsen and Taylor. He didn’t give it to me, he gave it to Jimmy. They can talk on background, but I think Anderson will appreciate it, and Jimmy will learn something.”

The Boss nodded. “Do it. Let’s get on it.”

As they filed out, the Boss pointed Jimmy to a chair and closed the door. He stood in silence than sat behind his desk and swiveled his chair back and forth. After several long moments, he said, “Four, maybe five, deaths, and implications of corruption in major institutions. Are you concerned the case might be getting out of control?”

“Yes sir, I am.”

“Well, it may be, but it’s yours. Go after it. There’s no formula, just sink your teeth in their hind quarters and hang on.”

McFarland almost laughed thinking about his teeth in the Deputy Chief’s hindquarters.

“Thank you, I will.”

How had the Boss known, McFarland wondered, that he was sitting there thinking they probably would and should bring in someone else? The Boss looked up at the ceiling and spoke slowly.

“One piece of advice about our friend Anderson. He’s a very good reporter. He has fabulous sources. You can trust his word, *but* he is a journalist, he’s not your friend. He knows that he benefits from our trust, and that we use him to get the story out, but his job is to get the story not to help you get a conviction.”

Chapter 45
Leaking

McFarland walked the thirty yards of polished granite back to his office buoyed by the Boss's unequivocal support. The day was fading outside. He had a lot to do. He picked up his phone and dialed his home number. Sally answered.

"McFarland-Brown residence." Which Brown, he wondered.

"Sally, you doing ok?"

"I miss you."

"I'm having a rough day. Taylor is dead. Things are completely crazy. I won't be home for a while, and I don't see how I can drive you to Philly tomorrow."

There was a silence, then Sally said, "Jimmy, you promised you'd get me there. I counted on you."

"Yeah, I know I did, but I'm leading a major investigation. I have responsibilities."

"So do I," she said, and hung up.

What did that mean? He had another death to deal with. She must understand that.

He asked Mrs. Bynum to get the manager of the bank where Conway had its accounts, a Mr. Wright. She seemed able to get through to anyone, and he was starting to enjoy the advantage gained by making the person he was calling wait while Mrs. Bynum put the call through to him. He wanted this man uneasy. When the call came, he didn't bother to introduce himself.

"Mr. Wright, I am investigating several murders connected with the large-scale theft of government funds. Currency found in the possession of one of the perpetrators came from your branch. It is essential for us to confirm which account those funds came from and who withdrew them. Agents will be there with a subpoena very soon, and I need the information immediately."

"Does this have to do with the terrible accident in the Metro today?"

McFarland let the question hang. "Can we count on your cooperation?"

"Yes sir, of course. I'll have to check…"

"The agents can answer your questions."

"It's past four o'clock. It'll be difficult…"

"They're on their way."

He called Harry Maddox, the Conway counsel in San Francisco, and learned he was out of the office. Where? In Washington. Would he be in the Conway Washington office? Yes, probably. McFarland sat and organized his tumultuous thoughts: We get evidence that money given to Blackstone is from a bank Conway uses; Maddox comes to Washington; Taylor falls in front of a train. Jeezus, this is unbelievable.

He called Taylor's office and got Kelsey. He asked if she was OK.

"Yes—well, no. I don't understand. Mr. Taylor left here this morning and he seemed ok. Why would he jump in front of a train?"

"When did he leave, Kelsey?"

"He got a call around nine-fifteen and left right away."

"Who was the call from?"

"I don't know."

That seemed improbable. "You answer his calls and don't get a name? Come on, Kelsey."

"No—I…"

"An FBI agent will interview you. You need to tell them the truth. Is Mr. Maddox there?"

"No, he left about half an hour ago."

"Do you know where he went?"

"I think he went to his hotel, and then he has a dinner at the Palm."

"We'll find him there."

"It's a personal dinner."

"Oh, I don't think the agents will mind."

He was reasonably certain Kelsey would alert Maddox. That was fine. He was interested in seeing how the man would react when a pair of FBI agents interrupted his dinner.

Donatelli stuck his head in to say he should call Anderson. "Suggest that he look at the connections between Conway, the fraud, the murders, and Taylor."

McFarland stiffened. "No, no, Vic, that's way off base."

"Just make sure he's pointed in the right direction."

"Aren't we prosecuting Olsen for leaking the same sort of stuff?"

"Anderson already knows Taylor was involved. He gave us that story. And he knows we're looking at the Deputy Chief."

"Jesus, Vic..."

"Uh-uh, not from me, kiddo, not from me. He's a reporter. He's digging. You serve the truth by directing him."

McFarland didn't think of himself as a leaker. He'd never considered Deep Throat a hero. Donatelli reminded him that he was acting on instructions from the Boss, and they were trying to make sure the coverage didn't go weird. "There is nothing wrong," Donatelli said, "with giving a good reporter accurate information."

"Why not on the record, then?"

McFarland knew that was a cheap shot, and Donatelli reacted. He leaned toward McFarland, eyes narrowed, blotches of color staining his smooth face, and said, "Don't play sanctimonious with me. You angled for this assignment. This is part of the job. We enforce the law, and we want people to know and understand what we're doing. Perception matters. Anderson defines the perception."

Had he, McFarland wondered, 'angled for' this assignment? He leaned away from Donatelli's anger and said, "Let's talk about what I can actually say and keep my self-respect."

When McFarland, a yellow pad with careful notes placed neatly on the desk blotter in front of him, reached Anderson, he could hear the laughter in his voice as he said, "Mr. McFarland, for a man who doesn't like talking to reporters you and I talk a lot."

"Yeah, we seem to."

Anderson waited, then asked, "Was Taylor murdered?"

"I don't know, he may have been."

"Why?"

McFarland was taken aback. The question was so obvious and so important. He forgot his careful calculations of the appropriate boundaries for the conversation. He said, "We were getting closer to a real connection between Conway and the murders."

McFarland wished they were meeting face-to-face. He wanted to know how Anderson was reacting. If he were the reporter, he would have followed-up on that answer. Instead, Anderson asked, "Do you trust Taylor's assistant, Olsen's girlfriend Kelsey?"

"You think the naïve little girl stuff is an act?"

"I do. You know she's from San Francisco?"

"A city sunk in sin?"

"The Conway office sent her to DC to work for Taylor."

"To watch him?"

Anderson mumbled something and then said. "Ask her, or even better, get Farwell to ask her."

"You know Smith and Farwell?"

"I've known Hank for years. My sources know Farwell. She's gonna be a star."

McFarland stared at the streetlight glow outside the dark window. He had prepared to carefully dispense information without disclosing too much, but it was Anderson who was disclosing. What was he after? "What do you know about how the San Francisco office is involved?" he asked.

Anderson responded with his own question: "Why is Maddox in town? Why was he at the White House the afternoon of the inauguration? Helping them unpack?"

"How in hell do you know that?"

"This is the new era of openness. We check the White House logs every day." McFarland looked at the notes in front of him, pushed them away, and said, "We have identified at least one person involved in all three killings, and we have some evidence against another. We tracked the one we identified to Philadelphia. The Philly police got him, and they almost beat him to death. The FBI searched the apartment where he was staying and found nearly five thousand in new bills—his prints on them."

"Can you track it?"

"We served a subpoena on the bank the money came from this afternoon. It's the same branch where Conway does its local banking." McFarland heard Anderson whistle. "You," Anderson said, "are starting to turn over some big rocks."

McFarland didn't mention they had found other prints, yet to be identified, on the wad of bills, quaintly stuffed in a sock. After the call, he sat trying to figure out whether he'd been played. He'd given Anderson information he'd never intended to reveal, but he'd gotten more than he'd given. It was as if they were developing a tacit understanding, a set of implicit rules for their conversations. He started to write a memo of the call, thought better of it, and wandered down to see whether the Boss was still in. Rushford saw him and yelled through his open door, "Friday night. It's his poker night. You wanted to pass something on?"

McFarland described the call with Anderson, Rushford nodding when he heard about Maddox's White House visit. McFarland asked whether he should make any written record of the call and Rushford just put his head in his hands, shaking, perhaps with laughter.

It was long past eight o'clock when he got home. He was tired and uneasy, and he needed to talk to Sally about why she had hung up on him. It had not occurred to him that she might not be there. He unlocked the now fortified door, went in, dropped his coat and briefcase, and yelled, "Hello!" The living room was dark, the kitchen empty. He went upstairs. "Sal?" His room was dark as was the little guest room. Paul's door was closed. He knocked and went in. The room reeked. Paul had his headphones on and his eyes closed.

"Where's Sally?"

Paul looked at him balefully.

"Gone."

"Gone where?"

Paul rolled his eyes back as if he were trying to recall, but his lips were compressed, and though he was obviously stoned, when McFarland looked back his eyes were blazing. He remembered years before, one late night when they had first roomed together, Paul had been sitting with a gentle smile on his face, listening to music and apparently doodling. McFarland had told him to kill the music. Paul had looked taken aback, "Why?"

"I'm trying to understand John Rawls on justice and you're daydreaming."

Paul's eyes had blazed then, too. He'd said, "I'm doing mathematics. Don't fucking assume whatever you're doing must be more important."

Now he said, "When you blew her off, Sally got the last train back to Philly."

"I didn't blow her off. There was another death. I have to…"

"Yeah, right, you're an important man and you have serious work to do."

"I do."

"And…?" McFarland turned and walked out, thinking, 'I'm an idiot.' He walked back into Paul's room. "What time was the train?"

"Seven o'clock, I think."

He looked at his watch. It was just past nine. She wouldn't be in Philly yet. Should he leave a message with one of her roommates? No, better just arrive so as not to give her the chance to tell him to go to hell. He changed into jeans, made a thermos of coffee, grabbed cold chicken, a piece of cheese, and two elderly apples from the refrigerator and headed for Philadelphia. Screw the case.

Chapter 46
Dan Adams' Story

It had been tedious. Trained in plodding patience, Adams' interrogators were losing theirs. For hours after Smith and McFarland abruptly left the little apartment, he dilly-dallied. He repeated bits of the ghost workers scheme that they'd heard before, asked for coffee or cigarettes, went to the bathroom. He was always shading the truth. Everything he said was a bit askew from what they already knew. The agents were meticulous and infuriating in their own way, like perseverative children. Adams led them off the subject, they pulled him back. They asked about Taylor, Adams started to answer, but then meandered, speculating on the prevalence of corruption. He seemed to swerve aside every time the subject was Taylor.

Williams watched, trying to understand. Adams knew he needed a deal. If he continued to jerk them around, Jimmy would pull the plug. Williams imagined holding the man by his ankles and shaking him, cigarettes, change, reading glasses, wallet slipping out of his pockets.

He said quietly, "Stop fucking with us. You know you ain't fooling nobody. What did you and Taylor have going?"

"You need to ask Taylor that."

"Taylor is dead. He fell in front of a Metro train this morning. That's why Smith and McFarland left."

Adams gave a low moan of anguish and crumpled forward onto the table. He looked at Williams, as if to challenge him, then covered his face and sobbed, apparently shattered by the news. Why did he care? Just another omen of the danger he was in? But this was pain, not fear.

Williams leaned toward him and asked, "What's going on, man, what was Taylor to you?"

Adams looked up, face blotchy with emotion and said, "He was my friend…"

"He was management. You said you didn't know him. You can't have been that close."

"You don't know shit, Sergeant." Adams was breathing hard, shaking, tears tracking down his face. "For Chrissake, he was my brother-in-law." Silence.

Williams held his eyes, and said quietly, "I'm sorry, Dan. Your little sister?" He glared at the agents to warn them to remain silent.

"I need to call her. I need to go to her."

"No, man, that ain't happening. You are stuck here with us. Help us find the SOB's who killed him?"

"I need to talk to her."

"Tell us the story. The truth this time." One of the agents tried to reach McFarland to let him know what Adams had disclosed. The message lay on Mrs. Bynum's desk. McFarland never saw it.

*****

By dinner time, Adams was seething with anger, demanding to speak to his sister, calling them heartless bastards.

Williams exploded. "You weaselly son of a bitch! You stole money, you conspired with murderers, you tried to throw us off the track, and now you blame us because your little sister's hurting. You're a gutless lying slimeball. Your sister deserves better."

The two agents told Smith later that it was an incredibly effective piece of interrogation. Williams was thinking about Little Ernie with no father and Claire with no husband. Ernie had been killed for trying to ensure justice. Taylor was a crook connected with a bunch of thugs. Adams drooped, settled, and then began to tell his story, almost as if he were reciting it.

"I'm the second oldest of six kids. I grew up in Southie—South Boston. My daddy worked construction and was big in the Union. Family. Church. Union. Country. We didn't have much, but he had a job, and in the thirties that was something. My older brother and I both quit school when Daddy found us work. We had a world. When Japan attacked Pearl Harbor, my daddy went right out and enlisted. He made it through the whole damn war in the Navy. As soon as he could, my older brother went out, enlisted in the Marines, and got killed."

Williams wondered, was this another diversion? He thought about his war. Fighting for nothing. Plenty of death. No honor.

Adams continued, "I was the oldest. It was my job to take care of the family. By the time they started drafting for Korea, Daddy was goddamned if I was going to get killed. He worked through the Union and our congressman and got me into the Seabees. Moving dirt, digging holes, building airfields. I was good at it. I loved it. I was good with people. I came home a sergeant figuring I was going to be someone. I married, had a family, started working my way up in the Union. The old guys knew my dad and they liked me. But it was slow. I got restless. I was stuck there waiting for the old guys to die off."

He looked up, eyes dull, face sad. Williams sat absolutely still and hoped neither of the agents would feel he had to ask a question. This was a story Adams needed to tell. Adams lit a cigarette, exhaled, compressed his lips, took another drag.

"In the Summer of 1968, I wangled a trip to a national meeting of the Union leadership in Houston. I thought it would be about strategy, organizing, wages. Crap no, it was a complete cluster fuck. A bunch of old guys with big guts fighting over whether to endorse Nixon. Humphrey had been a friend of labor since way back, but Humphrey had turned against the war and sided with the hippies. They hated war protesters and civil rights activists. They really liked George Wallace, but figured he'd just steal votes from Nixon."

"One afternoon I heard some guys gossiping about the subway in Washington. It was going to be the biggest union job in the country, and there was a fight about who'd run the DC office. I thought, *What the hell,* and I began to go after the job. I was a 'good boy' from a union family, and I'd been doing stuff for union officials for years. They wanted somebody they could control, and they were damned if they'd let themselves be pressured to put in a Black man. Half the city of Washington had burned down in the riots. The city was going to have a Black government, the rank and file were increasingly Black. I guess they thought that being an Irish kid from Southie I'd hold the line."

He looked defiantly at Williams, who sat impassively, thinking, this sounds might be the truth.

Adams' face grew animated. "They gave me the job. Told me I was their 'boy'. It worked good for me. I'd wrecked my marriage. The Italian mob guys were trying to get control of the local. And I was just sick of—I don't know—being a blue-collar Irish guy in Boston. I got in my car and drove south. Flying high. I had my own office. People working for me calling me 'Mr. Adams'."

He sighed, tapping one hand on the table, and drawing an invisible line with the other. He seemed more and more a man who loved to tell stories.

Conway began digging tunnels, leveling ground, and laying track where the line would be above-ground. Big machines. Operating engineers, carpenters, iron and steel guys, and an army of laborers—our guys. I was like a pig in shit. I was out on the job sites every day. Important work, you know. The membership was growing fast, and to those guys I *was* the union. The foremen and engineers on the job got to know me and figured out they could rely on me to solve problems.

"In nineteen seventy-one, I met Elliott Taylor at a party. He was a golden boy from the West Coast who'd just made vice president, and I was a high school dropout from Southie, trying to keep a bunch of construction workers happy. When I first met him, he was stoned, funny and easy going. Before we ever realized he was management and I was Union, we got to be friends. We were both recently divorced and both liked to party. One weekend in '73, my baby sister Chrissy came to visit. She'd always been trouble—in a wild, fun way. She went out with me and Elliott, and they began teasing and flirting. Before the evening was over, I saw that they were—well—it was pretty obvious they were crazy about each other. She moved down to DC, and in '74 they got married. My mom was furious, 'cause he's Episcopal, but I was happy. She'd have a good life. He's a good—he was—a good man. Elliot's been good to her, and he's bailed me out a couple of times when I got behind on my child support."

He stopped as if that were the end of the story. Williams wondered whether they should take a break but thought they had to keep Adams' head in his narrative. He finally asked, "You told us how the ghost worker scheme started after the cave-in and the hurricane. Taylor knew about it?"

"Shit, yes, the whole world knew. We talked about it. Every job I ever worked outside of the military a bunch of people were getting paid off or stealing. This was just the same old, same old, except it got big, and the company benefited almost more than anybody. The whole thing was cool except for that doddering prig, Douglas. He didn't know how things worked and he couldn't leave it alone. He went to Elliott and was told to leave it. Nah, he was a sad, lonely old guy who couldn't let things be. I think we could have shut him up—or scared him off, but he started talking to that Black lawyer, Hills."

Williams stiffened. "How'd Douglas meet Hills."

"I'm not sure. I heard Douglas was at a Senate hearing trying to see if he could get some senator's ear. He couldn't get close to the members, but I guess he saw Hills testify and decided to talk to him. Hills was a different kind of problem. Douglas worked for Conway, he could be squashed, but Hills worked for WMATA, and if WMATA decided to make a big deal of it, we had a problem. I told Elliott to leave it to me and let the Union take the hit if the whole thing blew up. I thought he agreed, but he heard Hills was slated to talk to the Senate Committee staff, and he wanted something done fast. I think he maybe got pressure from the suits in San Francisco. He went to the Deputy Chief, and Herman Dixon is a guy who likes to have people in his debt. He sent his nephew to warn Hills off—I guess they'd been buddies. That turned into a complete cock-up and the Deputy Chief asked Rankin to get it sorted."

Williams felt throbbing in his temples and rage seething in his gut. Adams leaned back casually, gesturing expressively as he told his story: A proud thief resentful of anyone who would blow the whistle on a beautiful scheme to steal the government's money. Ernie was a problem to be 'solved', Dixon a 'cock-up' to be corrected. Williams gripped the edge of the table. He couldn't hear what Adams was saying. He could barely breathe. He wanted to lift the table and smash it on this smug, uncaring Irishman. He stared at the dark window behind Adams, took a slow breath, and carefully relaxed his hands.

Adams saw all this and seemed interested, stopping his tale and asking, "Did you know those guys?" The two agents, seated off to the side, shifted in their seats.

"Yeah, I did. We served together in Viet Nam."

"I'm sorry, Sergeant."

"Are you?"

They sat in silence. It was growing dim, but no one had moved to turn on the lights.

Williams asked, "Did you hear what had happened?"

"Eventually. I heard that Hills had been shot. I asked Elliott. He just shook his head and said it was really screwed up. Then I heard when Douglas's body was found up at Fort Totten, and I went and saw Elliott at home and told him he had to tell me what was going on. I sorta lost it. Chrissy was screaming at us like the washerwoman she's descended from. Elliott took me out on a walk. He wanted to make sure Chrissy didn't know anything—as if. Rankin had sent his guy, Detective Ransome, and an ex-cop who's been busted out of the MPD—to 'talk' to Hills and convince him it wasn't in his interest to pursue this case."

Williams could hardly bear to listen. He said quietly, "That was never going to work."

Adams again looked at him with open interest. He waited and then went on. "They were in civilian clothes—suits, hats, overcoats and scarves—and it sounds like Hills maybe thought they were union guys and let them right in. He told them no way was he backing off, he had a sworn duty, and he'd do it. The story is that he called them dumb thugs. Ransome slugged him. The ex-cop was on some sort of speed and pulled his gun, hit him with it, and then shot him."

Williams held himself rigid to keep from screaming—or sobbing. He saw the two burly figures in their overcoats standing over Ernie, and Ernie just couldn't back down. Even if he had known that Blackstone was stoned and out of control, he wouldn't have backed down. Dixon had known what happened. When he and Jimmy questioned Dixon, it had eaten at him. He was going to tell them. But Al Dixon was just another problem Rankin sent Ransome and Blackstone to take care of, and then, even better put on him.

Adams was still talking, saying they'd roughed up Douglas, and then decided they couldn't risk having him go to the cops. "They just threw him in that hole to be done with him."

"No, Dan, that's bullshit! They chose that footing hole because it was going to get filled with concrete the next morning."

"I don't know, maybe they did."

"You told them. You were at that job site earlier that day."

Adams gazed at Williams calmly and responded, "They didn't tell me what they were going to do, but they asked to meet with me out there, and it was obvious. Douglas knew that Hills was going to blow the whistle. We'd heard that Douglas had been to see your DA friend."

"How?"

"That schmuck, Olsen. Elliott was panicked. He called the Deputy Chief who told him to keep his fucking mouth shut, but he went ahead and met with Olsen in that ridiculous parking lot."

Chapter 47
Philadelphia Quest

Late on the Friday evening after the inauguration, there was still traffic on I 95; a stream of oncoming headlights in the southbound lanes, and a swirling flock of taillights in front heading north. McFarland thought he might get to Sally's apartment by eleven if he didn't get lost. The chicken he'd grabbed from the refrigerator was old and cold, but he was ravenous and wolfed it down. Why had it taken him so long to realize he was in love with Sally? He thought of walking through Georgetown with her feeling happy, and of sitting, transfixed, as she explained the Hindemith Concerto, full of passion and humor. It had taken him a long time to allow himself to think of her as someone other than Paul's little sister who wrecked their games and begged to come when they went to a ball game. A brat. And now an incredibly sexy, funny, and talented young woman.

This trip was a quest. He needed Sally to know how much he loved her. She meant more to him than the damn case. He was walking away from it amidst a crisis to—to tell her he was wrong, and he was sorry. Sorry? He wasn't just sorry, he felt desperate. He could have called to say he was sorry. But he needed to make this trip. Not just talk, be. He needed to show *himself* he cared this much. He imagined arriving at the door to her apartment. A big concrete and glass building, he thought. One of her roommates would answer the door. He'd introduce himself and ask for Sally.

Would the roommate try to protect her? Or yell, "Sal, your friend Jimmy..." or maybe, "the Idiot is here. Do you want to see him?" He'd get himself in the door somehow. Would her roommates clear out so they could talk? *This,* he thought, *is crazy. I won't know what I feel until I see her. Maybe I should kneel and beg?*

He tried to control his galloping thoughts—to force himself to review where they were on the case. He pictured the dreary little apartment where they were holding Adams with its plastic furniture, bare floors and empty white walls. *Sarge,* he thought, *would be sitting in brooding silence while the two agents asked plodding questions.* He had believed the story Adams told them when they met in Cartwright's office, convinced by Adams' evident fear. Was any of it real? He wondered what Maddox had said when Smith and Farwell showed up at his table in the Palm? Or had Kelsey warned him so he could go elsewhere? What about Rankin and Ransome and the DC? He was an idiot indeed to disappear just now. Oh, the hell with that. He let his mind wander, recalling the utter joy of having Sally's smooth warm body curled up against him after they had made love.

He found the apartment without much difficulty. It was on the ground floor of a dingy, three-story brick building in a small development. He rang the bell, his heart racing. A tall, square shouldered woman, whom he recognized from Sally's description as Dana, a French horn student, opened it looking uncertain, but friendly.

"Hi, you must be Dana, I'm Jimmy."

Her face brightened. "Oh, I'm so glad to meet you. You're as—you're just as handsome as she said you were." Of course, his face got hot. How in hell can you stay cool when your face lights up like a neon sign saying you're embarrassed?

"Is Sally here?"

Of all the answers he'd considered, he had not imagined the one he got. "No, she's not. We thought she was in Washington with you?"

He was stunned. She hadn't come home? She wouldn't have lied to Paul about where she was going. The train, the goddamned train, it must have been delayed. Dana was watching his obvious confusion with dismay.

"Was she going to meet you here, Jimmy?"

"I was going to meet her, but she didn't know I was coming."

Dana looked at him, her face puckered in disbelief.

McFarland said, "It's complicated. I was a jerk. She told her brother she was catching the last train to Philly. I came to apologize."

"Oh—that's so romantic."

"Not if I can't find her. Can I use your phone?"

"Of course. Come on in. Carla, Jimmy's here! Sally's Jimmy."

He was beyond blushing. He went to the phone, found the Amtrak number and learned that the train from Washington had arrived over an hour ago. He was frantic. She could be a hostage. The two roommates watched him as he sat trying to think what he could do and whether he should call Smith's emergency number. Paul would know. If the son of a bitch had let him drive up here when he knew she wasn't heading for Philly… He called Paul. Sally answered. He couldn't speak.

"Jimmy?" She heard choking silence and mumbled, "Jimmy, I'm so sorry."

"You're—sorry? You can't be sorry. I was a complete fucking jerk."

"Yeah, you were, but…"

"What the hell are you doing there?"

"I got as far as Baltimore, and I decided to come back. I was crying too much. It was embarrassing."

"Oh, God, I thought they might have gotten you."

"Who?"

"Don't leave, I'm coming back."

"Tell Carla and Dana to make you some coffee."

"Wait up."

"Paul's going to drive me back to Philly tomorrow early."

"No, no, he doesn't have to."

"When you see the stack of messages from Sarge, and some really pissy lawyer named Maddox, and your FBI girlfriend…"

"No, it doesn't matter—I mean, you're more important."

Now she was speechless. He heard Paul shouting in the background. "Hang up the damn phone so he can start driving back."

He waited restlessly while the roommates made coffee and assembled PB&Js. Carla asked what was happening.

"All good," he said, and gathering sandwiches and coffee, floated to his car.

Chapter 48
To the Wolves

All three of them were bleary-eyed when Paul and Sally said goodbye to Jimmy and set out for Philadelphia at six the next morning. McFarland saw Officer Ross waiting just down the block. He went over and stood by the driver side window.

"How long have you been here, Ed? I had no idea you were waiting."

"Agent Smith said I should track you down and bring you in." Ross grinned.

"Am I under arrest?"

"Pretty much. You know Agent Smith when he gets set on something."

Twenty minutes later, showered and shaved, McFarland looked wistfully at the espresso machine and dutifully headed out the door. Officer Ross had evidently read his mind, telling him as he climbed in, "They said to assure you they'd have a good breakfast and coffee you'd like waiting at the FBI office."

McFarland, smiled, then thinking about the night before, he chuckled. "I was," he told Ross, "up all night."

"They figured that out. Agent Farwell chatted with your girlfriend, and I believe she got pretty much the whole story."

McFarland slapped his head and groaned. "Jeez, I can't go off the map even for a night."

"They are FBI agents. They were concerned when they couldn't find you."

McFarland was overcome with a wave of gratitude for the people he worked with. Why was everyone so good to him?

*****

Sergeant Williams had been concerned and impatient the night before when McFarland was driving north to find Sally. It was time to put Adams in front of a grand jury and lock-in his story. Williams had an uneasy feeling that someone had figured out they had Adams. He took elaborate precautions when a scruffy guy in an old overcoat arrived at the door with the Moo Shu Pork, Fried Rice, and Kung Pao Chicken they'd ordered. Williams insisted that Adams lock himself in the bathroom and stood hulking in the doorway to block the man's view of the apartment.

He had learned to trust his instincts.

They had eaten the chicken greasy and the pork cold, drunk beer, and argued about why Wes Unseld wasn't throwing up more shots and whether the Bullets could make the playoffs. Williams was sure they would.

"They got defense. That'll get them there. Hayes scores when he has to." One of the agents, an avid fan, screeched at that. "They gotta put the ball through the hoop. That's why it's called basketball."

As soon as they were done with dinner Williams told the two agents, "I think someone's figured out we're here."

"Nah, Sergeant, no one in our shop would leak it, and the MPD doesn't know."

"Yeah, but I got a feeling."

The older of the two agents asked what Williams had seen.

"That deliveryman gave me the creeps. He didn't check that this was the right apartment, he didn't count the money I gave him, and he didn't wait for a tip."

"How in hell would they know we'd order Chinese food?"

"I don't know, but we need to be careful. Maybe move."

*****

At 6:45 the next morning as Williams made his way to the FBI office, Washington's streets and sidewalks were empty. It was a January Saturday. The winter sun, just rising above Washington's low skyline, was bright. It did not loosen the knot of dread in his gut. He found Farwell unwrapping packages of bacon, eggs, grits, potatoes, biscuits, hash and a quart container of thick cream gravy. When McFarland arrived, he was met with shouts of derision. Lover boy is back. Doesn't know if he's coming or going. Talk about fruitless quests. Sir Lancelot trekking the Interstate in pursuit of Guinevere while she was safe at home.

Farwell shook her finger at him. "You should have just told us you had to drive her back to Philly."

He held up his hands and said, "I'm complaining to the director, Farwell, there's got to be something improper about using all your finely honed federal investigative skills to wheedle private information out of my girlfriend."

"Somebody had to figure out what the hell was going on."

They settled down to eat breakfast.

Williams said, "I got a bad feeling, Jimmy. I think they may have figured out where we've got Adams."

McFarland frowned. "How?"

"I'm not sure. They could have followed you and Officer Ross yesterday morning."

Smith nodded. "A sergeant gets home from Viet Nam alive, he damn well has to have good instincts. The last thing we want is some sort of fricking shootout."

McFarland asked, "You think they followed us yesterday morning?"

Smith shrugged. "It could be. I'll ask Officer Ross to be more careful. If they're watching your house, that's important information. And we can think about moving him."

Williams recounted his interrogation of Adams. When he told them Taylor was married to Adams' sister, McFarland closed his eyes and moaned. "Oh, shit! Did he ever play us? I bought the whole terrified act. He was just trying to protect Taylor."

"Apparently, and it worked. Threw us right off the trail."

"Sarge, did he say why he bolted?" McFarland asked.

"He said he hoped that we'd think he was dead and we'd go after Ransome and Rankin."

"How much of it do you believe?"

"What he told us fits with things we know that he doesn't know we know. But I don't believe we've gotten the whole story. He's a natural liar."

Smith and Farwell described calling on Rankin and Ransome. Nothing. They were Ready. Rankin at his desk, Ransome standing behind him. Rankin announced they wouldn't answer any questions, and if the agents didn't have arrest warrants, they should leave. They had looked for the DC, but he was not in his office.

Williams, frowning, asked, "Did the ladies in the DC's office tell you where he was or when he'd be back?"

"Nothing," Smith said, "but I imagine he told them not to give out any information."

"The last time I went in to see him," said Williams, "there was all that tension between him and Rankin. We ought to find him."

McFarland nodded his head in agreement. "With what you got from Adams, we can get warrants for all three and bring in Ransome and Rankin. Then we'll find the DC and interview him. Do we have anything new from the wire taps."

"Nothing."

McFarland sighed. "What went on with Maddox? Sally said he was belligerent when he called last night."

Smith turned to Farwell and she grinned. "Yeah, belligerent, that would be Maddox. We found him at a back table at the Palm eating oysters. It may have been business for the two women, but not for him. He was wearing a suit, silk shirt, no tie, and a gold chain. Lounge lizard. He accused us of harassing him as soon as we showed him our credentials. You could see he was trying to figure out how much of a scene to make. Then he decided to switch on the charm and invited us to sit down and have a drink. He claimed he wanted to help and said he would come in for an interview at eleven this morning."

McFarland said, "I want to question him. Two Conway employees are dead and he's obstructing us every way he can. He certainly wasn't turning on the charm when he called my home last night."

Farwell chuckled. "We probably spoiled his evening. The two young ladies looked like they wanted to get the hell out of there. He volunteered one thing as we were leaving. He said he was shocked and horrified by Taylor's death, and that when Taylor left the Mayflower dining room where they'd met yesterday morning, he seemed fine."

A few hours later, dirty cups and paper plates cleared away, they arranged three chairs at the table in the interrogation room. Smith said it would bother Maddox to be interrogated by a DA and a female agent while Smith and Williams sat against the wall where he'd have to twist to see them. When Maddox arrived, he was wearing jeans and a sweatshirt, a long leather overcoat, and a broad brimmed black hat. He was carrying a soft leather suitcase and a briefcase, explaining he had a 2:30 p.m. flight out of Dulles back to San Francisco. McFarland said nothing but pointed to the chair across the table from him and Farwell. Maddox looked around uneasily.

"Am I a target of your investigation?"

McFarland thought, *Not yet, but I hope soon.* He said, "Mr. Maddox, your company *is* a target and you represent them. Two of your employees are dead. We are investigating crimes that include extortion, murder, and fraud that appear to involve your company. We'd like your cooperation in our investigation, so far you have refused to comply with two subpoenas. You don't return phone calls, and when approached by investigating agents you have been unforthcoming. As of now we are moving to enforce our subpoenas and to compel the testimony of several witnesses." Maddox sat in stony silence. McFarland paused, then asked, "How often did you speak with Elliott Taylor over the past year?"

Maddox was taken aback by the abrupt shift. "Not often."

"Once? Twice? Every week?"

Maddox hesitated, wondering what they already knew. "A few dozen times."

"So, pretty much every week? What did you talk about?"

"I advised him."

"About what?"

"That's privileged."

"No, it's not. He's dead, you didn't represent him, and you weren't giving legal advice, were you?"

"He talked to me about problems."

"Like ghost workers."

"He was very troubled about that when he learned about it."

"When Mr. Douglas told him, was that when he learned what was going on, or did he already know?"

"Douglas was way off base."

"You and Taylor talked about Douglas."

"Not as such."

"As what?"

"Just a—the source of the information."

"And he was the guy who'd dug up that safety report."

"No."

"No, he didn't dig it up, or no Taylor didn't tell you?"

"I don't know what you're talking about."

"I'm talking about the TheoryQ safety analysis you told Taylor to bury."

"I didn't."

"Oh, he did that on his own? I doubt that. He wrote you a memo about it, didn't he, Mr. Maddox?" This was a wild guess, but McFarland could see Maddox was startled, his face was tight, and his eyes narrowed as he struggled to keep control. McFarland leaned back, stared at the calendar hanging on the wall behind Maddox, and gestured to Farwell who began to question Maddox about his activities the preceding day. Why had he called Taylor? Where did they meet? What had he ordered for breakfast?

"What did you and Mr. Taylor talk about yesterday morning?"

"I'd been to the White House," he said, "I needed to tell him where we stood."

"Where was that, sir?"

"This project has their full support."

"That's good to know."

"They don't want it derailed."

"They must have been concerned about the fraud and violence."

"It's a six-billion-dollar project to provide fast modern public transportation to the nation's capital. That's what we talked about."

"You didn't report the fraud and violence to them?"

"I told them that we hope to complete the system on time if the Congress and the local governments provide the resources."

"Do you log your phone calls?"

"Yes."

"We'll need to see your log for the past two years."

"No. No way."

"Yes, sir. Here is a copy of the subpoena we are serving on your office today."

"You can't have my working notes."

McFarland leaned forward, ready to respond, but Farwell, unperturbed, said, "We are not seeking working notes. The case law is clear. Your phone log is a record, and the grand jury has a right see it."

McFarland saw Williams smile. The phone log had been Farwell's suggestion. It had become a key object of the interview. Judging by the look of panic in Maddox's eyes, the record of whom he spoke with and when would tell an interesting story. Farwell began working through a list of names, asking if Maddox knew them. He turned toward McFarland with an expression perhaps intended to resemble candor.

"Look, Mr. McFarland, this is uncomfortable. Taylor was a friend, but not my client, the company is my client. Taylor doesn't need protecting any more. It's in the company's interest for you to get the people who committed these crimes. I'm sure we can work together." McFarland pictured a sleigh drawn by lathered horses racing across the taiga pursued by wolves with fierce yellow eyes, a terrified peasant thrown from the sleigh to distract the wolves.

By the time he left, Maddox had agreed to release the financial data from the Washington bank and to negotiate the terms of the disclosure of information from the company's files and his own records.

Farwell sat at the table looking disgusted. "Slimeball. A goddamn putrid, oozing slimeball. I need a shower."

Smith looked at her with a slight smile and gave her a thumbs up.

"Now, Jimmy, about your love life…"

Chapter 49
Witnesses

Farwell was typing up notes of the Maddox interview, McFarland reading over her shoulder, when Smith came back in from the restroom waving a pink message slip.

"Look what I found on the front desk, dated yesterday afternoon. A witness." They looked up like dogs hearing a siren.

"A witness to what?" McFarland asked.

"Taylor's death," Smith said. "You might have thought someone would have alerted me."

Farwell was already on the phone. "Would you tell him Agent Farwell called? I would very much appreciate a call back."

*****

Aaron Norton was a Stanford junior doing a semester in Washington. Pale and freckled with a reddish ponytail, watery blue eyes, and a flat Midwestern accent, he was pleased to have the attention of a pair of FBI agents. He would have been even more pleased if he'd known the excitement with which his message had been greeted.

Smith and Farwell sat with him in a corner of the common room of the apartment building the university owned called The Cardinal. Students were draped over sofas, reading, or talking, and there was a regular traffic of people coming in to get coffee or sodas.

Farwell smiled and said, "This is pretty sweet, Mr. Norton. How did you get to live here?"

“It’s part of the semester in DC program. I guess the whole thing was endowed by a wealthy alum who wants more of us to get involved in government.”

“And you saw something yesterday morning? Why don’t you just tell us what happened?”

He had, Norton told them, been waiting on the northbound platform Friday morning, planning to ride one stop to the end of the line at DuPont Circle where he was meeting a friend for coffee. “It was kind of silly. Just one stop, but I love the Metro, and the DuPont Circle station just opened. There wasn’t anyone else on the platform on my side, but there were a bunch of people on the other side waiting for the train toward Union Station. So, I’m standing there, and I notice a guy on the opposite platform. He just caught my eye because he was like trying way too hard to be cool. Long leather overcoat, black hat, dark mustache. I was thinking what a doofus he was. I heard the train arriving. Then a guy standing near the poser falls on the tracks. There’s a lot of screaming and commotion, I’m standing there thinking, What did I just see?”

Smith inclined his head thoughtfully and asked, “What made you ask yourself that?”

“I saw the guy’s face as he fell. He had a look of shock—and terror. And I began to think I might have seen someone move behind him. Maybe he was pushed? Some of the people in my office were saying obviously he was pushed. Probably the CIA.”

Smith let out a long breath. It would be near to impossible to disentangle what the young man had seen from what people told him he had seen, and the description of Maddox in his overcoat standing near Taylor, as accurate as it was, contained a flaw. Maddox was clean shaven.

“Did you see who was behind the man who fell?”

“It happened really fast. I saw the fall and the expression on his face. The rest is just kind of a feeling.”

“Could you recognize the guy in the hat if he didn’t have his hat and coat on?”

“Was he involved? Do you think you know who it is?”

“It’s important for you tell us if you think you could recognize him.”

“Yeah, I think so.”

They thanked him and asked him to come by the field office the following Monday to give a statement. Norton walked them down to the busy lobby, shook their hands and said solemnly, "Agent Smith, Agent Farwell, I really hope I was able to assist your investigation. It was an honor to talk to you."

Farwell rolled her eyes and chuckled as they walked out. "Who would believe it, a pro-FBI long haired college student?"

Smith suggested they stop at the Farragut North Station to try an experiment. He would stand on one platform, Farwell on the other. What could young Aaron have seen standing on the northbound platform looking across two sets of tracks to the southbound side? They trotted down the wide granite steps and over to the station manager's booth. Smith tapped on the glass and smiled.

"Mr. Anthony. We met yesterday morning. I'm Agent Smith. I'm glad to see you're on duty today."

Anthony looked out at them dolefully. "It has been a terrible time, Agent Smith. Police coming and going. Reporters poking around everywhere. Delays. Angry passengers, and that poor man dragged and mangled and bleeding on the tracks. The operator was sick with shock."

"Yes, I can imagine, Mr. Anthony. It was lucky you kept your head, and so helpful that you took the names of the people on the platform."

Anthony's long face fell still further. "I didn't think of it right away, and some of the passengers left before I could get their names."

Smith understood. It would have been chaos. Easy for anyone to quietly slip his card in the gate and walk out. He asked, "Anything—anyone—draw your attention?"

"No, I don't recall?"

"Did you see a man in a long leather overcoat and a broad brimmed black hat?" Anthony narrowed his eyes, trying to picture the scene. "Maybe, yes, I think I may have seen him. I recall a gentleman struggling to get the machine to read his fare card. And I did notice a shiny leather overcoat."

"When was that?"

"Less than a minute or so after the accident. As soon as I realized something serious had happened, I went down to the platform."

Smith explained that they wanted to look at the two platforms. Anthony came out of his booth, let them in, and led them first to the eastbound platform. The pristine Cathedral space of the Metro station was softly lit by indirect lights. Warning lights built into the edge of the platform brightened and dimmed as a train arrived. A deep voice advised them to stand clear. The doors opened silently. The cars were upholstered in brown, tan, and orange and smelled new.

Anthony took them to the middle of the platform and said, "This is where he was hit." They walked on about seventy-five feet. "And this is where the train stopped. They worked all night last night to clean up the blood after your people had photographed everything."

Farwell remained at the spot where Taylor had been struck while Anthony and Smith walked to the end of the platform, rode the escalator to the mezzanine, and went down onto the opposite side. She had no trouble seeing Smith's face. She held up her hand to see if he could count how many fingers she had raised. When they met again at the station manager's booth, Smith lifted his eyebrows and said to Farwell, "He could have seen what he said he saw." He turned to Anthony and asked, "Do you know whether they've gotten a statement from the operator yet?"

"I'm not sure, but he told me he was looking down the tracks and just saw something tumbling."

"Mr. Anthony, thank you for your help."

At their office Farwell set off on a fruitless search for copies of the statements that had been taken by the Metro police from passengers on the platform. No one at Metro police headquarters had any idea where the statements might be or who was in charge of Metro's investigation. Smith sat fuming.

"Everybody has their own police force—Congress, Metro, the Park Service, and none of them share what they know." He closed his eyes and leaned his head back as if he were going to howl and then, grabbed the phone and called a friend. "Stan, it's Hank… Yes, of course I'm working. It's too goddamned cold for fishing. Listen, I need a number. I need the home phone for the general manager of Metro." There was a pause. Smith wrote down a couple of phone numbers. "Thanks, my friend, you're right he may be at work."

It took less than ten minutes after Smith had explained his problem to Theodore Lutz, the general manager of Metro, for Captain Gaines, who was in charge of the investigation, to call. Captain Gaines was barely civil. The Chief of the Metro Police had called him at home after hearing from Lutz. Friday's death had been classified as an accident. Why in hell did the FBI need to see the interview notes in such an almighty hurry on a Saturday afternoon? They sure earned their reputation as arrogant bullies. He would get the notes copied, the captain said, and deliver them later that afternoon.

"No need to copy them. We can get over to your office and read them there." There was a silence, and the captain finally said, "Thanks for the offer, but the Chief told me to take care of this myself, and I better do it. I'll be there with a copy in an hour. Agent Smith, is there something going on with this that I don't know about?"

"I don't know, Captain. The victim was a person-of-interest in a case we are working on."

There had been sixty-one interviews with people who had been spread along the southbound platform. They revealed little other than the witnesses' horror at what had happened and the fear that had spread in the ensuing chaos. Only one witness had seen Taylor falling, and that was out of the corner of her eye. She turned in time to see him struck and dragged, and then she vomited. Four other witnesses said they had been standing near where Taylor was hit but had not seen anything. The two agents called each of the five, reaching three, to ask whether they recalled seeing Taylor with anyone—a question the Metro police had not asked, assuming that if the accident victim had been with someone that person would have come forward. None of the three had noticed whether Taylor was with someone, and none had seen anyone leaving immediately after the event. They got nothing.

Smith called McFarland to report. When Smith told him they had two witnesses who described someone who looked like Maddox in the station when Taylor was killed, McFarland groaned and said, "And he's on a plane back to California. Shit he's probably going to disappear?"

"He doesn't know what we have, and it isn't enough to arrest him anyway."

"We know he lied. He'll probably burn that phone log. Crap. What next?"

"I think it's time Farwell and I paid a call to on the Deputy Chief at his home."

"Good, I'll come."

"No, Jimmy. This'll be just a couple of plodding, obtuse FBI agents. We may have to be a bit annoying. It goes with the turf for us, but I don't think you should be part of it. Not a good look."

Chapter 50
Diminished

Smith and Farwell found Deputy Chief Homer Dixon's home in a newly constructed community of *faux* antebellum mansions in suburban Virginia, a landing place for white families fleeing Washington. Painted brick houses with two-story porticoes, gabled roofs, and high double entries faced onto four-house *cul de sacs*. A few streets down, big yellow machines rested by piles of red earth where construction was still underway. Farwell leaned her head back against the headrest and grumbled to Smith, "Just the place for a DC cop to live."

As they expected, they found the DC at home. He came to the door in sweats, looking diminished. The sleek self-confidence had ebbed from his face, frown lines ran from his eyes across skin that seemed no longer anchored to his cheek bones and chin. He made no effort to disguise his odium.

"Smith, you have no damn business showing up here like this. This is my home. It's the weekend. You can call my office to make an appointment."

"Well sir, you haven't been in your office, and they say they don't know when you'll be back."

"I haven't been well."

"No, you don't look well. It's probably best for us to meet here so you don't have to go out."

"I don't want to talk to you."

"But you need to, Chief Dixon. We're about to arrest several of your Palace Guard on murder charges."

He looked at them, tired eyes narrowed. Farwell noticed his breathing was shallow and rapid. He gave off a sour odor. "I don't have a 'Palace Guard'. That's insulting to a loyal group of professionals."

Farwell moved forward, sure that the sagging figure before her no longer had the nerve or the energy to force them to leave. He was already defeated. Without a word, Dixon turned and walked away, leaving the door open. The two agents followed. The house was stuffy and smelled of stale cigar smoke. It felt almost institutional, furnished impersonally, the trim stained a dark mahogany color, the walls painted a neutral cream shade. Had the developer marketed these places fully decorated?

Dixon walked into a large sitting room with chintz covered sofas and armchairs, flowered cushions, and a white carpet. He sank heavily into a chair and waited, sullen, focused on Smith and ignoring Farwell. He made a guttural sound that might have been a cough or a snarl.

"You and Donatelli have been trying to get me for years. Last time, the judge slapped your hands. You should have been fired. Now you're doing it again. Tapping my goddamn phones, harassing my people, and turning police officers into spies. You're not going to get away with it this time any more than you did last time."

"You know, Chief, we did screw up. We had all that evidence of how corrupt you are and we couldn't use it. It was a shame."

Farwell roamed the room, ostentatiously examining photographs and papers lying on a side table. Smith focused on the man, Farwell on his habitat. She hoped this invasive survey would discombobulate him. Smith saw Dixon's eyes following Farwell. He leaned forward abruptly and asked, "Do you know who killed your nephew?"

"Yeah, sure, that street bully Sergeant Williams."

"No, that's crap. You know damn well he didn't."

"He came and begged me to help him beat the rap."

"Uh huh. And you thought you could use him against McFarland." Smith looked into Dixon's eyes, and continued, "We sent him, and he recorded your conversations. We have you on tape saying you know he didn't kill Dixon."

"That's entrapment."

"Nah, not even close. You suggested it to Williams. You knew Williams didn't kill your nephew, Blackstone and Ransome did."

"That's a load of crap."

"Oh no, Chief, it isn't. We've got the gun, and we've got witnesses. Did Rankin not even tell you he'd ordered that hit?"

A rivulet of sweat slid down Dixon's forehead to his chin. Smith continued, his voice soft, almost singsong. "You told Taylor you'd take care of Ernie Hills, and you sent your nephew to threaten him. That was stupid because you knew your nephew was a coward. And he lost his nerve and never even talked to Hills, but he was made by a couple of witnesses. So, you—or was it Rankin? You sent a couple of your thugs to get the job done. Time was running out."

"Is that what that crackhead Taylor is telling you?"

There is a heavy silence. Smith was inexorable. "The thing was, your nephew owed his life to Larry Williams and Hills was a buddy. He couldn't bear lying to Williams. He was going to tell Williams what had happened."

"No."

"And you told Rankin that you thought he was going to crack."

"No, I didn't."

"Oh, come off it, Chief, those were your guys who went to kill Alan."

"Rankin overheard me yelling at him. He told me we needed to get this under control."

"Oh, and that's different? You knew and you didn't stop him? Or you couldn't stop him? You are losing control. You might as well have loaded the gun, that chrome-plated, pearl-handled gun your man Blackstone used."

Dixon lowered his head and groaned. He seemed unable to focus and stood up shakily, looking wild-eyed. He staggered toward Farwell and grabbed the sheaf of papers she was holding and threw it across the room at Smith, sheets falling on the white rug and the glass coffee table.

"Get out. Now. Get out!"

Smith watched, imperturbable, and then said, "You know Taylor is dead?"

Dixon's head jerked. "Jumped—or maybe pushed in front of a subway train."

Dixon seemed to deflate. "Oh God."

"Are you concerned they might come after you?"

The hunched figure shook. "It's crazy."

"What is, Chief?"

"Rankin—thinking he can take over."

Smith looked at Farwell. She nodded, slipped quietly behind Dixon, gently pulled his arms back and cuffed him.

"Chief Dixon, you're under arrest as an accessory to murder." She recited his rights as he stared dazedly at Smith who nodded sadly.

"Chief," he said quietly, "I think you'll be safer this way."

Chapter 51
Baby Sister

As Farwell took Dixon out to their car, Smith picked up the hall phone in the DC's house and called McFarland. "Jimmy, I'm calling from the DC's home so we're on tape. We've got him under arrest, and I'll call my office to roll up Rankin and Ransome. He's given us more than enough."

"Whoa. Apart from that, anything going on?"

"Yes. We'll meet you at your office as soon as we finish papering the DC. About an hour."

*****

Once again they gathered in McFarland's office. The building was quiet. A shaft of late afternoon winter sun crossed the room and shone on the conference table. It was strangely peaceful. Smith and Farwell recounted their interview with Aaron Norton, the Stanford student. McFarland shook his head, "The ID is pretty weak because of the mustache and all the other stuff he told you."

"But we have the station manager as well."

"Nah, you suggested it to him. We know he was there, but a jury wouldn't be convinced. I hope you get something from one of the witnesses you didn't reach."

They described their conversation with Dixon. "He looked broken," Smith said. "Sarge, you saw there was something weird when you went to the Deputy Chief's office, now we know."

"Rankin is meaner than the DC," Williams said, "and the word was that he was pissed off that he was still a lieutenant when there was already a Black captain."

McFarland asked, "Adams opened up only when he heard Taylor was dead?"

"Yeah."

"Do you think it's the truth this time? I mean, it's convenient. He can just put it on Taylor the same way Maddox was trying to do."

Williams responded, "The man makes stuff up, but if this was smoke, I don't know what game he's playing."

"That's the thing, Sarge, he's always got a game. He's an Irish charmer. He was born with the blarney in his heart and a mouth full of bullshit."

Farwell leaned over the table and said, "Wait, wait, Jimmy. Don't you think he's trying to protect his sister?"

"From what? From losing her husband? I don't see it. But you're right, we need to talk to her."

"We'll do that."

"No, I mean now, tonight. Something's not making sense. What did Dixon say about Taylor?"

"You mean, calling him a crackhead?"

"Why'd he say that?"

The phone rang. Farwell picked it up, hoping to intercept a call from Sally, but immediately turned serious. "Yeah, we're all here—you don't know where he is?" She listened, nodding. "Thanks for the heads up." She turned to the group. "They got Rankin, but they can't find Ransome." Williams closed his eyes and groaned.

Farwell looked at him and smiled. "What's up, Sarge? We'll get him."

Williams put his hands to his head and said, "You don't understand who he is. The man knows how to kill. His unit has been attacked. He's not thinking about getting away, he's thinking about hitting back."

Smith asked, "Who's he going to come after?"

"Me. Jimmy. Ernie's family because that's where it all went wrong. Adams, if he can find him."

McFarland screwed up his face and compressed his lips. He looked pugnacious and faintly silly. He said, "Let's be visible so we tempt him out in the open. Hank, you and I need to go talk to Chrissy Taylor. Farwell, you and Sarge need to go out and find Ransome's slime trail."

Farwell held her palm out. Whoa. "With respect, I think I should go see Chrissy. She's a young woman. She's frightened and grieving. Hank should go with Sarge."

McFarland hesitated, but Smith said, "She's right."

*****

McFarland and Farwell drove to Georgetown. It was after 9:00 p.m. on a Saturday evening. Farwell asked whether they should wait until Sunday morning. McFarland insisted they push ahead. He rang the polished brass bell by the door of the townhouse on Q street in upper Georgetown. An engraved plate said Taylor. The woman who answered the door was pallid, bleary-eyed, and obviously pregnant. McFarland started to explain who he was. She waved a hand. "I know who you are. I've been expecting you."

This was the baby sister? The mischievous party girl, whom Taylor fell for and Adams adored? She was unkempt, her eyes were dim. Could grief do this in a day?

She said, "I've just gotten my son down—I don't know whether he's really asleep." They heard a wail, she closed her eyes, took a breath, and said, "I'm sorry. I don't want to leave him to cry. I'll be down in a few minutes." McFarland watched her climb slowly up the stairs. Mourning her husband? Her life?

Farwell began her usual tour of inspection, pausing to look at a picture of Taylor and Chrissy with their son. He had made the effort to smile, she had not. Neither looked happy. She wandered into the messy kitchen, inspected a jumbled refrigerator, and took several minutes to examine the cork bulletin board on the wall above the phone. Cards for an electrician, plumber, an exterminator; a flyer from St Columba's Nursery School; letters from friends; and an old picture of her with Dan and what looked like his brothers at an amusement park. In the lower right corner, an appointment card for a session with a marriage counselor. Nothing to suggest she attended Catholic mass.

Chrissy came back down the stairs, her two-year-old, sucking on a pacifier, in her arms. "He's not ready to sleep. He must know something's wrong. I'll just get a bottle."

"Let me take him," Farwell said, "I've got four younger brothers."

Chrissy handed her the baby, and Farwell smiled, asking, "How old is he? He's a big guy."

"Almost two, and he's a hulk. I hope this," she patted her stomach, "is a *little* girl."

McFarland was in the living room, but he got up to join the women in the kitchen. They were chatting about the difficulty of getting childcare. McFarland realized he didn't even know whether Farwell was married. Would a female agent get penalized if she took maternity leave? Of course, she would. Chrissy stood at the stove warming a bottle and turned her large eyes on McFarland.

"Mr. McFarland, did Danny kill Elliott?"

It seemed a genuine question, and he was aghast. "We don't know that your husband was murdered, and we had your brother in custody when your husband died."

"I'm glad it wasn't Danny."

Farwell asked coolly, "Why would your brother kill your husband." McFarland was struck by the incongruity of the baby on her hip exposing the butt of her pistol.

"Obviously he didn't," Chrissy said.

"Yeah, but Chrissy, why'd you ask the question?"

Chrissy looked at the floor, then took the bottle out of the hot water, shook some milk on her wrist, and said, "They weren't getting along so well."

"Like *murderously* not well?"

Chrissy took her son from Farwell and walked back to the living room. She sat on a small rocking chair and her son attached hungrily to the bottle. She was silent.

Farwell sat next to her and asked, "You and Elliott weren't getting along either?"

"We were ok."

"You were going to counseling."

Chrissy laughed derisively. "I wish. He wouldn't go."

McFarland leaned forward, and Farwell gestured with her left hand for him to shut up while she held Chrissy's arm with her right hand.

"He hit you?"

Chrissy looked at Farwell blankly.

"Your brother wouldn't have let that happen, would he?"

They stayed another twenty minutes, but Chrissy had shut down. Farwell asked whether she needed help. She shook her head miserably. Nothing they could do would help.

It was Saturday night. Georgetown was a zoo. M Street and lower Wisconsin Avenue seethed with noisy life. The traffic was chaotic. Cars stopped suddenly so people could jump out to join noisy packs of students. Or vomit. The bars spilled noise onto the streets. They were stopped behind a car full of young women yelling to someone looking out of a second story window above a shop.

Farwell pounded on the steering wheel. "People pay a fortune to live here. Jeezus, you couldn't make me." McFarland started to respond, and Farwell muttered, "To hell with this," turned on her blue flashers, and swerved left through two lanes of traffic onto a side street climbing away from the nightlife. The rest of Georgetown was quiet and dark, brick town houses with yellow eyes looming close to the narrow streets. Farwell grinned. "Sorry about that. I didn't even like that scene when I was an undergraduate."

"Did you go to college here?"

"Sure did. College and law school at Georgetown."

Unexpected, McFarland thought. He had her down for a big state school in the Midwest. He asked, "What did you think of Mrs. Taylor? Just grief?"

She stared ahead and then shook her head saying, "You know what the Deputy Chief called Taylor? 'That crackhead.' A golden boy who loved to party and got in too deep. Huge mood swings. A noisy toddler. His pretty, fun-loving girlfriend gone mousy and domestic. Pressure from our investigation. I think he was beating her, and she knew her brother was going kill him."

"But we had him."

"There is that—so someone did it for him. She wouldn't have asked the question if she didn't think Danny was going to kill her husband."

"Or—she's as much of a liar as her brother, and she was playing us."

*****

Adams and the two agents were arguing about dinner. He wanted pizza; they preferred ribs, or fried shrimp. "Look, I know this place, Sebile's, you'll thank me. Their pizza is unbelievable." They called Sebile's to order. Adams wanted pineapple pizza.

“They want to know what else you want on it.”

“Tell them to tell Sebile that it’s for Danny.”

The agent hesitated and then thought, *It’s a pizza parlor for Chrissake*. He made the request. Forty-five minutes later the agents were riding Adams about how slow the delivery was. Yeah, but worth it, he answered. There was a knock. They looked. It was the pizza guy. They opened the door. He threw something in. Adams hit the floor and covered his head with his hands before the stun grenade went off. Two figures pushed in through the smoke and grabbed Adams. One of the agents rolled over trying to clear his head, got his weapon, yelled stop, and fired. Someone fell. One of the figures fired back. The agent crumpled. The door slammed.

The second agent found his partner wounded in the thigh, but alive and cursing.

He called an ambulance, then the field office. Adams was gone. There was a trail of blood down the hall. Within an hour, a massive search was underway. They called every hospital in the area looking for a man with a gunshot wound. Already, there were several. But not Adams

McFarland and Farwell, driving back from Georgetown, got a call on the car’s radio. Adams had been taken, an agent wounded, and Adams or one of the attackers shot. McFarland was stunned. How could they let this happen? He saw that Farwell was desperate that she was not where she should be. He told her to head for the FBI office where they found Smith angry, his face dark. They’d missed Ransome, lost Adams, and nearly lost an agent. He suspected the three things were connected and wondered how Ransome had found Adams. And how the hell the agents guarding Adams had been so careless. But he knew the answer. Adams was a charmer, a wonderful teller of tales. He’d become friends with the agents. He, Smith, should have rotated in new agents every few days. It was on him.

Smith was perplexed by the tale of the visit to Chrissy Taylor. Adams had apparently been spinning them—again. What seemed like a train of murders—all growing out of an effort to cover up fraud in the construction of Metro—might be at least partly, personal. Adams’ defense of his sister. He wondered whether the people who had taken Adams had come to rescue him or dispose of him?

McFarland swallowed some old, burned coffee, grimaced, and asked, “Hank, where are we?”

"A lot further behind than we ought to be. Neither of the two agents who were with Adams is able to say whether the second man at the door when they lost Adams was Ransome, but I think we should assume so. No ID on the guy dressed as a delivery man."

"Are they certain Adam's was taken against his will?"

"They aren't goddamned certain of anything. He insisted they order dinner from Sebile's, and then persuaded them to let Sebile know that the pineapple pizza was for Danny. We've been up there. Sebile claims she never got that message and wouldn't have understood it if she had. Says she doesn't know who Danny is."

"Did they deliver an order to that apartment?"

"The delivery man says a guy met him outside the building, flashed a badge, paid him and took the order."

"So somehow they knew."

"Yeah, well, that's two nights in a row it seems like they knew. We've alerted every hospital in the area to let us know about gunshot victims."

"It's Saturday night in DC, Hank. That'll be a lot of calls."

They trudged through the whole case again. McFarland shook his head. "The more we find out the less I understand. I thought it was about fraud and cover-up, but now it seems like it's about Adams, Chrissy, and Elliott Taylor." He looked at a set of notes on a yellow pad and groaned.

"What?" Farwell asked.

"We need to get a warrant and search Taylor's office. They've probably sanitized it already."

Farwell grinned, "Well, no, actually. I had it sealed. I don't know whether we had the authority, it isn't a crime scene, but no one objected. I don't think we'll need a warrant."

"It sure is fortunate," McFarland said, wincing, "that you have a highly trained prosecutor heading up this investigation. Thanks for getting on top of that, Nora." This drew a wan smile from Smith.

McFarland asked, "Do you know what Sarge is up to?"

"Trying to find Ransome before he does more damage."

Smith looked at McFarland. He was having trouble focusing. He had barely slept the night before and he was fading. He laughed. A good sound.

"You aren't actually adding anything being here. Go home. I'll call if something happens."

When he got home, McFarland found a message from Sally. Call when you get home—*whenever you get home.* By the end of the call, it was understood that being apart was impossible, and as soon as she finished at Curtis, Sally would come live with him.

Chapter 52
D.C. General Hospital

D.C. General Hospital had been a hulking presence off Massachusetts Avenue southeast of the Capitol since 1846. Built as a combination hospital, poorhouse, and asylum, it had been over-burdened, under-resourced, and disreputable for a hundred and thirty years. D.C. General always cared for the indigent, the uninsured, and the desperate who were not welcome at other hospitals. Often chaotic, on Saturday nights it tended toward the charnel, its hallways cluttered with gurneys, overdose cases competing with shooting victims and car crash survivors for the attention of harried doctors and nurses, blood and vomit marking their passage. The triage nurse exercised the power of a god.

It was past 1:00 a.m. when the ambulance delivered a white male identified by a tag pinned to his coat only as 'Daniel'. The triage nurse saw that he was bleeding from a gunshot wound to his shoulder that had probably shattered the joint. He was unconscious but had a strong pulse. She sent him directly to the OR where a weary surgical resident scrubbed up while the shoulder was x-rayed. The bullet had passed out of the back of the man's shoulder, but the work of removing bone fragments was difficult and tedious. Later an orthopedic surgeon arrived from another case, and they began reconstructing the shoulder. By the time the man was wheeled out into recovery nearly five hours later he was stabilized. The nurse told the surgeon that a young woman who said she was the patient's sister was waiting for news.

The waiting room was hot and crowded. It reeked of disinfectant, French fries, and human bodies. When the surgeon came through the door, his scrubs soiled with blood, he was beset by imploring looks from every side. The patient's sister was easy to identify. She was the only white person in the room. The surgeon wove through the rows of relatives and friends slouched in dilapidated seats waiting for news. He tried not to make eye contact. He had nothing to offer them. He approached the young woman, obviously pregnant, her face gray and tear stained.

"Mrs.…?"

"Taylor. Chrissy Taylor."

"You're here about your brother?"

"Yes, Dan—Daniel Adams."

"We have a patient here who was identified to us just as 'Daniel'. Are you sure that's your brother." He felt silly asking. She was here, somehow, and she looked like the unconscious man in the recovery unit.

"They called me and said he was here with a gunshot wound."

"Who called you?"

"I don't know. They wouldn't say. They just said they'd put him in an ambulance to D.C. General and they weren't sure whether he'd make it. Is he alive?"

By this time a stern-faced older woman was tugging on the doctor's sleeve.

Without turning, he said, "Ma'am, please let me finish speaking with Mrs. Taylor." The woman, who knew better than to back off when she'd gotten the attention of someone in authority, moved closer. Faces all around the room were turned toward them. The doctor tried desperately to maintain a calm professional demeanor. He couldn't help them. He turned and said, "Ma'am, I've been operating on this lady's brother for nearly five hours. I don't know anything about any other cases."

"An' I been here waiting for almost nine hours, and nobody's told me a thing."

Voices rose around the room.

"We ain't heard nothin'."

"How come this white lady comes in an' the doctor comes to see her?"

The doctor bit his lip and looked for help. A nurse came in with a security guard and said sharply, "You all need to sit down and wait 'til we have something to tell you. Doctor, why don't you take this lady to the recovery room to see her brother."

"Will you get these people some information?"

"Yes, doctor, just as soon as we can."

The doctor led Chrissy through a hallway littered with stored equipment and a few gurneys with patients awaiting treatment. He wondered how she would react when she saw her brother unconscious and wired up. She stood very still looking at her the pale figure in the bed.

The surgeon said, "He's still under the effects of the anesthetic. He'll come around soon, but he'll be groggy and confused. He's going to make it, but his shoulder is a mess. He'll need more surgery when he's stronger."

She nodded and asked, "Can I hold his hand?"

"Yes."

Half an hour later, at 6:30 Sunday morning, Smith and Farwell arrived at

D.C. General and found her there still, sitting by the bed, holding her brother's hand. She didn't look at them, but said, "He seems to be about half-conscious. Did you shoot him?"

The two agents looked at each other.

"One of our agents may have," said Smith. "A couple of men came to take him from where we had him, and there was an exchange of gun fire."

"Danny lives hard…"

"Do you know who brought him to the hospital?"

"A man called and woke me up. It was after midnight. He told me Danny had been shot and was in an ambulance to D.C. General. I got a neighbor to come over to watch the baby and I drove over here."

"Did you know the voice?" She shook her head.

Farwell said, "You've had a real rough couple of days, Chrissy. Are you sure we can't get you some help?"

She shook her head sadly and asked, "You think they're going to come after him again?"

Farwell frowned and said, "I hope not, but we'll put a guard in the hall." A lot of good that did last time, she thought as she said it. She saw Chrissy looking at her with the same thought. Smith thought, *If they put him in an ambulance, they weren't his enemies.*

Chapter 53
Another Witness

"Agent Farwell?"

"Yes, that's me."

"This is Elaine Davidson. I wasn't sure whether I'd get you on a Sunday morning, but your message said it was important."

"Yes, ma'am."

"Is this about that terrible accident in the Metro?"

"Yes."

"I'm sorry I didn't get back to you sooner. I was—away."

"Your roommate said you might not be home until Sunday. Do you have a minute to answer some questions?"

"Sure, of course. As I told the other officer, I saw the poor man falling."

"Would you just go through it from the beginning Ms. Davidson?"

"I was on my way in to work. I was late. I'd been to the dentist."

"Where do you work?"

"At a small law firm, Jackson and Connor. They have offices in that new building at four hundred North Capitol. It's just a block from the Union Station stop."

"Uh huh."

"I was on the platform waiting for a train. It was pretty crowded, and I was wondering what it's going to be like when they have the whole system open. Then I heard the train announced. I turned to look at it, and I saw this man falling. It was horrible. The train was right there. There was nothing the train operator could do. I heard the brakes and someone screaming, and the train swept by and stopped a ways down the platform. I was stunned. I couldn't move. I couldn't scream. I wasn't even sure what I had seen."

"You did well. Had you noticed the man who got hit before you saw him falling?"

"No, not really."

"Did you notice anyone else who was standing there?"

"No. You know, you don't really pay attention when you're standing in a crowd. But just after the accident, a guy pushed past me leaving the platform. Rude. He had a terrible expression on his face, like he was trying to keep from getting sick."

"Could you describe him?"

"Yeah, he stood out. He had on a long leather overcoat and a big black hat."

"Was anyone with him?"

"I have no idea. Another guy left, a big man with a dark overcoat, but I don't know whether they were together."

"That is very helpful, Ms. Davidson. We'll send someone over to your office tomorrow to show you some pictures to see if you can identify the two men."

"Did they do something? Did they push him?"

"We'd just like to talk to them." She thanked the young woman again, placed the phone back on its cradle, turned to Smith and said, "We've got Maddox on the platform by Taylor, leaving right after the event. And I think maybe Ransome was with him."

Smith called McFarland to tell him about finding Adams in DC General and Elaine Davidson's confirmation of the presence of the man with the leather coat and the black hat.

McFarland laughed. "Now we have two defendants lying unconscious, a third I let leave for California, and possibly a fourth who's dead."

"Well, no, actually Blackstone is conscious, and we're hoping to go up to talk to him tomorrow. Adams was coming around by the time we left. Nora and I are going back this afternoon."

"Can you get them to shoot him up with truth serum and keep anybody else from shooting him with anything?"

Chapter 54
Shambles

On Monday, he walked down the hall to find Donatelli tell him what had happened over the weekend. The older man sat and listened without expression. No nods. No questions. No sarcastic chuckles.

McFarland finished his recounting, and said, “We know who killed Hills. We’re pretty sure we know why. We have the gun. We can tie it to Blackstone. We’ve got a fingerprint that ties Blackstone to the Douglas murder and witnesses who put Blackstone, Ransome, and Adams at the murder site earlier in the day, but it’s thin without testimony. The strongest case is the murder of Dixon. We’ve got the gun and a witness, but the evidence we have of why Dixon was killed comes from Adams and maybe the Deputy Chief. Then there’s Taylor. We don’t have evidence that Taylor was pushed, we just know that Maddox was there and lied to us about it. We’ve got a partial story from the DC and several different stories from Adams. And we don’t know whether any of this involves more people at Conway than Taylor and Maddox.” He stopped. Donatelli was still quiet.

“I guess the question is, which of the unknowns am I trying to solve this equation for?”

“You’re a prosecutor. Knowing who’s guilty isn’t enough. You have to get convictions. You need evidence that tells the story of who did it and why. You don’t have it yet. Somebody’s going to have to talk.”

“Wait a minute, Vic. You ducked my question. Is the Taylor killing the key? Is this about MPD corruption or corporate corruption? Or is it personal?”

Donatelli held up his right index finger and tapped his left hand. “Who are you going to deal with? You’ve got Adams.”

“He’s a suspect and a liar.”

“They all are. You still need to know what he’s saying now.”

"True, but I'm skeptical of cutting him a deal."

Donatelli prowled imperiously like a professor in front of a law school class and asked, "The Deputy Chief?"

"According to Smith and Farwell he's a broken-down wreck and maybe didn't know all that was going on. But he is certainly a greedy, corrupt SOB and he knows a lot."

"So," said Donatelli, "still a possibility for the role of star witness. He sure as hell doesn't want to go to jail."

McFarland looked at him in horror. "You've been waiting years to nail him. You'd bargain with him now?"

"Point taken, but we have a lot of leverage on him. We need to go after him soon, before his legal team stiffens his spine too much. You have an arraignment today?"

"In an hour."

"That'll be a circus. Did you call Anderson?"

"No."

"You need to call him. Pay your debts, Jimmy."

McFarland called, told Anderson what evidence they had, and said they were planning to go with fraud and conspiracy. Not murder. Not yet. Anderson asked whether they'd arrested any of the Palace Guard.

"Yes, Lieutenant Rankin. But, again, not on murder, not yet."

"Are we on the record, Jimmy?"

"A source in the U.S. Attorney's office."

McFarland and Donatelli went back to the list. Not Ransome. Barely verbal. Rankin was a vicious, calculating SOB. If he thought it was worth it to him, he might say what he had to, but he'd make it obvious he was just fulfilling a deal. Worthless, and he belonged in jail.

"You need Maddox and that young woman whom Olsen was dating, Kelsey."

McFarland nodded agreement, and asked, "Fear or favor?"

"Fear, I think."

"We should get Maddox's phone logs today, and a guy from the U.S. attorney's office in San Francisco is going to negotiate a schedule for the production of the other records we subpoenaed."

"Screw the records. You need to go out there and put the heat on Maddox. He doesn't know that you have him on the platform with Taylor. That will shake him. Even if you don't think he killed Taylor, you need to scare the shit out of him, because if he didn't, he probably knows who did…and why."

Mrs. Bynum knocked on the door. "Agent Farwell and another agent are in your office with a couple of boxes of papers."

McFarland walked back down the hall with Mrs. Bynum and asked, "Who's the other agent?"

"He was here a few weeks ago. Agent Rohrig."

"Aah, the accountant. Nora must have found something."

Farwell and Rohrig were standing at the conference table laying out copies of bank statements. The bank had provided records for both the Conway Corporate account and Taylor's personal account, and Rohrig was highlighting entries here and there. He stopped when McFarland came in and greeted him with a knowing smile.

"Mr. McFarland, good morning."

"Good morning, Agent Rohrig. You look pleased. Pay dirt?"

"Oh, yes sir. Just that. Payoffs, and a lot of dirt I should say. I need more time to get the full picture, and I certainly need to see more of the company's financial records."

"And…?"

"There are dozens of entries that warrant investigation. If you look at March 1976, for example…"

"What did you find?"

"This man Taylor wasn't even clever. He left tracks everywhere."

Rohrig gestured grandly toward the piles of paper spread across the table.

McFarland remembered Rohrig happily sorting the piles of paper taken from the union office at the start of the investigation.

He grinned and wagged his finger at him. "Jim, please just humor me. Who was doing what?"

"Well, our Mr. Taylor was embezzling. And the money that was found in Philadelphia in former Detective Blackstone's apartment, that came from the Conway account." Farwell smiled, and added, "And the prints, in addition to Blackstone's, were Taylor's."

McFarland punched the air and hissed "Yes! Taylor tied to the shooter." But Farwell said, "Wait, Jimmy, there's more. Jim, give him the good stuff."

Rohrig, looking smug said, "I noticed some interesting deposits in Taylor's personal account. I had a feeling... The good people at the bank were extremely helpful. Taylor was getting payments from Adams."

"*From* Adams?"

"Yes sir. Quite a lot. I think we'll be able to track that money back to the ghost workers."

"When did it start?"

"Last summer."

McFarland pushed his eyebrows together. "What the hell was that about? I thought Taylor was the wealthy businessman and Adams was the poor working schmuck."

"Mr. Taylor may have had other accounts, but from what I've seen so far, it looks like he may have been in difficulty."

McFarland struggled to fit the idea of payments from Adams to Taylor into his map of the case. The image he had of Taylor trying to protect his family and job was in shambles. Was Adams paying him off or helping him? Why would Taylor need money? Chrissy didn't look like a woman who was expensive to maintain. He turned to Farwell.

"Nora, if you and Hank talk to Adams this afternoon, ask him what he was paying Taylor for. When he says he was helping his sister, ask him why the hell a big-time corporate executive needed help from a small-time union boss?"

Rohrig, oblivious to McFarland's confusion added, "When we can look at these statements with care and use the Conway records, we can probably see what was really going on."

Chapter 55
Who *Was* Taylor?

Smith and Farwell arrived at the Conway offices later that morning. Smith broke the seal on the door to Taylor's office and went in raising his eyebrows. The Conway premises were spare and utilitarian, but Taylor's office was large and full of light. A lustrous mahogany Queen Anne writing desk stood in a corner between two windows, an upholstered Chippendale chair behind it. Behind that a two-drawer wooden file cabinet on which stood a ceramic vase of wilted tulips. To one side a superb model of the Schooner America stood on a brightly polished armoire. On the other side, a red plush sofa, marble coffee table, and two wingback chairs covered in a brocade fabric were gathered beneath a Hudson River landscape in a heavy gilt frame. A richly colored Persian carpet covered most of the floor. Everything was in order and the surface of the desk was clean. Smith wondered whether that was the way Taylor had left it—or had the place been scrubbed of evidence before Farwell sealed it?

Farwell looked around and said, "This sure doesn't look like a construction office."

Smith laughed. "You got that right. Makes you wonder."

"What? Where he got the money?"

"That, and what was he trying to prove?"

They pulled open drawers, leafed through files, and put anything that looked interesting in a box to take back to the office. But there wasn't much. The armoire and the coat closet were locked. Smith went out to look for Kelsey Darrin to see whether she had keys.

"I have the key to the closet. He kept the other key himself."

"Okay, we'll need to find it or we'll force the lock."

She looked stricken. "It's an antique, Agent Smith. I hope that you won't have to break it."

He nodded, and asked, "Did you clean up the office?"

"Oh yes, whenever he goes out—went out—he wanted me to neaten things up. So I did, right after he left on Friday."

"The desk is very clean. Did you move things off it?"

"Anything on the desk, I either put in one of the drawers or in that box on my desk for things that need to be dealt with."

"Did he have a phone log?"

"Yes, it's company policy. I kept it for him. It's right here. I know you've subpoenaed Mr. Maddox's log, so I thought you'd want Mr. Taylor's."

"How about his calendar?"

"Yes, I have that too."

"Did he have one he kept with him?"

"Yes—didn't you find it?"

"I'm afraid his body was badly mangled."

She covered her mouth and leaned back against her desk. Farwell looked at her with sympathy. "Was he a good man to work for?"

"Yes, he was funny and mostly kind."

"Mostly?"

"Well, lately he's been weird—erratic. He'd been under a lot of stress."

"Why?"

She looked horrified and stammered while she gestured broadly. "All, all this. The investigation. Gareth meeting him in a parking lot and then just disappearing. And his personal life was—I don't think his marriage was so great."

Smith looked hard at her and asked, "Miss Darrin, did Harry Maddox send you to Washington to keep track of Elliott?"

She was startled, but not frightened. She answered immediately. "I had asked to be transferred to DC. I worked for Harry in San Francisco, and he said it would be fine for me to move to the DC office, but I had to do him a favor. He told me he knew he could trust me, and they were worried that Elliott might be in over his head, and could I just let them know how things were going from time to time. I was flattered and I said I would."

"What did you report?"

"It turned out they wanted to know specific things. Who he was meeting with, stuff like that. They asked me to listen in on his calls, but I said I wouldn't do it."

"Did they find out about the ghost workers?"

"Ghost workers? You mean the payroll fraud. They knew all about that."

"Did Elliott know what your boyfriend Gary was up to?"

"Yes, he figured it out."

"Did you tell him?"

"No. He asked me. I just said I didn't know."

"Did you tell Maddox?"

For the first time, her eyes flickered away. "Yes."

"Thank you, Miss Darrin. We'll need to talk again. We'll let you know." He saw the tension around her mouth ease. There was clearly more to learn from her. He took the calendar and phone log and went back into Taylor's office. He unlocked the closet and found nothing more sinister than several loud suits, flamboyant shirts, and alligator boots.

It wasn't too difficult to find the key to the armoire. Taylor had hidden it in the case for a pair of reading glasses. In the armoire, they found a small book of phone numbers, a pistol, and a locked metal box, which Smith pried open. It contained cocaine, a small mirror, straws, razors and other equipment. "That's one thing she wasn't telling us," Smith said, turning to Farwell. "It makes you wonder who the hell Taylor was."

Smith went back out, found Darrin again, brought her in, and pointed to the paraphernalia.

"You knew your boss was using." She nodded. "And his friend Adams knew."

"Danny was trying to stop him for Chrissy and the baby's sake."

Smith leaned his head to one side and gave her a knowing look. "You told Maddox."

She wanted to lie but gave up. "I had to. It was getting bad."

"Did he have a supplier who came to the office?"

"I think so. A horrible man with crazy looking eyes. He really scared me."

Farwell grimaced and said, "Blackstone. They had Taylor nailed."

They packed up the evidence, sealed the room again, and took Darrin back with them to the FBI office to give a formal statement.

McFarland arrived back from District Court indignant. He was chagrined that the judge had let Dixon back out on the street. He wasn't afraid Dixon would disappear, he was afraid he'd be killed.

When he opened the door to his office, Mrs. Bynum held up a wad of messages from reporters, some pleading, some angry. "These are the ones that left messages. I think people who get jobs in the press must practice being rude. Also, Agent Smith called. He would very much appreciate a call."

McFarland nodded glumly. "Cora, would you check when I can see the Boss, and let Vic know I need to talk."

"Mr. Donatelli is coming with the sandwiches. The U.S. Attorney is testifying. They'll let us know when he gets back."

By the time McFarland got the call to go down the hall, he'd heard what Smith had found, spoken with Anderson, and put in a call to his old colleague KA. Old colleague? It was only three weeks ago that he had been uprooted from the rat-infested precincts of the Pension Building. He wanted to know what she and David were hearing about the arrests of Dixon and Rankin.

Mrs. Thomas, the Boss's assistant, looked at them glumly. "Gentlemen, a word to the wise. He had a bad morning on the Hill and got ambushed by a TV crew when he was leaving the hearing. They wanted to know why the Deputy Chief of Police was pulled from his sick bed and arrested at his home on a Sunday. He hates being taken by surprise."

McFarland took a deep breath, thanked her, and looked at the door to the Boss's office. Mrs. Thomas smiled. "Go right in. He's waiting."

The Boss had his chair turned toward the window and his back to the door. He didn't move when they entered. "Mr. McFarland, you seem to be attracting attention again."

He thought of reminding the Boss that he had said it was time to increase the pressure on the Deputy Chief. This attention was exactly what they needed.

"Yes sir."

"I urged you to crank up the heat, and you seem to have cranked."

"Yes sir. To be fair, the Deputy Chief wasn't sick and he wasn't in bed, just depressed and hung over."

"That's good work, McFarland." He turned and pointed at Donatelli. "You should have had the SOB a long time ago."

He leaned forward, elbows on his desk, chin on his fists, hard eyes fastened on McFarland. McFarland heard sirens going by outside and the big clock on the sideboard ticking. He waited. Finally, the Boss said, "Goddammit, Jimmy, I'm giving you all the space and resources you need. I am covering your tail each time somebody in Main Justice starts muttering that maybe this should be their case. That's fine, and I'm used to fending off the West Wing, although Carter's people are neophytes and require a lot of educating. I just ask, for Christ's sake, that you keep me informed."

McFarland nodded miserably. The problem, he thought, was that he was so puffed up with his own importance, he had forgotten that he owed it all to others.

Donatelli interrupted his gloomy self-recriminations. "Jimmy is too new at this to have known what was coming. I should have warned him."

"Yes, Vic, you should have. Well, they smell blood and they're baying for more. Let's see how the defense plays it, then you can work it some more. And, Jimmy, keep an eye on the Deputy Chief. Let's not lose him."

Donatelli leaned forward, pulled on the bottom of his vest, pursed his lips, and said, "I think we should send Jimmy to San Francisco. He ought to turn the screws on Mr. Maddox and see if he can shake up top management. Olsen's girlfriend Kelsey told Smith the guys in San Francisco knew all about the ghost workers and sent her to spy on Taylor."

A malevolent smile spread across the Boss's face. "Mr. McFarland, I like what Vic is thinking. Let's get you out there. Pack your bag and ask Mrs. Bynum to get you a flight tomorrow morning. Let's not settle for the little guys. I'll call my friend Browning, the US Attorney in San Francisco, and smooth your path. The guys in the Northern District of California will want to get a piece of this. They'll send someone with you to interview Maddox."

"Won't they just want to handle that part of the case themselves?"

The Boss picked a red and white striped peppermint out of the bowl on his desk and offered one to McFarland. "Vic doesn't approve of these, but I find they wake me up." He unwrapped the candy with elaborate care, popped it in his mouth, sucked thoughtfully as he flattened the cellophane, folded it, and put it in the trash.

"Like me, Browning is wondering how long a Democratic administration will keep him in his job. Big cases help. The guys out there will certainly want to handle as much as they can get their paws on, but it's our case. You, my friend, are in the lead. Browning has a crew of sharp, hungry lawyers so I suggest that you—watch your wallet."

Donatelli remained straight-faced but shook gently with suppressed laughter.

Chapter 56
San Francisco

A pair of U.S. Marshals met McFarland at the gate and whisked him out of the airport and into San Francisco. If he was supposed to be impressed, it worked. He had Officer Ross chauffeuring him around in Washington and now this. *Time to check my wallet*, he thought, recalling the Boss's advice.

He had caught an early plane, and his escorts dropped him at the U.S. Attorney's office a little past noon, West Coast time. The receptionist looked at him with curiosity, then smiled, welcomed him, and pointed him to the restroom. When he returned, she said, "Mr. Browning and Mr. Gopnik are going to take you to lunch when you're ready."

He smiled sheepishly, "You folks certainly are taking care of me. An escort from the airport, lunch with the boss…"

"You're a distinguished visitor."

He looked at her sheepishly. "Do I look distinguished? I'm just an AUSA from the Washington office." He grinned.

She returned the smile and said, "You do look younger than I expected—oh, here is Mr. Browning."

A long-limbed man with short cropped gray hair and bushy gray eyebrows, wearing a loosely cut tan suit and a bow tie, appeared from a door behind the receptionist. He shook hands with McFarland betraying no surprise that the big-time prosecutor from Washington was a kid just off a clerkship.

"Mr. McFarland, I'm Jim Browning, the U.S. Attorney. This is Timothy Gopnik, the Chief of our Criminal Division." He gestured to a beefy, red-haired man who'd followed Browning into the reception area. Gopnik grabbed McFarland's hand and crushed it, looking at him with obvious surprise. Nevertheless, he smiled warmly, his whole ruddy face lit up with warmth and good cheer. He said with obvious relish, "Let's head to lunch. Lucy, would you let them know we're on our way."

"Yes sir, I already called. They're holding the table."

Browning turned to McFarland. "We're going to Sam's. It dates back to the gold rush days. It's a bit touristy, but they have the best fish in the city." He turned to his companion. "As you can see, Tim likes to eat. He's tried them all." Gopnik beamed, and McFarland pictured him eating his way across the city wearing a red and white bib and stuffing leftovers into his pockets.

The dining room at Sam's was dim, paneled in dark wood, the daylight blocked by heavy damask curtains. There were polished tables and plenty of white linen. It looked as if it hadn't changed much in a hundred years. They were taken to a curtained booth at the back, brightened by a vase of spring flowers. McFarland saw that it was a place they could talk without being seen or overheard by customers in the rest of the dining room. Once they were seated and McFarland's efforts to limit himself to a light meal were overruled, Browning turned to business.

"Your Boss is one of the best prosecuting attorneys I know. He's tough, smart, and a good politician. He's one of my heroes. He says you have the makings of a prosecutor, and you've got your hands on a case that matters. Let's hear about it."

He told them. The unemployment fraud. Douglas. Olsen trying to bury the case. The murders of Hills, Douglas, and Lt. Dixon. Feeling sheepish, he described his unofficial involvement in the murder cases and getting the tip that Olsen was feeding information to Conway. Browning stared at him with grim intensity. Gopnik rolled his big florid head and growled. McFarland described the scene when the agents brought Olsen to the AG's conference room. Browning muttered, "Brilliant." By the time he got to Maddox, their plates were empty and the coffee was cold.

"We have witnesses who puts Maddox on the platform with Taylor," McFarland told them. "We have calls among Taylor and Adams and Rankin. We have the money that went to Blackstone coming from the Conway account with Taylor's prints on it. We have Taylor embezzling, and we have Ms. Darrin saying Conway knew about the ghost workers and that Taylor was using."

Browning stared at him. "You know, Jimmy, I've been in this business off and on for decades, and I've never seen a case like this. You walk in with no trial experience and no investigative experience, and they let you lead the investigation." McFarland stiffened, feeling the familiar rush of heat and color to his face. Before he could respond, Browning smiled and added, "But if your boss decided that was the way to go, I'm not going to second-guess him."

Gopnik tried but failed to hide a look of envy and pique. McFarland knew he'd been told to be cautious, but their reaction seemed reasonable. He liked them and decided he would trust them. He admitted, "I'm not sure why the Boss decided to put his confidence in me, but I'm not going to let him down. I'll use any help you can offer. If top management at Conway knew what was going on, they should be held accountable. Maddox is the entry point. We can't prove he pushed Taylor in front of that train, but he sure as hell lied to us. He knew exactly what was going on, and Taylor had become a huge liability."

Gopnik said, "That makes sense, Jimmy, but if Maddox wanted to dispose of Taylor, he'd never do it himself, and he wouldn't be around when it happened."

Browning waved off a hovering waiter and said, "Timothy's right, there's something screwy here. The moment when you confront him with the evidence is crucial. When you hit him, he'll be vulnerable. You have to go right after him. Make him feel he's got to explain."

It was past three when they left the restaurant, and though it was late January, the sun was warm. Sun starved Easterner that he was, McFarland would happily have turned and walked along the waterfront or just found a place to sit. Browning was telling a story about embarrassing himself trying to get drug evidence admitted in front of a punctilious and vindictive judge. "Everyone in the courtroom knew he was going to admit the evidence in the end, but they sure did enjoy watching the young AUSA flounder." Was that a jab, he wondered? With what purpose? Or was it just a 'we were all young once' parable?

McFarland and Gopnik spent the rest of the afternoon working out a strategy for the visit with Maddox. Gopnik would start the questioning, reviewing Maddox's previous statements about his interaction with Taylor before his death and asking what he knew about Taylor's contacts with the Deputy Chief. Then McFarland would tell him that they knew he was lying. The trouble is Mr. Maddox… Maddox would be in a difficult position. He faced personal criminal liability in a case where his firm was also at risk and might have interests different from his. They would press him about his ethical obligations as corporate counsel and demand to interview senior management at the company. They did not expect him to agree.

McFarland was drooping by the time he got to his hotel. He thought about dinner, remembered lunch, and decided on a bath and bed.

*****

He woke, of course, at four a.m. West Coast time. By the time he was showered and dressed, it was eight a.m. in the east, and he thought it would be reasonable to call and check in with Mrs. Bynum.

"Yes, Mr. McFarland, things have been busy, but Agent Smith and Mr. Donatelli have been handling everything." He knew he could probably get Hank at the FBI office, but Vic wouldn't be in yet. He decided to wait until he had something to report.

Mrs. Bynum was trying to get his attention. "There was one call—from Mr. Anderson. He didn't want to talk to Mr. Donatelli. He just said to tell you that 'they're worried' and 'good hunting'." McFarland thought, *If I had his sources, the case would be solved.*

The Conway offices were in a gleaming new high rise with expansive views of the harbor and the Golden Gate. McFarland had only been in San Francisco as a teenage tourist with his family. He didn't remember it this way. Tall and busy. This city proud of its distance from Washington and New York was new to him. Apparently, he thought wryly, they didn't fully understand that Washington was the center of the universe.

He and Gopnik were shown to a small conference room. A briefcase was in one of the chairs with its back to the windows and the view. Gopnik scowled, shook his head and said, "Sun in our eyes and the view to distract us. I don't think so." He picked up the briefcase and moved it, sat in the chair where the briefcase had been, and spread some papers in front of him. "Our space," he said. *Fair enough,* McFarland thought, *an assertion of control.*

Maddox came in, his face tight and unfriendly. He barely acknowledged McFarland. He was followed by a tall man with a surfer tan and blond hair tied in a short ponytail. Maddox started to introduce him, but Gopnik rose with a broad smile and boomed, "Jack, this is a pleasure. Jimmy, this is Jackson Diehl, the best trial attorney in San Francisco, at least according to him." Gopnik guffawed.

Diehl extended a hand to McFarland and looked at him steadily, "Pleased to meet you, Mr. McFarland. Mr. Maddox has retained me to represent him."

There, thought McFarland, *goes our hope of getting much of anything out of Maddox.* "You represent him, not the company?"

"Yes. My client has advised the company that his personal interests may diverge from theirs and he cannot represent them in this matter."

"Who's representing the company?"

"A San Francisco firm. I'll put you in touch with them."

Gopnik broke in. "Jack, we're here to interview Mr. Maddox. Can we start?"

Diehl shook his head. "Before you do, there are some matters that my client needs to correct from his previous statements to the FBI."

McFarland had to remind himself to breathe. What the hell was going on? Maddox, who had sat with his face in a mask of misery, shifted uneasily. Diehl turned to look at him and nodded. Maddox cleared his throat, looked at McFarland, and began to speak, his voice almost a croak. "When I told you that the last I saw of Taylor that morning when he—died—was when he left breakfast, that wasn't the truth. I went with him."

"To the Metro?"

"Yes. I was with him on the platform."

"What happened?"

Diehl held up a hand and shook his head. "Mr. McFarland, just let my client tell his story and save your questions." McFarland clamped his lips and sat back.

Maddox looked down at the yellow pad in front of him as if there might be an answer written there, then looked up at McFarland and continued, "I was standing on the platform next to him—next to Elliott. It was actually my first ride on the Metro, and we were talking about how beautifully the station was designed, how it felt more like a monument than a subway tunnel. He was on my left, close, it was crowded. We saw the lights blinking to announce the train was approaching. All of a sudden, someone pushed me hard from behind. I reached out trying to keep from falling. I grabbed Taylor to keep my balance. He fell. It was me. I pushed him in front of that train, but I never meant to. I was stunned. Paralyzed. I knew he must be dead and that you'd think I meant to kill him. People were screaming and crowding to look at the body where the train stopped. I just turned and walked out."

He stopped, a look that seemed like genuine sadness on his face, eyes heavy, mouth turned down. The hand he had resting on the table trembled slightly. McFarland sat immobile while his mind raced. Had someone tried to kill Maddox? He looked at Gopnik and shook his head very slightly to signal him not to jump in. He could picture the station platform with its red tiles and rough granite edge, the round lights in the granite blinking as the train neared, the two men standing next to one another just back from the edge. How would you accidentally push someone over the edge?

He asked slowly, "When you grabbed Taylor, did you throw your arms out to both sides? Could you show us?"

Maddox stood and closed his eyes, perhaps picturing the scene. Then he turned slightly and pantomimed while saying, "I was slightly turned toward him, and I just grabbed." He leaned forward and reached out with his left hand as if wildly trying to grab something.

"Did he try to hold you?"

"No, no, it was much quicker than that. I was going over. I grabbed. I must have gotten his right arm. Maybe just his coat sleeve. I hauled myself back and he went over—headfirst, as if he was diving."

"Could the push behind you have been an accident?"

"No, no. Never. It was sudden and violent."

McFarland turned to Gopnik who asked, "Did you see anything about the person who pushed you?"

"No."

"How high on your back was the push?"

"High. Between my shoulder blades."

"You're a pretty big man, so the pusher must have been big."

"Yeah, I guess."

"Was there anything that gave you any sense of who it was? Did you hear anything, or smell aftershave?"

Maddox closed his eyes again. "Not that I noticed." There was a pause, then he said, "When I was leaving the station, fumbling with my fare card to figure out how to get out, there was another man leaving. I didn't see his face, but he had on a dark tweed overcoat, and he seemed big. He ran up the escalator two steps at a time." *That,* thought McFarland, *could be Ransome.*

Gopnik was still going. "What was your first reaction?"

"I was terrified—panicky. I thought if that was the guy, he might wait for me and try again. And I thought those FBI agents would find someone who saw me pushing Taylor and they'd think I wanted to silence him."

"Did you—need to silence him?"

"No, if anything he'd want to get rid of me. I hadn't told him yet, but I knew that he was using, and I suspected he'd had some role in those murders. I think he guessed I was going to fire him."

"You hadn't told him that morning?"

Maddox looked down. "No. I wanted to have one more talk with Kelsey."

McFarland broke in. "Did you know he was embezzling?"

Maddox's eyes widened. He breathed deeply. "No, I had no idea—I should have checked."

"Did you know he used corporate funds to pay off the ex-cop we can tie to the three murders?" Maddox's head fell and he just shook it back and forth.

This guy, thought McFarland, *is in deep shit with his company.* He felt his anger rising. Were they supposed to believe he had no idea of the scale of the crime that was accumulating amidst their six-billion-dollar project? It was all Taylor, and, oh dear, now he's dead? He looked at Maddox coldly, and asked, "How many people here in the San Francisco office knew the company was paying hundreds of ghost workers?"

Maddox raised his head, his face drooping with self-pity. Diehl said sharply, "Harry, they've subpoenaed the records. They're going to get it all. Tell them." So, he did.

"Taylor wasn't an idiot. He told us what was going on. He said it was a cheap price to pay for having the union on our side. And he wrote it down." This whole interview seemed incredible. Maddox had given them a completely different view of Taylor's death. He was implicating the company he was supposed to have protected.

Gopnik hauled his bulk upright and said, "When Taylor asked you what the hell he should do with the consultants' report that warned you about the risk from the buildings that weren't underpinned, what did you tell him?" Both Maddox and MacFarland jerked around to look at Gopnik. Maddox's eyes widened and his jaw literally dropped. Gopnik lowered his voice to almost hiss, "That puts the company in a difficult position, doesn't it? When did he tell you?"

It was obvious Diehl hadn't heard about this. He put his arm around Maddox and whispered something, then turned to them and said, "We need a couple of minutes to consult. Let's take a break."

Gopnik growled, "Jack, we all saw his reaction. He knows about that report, and he talked with Taylor about it."

"I didn't see anything."

"That's crap."

MacFarland saw no benefit in a dog fight, especially not since this one seemed to be freighted with baggage from past encounters. Diehl knew his client had reacted and he was smart enough to want to cut off the questions and get the interview back under control. They couldn't force Maddox to answer, not here, and they'd blown up what had been a very productive conversation.

Diehl and Maddox left the room. A secretary came in to offer coffee and the keys to the restroom. They both took advantage of the restroom, and as they stood side-by-side in front of very clean urinals that smelled like lilies, Gopnik said, "Sorry, man, that arrogant SOB just rattles my chain whenever we're on opposite sides."

"He seemed to have advised his client to tell us the truth."

"You believe that concoction?"

Gopnik sounded scornful, but McFarland wasn't daunted. "His story is plausible. And he told us without knowing we already had witnesses that put him on the platform."

"I don't know, it sounds like a tall tale to me."

"Tim, you said yourself he wouldn't have killed Taylor himself, he'd have had someone do it for him. And he certainly wouldn't do it in a public place." Gopnik grunted. McFarland continued trying to shift away from the question of whether Maddox was telling them the truth. He decided a little butter would help. "You were brilliant to just ask about the report out of the blue. He looked like you'd driven a spear into his belly."

Gopnik backed away from the urinal zipping his pants. "He's a lawyer. His job was to protect the company from just this kind of shit. How could he let Taylor hide that report?"

They walked back to the conference room, poured themselves coffee, and stood staring out the window. Gopnik asked, "Are we going to arrest him?"

"What do you think we should do?"

Gopnik leaned back against the long table. “If Maddox’s story is true, he’s in danger and he knows it. Let’s get him off the street.”

“Lying to a federal officer? Conspiracy?”

“Both. I’ll get the office to start work on a warrant.”

When Diehl and Maddox walked back in, Maddox looked beaten. He remained silent and Diehl said, “We’re done for this morning, gentlemen. We’ve discussed the so-called safety report. Mr. Maddox did talk to Mr. Taylor about it, but he never saw it and has no personal knowledge that it exists. Mr. Taylor said it did and said he had buried it.”

McFarland wondered whether to push back. Why the hell was Maddox shutting down now? It sounded as if he was trying to protect the company. Should McFarland stage a tantrum? This sudden reticence threw the whole story into question. The report existed. They had solid evidence, and it wouldn’t be hard to subpoena the consulting company. Of course, Diehl knew that. His client didn’t want to be the one dropping a dime on the company.

McFarland decided to leave it. “The consulting company will confirm the existence and delivery of the report. Mr. Maddox, we are going to get a warrant for your arrest on charges of lying to federal agents and conspiracy to defraud the United States Government. We would ask for your assurance that you will turn yourself in to the FBI when the warrant is issued.”

Maddox didn’t react.

Diehl just said, “He’ll be there.”

Chapter 57
Everything Is About Race

Sergeant Williams and Agent Smith were cruising north on Maryland Route 1. The day was unseasonably warm—false spring. Smith had told Williams he wanted to drive to Philadelphia the back way, through the southern Pennsylvania towns of Kennett Square and Chadd's Ford where he had grown up.

It was a week since the Philadelphia Tactical Squad had caught, beaten, and nearly killed Blackstone. He had been in Pennsylvania Hospital under guard and in a coma for five days, but he had regained consciousness the preceding day. The neurosurgeon had told Smith that Blackstone might never fully recover. He seemed to be awake but was not responsive. He was certainly suffering from the symptoms of drug withdrawal. Knowing him, Williams suspected he might not see much reason to be responsive. The two men had been in conflict before, and Williams expected a tough session with Blackstone. Smith had told the Philadelphia Field Office not to question Blackstone and not to let the Philadelphia police anywhere near him. Williams believed he could get through to Blackstone, and Smith thought it was worth a try. But there was no rush. Blackstone wasn't going anywhere.

They crossed the Susquehanna River, Smith chuckling about saving the Federal Government the cost of the Delaware Bridge toll. He turned off Route 1 to wind along a small road lined with stone walls and leafless oak trees. Low hills and tawny fields glowed in the midday sun. Everything was quiet, basking in the respite from winter.

"You grew up here?" Williams asked. Smith nodded. "Doesn't seem like there's much going on. What was it like for a kid?"

Smith responded almost dreamily, "Easy. Small town. Just a little world of its own. You had to go to Philly for excitement, but my dad was a Methodist minister, so excitement wasn't part of the program. He kept me on a real short leash." Sun and the shadows of overhanging oak branches played on Smith's face. He smiled and went on, "I was going to join the Navy to get away. The Reverend said no way, I had to go to college. I said I'd go someplace warm and far away. We compromised on Penn State. Cold, close, and cheap."

They drove on in silence then Smith pointed, and said, "I'll be damned, it's still there."

He pulled into a gravel parking lot in front of a diner pressed back under the woods. A faded sign read, 'Red's'.

"Let's have some lunch."

Williams, looking straight ahead, said, "Why don't we get to Philly first?"

"Naw, this place is great. Have you ever had scrapple?" Williams rolled his eyes but said nothing.

Smith led Williams into a metal and Formica atavism: Booths under the windows, a long counter lined with round red upholstered stools, and the sounds of the kitchen flowing through a long opening behind the counter. Red's champion Smallmouth Bass hung on the wall behind the cash register. Smith walked happily to a booth lit by a slash of sunlight coming through the bare trees. He slid in and started flipping through songs on the juke box saying, "Oh, yeah, nothing's changed." Williams sat back quietly. Smith pulled menus out of the stand that also held the ketchup, mustard, vinegar, salt and pepper. He crooned about scrapple with biscuits and cream gravy. A waitress in a light blue uniform and white apron was wiping down the booths at the other end of the row.

Smith smiled and waved. "Could we get some water, and I'd like a Coke." She turned, walked to the counter, and brought a glass of water. Smith smiled again, and said, "I think we're ready to order. I haven't had anything like Red's scrapple in years."

She stood, unsmiling and hostile. "The kitchen is closed, Hon."

Smith wrinkled his face. "Huh?"

"The kitchen is closed."

He looked toward the long window behind the counter. A cook was busy at the grill. There were customers in other booths. Behind the counter another waitress stood and watched. Smith's eyes narrowed. He leaned back, his face tight.

"I've been eating here since before you were born, Miss, and I'm going to eat here today. Is Red still alive?"

"His daughter runs the place."

"Cheryl? Tell her Henry Smith is out here and wants to order some food."

Williams sat silent and still. Smith didn't look at him. His eyes followed the waitress as she walked back to the kitchen. A sharp featured woman with short red hair emerged. She looked cross, but that might just have been her look. She stood at their booth, arms folded. "Henry, it's been a long time."

"Yes, it has. Is your dad still alive?"

"He passed eight years ago."

"I'm sorry. He was a good man."

"I don't want trouble, Henry. We'll make you some food and you can just take it with you. My treat."

"I want to eat here."

"Then I'll have to close the kitchen."

"Why?"

She looked at Williams and said, "There are other places for people like him to eat."

"Cheryl, this man is my guest and my friend. He's a police sergeant and a war hero. You have no right to refuse to serve him."

Conversation in the diner had stopped. Everyone else in the diner watched.

"I can close my place if I want."

Williams caught Smith's eye and shook his head. "Leave it, Hank, we've got work to do." Smith was angry, and embarrassed. He did not look ready to back down.

Williams said quietly, "We've got more important fish to fry, man."

Smith stood, looked at Cheryl, and muttered, "Your father never…"

She turned on her heel and walked away.

Back in the car Smith said, "Sarge, I'm sorry. I had no idea."

"No, you wouldn't."

*****

They arrived at Pennsylvania Hospital after a silent ride, grabbed sandwiches from the cafeteria, and ate while they waited for the nurses to track down the neurosurgery resident who had spoken to Smith. He was not encouraging. Blackstone's brain, he said, was fried before it was battered. He chuckled at his cleverness and said, "He's stabilized and appears conscious, but I doubt you'll get much out of him. He moans and babbles a lot."

Blackstone was wired and tubed and surrounded by machines. His face was sunken, his jaw broken and wired. The eyes that had frightened people with their maniacal gleam had faded. His right hand, shackled to the bed frame twitched spasmodically. Smith stood at the door trying to focus. Williams found a chair brought it to the bed and sat leaning over Blackstone. He laid a hand over the shackled hand lying on the tightly tucked sheet. Blackstone's eyes in their dark shadowed spaces moved from Williams to Smith and back.

"Sergeant Silas Blackstone, it's Sergeant Williams. You're fucked, man. You totally screwed up. You killed my best friend. You killed my buddy Dixon. And you killed that poor old engineer, Douglas. We've got your gun. We've got your prints. We've got witnesses. Chief Dixon ain't saving you this time. We've arrested him. Rankin's locked up too." The eyes moved. Both Smith and Williams saw the flicker. It wasn't the arrest of the Chief he reacted to, it was Rankin. Williams's voice was gentle, almost tender. He leaned closer. Blackstone reeked of disinfectant, adhesive, and decay.

"It's rough Silas. Your boys are in jail, and Elliott Taylor, the dude who gave you the money? He's dead, pushed under a train. Here you are, chained to a bed with the guy you been trying to frame for years hanging over you like a thundercloud."

Blackstone's jaw moved. The thin lips parted. "Fuck you."

Williams looked at him steadily. "We know what you did, but why don't you tell us why?"

Blackstone almost managed a sneer. "I killed your friend. We were going to scare him. Uppity…"

"Not scared enough?"

"He laughed. I told him, 'You gonna die dog, an' I killed him."

Williams knew now what Claire had heard: not 'Y-Dog', but 'die dog'. He gently took the bandaged head in his hands. Smith took a step toward him, but Williams gently turned the face toward him and peered into the fogged eyes.

"Listen, Silas. We are going to keep you alive and safe. You are going to go on trial in Washington, D.C., in front of a mostly Black jury. They will convict you. Multiple murders, including killing a cop. Death sentence, maybe, but you'll sit waiting on death row. You won't be alone. There are people there who remember you. You know what they'll do, don't you? How do you think your balls will taste when they feed them to you?"

Blackstone had heard. His eyes flickered. Williams asked, "Why'd Rankin want Ernie scared."

"Al didn't give a shit. Just fixin' a problem for a friend."

Williams decided to risk a guess. "Taylor?" The eyes faded. Williams bit his lip.

Smith said, "No, no, Sarge, you got it all wrong. Silas doesn't even know. You don't know much, do you?"

Blackstone liked this game. He managed a sneer and said, "Who's your friend, Sarge. You just the muscle? He must be in charge 'cause he's got brains."

Williams smiled and said, "Yeah, he does. Do you?"

Smith broke in. "Maybe you were so stoned, you don't even remember. You had Ransome with you for all three murders. They didn't trust you. Now they're trying to protect Ransome, but you? You're so worthless nobody cares that you got arrested—or beaten just about to death. You aren't one of Rankin's guys. Not like Ransome. The unit's not going to take care of you."

A nurse entered. Smith rose easily, took out his credentials, and drawled, "Ma'am, we're going to need you to go on back out. We'll let you know when we're done." She looked at her patient, then at Smith, and backed out the door. Smith followed her and returned with another chair which he set at the foot of the bed turned backward. He folded himself carefully around the ladderback, all the while never taking his eyes off Blackstone's battered face. He said, "Sarge, the man's brain isn't working."

Williams shrugged. "He shot my friend for being Black and not being afraid. He shot my chickenshit lieutenant, a guy I kept alive for two years. I don't care how this broken-down pile of shit dies. I'd pull the plug on him now," he ran a hand over some of the tubes, "but his old friends in jail will do the job so much better—or worse, depending how you look at it."

Blackstone's eyes swing back and forth. His shackled hand shook. His wired jaw jutted slightly. "I was just doing the job they paid me to do."

Williams and Smith listened in silence. Then Smith smiled thoughtfully. "We've got the money they gave you, Silas. It came from Taylor, and now it's in an FBI safe. But you're going to have to tell us why Taylor paid you and why Rankin sent you to kill those guys."

Blackstone's eyes narrow. "You've got Rankin?"

"Mmhm"

"What about Ransome?"

"Not yet."

Blackstone rose slightly from his pillow. "You gotta get Ransome. If you got Rankin, Ransome is gonna start doing bad shit. He'll come after me."

"Where does he hide when he doesn't want to be found?"

Blackstone seemed to struggle to breathe. His nostrils flared. He moaned and began to whine. "I'm all fucked up. You need to help me."

"Yeah, sure, when we take Ransome…"

Williams lit a cigarette and put it between Blackstone's lips. He watched him inhale, and then reached out and took it, snuffing it out between his thumb and forefinger.

"Tell us where."

"He has a hidey hole somewhere, maybe in PG County."

"Where?"

"Who knows?"

Williams took a deep breath, rose out of his chair, looming over Blackstone. He turned to Smith. "This isn't worth our time, Hank. I'm done."

Smith walked over and bent close to Blackstone from the opposite side. He said softly, "You are going to wish you had used this chance to get us on your side."

Blackstone had lived at the ragged edge of violence and brutality, hurling himself half insane at anyone who stirred his loathing. Now he was chained to this bed in pain, and afraid. He depended on nurses to feed him and wipe his ass. He knew Rankin would give him up if it suited him, and Ransome would surely kill him if he got the chance. He knew he was alone and powerless. He hated Williams, but he knew him, and knew he was implacable.

"Burton's Cabins."

"Huh?"

"Ransome's place. Burton's cabins in Clinton."

Smith slipped out of the room to call his office and get a watch on Burton's Cabins. Over the course of twenty-five minutes, they extracted the confused fragments of a story about Rankin. He had been disgusted that the MPD was being 'negrofied' and decided to fight back. A Black city council and their white liberal supporters might put in weak chiefs, but they couldn't run the real police out of the force. Rankin had thought the Deputy Chief was the man who'd stand up. They kept a lid on things for a while, but when the new Chief came in the Deputy Chief had played along with appointing 'Blacks and women, for Chrissake' to senior positions. Dixon wasn't tough enough, and he liked his big house and his expensive cigars. Blackstone said Lieutenant Rankin was angry and said Dixon had forgotten who he was and who his friends were, and "we had to remind him." Blackstone stopped, asked for a cigarette, smoked hungrily and went on, "You know Rankin, Sarge, when you guys set me up…"

"No man, we didn't. You went fucking crazy and every cop working drugs knew what you were doing."

"Well, why the hell not. Bein' more careful doesn't mean you're not dirty. You're like everyone else, you get your cut." Smith watched Williams as Blackstone needled him, searching for a reaction.

Williams smiled broadly. "You've spread that shit for a while, Silas, and you don't even expect anyone to believe it. You just enjoy smearing shit on everything around you. But now you are telling me that you had to deal with Rankin, not the Deputy Chief, to get IAD off your back for pedaling the crap the rest of us managed to get off the streets? What'd it cost you to get that buried?"

"That's what we're here talking about, Sarge. I worked for him. Hills, Al Dixon, that engineer. That's what I did."

Smith lifted his hand to signal to Williams. They both watched Blackstone, then Smith said, "You're saying Rankin didn't have an angle, it was just business?"

Blackstone shrugged. Smith leaned his head to one side, as if trying to see Blackstone from another angle. "Well, damn it, who was *he* working for?"

Blackstone shook his head.

Smith said, "I'd say if Taylor was paying you, he must have been paying Rankin."

"No," said Blackstone with some disgust, "Taylor is—was—a pussy. The only thing I did for him was sell him expensive white powder."

Williams rested his hands on the rail of the bed. The smell was worse. Blackstone reeked of shit. *No,* thought Williams, *Blackstone was shit.* "Are you saying you don't know who, but you know who it wasn't?"

The door flew open, and the nurse returned with a doctor, a small man with very large ears and bushy eyebrows pursed in indignation. He marched over to Smith. "This is a very ill patient. He is here under my care. You're putting him under stress and obstructing his treatment."

Smith nodded in agreement. "Yes, I guess that's true. But see, this man is a triple-murderer, and we need to get his help to make sure there aren't more murders." The nurse recoiled. The doctor's ears and eyebrows lifted. It was hard not to laugh, but he held his ground.

"He is a patient. He has a right to treatment."

They looked at Blackstone, apparently asleep. The doctor advanced toward the bed, caught the odors and saw the cigarette ashes at about the same time. He rounded on them. "This is appalling. The man is lying in his own filth, and you're giving him cigarettes that will just make his withdrawal worse—but you knew that. You need to leave. You can come back tomorrow."

They left, instructing the Guard at the door to admit no one except medical staff he recognized, or whose credentials he'd examined. They told him that local FBI agents would come to take a statement from Blackstone the following day.

*****

The light was fading, and high clouds were drifting in from the west by the time they had retrieved their car from the hospital garage, pumped some gas, bought coffee and pizza, and set out for D.C. They talked about the strange vile figure they had spent their afternoon trying to manipulate.

Smith said, "For all the drama, he mostly confirmed what we suspected."

"Honest to God, Hank, it just breaks my heart. He killed Ernie because he's a Black man and he wouldn't cringe. You can't know how much I loved that man and his family. It hurts. A part of me wishes I'd just killed the motherfucker right there. It'd be done with, and you could arrest me."

"That would have broken *my* heart, Sarge. We're going to get the whole putrid bunch of them, and we're going to do it right."

They were surrounded by commuters wanting desperately to get home. Williams, however wanted to turn back to the hospital and demand that the doctor let them go on grilling Blackstone. He was imagining the interview when Smith asked, "Did you notice how much he didn't want to talk about

Adams? When Nora and I talked to Adams again in the hospital and asked about those payments he was making to Taylor, he said Taylor was his brother-in-law and was in trouble. He had to help. But I imagine he figured he needed Taylor to keep Conway from causing trouble. Adams has spun a lot of stories trying to keep us away from something, and it seemed like Blackstone was doing the same."

Smith handed Williams a slice of congealed pizza and a napkin. They agreed it was awful, almost criminal, without even a beer to wash it down.

Then Smith said, "Sarge, can I ask you about what happened back in Kennett Square today?"

"Okay."

"I had no idea how it was. But you knew what was going to happen as soon as I pulled into Red's."

"Yeah, I did."

"I've gone through life not seeing, thinking it's somewhere else, someone else…" Williams kept his eyes on the road and waited. Smith continued, "And then there's the Deputy Chief who has Rankin running a bunch of white enforcers to keep Blacks out of power in the department, and nobody does anything. Does it make you want to give it up?"

"And do what? It's a Black city with a Black mayor. Rankin's going to lose."

Smith frowned and asked, "Is this case about murder, graft, and corruption, or about race?"

"Everything is about race, man."

Chapter 58
Numbers

Agent Rohrig hummed a Beach Boys tune to himself as he organized piles of documents on the long table in the conference room. There were four stacks of boxes: the records they'd seized weeks before from the union office; the records from the Conway DC office; the account records supplied by the bank; and now the four heavy boxes of papers McFarland had gotten from the Conway Headquarters in San Francisco. Rohrig wasn't comfortable with people, but he reveled in the close examination of financial records, especially when, as in this case, the records tracked the same transactions from different angles. He was going to find some weird inconsistencies that would lead him to the crux of a series of poorly-hidden and corrupt decisions. He could feel it—no—he could smell it. He leaned his head back, inhaled deeply, flaring his nostrils, then, playing air guitar, he wailed:

You shouldn't have lied, no, you shouldn't have lied
But we'll have fun, fun, fun now that Daddy took the T-Bird awaaaay

If one of his colleagues had walked in, they would have smiled and left. Jim being Jim, but, oh man is he good at what he does.

He began scanning pages, marking them here and there with sticky tabs, which he numbered and noted in small precise handwriting on a long, lined pad. Three hours later he was still there, walking back and forth among neat stacks of documents on both sides of the table, and muttering to himself. "Mmhm, I see. Oh, dear they didn't? Yes, they did, tsk tsk. Now you really can't put me off the track that way, no, *non, nyet, nein,* no way my friends. I've got you."

And he had, although he wasn't sure whom it was he'd gotten. He called and left a message for Agent Smith, and after a moment's hesitation said, "Tell him it's urgent." He circled the table several more times, grimaced, and then called the U.S. Attorney's office.

"Mr. McFarland?"

"Hello, Agent Rohrig. What's up?"

"Well, I tried to reach Agent Smith…"

"He's here with me."

"Oh, that's good, that's excellent, sir. Perhaps you could put me on speaker?"

McFarland fussed with the phone.

Smith greeted Rohrig. "I heard you were singing Beach Boys songs when I left this morning, and I figured someone was in trouble."

"Ah, yes, I've found several things. The first is pretty shocking." He paused for effect. "The ghost workers? They're still being paid. The checks are still being cashed, and it almost seems like they're trying to shovel as much money out the door as they can."

Smith and McFarland stared at each other, looking like amateur actors portraying shock and horror. Rohrig was about to repeat his finding, unsure they'd grasped what he was saying, when McFarland finally said, "Oh, shit. This is unbelievable."

Smith held his head in his hands and said, "Of course, of course. They went right on. They'd already been caught. They had nothing to lose. And who was going to cut it off? Taylor would've been the one, and he was way too frightened and messed up. He probably thought that shutting it down would be some sort of admission."

Rohrig cleared his throat. "There's more, sir. When we first got the Union's records and Adams' book, I told you there were some screwy numbers that didn't add up, but we thought it might be skimming or maybe just incompetence. These records show that someone, almost certainly Mr. Adams, was taking a lot of what came in *before* it got into the distribution pipeline. A lot. More than a million dollars I'd say."

"Jim, can you come up here?"

"I think you should come here, sir. I have a few hundred pounds of documents all laid out so you can follow the trail of the money."

"We're on our way."

They found Rohrig, sleeves rolled up, reading glasses perched on his nose, wrestling an overhead projector into position. He led them through his analysis literally bubbling with excitement, running back and forth between the screen and the projector. "You can see, the job was hemorrhaging money. A lot of it seemed to disappear into a black hole." McFarland sighed and asked, "Jim, would the company have known this was still going on? Not just the DC office, headquarters?"

Rohrig put his hand to his face and rubbed his chin. "Yes, absolutely. If they can't see millions of dollars leaking, they aren't looking."

"How do we shine a light in the black hole?"

"Someone in the union office is managing the money."

Farwell had been quietly circling the table trying to follow Rohrig's notes. She looked up in response to Rohrig's comment and said, "I know who it is. It's the office manager, Mrs. Drayton, and she seemed very protective of Adams."

McFarland held up his hands and said, "Okay, we need to stop this now. I'm going to call our friend Gopnik in the office out there. Hank, Nora, I'd like you to go get Mrs. Drayton, bring her down here, and find out where in hell the money's going. Make sure news of that doesn't get to Adams."

One of the office assistants came in and handed Smith a note. He read it, closed his eyes and groaned.

"What is it, Hank."

"Blackstone's dead. Somehow, he administered himself an overdose in a secure ward in the hospital. Goddamned sanctimonious doctor threw us out so he could 'care' for his patient, and then he let this happen."

"Did Ransome get to him?"

"Nah., we pushed Blackstone hard to face reality and talk to us. He started to, but I don't think he cared for reality. He just copped it." He looked at the time on the message. "It took them eight hours to decide to let us know."

"Let's make goddamned sure Adams doesn't do the same."

*****

They found Peg Drayton at her desk in the Union office. She looked at them, calmly, and said, "You're here for me." She quietly collected her coat and purse, instructed a young woman to close the office, and went out with the two agents.

Farwell extended a hand. "I'm sorry ma'am. I have to search your purse." Smith thought, *That's interesting.* What's she after? Farwell emptied the contents onto a desk. The usual stuff. And a small ledger. Farwell didn't even pretend she hadn't been looking for it. "This is the record of the skim?"

"Skim? No, Mr. Adams' discretionary fund."

"Yes, of course." Farwell smiled. "He really trusts you. Will this show us where the money went?"

"If you know how to read it. I kept good records. Mr. Adams knew what he was doing."

"How have you handled it since he's been—out of touch?"

"I've done my best."

"Mrs. Drayton, I don't want to get this wrong. Will you help me understand what's in this book?"

She looked at Farwell for a long moment. "You'll figure it out eventually anyway. He wasn't corrupt. He was doing this for the working people."

Chapter 59
The Tapestry

When McFarland returned to his office, Mrs. Bynum handed him messages from KA, Donatelli, and Tim Gopnik. He looked forward to telling Gopnik what they'd found.

"Hey Tim, how're you doing?"

"I didn't fly back to DC on the red eye last night. The question is, how are you?"

"Okay. I managed to sleep. I have some news…"

"Ya gotta hear this Jimmy. The company is gonna feed Maddox to the sharks."

"Wolves."

"Huh? Yeah, us. They are shocked and disgusted by what has been happening. They left it to Maddox. It was all Taylor and…"

"Tim, the unbelievable fact is, they're still paying the ghost workers."

"They what?" McFarland imagined Gopnik's broad face, the small eyes narrowed in consternation. His news has been upstaged.

McFarland continued, "It's three weeks since we executed a search warrant on their DC office, and they somehow haven't figured out something was going on."

"Incredible. I imagine they're still going to try to blame Maddox."

McFarland grunted and asked, "Do you think they have a deal with him? Take the rap, go to jail, and he'll be taken care of in a few years when he gets out?"

Gopnik guffawed. "You're such a cynic, McFarland."

"Let's start by getting them to shut down the scam."

"It'll be my pleasure. I'll go over there this afternoon."

"What about the safety report."

"It was just a misunderstanding, they claim. They produced a copy of a so-called 'final' report that doesn't contain a warning about collapsing buildings, just a reference to a theoretical possibility. They claim Taylor got an early draft that the consultants produced using flawed data. He was upset because he didn't understand what it was. Obviously, Conway got to the consulting firm. They're a very big client."

"Let me know what they say when you tell them they're still writing checks to people who aren't actually working on the project."

McFarland sat glaring at a darkening window. The company seemed to be doing serious damage control, and it felt like they were slipping away. With the murders solved and the culprits dead or in jail, he wondered whether the appetite for pursuing an apparently repentant company would wane. The thing was that knowing *who* had done *what* was different than understanding *why*. He wanted clarity. He had expected to discover a story he could follow from beginning to end. But there wasn't just one story. There was family, race, greed. A battle for power. Hunger for vengeance. He wanted to know what it was all about, but it was about something different for each of the players. For Conway, it was money and reputation. For Rankin, it was about power and excluding black people from power. For Taylor, it was the chance to be a high rolling player. There was no clear picture, more of a tapestry, one of those fabulous portraits of medieval life that contained elements of many stories. He thought of his mother leading him and Miggy through French castles, searching the walls for unsung masterpieces, exclaiming, 'Jimmy, Jimmy, see, this is how they want their lives to be. Everything around them was brief and uncertain, but here it is all woven together.' He thought of the District Court downstairs. 'Ladies and gentlemen of the jury. This is not a case, it's a tapestry…'

He called KA, wondering what news she might have for him.

"U.S. Attorney's Office, Abbott speaking."

"KA, it's Jimmy, how're you doing?"

"Jimmy, it's great to hear from you. You have really shaken things up."

"What're you hearing?"

"The Deputy Chief is done, and everyone is trying to figure out who's going to come out on top."

"Who will?"

"Well, that's what I called about. They've contacted me about becoming Deputy Chief. They need someone squeaky clean, and apparently I had a reputation when I was in the MPD as a pain-in-the-ass stickler for the rules."

McFarland hooted. "Oh, KA, that's fabulous. If anybody can whip them into shape, it'll be you."

"We'll see. Do you feel you can tell me how bad it is?"

McFarland was taken aback. KA and David were a totally wired couple. "Doesn't David have all the gossip?"

"Jimmy, right now you are the man who holds the future of the MPD in his hands. Everyone is wondering who you are going to indict next."

"I know that a guy in the Deputy Chief's Palace Guard and ex-Sergeant Silas Blackstone murdered Ernie Hills, Aubrey Douglas, and Alan Dixon. I know they were acting on orders from Lieutenant Rankin and that the Deputy Chief had lost control. I'm not sure who Rankin was acting for or who killed Taylor. Rankin's in custody. Blackstone is dead. And Ransome is out on his own, probably still trying to kill Sarge. Am I supposed to be thinking about reforming the MPD?"

KA sighed, "I've got a lot at stake. I think you'd better discuss that with the Boss. He probably had this all thought out when he put you on this case—and Jimmy, you have done an amazing job. We're all in awe—jealous, but in awe."

"Sure, two suspects dead. One in DC General. A robokiller on the loose, the criminal enterprise still going on under our noses—it's a hell of an achievement."

She chuckled. "Yes, if you put it that way…"

The team gathered and settled in to, as Donatelli put it, "Figure out what we know and what the hell we still can't figure out." McFarland passed along KA's news—she had not asked that he keep it confidential. "No point," she'd said, "the rumors are all over and I'm already getting press calls."

Donatelli slapped his thigh and gave a hoarse cheer. "I sure hadn't heard. That's a revolution. What do you think, Sarge?"

Williams's eyes were gleaming. "If it's true, if that nest of racist vipers is going to get cleared out, its…" He choked up, but did not cheer, he looked grim. "Ransome is on the street along with the rest of the unit. They won't go peacefully."

They reviewed Maddox's story of having been pushed, Blackstone's fragmentary revelations, the evidence Rohrig had found in the documents, and Adams' explanation of his payments to Taylor. McFarland asked Smith to explain his hypothesis about Taylor's death. Smith got up and leaned against the desk, occasionally going to one of the sheets of newsprint they'd hung on the walls scrawled with names and events.

"I start by believing Maddox. He admitted he killed Taylor, albeit unintentionally, *before* he knew about the evidence, we had against him. His story feels true—any one of us would grab wildly for support if we were pushed onto the tracks. If that much is true, the rest kinda follows naturally. Who'd want Maddox dead? Taylor might have, but he wouldn't have arranged for it to happen while he was standing there. I rule him out. Rankin on his own? No, he didn't care one way or another what Maddox was doing. Not plausible. Rankin was involved but acting for someone else. The obvious suspect is Adams. He wants Maddox dead to protect his brother-in-law, and he wants him dead to protect his own scam. That leaves us with the question how the hell could Adams have arranged it while we had him? The only explanation I can think of is that he didn't arrange it while we had him, and it was already set up when Sarge found him. *That's* why Adams caved when we told him Taylor fell in front of a train. He realized it was his contract on Maddox gone wrong."

Donatelli stroked his smooth face and asked, "Do we believe that all four murders were contracted for by Adams? Just to protect some routine graft?"

Smith looked at McFarland who explained, "I think it was more than that, Vic. Adams wants power. He covers it with his Irish boy act, but he wants to be a big man. He saw this as the path to build himself an empire. He was going to push aside a bunch of fat superannuated old bosses. The more we talk to Mrs. Drayton, the clearer it gets that Danny Boy was using the money to build himself a power base. Even if he got caught and spent a little time in jail, it would just be a badge of honor. He'd say that the government was out to get him for fighting for the little guy. Rankin was a ruthless and reliable ally. Of course, Adams wanted to protect his little sister, and Taylor was useful, but he believed that the money would solve any problem."

"We've got 'em all," Smith said, "But can we make it stick?"

Williams closed his eyes and held up a big hand. He spoke in a low, tense voice.

"We have got to find Ransome. I don't think you understand who he is. He's not just a stoned sadist like Blackstone. Serving in 'Nam was where Ransome felt he belonged. His squad was his family. His code of honor was unit loyalty. Now it's loyalty to Rankin and the guys around him. Ransome will die to get vengeance. He is out there. He knows we're looking for him."

They heard a janitor running a cleaning machine on the granite floor of the hallway. Somehow the sound seemed threatening. The room filled with a slight odor of wax. McFarland had never heard Sarge speak with such grim concern.

Smith asked, "Who will he go after, Sarge?"

"Me, Jimmy for sure, maybe Ernie's family because he knows how much they mean to me. Maybe Adams. Probably the Deputy Chief. He doesn't have anyone to tell him what to do. He'll go with hate."

Farwell broke in. "When Ransome came down to lecture at Quantico, he taught us sniper tactics. He had a mantra, something like, 'plan, position, pull'. The plan puts you in the right place at the right time and gets you out again. The perfect position is somewhere under five hundred yards from the target. Someplace where you can see them, but they won't see you, and where they'll be exposed for at least five seconds. The plan puts you there at the right moment to pull the trigger for the kill."

Donatelli looked stricken, his gleaming face blotched and lumpy. He muttered, "Ransome's a sniper?"

Farwell shook her head and answered, "Was, I guess."

Williams, sounding impatient, said, "Man—that's what I'm trying to tell you. He's cold and he's got the skills." Donatelli looked at his watch and scurried wordlessly out to use Mrs. Bynum's phone. He returned ten minutes later, grim-faced.

"I hadn't had a chance to tell you, Jimmy, but the AG pulled your driver. Somebody over there in Main Justice who's pissed you have the case convinced the AG they'd look like idiots if the press got the story that a twenty-something kid was being chauffeured around town by an armed guard."

McFarland grinned. "Whoever he is, he's right."

Smith growled, "No, no he's not. You're not a combatant."

McFarland laughed. He hadn't liked being treated like a helpless kid who had to be protected. This was a relief. He told them, "Well, we're all in the same boat now."

He remembered reading that was what Roosevelt had said to Churchill when the British Prime Minister called the president after Pearl Harbor, and he'd wanted to find a moment to use it.

Williams rolled his head and groaned. "McFarland, you just ain't taking this seriously, and goddamnit, you need to." He loomed over McFarland. "You're driving home. Cool, listening to music. You're on that section of Mass Ave. just above the Observatory. Some idiot swerves in front of you. You slam on the brakes and swerve. You end up halfway onto the sidewalk with a flat tire. You get out to see what the hell is going on. There's a pop from on top of one of those buildings. The last thing you ever feel is a white-hot sledgehammer slamming your back. You are dead. He doesn't miss. He doesn't need two shots. You are dead. No trial. No career. No Sally. You are dead, and I have to go hunt the sonofabitch and kill him."

McFarland could see the scene, he felt the fear, but it was obliterated by the emotion elicited by Williams's matter-of-fact statement that he'd have to hunt and kill Ransome.

Smith said, "He'll go for you first, Sarge, to get you out of the way, then Jimmy. He'll figure there's no use going after the Hills family if he kills you first."

Williams had an expression McFarland had never seen. Hard, intense, scary. He said, "He's not going to kill me."

No one in the room doubted his word. He stood with folded arms and spoke quietly and slowly. "I'll ask Amel to watch at Varney Street. Keep Claire and Ernie safe. Hank, you have a watch on Ransome's cabin?"

"Uh huh."

"And Adams?"

"Uh huh."

"Will you and Nora get Jimmy home?"

"Yeah, we will."

Chapter 60
Plan, Position, Pull

Detective Caleb Ransome walks slowly across the cracked and pitted parking lot in front of Burton's Cabins. He had spotted the agents staking out the property long before they saw him. He correctly concluded they would watch, but not immediately try to arrest him. He unlocks the cabin, sees that it has been searched, shakes his head, and mutters, "Dumb fucks." It takes a few minutes to shed his uniform and don black pants, sweater, and sneakers, the white soles carefully painted black. He hangs the uniform in the closet above the perfectly polished black dress shoes. He switches on the light in the bathroom, pulls down the shade, and then, moving quickly, shoves the bed aside, pries up a section of floor boards, pulls out the aluminum case with the name Anschutz emblazoned on it, and puts things back as they were. The case goes in a black backpack along with an automatic pistol, a thermos of coffee, two chocolate bars, and a small packet of papers. He may not get to sleep this night. He pulls on a black knit cap and slips out a back window, crossing through the strip of woods to where he has parked his car—the city's car—half a mile away.

He heads for Anacostia. He has spent several nights scouting the block opposite the apartment building where Williams lives. He has identified two good vantage points. He knows that tonight Williams is scheduled to go off duty at six. Ransome will be in position a good half hour before Williams drives up and emerges from his car into the target zone.

Ransome parks on a side street a few hundred yards behind the squat building that is his first position option, a two-story brick apartment complex with a flat roof. He can reach the roof from stairwells at either end of the building or several fire escapes. He takes his backpack and climbs the stairs. The stairwell is full of the smell of dinner and the sounds of families. He emerges onto the roof, spreads a small tarp, and sits down. He opens the Anschutz case. It is a beautiful weapon, a product of meticulous German craftsmanship. Not a sniper weapon—there were no sniper rifles available for him to steal from the evidence locker—but this is an exquisitely accurate target rifle. It will not stop a grizzly, but at this distance it will do the job.

Methodically, he assembles and loads the gun, lays out the case and his backpack so he can leave quickly, and settles in. A familiar sense of calm control settles over him. The job demands mindless concentration. He slows his breathing and tunes his senses to the night and his surroundings. A woman is shouting up the street. An aged car dragging its muffler passes slowly. Ransome sees Williams pull his old blue Ford into his accustomed spot, turn off the headlights, and gather bags of groceries from the front seat. Williams is shrouded in an enormous overcoat and a dark hat. He is unmistakable. Ransome watches him through the telescopic sight, waiting until he has turned to walk up the path to the apartment building. With infinite gentleness, he squeezes the trigger. There is a pop in the darkness. Williams jolts forward, the bags fly, he falls, and lies still. Ransome watches without emotion, turns, packs his weapon, and walks easily back down the stairs and to his car. He has the ability to move quickly without haste. He finds his car and follows back streets through Anacostia to the quiet wooded curves of the Suitland Parkway. He'll cross below Georgetown on the Whitehurst Freeway and then swing up Foxhall Road and over to McFarland's house the back way. He has watched. He knows that McFarland rarely arrives home before eight. There will be time. He has chosen a neighbor's roof to shoot from. He will need to be careful climbing up the back of the house from the little garden. But he has practiced. It will be an easy shot. The street is narrow, the light from the streetlamps is sufficient, the only issue is whether the trees will obstruct his shot.

He is in position. He thinks for a moment about his route back to the Deputy Chief's house and then empties his mind and waits. Two cars pass in the next thirty minutes. Neither stops. He expects McFarland to arrive in the black Mercury driven by Officer Ross. McFarland will be in the front seat. He will get out and turn toward his house. Officer Ross will wait while McFarland climbs the three concrete steps, walks the fifteen-foot path, and mounts the four wooden steps up onto the porch. The walkway will provide the easiest shot.

This night, however, is different. Ransome is surprised when a different car carrying three people stops. A woman emerges from the front passenger side door and seems to peer right at him. The driver steps out and looks up and down the street.

Agent Farwell has been turned inward during the drive from McFarland's office. She is replaying Ransome's lecture to the trainees at Quantico again and again in her head. Ransome will be there. Tonight. She feels it. He will have a plan to remain invisible. One shot, and then he will disappear. The more she thinks about it the more sure she becomes that Ransome will be on a roof opposite McFarland's house. They should have scouted the area to figure out where, but there was no time.

"Hank, when we get there, drive up slowly. I'll watch the roof tops, you cover the street. Jimmy, please don't get out until we say it's clear."

McFarland rolls his eyes.

Smith and Farwell get out scanning the street and the roof tops, but Ransome is well-hidden. Farwell says uneasily, "It looks clear," and McFarland pushes the door open. Ransome sees the figure in the back seat getting out and that it is McFarland. He decides he has to take his shot as soon as McFarland is out. He lines up his shot. The woman moves. He pulls. She shouts, "NO!" and shoves McFarland. The shot grazes his arm and ricochets off the concrete steps. Farwell catches a glimpse of what briefly looks like a man's head. There is a loud crack. The head explodes. The two agents stand, tensed, weapons drawn. Porch lights go on along the street.

McFarland says, "Damn, I'm getting blood on everything."

Farwell looks at Smith. He nods, and she ducks into the car, finding it is indeed a bloody mess. She looks at McFarland. He is holding his right arm with his left and looking embarrassed.

"You saved my life, Nora."

"Damn you, you didn't wait."

She reaches over and pulls his hand away from his arm, then slides into the front seat, grabs a first aid kit from the glove compartment, and gives him a wad of gauze to hold against the wound. She gets on the radio to call for an ambulance and a crime scene team. Someone has already called the MPD. She hears sirens approaching. There is a shout from down the street.

"Hank. It's Sarge. Don't shoot me, OK? Ransome's dead."

Farwell wonders how the hell he showed up at just the right moment. Paul Brown has emerged from McFarland's house and seeing his blood smeared housemate, fears the worst. McFarland, seeing Paul, breaks into almost hysterical laughter, all the fear and tension bursting out of him as braying guffaws.

"If you could see yourself…" he struggles to say.

A pair of MPD squad cars arrive, their flashing lights turning the scene psychedelic. The officers leap out guns drawn. Williams holds out his badge saying, "Whoa, whoa, guys! It's cool. These are FBI agents. There's a dead cop on the roof over there. We need to control the site and get AUSA McFarland into an ambulance. He's been wounded. Can you send someone to the rear of thirty-six twenty to keep the scene stable?"

There is a moment of uncertainty and then they do as Williams instructs them. Neighbors emerge onto their front stoops. Smith and Williams go over and ring the bell at thirty-six twenty. There is no answer, and a neighbor calls out, "The Darnells are out west skiing."

The ambulance arrives. McFarland half hopes they'll just bandage him up and leave him. Williams walks over to make sure McFarland gets in the ambulance. "How you feelin', man? You're lucky Nora saw something and got you out the way."

"I sure am, Sarge. How did you happen to turn up here?"

Williams waves Smith and Farwell over. "They asked the same thing."

The ambulance driver tells McFarland he needs to get in. Williams smiles and tells him to chill a minute. He turns back to McFarland and unbuttons his overcoat. Underneath is a stained and tattered flak jacket, bulky with its armor. He takes it off and shows them where Ransome's shot had hit him just below his left shoulder blade. "That," he says, "kinda stung."

Smith asks, "What kind of weapon did he have? It sounded like a small bore."

"A single shot .206, an Anschutz target rifle."

"You were lucky he hadn't gotten his hands on a sniper gun, Sarge. That thing wouldn't have saved you."

"It wasn't luck. I knew he was supplying himself with weapons from the evidence locker—hard to trace back to him. I had a friend remove anything high powered. I knew he'd taken the Anschutz, and I figured it's such a beautiful gun he'd want to use it. I let him think I was dead. I figured he was coming here, and I'd—well—I'd staked Jimmy out some without him knowing, and I went and checked where Ransome would probably wait. I got here and saw Ransome, but I didn't shoot quick enough."

McFarland watched Williams's face and felt emotions welling up.

"Sarge, I don't know what to say. You are an incredibly brave and wise man. With Nora saving my ass, I'm glad you didn't shoot first."

Chapter 61
The Rats Turn on Each Other

The senior prosecutors who'd persuaded Judge Bell to cancel the car and armed driver pointed out that McFarland had, after all, been protected by a pair of FBI agents, but that wasn't the way it was covered. The story was that Department of Justice bureaucrats had recklessly endangered a young prosecutor because they were jealous. He'd been saved by an alert and rather good-looking female agent and a heroic and streetwise police sergeant.

Anderson had told McFarland, "Jimmy, m'boy, if you'll just take your shirt off and show them your scar, the networks will swoon. You have the luck of the Irish."

McFarland knew that was true. Luck and very good friends.

The Deputy Chief—the former Deputy Chief—wanted a plea deal, and hearing what Blackstone had said about him, unloaded. Rankin was a vicious, conniving, racist SOB who'd had Blackstone kill his nephew to keep him quiet and had laughed when he heard how Ernie had died. Meeting with him the next day, his arm in a sling, McFarland listened quietly, thinking, 'Takes one to know one.'

Smith told the DC, "You were next on Ransome's list. He had a map of your house and the password for your security system in his pack when we got him." The Deputy Chief's sagging jaw fell, then through tight lips he said, "Bastards. I made every goddamned one of them. You can put me in front of a grand jury. I want to nail that motherfucker, Rankin."

Adams, hearing that Ransome and Blackstone were dead, had said nothing, but when he learned that Mrs. Drayton was in custody, he seemed deeply affected. He sat up off his pillows and said angrily that she had done nothing but follow his instructions.

"I want you to leave her alone," he moaned. "You can have the whole story from me."

He admitted paying Rankin to take care of Ernie and Douglas but remained evasive about Maddox and Taylor. He confirmed skimming huge sums for a slush fund, but insisted he was doing it to strengthen the Union. "I was only doing what everyone in my position does, I just stumbled on a big productive cash cow. Nice boys don't make their way in my world." When they pushed him about Maddox, Adams said, "Well Ransome screwed that up, didn't he? Talk to that slimy toad, Rankin."

As they drove from DC General to the jail where Rankin was being held in protective isolation, Smith said, "I love it when the rats all turn on each other and bare their dirty yellow teeth."

Rankin was brought into the bare and windowless interview room in handcuffs. The guards removed them and looked at Smith who motioned them out.

Rankin had not heard Blackstone was dead, and when they told him, said only, "He won't be testifying then, will he?" He reacted more strongly to the news of Ransome's death the night before, saying he'd been 'a brave boy' and 'absolutely loyal'.

McFarland had not met Rankin before and reacted with such visceral dislike that he had to get up and stand back against the wall, something Rankin noticed and responded to. "You don't like evil, do you, sonny? Now you can believe…"

Smith cut him off. "Lieutenant, you're not in a good place. Your boys are dead. Both Adams and the Deputy Chief have opened up, and they want to see you go down. Adams' office kept surprisingly detailed records of what you were paid and when and for what."

Rankin's face was stony, but his eyes shifted from McFarland to Smith, and back. Hate? Calculation?

"What're you here for then?"

McFarland came back to the metal table, sat down, stared hard, and said, "Who knew about the killings?"

Rankin looked away for a long moment, then turned back and smiled.

"Yeah, well, here's something Danny Boy won't have mentioned. You know who paid me to get rid of Maddox?"

"Adams?"

A tight smile slid across his face. “Nope, and he’d never tell you who it was.”

Smith and McFarland waited in silence. “What’ve you got for me if I tell you?” It was obvious he wanted to tell them in order to inflict pain on somebody. They waited.

“It was that little sister of his. Fucking Taylor was an addict and a liar, and he beat her, but all she wanted to do was protect him. She wanted to get rid of Maddox before he fired Taylor, and she told us to make it look like an accident. She thought that an accident in the Metro was hilarious. I thought it would confuse you.”

“You screwed that up.”

“Taylor wasn’t supposed to be there.”

*****

Late that afternoon Smith dropped McFarland at his office. He was exhausted, in pain, and felt strangely let down. He would drop off his briefcase and treat himself to a cab home. Donatelli was waiting in his office and gestured with his thumb that they were going down the hall to the Boss’s office. He winced. The Boss had warned him to stay out of the action and now here he was with his arm in a sling and the media calling him the Bloody Boy Wonder. He pictured the Boss standing at the window with his back to the door.

He was surprised to find Rushford, the AG’s Chief-of-Staff, Jim Jefferson, and KA seated around the table. Several bottles of champagne stood on a tray surrounded by tall, elegant crystal flutes. The Boss grinned, obviously enjoying McFarland’s confusion.

“Mr. McFarland, do you know why you are here?”

“For you to remind me that you told me to stay out of the action?”

The Boss did something bizarre. He hooted and shook his head. “My warnings never seem to have much effect on you, but no. You’ve wrapped up a hell of a case, cleaned out an MPD cancer, and earned the government some money.”

“Sir?”

"Conway has approached the Attorney General to say they feel terrible about what has happened and they will reimburse the government *all* of the costs of the ghost workers."

"But they're not victims, they were part of the conspiracy. They should be indicted."

Jefferson was once again looking twitchy, and Rushford was looking like he was going to explode. The Boss watched McFarland with calm level eyes. "They've cleaned up their mess. It would be a foolish and quixotic gesture to indict them and lose. Paying us back makes the point."

"Four people died. Two senior executives were directly involved. They let it run as long as they thought they could get away with it. Somehow, they've convinced Maddox to take the fall for the company, but you can't tell me senior executives weren't briefed. Now they say they're shocked to find there was fraud going on and they hold out a fistful of money and the United States Government says, Oh, thanks so much? We have an obligation to equal justice..."

"You've made your point, Mr. McFarland."

"Sir, I'd like a chance to meet with the Attorney General."

"No, Mr. McFarland, you would not like that at all. He has not asked for your opinion, and he isn't going to be interested in your indignation. You did your job, and you did it well. Mr. Jefferson, you had something to add?"

Jefferson looked miserable, but took a breath and said, "I want you to know that I take full responsibility for pulling your protection detail. It was a poor decision made for the wrong reasons. I'm sorry."

"Mr. Jefferson, if you hadn't made that decision, I'd probably be dead. Agent Farwell had heard Ransome lecture about sniper tactics at Quantico. She knew where he'd be, she saw something, and she got me out of the way."

Jefferson smiled gratefully and said, "I'm very glad it worked out that way."

KA had been watching this exchange and said, "Gentlemen, I appreciate the pleasantries, but I have a proposition for Jimmy." He turned to her in surprise. A proposition? The smug looks told him he was the only person in the room who was surprised. He waited.

"Jimmy, I'm going to accept the deputy chief job. The chief and the mayor have given me strong assurances I can clean things out. David's going to take a leave to teach criminal justice at GW."

"KA, that's amazing. Congratulations! You are the right person for sure."

"I want you to come work for me. The Boss has agreed to a six-month detail."

"What? I mean, doing what? I'm not a cop."

"You just cleaned out the core of the corruption in the department. We all knew about it. We all hated it. You came in and just blew it up. Every crooked cop in Washington thinks you're coming for him. I need your help."

The familiar heat rose from his neck through his face. He couldn't speak. He'd stumbled through to the right answers because of Sarge and Hank and Nora. They were honest, dedicated, and smart, and they had been willing to take care of him. Now he was supposed to be some sort of avenging angel?

"I'll take your blush as a yes."

"But it wasn't me, it was Sarge…"

"*Lieutenant* Williams is going to work with you. You can even continue to call him Sarge—in private."

Rushford reached over and began opening champagne. This was the first real cooperation with the MPD he'd seen since he'd come to DC.

Chapter 62
Lieutenant Williams

James Henry McFarland sat in a dejected heap in the rear seat of an elderly DC cab. It was the nation's capital, and it was served by shuddering twenty-year-old land yachts with no meters. McFarland was shivering. He couldn't keep his thoughts straight and wondered whether he was starting to hallucinate. Probably painkillers and champagne weren't such a good combination. As they pulled up to his house, the driver was saying something about how there'd been a shootout here the night before. A bunch of federal agents had raided a drug factory in one of the houses. There had been seven or eight people killed. McFarland looked up and saw the walkway and the front porch, and for a moment couldn't move.

"That's ten dollars, sir."

"No, it's not. It's two zones. It's five-fifty. Here's seven dollars."

He forced himself to open the door and step out. Nothing happened. He walked slowly up the path, climbed the steps, and almost fell against the door. As he fumbled with his keys, it flew open and a figure in jeans and a green sweater hurled herself on him.

"McFarland, you are not, just absolutely not, allowed to get yourself killed in the line of duty." She dragged him inside, looked at him and wailed, "What've they done to you? You *look* like death."

"I thought you had a concert this weekend?"

"I do, *but* nobody's going to try to assassinate me."

"Don't you have to rehearse?"

"Stop! You sound like my mother. They tried to kill the man I love. I need to be here."

Paul appeared. "C'mon, Jimmy, we've read the story in the *Post*, and I saw the results. What the hell was going on?"

"There was this former army sniper who was part of the Palace Guard and was involved in all the killings. As we closed in, he wanted revenge, and he came for me and Sarge."

"Jeezus…"

"I don't think I want to talk about it."

The phone rang. Paul answered and turned to McFarland. "It's Sarge."

McFarland leaped for the phone. "Sarge, I heard your news."

"You did? But she just asked me. How'd you hear?"

"I saw her in the boss's office an hour ago and she told me, and—asked me as well."

"She did? Claire did?"

"Claire? No, KA."

"Ohhh, that. No, Jimmy, Claire asked me to go with her and Little Ernie to a dinner with her parents—in my honor."

McFarland's eyes widened. He said, "That is great, Sarge—Lieutenant. It sounds, well, formal."

"It is. She said she knew I'd find an excuse not to go otherwise."

"I am so happy for you. You deserve a little recognition."

"That's good, man, because you and Sally are coming too."

A couple of months ago, he had not known this man, had never investigated anything, and had thought of the woman standing in front of him as a friend's little sister. Their lives had intertwined, and he felt overwhelmed with gratitude.

Printed in the USA
CPSIA information can be obtained
at www.ICGtesting.com
CBHW062253081024
15600CB00027B/442

9 798889 107033